Praise for *Love's Rescue*

"Johnson initiates another swoon-worthy historical series with this emotionally charged romance in which passions run high and things are not always what they seem. Perfect for fans of Melody Carlson and Rachel Hauck."

—*Library Journal*

"*Love's Rescue* is a fast-moving story of forbidden love and shipwreck rescues. Elizabeth Benjamin's independence is refreshing, as she is a headstrong woman who is not afraid to pursue what she desires. This action-packed tale is one to keep readers engaged and rooting for her from the first page to the last."

—*RT Book Reviews*

"The first in Johnson's inspirational romance Keys of Promise series sails off to a strong start with a sweet love story that skillfully incorporates fascinating facts about the nineteenth-century salvage and wrecking trade into a quietly moving plot about the importance of family, faith, and forgiveness."

—*Booklist*

"Johnson has penned a tale worthy of anyone who has ever dreamed of high seas adventure with this first book in her Keys of Promise series. Filled with romance, adventure, and drama, *Love's Rescue* takes readers to the far South, where mannerisms and rules often stifled dreams and desires."

—*CBA Retailers+Resources*

HONOR REDEEMED

A NOVEL

Christine Johnson

Revell

a division of Baker Publishing Group
Grand Rapids, Michigan

Published by Revell
a division of Baker Publishing Group
P.O. Box 6287, Grand Rapids, MI 49516-6287
www.revellbooks.com

Printed in the United States of America

Library of Congress Cataloging-in-Publication Data
Names: Johnson, Christine (Christine Elizabeth), author.
Title: Honor redeemed : a novel / Christine Johnson.
Description: Grand Rapids, MI : Revell, a division of Baker Publishing Group, [2016]
| Series: Keys of promise ; 2
Identifiers: LCCN 2016001006 | ISBN 9780800723514 (softcover : acid-free paper)
Subjects: LCSH: Mate selection—Fiction. | Man-woman relationships—Fiction. |
GSAFD: Love stories. | Historical fiction. | Christian fiction.
Classification: LCC PS3610.O32395 H66 2016 | DDC 813/.6—dc23
LC record available at http://lccn.loc.gov/2016001006

Scripture quotations are from the King James Version of the Bible.

This book is a work of fiction. Names, characters, places, and incidents are the product of the author's imagination or are used fictitiously. Any resemblance to actual events, locales, or persons, living or dead, is coincidental.

16 17 18 19 20 21 22   7 6 5 4 3 2 1

To my Keys friends, whose support and encouragement
carry me through the tough writing days.

1

Nantucket Island
April 20, 1852

"What will you do now?" The gentle nudge came from Mrs. Franklin hours after Prosperity Anne Jones laid her mother to rest in the church graveyard.

They sat on sturdy wooden chairs in the only home Prosperity could recall, while neighbors bustled about preparing a meal for those who condoled with her. She had attempted to help, but they had shooed her away from the kitchen. Stripped of the ability to do something useful, she battled a barrage of conflicting thoughts and feelings that ultimately came back to Mrs. Franklin's question.

What would she do?

That question had never been broached until now. Prosperity always knew what she must do. As a child she had tended house for her oft-ailing mother. The year that fire had swept through town and the sea claimed her father's life, she added nursing and managing their meager funds to her duties.

Nearly six years later, Ma breathed her last, ushering in

overpowering loneliness. Prosperity's entire family was gone. No more could she turn to Pa for counsel or weep on Ma's shoulder. She had been set adrift on a vast ocean.

What would she do?

At some point she must have donned the black cotton mourning gown. Somehow burial had been arranged and the funeral carried out. Even now, mere hours afterward, disjointed memories ricocheted through her mind: the deep grave carved into the cold earth, hymns so familiar they flowed by without notice, mourners weeping uncontrollably while she could not muster a tear. Well-meaning statements about God's will drifted past like dandelion fluff on a breeze.

After tossing a handful of dirt on the plain pine coffin, she would have preferred to climb the dunes and gaze across the sea at the endless horizon, as she had for months after her father's whaling ship disappeared. Instead she had returned home with the neighbors who now buzzed about like a hive of bees. Only Mrs. Franklin's inquiry had managed to break through the fog.

What *would* she do?

Before Ma's passing, Prosperity had whiled away countless hours dreaming of her future.

David.

She touched the locket at her throat. He had given it to her after she agreed to marry him. It would one day contain tiny portraits of the children they hoped to have. Now it held a lock of his sandy blond hair. That's all she had to remember him by, for more than two years ago the army had sent him to faraway Key West, and he would not return for six more years. What would she do until then?

"Are you all right, dear?" Mrs. Franklin asked.

Prosperity knit her fingers together and nodded.

She was spared further questions by Mrs. Newton, who chased two boys from the kitchen with a scolding that they must wait until dinner was served.

Mrs. Franklin chuckled. "I think he nabbed a biscuit off the tray. That was my Donnie back in the day."

Her voice blended into the drone of the half dozen women gathered in the tiny parlor. Outside on the porch, the men clustered together, supposedly to keep the children in the yard. Their guffaws punctuated the knowing whispers and pitying glances of the women sitting on the chairs loaned by generous neighbors. Aunt Florence held court in the opposite corner, informing all who would listen that she'd known her sister would die and was amazed she'd hung on so long in this dreadful, drafty shack.

True, the rough slab-wood walls held no charm and retained little of the stove's heat. A scarred table occupied the center of the room, topped with a vase of daffodils, shadbush, and white violets brought by one of the ladies. Little else graced the room, for Prosperity had been forced to sell every item of value in the years following her father's death. Nothing frivolous or beautiful remained. Even the cold gray of late April refused a ray of sunlight.

"There is nothing left here," she breathed.

Mrs. Franklin, a kindly soul, clasped her hands with the warmth of a dear friend. "You must find the strength to go on. Your mother would have wanted it."

"I know."

Yet it was easier to say than to do. Once the condolers left, she would be alone with nothing but memories, a few personal items, and David's letters. Those had brought comfort in the most difficult days. He had pledged a life together. David Latham never broke a promise.

"He will return," Mrs. Franklin stated with a knowing nod.

"How did you know I was thinking of Mr. Latham?"

Mrs. Franklin sighed, her gaze far off. "A woman gets a certain look when she recalls the man she loves." She patted Prosperity's hand. "Never fear. You need only write, and your lieutenant will come back from that wilderness."

"Key West." It might as well be Tahiti, for both lay beyond reach. Ship passage, even in third class, cost far more than she could save.

"Wherever it is, your young man will set sail for home the moment he receives your letter. Mark my words, he will not hesitate."

Prosperity wasn't as certain. David had stressed that his tour of duty would last eight years. Even now she could recall how worry had pinched his brow that day. Eager to brush it away, she had promised to wait. A rare smile had flickered across his lips, and she had been pleased. Alas, she had not accounted for this day.

"I doubt the army will grant leave," Prosperity murmured.

"Nonsense. You must write. He will find a way to return to you. Then you can decide together what to do."

That was the fanciful talk of a woman seeking to comfort. The army would not grant David leave because his fiancée's mother had passed away. No, she must find her own way. She couldn't stay in this house. That much was unavoidable. She could not afford to pay the overdue rent, least of all continue the lease of an entire house on her own. Mother's rainy day jar had been emptied long ago. There were no secret bank accounts, no accounts at all. John and Olivia Jones had left this world as poor as they'd come into it.

Mrs. Franklin, short and portly and pink-cheeked beneath

her white lace cap, must have been chattering for some time, but just one statement caught Prosperity's attention. "You can stay with us, of course, if your relations can't take you in. Mr. Franklin would dearly enjoy your delicious currant cakes each morning."

Prosperity mustered a smile, though she could not manage the emotion to go with it. Her parents were gone, and life on Nantucket Island was slipping away.

"You are very generous," she said, though living with the Franklins was out of the question. No Jones accepted charity.

"Only until your young man returns for you, of course."

Prosperity nodded, unable to speak over the knot in her throat. Two years had passed since David offered for her. Each morning and night she recalled his handsome visage. The cornflower-blue eyes and curly hair the color of sand brought a smile to her lips. How stiff he'd seemed when she first met him. She had laughed at his formal bow, and he had acted affronted, but in time she'd grown to appreciate his careful ways. Nothing was out of place. No possibility had gone unconsidered.

He was a product of his demanding father and austere upbringing, so serious of temperament that she'd made silly faces at him to induce a laugh. Oh, how he resisted. First, the corner of his mouth would tick up a fraction. Then he would force a frown. Will would battle emotion until, in the end, a deep guffaw would burst out. Only then would the corners of his eyes crinkle and pleasure fill his gaze.

If only she could see that again. If only she could hear his voice and feel how the very air shimmered when he walked into a room. Then she would know all was well. She could endure any hardship. Alas, her David was beyond reach, and she had only memories to lean upon.

Over time his features had grown dim. Was that tiny mole above the right corner of his mouth or the left? Did his brows sweep high in an arc or duck low? Did the spectacles he used for reading leave the same red marks on the bridge of his nose? Had he succeeded in taming the tuft of frizz at the peak of his brow?

She closed her eyes and tried to recall.

The shifting shapes of memory faded like a dream in morning's light.

"He will return. You must believe it." Mrs. Franklin's voice dragged Prosperity back to the painful present.

Until he returned . . . Her breath caught at the daunting prospect. Alone. Impoverished. Without a home.

"He will." Mrs. Franklin patted her hand for emphasis. "He is a gentleman."

A man of honor. Yes, David was that. He never failed to write each Sunday. The letters might arrive late or all in one batch, as was the case right now. She had not received a letter in nearly a month, but tomorrow might be the day. Until then she treasured each written word, reading the letters over and over until his sentences wove into the fabric of her days. He was saving all he could. He would marry once he had saved enough. If that came sooner rather than later, he might send for her. No woman on Nantucket or Key West could compare to her in beauty and intellect. He kept her portrait on the desk in his quarters.

He was an ever-true, unshakable mark. To this she could cling.

At her side, Mrs. Franklin rose, pulling Prosperity from her thoughts.

Aunt Florence approached with a swish of her flounced skirts. "I'd like to speak to my niece."

Mrs. Franklin offered her condolences to Aunt Florence and trundled to the kitchen.

Prosperity rose, aware that her future might depend on good relations with her closest remaining blood relative, who had made the voyage to Nantucket Island from Boston with her husband. "Please have a seat."

She'd met Aunt Florence just once before, on her aunt's brief visit to the island when Prosperity was a child. How different Aunt was from her sister! While sunlight and love had creased Ma's face into a starburst, Aunt's face was pinched, her lips pressed into a white line. Thin and bony, Aunt wore a silk mourning gown that rustled as she moved. Its fine black-on-black striping took Prosperity's breath away. Never would she touch, least of all wear, such a gown.

Aunt Florence looked down her nose at the chair. "Given the option, I prefer to stand. After the grueling journey, I cannot endure another hard bench."

Prosperity swallowed. "I hope your accommodations were comfortable. Dumfrey Hotel is the finest on the island."

"It was barely habitable, but better than this," Aunt sniffed with a caustic glance at Prosperity's home. "My sister chose unwisely. I trust you have done better. Livvy wrote that you are engaged to marry an army engineer." She never once looked directly at Prosperity. "It's certainly better than a whaler, though a true gentleman would have married and brought you with him."

"He is a true gentleman."

Aunt didn't seem to notice that she had spoken. "I fear that your uncle and I must return to Boston at once. Harold can't be away from the bank for long." She opened the clasp on her elegant silk bag and pulled out a small ivory envelope that must have cost dearly at a stationer. "We want you to have this."

With trembling hand, Prosperity took the fat envelope. What on earth could it be? Perhaps it was a note of condolence or one of Ma's letters to her sister.

"Thank you," she whispered, her throat dry.

"Do understand that we can't take you in." Aunt Florence's cold smile revealed perfectly white teeth. "Harry and his family visit often, and of course Amelia is still at home. Between friends and family, there isn't a week that we don't use every bed in the house."

Prosperity averted her gaze. "I understand." Her last close relative was deserting her.

Aunt waved a hand toward the envelope. "Use this to make your way in the world. Livvy wrote that you are quite capable of caring for yourself, but we wanted to give you this assistance until you can secure a position as a governess or housekeeper."

Prosperity stiffened. She was the daughter of a whaler. Her fiancé was an engineer. Her future did not depend on going into service. Mrs. Franklin was right. David would help. And Prosperity would turn the other cheek on the affront.

Swallowing her pride, she managed to speak. "Do thank Uncle Harold for me."

"You can thank him yourself. We must leave now in order to catch the boat to the city. You may escort me to the carriage."

Prosperity could not regret Aunt's early departure. For her mother's sake, she expressed sorrow as she led her aunt to the door. Behind her, the women carried the food to the table. The moment Prosperity escorted her aunt off the porch, the men and children rushed inside, leaving Prosperity alone in front of the house with her aunt and uncle.

He tipped a hand to his beaver. "Miss Jones."

"Uncle Harold."

"I fear we must leave."

She nodded. "It can't be helped."

"Indeed."

"We will be late for the boat," Aunt Florence said.

He helped his wife into the hired carriage. Before climbing in himself, he turned back to Prosperity.

"Be a good girl, now." He too did not meet Prosperity's gaze. "That little sum should help you make a start of things." He cleared his throat, muttered something unintelligible, and then entered the carriage. With a final apologetic glance, he closed the door.

After the carriage rolled from view, Prosperity broke the seal on the envelope. A single sheet of paper, unmarked, cradled a number of large bills. She could not count the sum now, in the street, but it appeared enough to settle accounts and pay for room and board until David learned of her circumstances. A letter would take weeks or even a month or more to arrive. Then the same time for his reply to return. By then . . .

Prosperity pressed the envelope to her midsection, overcome by the speed with which the world was closing in upon her.

Help me, Lord. Show me Thy path and the way Thou wouldst have me walk.

The simple prayer calmed her.

"She's gone, is she?" Mrs. Franklin joined her in the yard. "Good riddance, if you ask me. Livvy deserved better from her sister, but there's no sense fussing over what can't be changed. Come, dear, let's go inside and have a bite to eat." She took Prosperity's arm. "There will be plenty of time to consider your future tomorrow."

Prosperity did not move, for the answer to her prayer struck with perfect clarity. Why wait for letters to wend their way south and then north again?

"I will go to Key West."

Mrs. Franklin's jaw dropped. "You cannot be serious."

"I am not only serious, I am certain."

"But my dear, you are letting your emotions speak. You have suffered a great loss and are not thinking clearly. Give yourself time to grieve. By the time your young man returns, you will be in a much better state of mind."

"I am perfectly sane. In fact, my thoughts have never been clearer."

"Naturally you want to see your fiancé, but do be practical. Even if you could afford such a voyage, someone must travel with you."

Prosperity clutched the envelope. "I shall travel alone."

"Alone? You cannot. Sea travel is neither comfortable nor safe. I speak from experience, dear. Mr. Franklin and I have traveled to Charleston in the past. It's not a voyage to be undertaken without great care. A woman alone?" She shuddered. "Your reputation and quite likely your person would suffer."

"It does not matter. David awaits me."

"You cannot mean that." Mrs. Franklin's voice rose with every word, her expression earnest. "I will account your rash decision to grief, but even if you will not guard your reputation, you must consider the uncertainty of the seas. Your father was a seasoned sailor, yet the sea claimed his life. The risk is too great. Better your fiancé return to you."

"He cannot. He would never leave his post."

"Then wait. You are welcome at our house."

Though Mrs. Franklin's concerns chipped at Prosperity's confidence, she would not be swayed. When weighed against servitude or destitution, the risk was small, for if she succeeded, her beloved awaited.

Prosperity squared her shoulders. "I am sailing for Key West, and you cannot persuade me otherwise."

⌒∞⌒

Key West
That Night

Lt. David Latham's hand trembled. A drop of ink splotched onto the white paper.

"Not again." His muttered frustration echoed off the walls of the small but adequate quarters.

Already the sheet of paper was a tangle of scratched-out beginnings and blotted ink drops. Once he got the wording right, he would begin anew with a fresh sheet of stationery, but two hours of wrangling had produced only the date. In thirty minutes, even that would be incorrect.

Ordinarily he handled any difficulty with calm precision. An engineer in the United States Army Corps must rely on logical analysis to conquer frequent setbacks. This one, however, was both personal and painfully unexpected. It drove a spike into the heart of his carefully drawn future.

It made this letter far from ordinary.

He returned the pen to its holder and flexed his fingers. To his right, the window opened onto a star-filled sky barren of suggestions.

How to begin? Every letter required a salutation, but no combination of words worked. His usual address bespoke an affection that would gladden his beloved's heart. What cruelty when a paragraph later he must crush that joy. On the other hand, formal address would send her into a panic before he'd cushioned the blow with careful reasoning.

No, this was a delicate affair.

He laughed bitterly.

Affair was too kind a word. *Debacle* fit much better, especially when he could not recall a single moment of the slip into temptation that led to this painful decision. To counter his disbelief, she had brought forth witnesses. The result could not be denied. He was responsible.

Oh, Prosperity, dear Prosperity, what have I done to you?

He ran a finger over the daguerreotype that he had commissioned immediately after she agreed to marry him. The frozen image could not capture the glow of compassion in her gold-flecked hazel eyes. The interminable wait without moving a muscle resulted in too severe an expression. Despite the hardships Prosperity had endured, she brought joy and light to the darkest day. Her plain gown and cap in this picture reflected her present lowly estate. He had planned to one day clothe her in the fine gowns she deserved.

That hope was gone, whisked away in a single night of shameful revelry.

He kneaded his throbbing temples. Why couldn't he remember? He had no recollection of Aileen Carlyle beyond some playful jesting when she brought the rum to the table he and his soldier friends occupied. The first toasts led to more and more until he awoke the next morning in the soldiers' barracks with a splitting headache and no idea how he'd gotten there. After a stern reprimand, the incident seemed over until Miss Carlyle approached him four weeks ago with news that chilled his bones.

Why hadn't he turned away at the grogshop door? Why had he even gone there? He never drank spirits, but the men had insisted, and he had been flattered by their attention. He'd let camaraderie draw him into temptation.

Why such a terrible price?

How many times he had prayed for God to relieve him of this burden. How often he had dropped to his knees pleading for a miracle that would absolve him, but this sin could not be whisked out the door.

The fruit of his error grew, and honor dictated he must set matters to rights. That entailed breaking the unwelcome news to his fiancée. Such a thing ought to be handled in person, but she dwelt nearly fourteen hundred miles north of this tropical island outpost. A letter was his only means of communication. Delivery would take weeks, perhaps a month if weather delayed the ship. By the time she received this . . .

He heaved a sigh.

It would be done.

Irrevocable in the sight of God.

Thus he must write the painful letter, and a letter began with a salutation. He drew a clean sheet of paper from the desk drawer.

As an engineer working on the construction of the new fort, named in honor of the late President Zachary Taylor, he would move to larger quarters sufficient for a family after the wedding.

The event that had once filled him with anticipation now churned up dread. He had always envisioned a proper ceremony back home on Nantucket Island. His parents and brothers, cousins and uncles would witness the joyous uniting of kindred spirits in their family church. He had promised to wed as soon as he finished his tour of duty in Key West. Though this meant years apart, the income he earned here would build a solid financial foundation to start a family. The reasoning had made perfect sense at the time, and she had gazed up at him with complete trust.

Oh that he had tossed reason to the wind and married her at once.

He raked fingers through his tangled locks. Nothing could be done now to alter the plans. Fate—or rather, despicable conduct—dictated his future. He would wed sooner rather than later, and not to the woman he adored.

She gazed at him sweetly from the daguerreotype. Despite the loss and hardship she'd endured, hope shone in her eyes. That hope had been rooted in his promise.

He slammed the image facedown on his desk. How could he look her in the eye?

She trusted him, and he had betrayed that trust. He must break her heart. Dear, gentle Prosperity deserved the best after all she had suffered, not another loss.

Unable to bear not seeing her, he lifted the image once more. He traced the curve of her cheeks to the dimpled chin. If he closed his eyes, he could still hear her resonant voice, surprisingly deep for one so small. He could still feel the softness of her hair, a lock of which was buried in his trunk. He could still smell the freshness of the sea upon her, as if she'd just climbed the dunes to look for her father's lost whaling ship.

"You deserve better," he whispered.

The cricket he'd not managed to evict from his room answered with a shrill taunt.

He ought to destroy the daguerreotype. That part of his life was over. But he could not bear to lose this last link to her, so he tore apart the frame and removed the silvered plate. He tucked the image between the pages of his Bible. Then he closed the volume and slid it into the bottom desk drawer beneath his engineering manuals and the army regulations that ordered his days. Tomorrow morning he would take them all to his office.

The time for regret was over. A man accepted his responsibilities, no matter how distasteful.

He picked up the pen, his hand steadier.

Dearest Prosperity, he scrawled, forgoing the initial *My*. She was dearest to him still, though he could no longer claim her affection.

I cannot ask your forgiveness, nor do I deserve it. Though I am tempted to soften the blow, your honest, practical nature would not wish me to couch what I must tell you in false cheer. Thus I will be straightforward, trusting that your affections have so sufficiently dimmed over the two years of our separation that this news will not inflict great suffering.

I fear that I must break our engagement.

The trembling began again, so violently that he had to set down the pen. Driven by torment, he sprang to his feet and paced to the darkened window. Yanking off his spectacles, he stared into the night. In the distance, a few lanterns dotted anchored vessels. Nearer, lamps brightened the commander's windows and glowed dimly at one end of the soldiers' barracks. Soon they would be put out, leaving only the moon and the stars to light the garrison.

No light could illuminate David's soul. Such sooty blackness could never be scrubbed clean. She was better off without him, but he was lost without her.

Despair welled again. Once more he pushed it down. Honor dictated but one course. Lives would be wrecked no matter which path he took, but only one protected the innocent.

Once again he sat at his desk and picked up the pen. He

could not profess what was in his heart, that he loved her still, that he would love her until the day he died. That would be cruel. No, this letter must sever their bond in a single stroke, break every connecting sinew, and leave not even a ray of hope. Only then could the wound heal. Only then could his beloved let go of the future they had planned together and turn her gaze toward another.

He dipped the nib in ink and touched it to the paper. The words did not come easily. His unsteady hand bore witness. He scratched it out as best he could.

I will marry tomorrow.

2

Five Weeks Later

Prosperity squinted into the dazzling sun and blotted the perspiration from her brow. The steamer had changed course, and the brim of her bonnet did little to shield her from the glare. The waters shimmered, and heat rose from the wooden deck in waves. Though she'd attempted to find refuge in the shadow of the deckhouse, this course change put her full into the sun.

Mourning black was not made for such climes. She pressed the handkerchief to her forehead again.

"You ought to go indoors," Mrs. Cunningham stated in her usual abrupt manner. The Cunninghams had graciously agreed to escort Prosperity on the final leg of the journey from Charleston, where the Franklins had disembarked. "Without a parasol, the tropical sun will wilt a Northerner like you."

Naturally the woman did not offer to loan her one of the many stowed in her stateroom.

"Yes, ma'am." Prosperity had learned early on that debate

accomplished nothing. She simply agreed with Mrs. Cunningham's counsel and continued on her course. This morning, that course included a first glimpse of Key West. Not even the oppressive heat could persuade her to miss that.

As the steamer glided nearer the small island, a substantial brick edifice rose from the water with only a narrow spit of sand to connect it to the shore. The wall stood a full story in some spots while other sections did not reach the gun ports yet. Even from this distance, the exterior walls looked several feet thick.

"Oh my!" Prosperity clapped her hands. "That must be David's fort."

Mrs. Cunningham lifted a dark, perfectly sculpted eyebrow. "David's?"

"Not his, strictly speaking. The nation owns it, but he has worked so diligently for two years that I think of it as his."

"All partiality aside, I believe the credit lies elsewhere. Mr. Cunningham often dines with Captain Dutton, who has taken charge of the project from the beginning."

"Naturally," Prosperity murmured, embarrassed by her outburst but not her excitement. Soon she would see David. So very soon.

Knowing David, he would be hard at work. Workers and cranes and all manner of mechanical devices crowded the site. As the steamer passed, Prosperity leaned over the rail to keep the edifice within view. How grand it looked, floating upon the turquoise seas, as if an island. David's island.

She touched the locket at her throat. Had he changed over the two years, or would he look as crisp and perfectly ordered as the day he marched aboard the ferry to Boston? Had his hair lightened in the brilliant sun? Had the clime darkened his fair skin? Was he thinner or had he gained strength from the hard labor? Would his eyes sparkle when he saw her?

Oh, that they would. His earlier writings had led her to believe that he would welcome her arrival, but the long-anticipated batch of letters did not come before she left. The unusual delay must have been due to an exhausting workload or even a wrecked mail ship, but she would not know for certain until she saw him. And he saw her.

He would know by her mourning attire that her mother had passed, but she would not allow sorrow to overcome the joy of their reunion. She would go to him and profess her undiminished affection. One look into his eyes would confirm her hope.

"When completed, it will protect us from those dreadful Spaniards," Mrs. Cunningham sniffed.

The statement snapped Prosperity from her daydreams. Her traveling companion must have been speaking for some time, but she caught only the last words. "Spaniards?"

"Havana is only a day's sail away, whereas the nearest American settlement of any size is at least three times that distance. We are completely unprotected."

"The army is here."

"A few companies. Ill equipped and ill supplied. Half at a time are sick with fever and ague, especially the Northerners. I will never understand why they don't send a good Southern regiment here."

Prosperity gritted her teeth, for David was one of those Northerners whom Mrs. Cunningham deemed weak. "You can have the greatest confidence in our soldiers. Lieutenant Latham will see the fort completed. He will ensure you are protected."

Mrs. Cunningham cocked her head with its beribboned straw bonnet. "You are very certain of your fiancé."

"I have known him for many years. We attended the same schoolhouse and church. He courted me three years before offering for my hand. Indeed I know him as well as any woman can know a man."

"If you were my daughter, I would have insisted you write for his return, not run off on some wild goose chase."

"It is not a wild goose chase. I know Lieutenant Latham. He holds honor in the highest regard. He will keep his word."

"Time changes men." Mrs. Cunningham must have said that because her husband spent his days in the gentlemen's lounge gambling at cards.

"Not Lieutenant Latham."

"I hope for your sake that you're right. I can't believe you did not send a letter ahead to warn him." Mrs. Cunningham shook her head. "He will be surprised, to say the very least."

"He will be overjoyed."

Prosperity had no reason to doubt David. He'd written faithfully of his love and affection. The language was as stiff as his posture, as if he took hours crafting each word. Perhaps he did. An engineer did not hastily place an arch or doorway. He considered it from every angle, calculating the strength of the surrounding walls. It made perfect sense that he measured words with the same care. No unbridled passion. No careless declarations. Even so, passion lurked beneath the surface.

She smiled. Yes, David would rejoice to see her. Nothing stood in the way of their marriage now. A simple church wedding would suffice. She did not require an elaborate ceremony. After all, he earned only a lieutenant's wage while she brought nothing to this union but love and a willingness to work.

"Ah, home at last," Mrs. Cunningham said.

The shoreline now displayed quaint houses reminiscent of

home. Many had two floors. Some boasted a veranda on each. Whitewashing was not in great use here. Instead many allowed the bare wood to weather to silver. Arching palms and brilliant flowers lent the scene an exotic appearance.

"Look at all the colors," she breathed.

Mrs. Cunningham offered an indulgent smile. "It must seem strange to a newcomer."

"Are there parrots and monkeys here?"

"Only those brought by sailors and kept indoors or aboard ship."

That disappointment vanished when another curiosity arose. "What are the round balls in that palm tree?"

"Coconuts."

"I've never eaten one."

"You will eat so many here, I fear, that you will grow to despise them."

"I can't imagine that."

As the steamer proceeded along the shoreline, Prosperity's attention shifted to the harbor with its huge warehouses, each labeled. "Tift. O'Malley & Sons."

"Local merchants," Mrs. Cunningham said. "They control the wharves and any cargo brought into port."

"Much like Nantucket. Do they fish?"

"Fish, turtle, and sponge."

Prosperity had a great deal to learn about this place, but she relished the idea of David showing her every street and shop and delicacy. He stood head and shoulders above her, a commanding stature. With his talent and skill, she had no doubt he would soon rise in rank until that fort truly was his, or at least under his command. Together they would make this town their own, just as Ma and Pa had claimed a spot in the fabric of Nantucket.

She stood on her tiptoes and leaned forward to catch a glimpse of the docks as they entered the harbor. Throngs of passengers crowded the rail, waving and shouting at people ashore, and she could not see past them.

She settled back on her heels. The steamer would soon dock, and everyone would disembark. Those waving passengers would hurry to meet family or friends. The Cunninghams would return home. Why did she need to see the wharves? No one waited for her. David didn't know she was coming.

Mrs. Cunningham touched her forearm. "Mr. Cunningham can hire a cart for your trunks."

Prosperity's luggage consisted of one small bag. "Thank you, but that isn't necessary."

"Of course it is. The army post is a goodly distance from the harbor. You certainly can't drag your trunks that far. If we had a carriage, we would gladly take you, but Mr. Cunningham refuses to buy one. He insists the cost outweighs the occasional need."

Prosperity smothered a smile. Mrs. Cunningham had made no secret of her dismay that her husband refused to purchase what she considered a necessity. "Thank you, but I prefer to walk, and I have only one small bag."

Mrs. Cunningham clucked her tongue. "You aren't accustomed to sea travel. You will find walking most difficult after weeks at sea. Trust me, dear. You need a carriage. Mr. Cunningham will pay the driver."

Prosperity could not let the Cunninghams incur an expense that she could not compensate. "Thank you for your kindness, but I insist on walking."

"Well then, have it your way." She looked past Prosperity and waved. "There you are. I thought you would never show."

Mr. Cunningham strolled toward them from the direction

of the gentlemen's lounge, looking a bit rumpled and not at all pleased that his wife was hurrying toward him with a stream of instructions.

Mrs. Cunningham's departure left Prosperity alone with her thoughts. She watched the dock workers wrap thick lines around the dock pilings. Friends, relations, and the curious crowded the length of the wharf, making the disembarkation process difficult. Stevedores and porters threaded through the crowds, but the crew had to push back the bystanders to move the gangway into place.

Prosperity looked for David. He would tower above everyone else. Her heart skipped a beat at the sight of a soldier's uniform, but then the man removed his hat to wave it at the ship, revealing black locks. Not David.

She pressed a hand to her midsection. If her nerves got into such a state at the sight of a uniform, what would happen when she finally saw David?

She forced out a shaky breath as the first passengers streamed off. She would soon find out.

⁓

David checked and rechecked the placement of every brick on the rising casemate arches. They would carry the weight of the second tier. Improper construction would bring the fort—and David's reputation—crashing down.

"O'er there, you darkies," the sergeant foreman shouted to two men carrying an impossibly large load of brick.

David cringed, as always, but he had learned to swallow his distaste for slavery. No small number of those under his command believed that the Negroes were inferior and needed direction—the rougher, the better. David saw instead men who sweated and toiled in the hot sun, while their wages went to masters who sipped lemonade on shaded verandas. His abolitionist father would preach against such men, but Reverend Myles Latham was in Nantucket, not Key West.

David made sure all his men rested and received adequate rations, much to the displeasure of his cohort who led an all-white contingent of laborers. In Lieutenant Ambleton's view, paid laborers deserved more rations and rest than a slave, though he never expressed that sentiment to their commanding officer. When given the same provisions, David's men bore up better under the heat and bouts of fever. That was proof enough for him.

"Message for you, Lieutenant," one of his men called out.

David stepped out of the casemate and squinted against the blazing sun. He lifted a hand to his forehead and absently wondered where he'd set down his stifling hat. They really ought to use the straw hats worn by the hired men. He scanned the parade ground until he spotted Private Jameson heading his way. The slender man was better suited for a clerk position, but the army in its infinite wisdom had sent him to labor in the hot sun. Jameson largely avoided work by running messages between the garrison and the fort.

The darkly handsome private stopped before him and jerked a hand to his cap in salute. "Lieutenant Latham, sir. Mrs. Latham sent this note." He handed over a folded square.

David still flinched at the term. His mother was Mrs. Latham, not Aileen Carlyle. Yet in the eyes of God and the law, Aileen was his wife and the bearer of his name and progeny. By now his parents must have received his letter informing them of his marriage. No doubt they were shocked. An Irish grogshop girl was not the type of daughter-in-law they had anticipated, though he had wisely not stated his new wife's former occupation or the reason for their haste.

He sighed and dismissed Jameson. His wife sent a message at least once a day. She always needed something: money, medicine from the apothecary, foodstuffs, or simply his presence. He was tempted to ignore the note, but she was heavy with child. The other wives at the garrison had informed him that he must attend to her needs at this delicate time.

He mopped his forehead. What he needed to attend to was his work. The fortifications would never get finished if he spent all his time catering to his wife's whims.

The short note was scrawled in a nearly illegible hand. Almost every word had been misspelled, and the improperly constructed sentences were peppered with language as raw as her speech. It took every ounce of restraint not to correct and rebuke her for speaking in a manner more commonly used by sailors and soldiers.

Once he got past the wording, today's message was clear. She wanted milk. Fresh, not from this morning. She expected him to ply the few men in town owning a milk cow to squeeze out a pint midday.

He groaned.

It never ended with the milk. Once he arrived home, she would devise all manner of excuses to keep him there. She was bored and lonely, but she refused to spend time with the other wives. Neither would she listen to reason. To provide for her and their child, he must work. She pouted and asked why he must work so much. He suggested over and over that she make friends. She insisted no woman would befriend her. He had even tactfully hinted that she might pick up the house or dust. Naturally she pointed out that a woman in her condition should not tax herself. A proper husband would hire a housekeeper, but he could not afford a servant. The arguments went on and on.

He would rather stay at the work site than go home.

With a sigh, he crumpled the note and stomped toward the gate. On the way he tossed the note in the cook fire. Work would have to wait.

❧

The town bustled with activity. Prosperity clutched the handle of her small bag as she walked in what she assumed was the direction of the fort. It was at least directly opposite the route the Cunninghams had taken. She did not relish Mrs. Cunningham's presence at her reunion with David.

The streets ran every which way near the harbor and were lined with houses and shops carrying all manner of goods. Most she could find in any Nantucket shop, but a few windows displayed oddities. Huge tortoise shells, piles of sponges, and large shells with pearly pink interiors drew her eye.

Very few wagons and carriages roamed the commercial district. The bulk of people were on foot. That made her feel a bit less conspicuous, though her black mourning clothes drew more than one sympathetic glance. By and large, the women here dressed in light colors and summery fabrics with straw bonnets and parasols.

A wagon-wheel intersection brought her to a halt. Five streets spread out in all directions except the one she wanted. She sought to ask directions, but foreign tongues coursed around her like the ebb and flow of the tides. Then she spotted a lovely, hatless blonde holding one end of a large sign outside a shop. A man held the other end. They appeared to be placing it above the door. They must be local.

She hurried across the intersection, but they had not heard her approach. She cleared her throat. "Pardon, but might I ask for your assistance?"

The woman turned around with a smile and brilliant blue eyes that reminded her of David's. She set down her end of the sign. "Good afternoon."

"Good afternoon. I'm sorry to interrupt."

The woman's warm smile spread into a grin. "You're from the Northeast. Boston?"

"Very close. Nantucket, but how did you know?"

"The way you said *sorry*.'"

"Oh. I didn't realize I said it incorrectly."

The woman laughed. "Not at all. Our friend Tom says it the same way, doesn't he, dear?"

The muscular, dark-haired man at the other end of the sign nodded. "That he does. If I'm not mistaken, he's from Nantucket also."

"He is?" The prospect of another Nantucketer in Key West made Prosperity feel even more welcome.

"Fancy that," the woman said in the same charming accent Prosperity had heard in Charleston. "You must meet someday."

The man leaned the sign against the ladder and cleared his throat. "I believe the lady asked for our assistance. Introductions might be in order."

"Of course, of course," the blonde bubbled. "I'm Elizabeth O'Malley and this is my husband, Rourke. You must be new in town."

"Pleased to meet you. I'm Prosperity Jones. I didn't realize it was so obvious that I've never been here."

The woman laughed. "Your eyes are wide as saucers, and

you're carrying a bag. Those are two fine clues. Are you looking for a particular inn or boardinghouse?"

"Actually, I need directions to the fort. My fiancé is an engineer with the army corps."

"He didn't meet your ship?" Mr. O'Malley frowned. "The army should allow a man to escort his lady."

"Oh, no." Prosperity hastened to correct his assumption. "That's not it at all. You see, he didn't know I was coming."

Mr. O'Malley's frown deepened, and his wife's eyebrows lifted in surprise.

"It was quite sudden," Prosperity explained. "There was no time to write ahead." She bit her lip, unwilling to spill the details of her circumstances to complete strangers.

"It's quite a walk to the fort," Mr. O'Malley said. "You might want to hire a carriage."

"No, thank you." Prosperity looked down the long street lined with houses. In the distance, a lighthouse rose above the roofs and trees. "I prefer to walk."

Mr. O'Malley chuckled. "Reminds me of someone I know." The gaze he cast on his wife left no doubt of his affections.

Elizabeth O'Malley laughed and blew him a kiss.

Prosperity turned away, embarrassed to witness such public affection yet longing for the same with David. "I should be going. If you will point the way . . ."

"Forgive me." Elizabeth joined her. "I don't mean to intrude, but I have some experience arriving without notice. He will be . . . surprised, to say the least. I'm sure that in the end it will turn out well, but don't be shocked if he is taken aback at first. Men, as a rule, don't much care for surprises."

Her husband loudly cleared his throat behind them.

Prosperity shook her head. "He loves me. He might be surprised at first, but once the shock wears off, he will be delighted to see me." She gripped her bag a bit tighter. "Now, if you will point the way, I will leave you to your business."

"Let's see. From here, go toward the water on the cross street and then turn left at the end and follow it to the part of town where the colored people live. Mind you, it's perfectly safe, but stay on the street all the same. Pass the marine hospital and go to the right. Soon you will see the fortifications."

Prosperity tried to calculate those instructions, but they didn't make sense. "Wouldn't that put me in the ocean?"

Mr. O'Malley shook his head. "My wife omitted a turn or two. You'd better walk to the fort with Miss Jones, dear."

No matter how nice Elizabeth O'Malley was, Prosperity did not want anyone with her when she first saw David. "I wouldn't want to take you from your work. Surely I can find it by heading in that direction."

Elizabeth untied her apron. "Nonsense. Rourke can manage the sign quite well without my assistance, and I could use the walk. But first I insist you drink a glass of limeade. A Northerner like you must be suffering from the heat, especially dressed in mourning black. My condolences on your loss."

"My mother." Prosperity's throat constricted. Unlike Mrs. Cunningham, Elizabeth O'Malley spoke with genuine sympathy, not pity.

"I lost my mother also. Two years ago next month. It will get a little easier over time, but she'll always be in your thoughts."

Prosperity nodded. She could do little else, for tears rose despite the fact that Ma seemed a lifetime away from this hot, tropical port.

Elizabeth stepped into the building and returned with a glass of cool liquid that looked like lemonade. "Try this."

Prosperity took a sip and coughed. "My, it's tart!"

"I told you it needed more sugar," Mr. O'Malley said.

Elizabeth made a face at her husband. "None for you, then."

He shrugged. "Florie left a jug of tea inside, if you prefer."

Prosperity shook her head and managed to down the somewhat bitter liquid. She would not refuse such kindness from a woman whom she hoped might become a friend. "Thank you very much."

"See? Some appreciate my efforts," Elizabeth said to her husband as she took the empty glass from Prosperity. "Now, let's go find your beau. Rourke can take care of this." She handed the glass to her husband, who took it without protest. Prosperity couldn't imagine any of the men she knew handling dirty dishes.

The couple set Prosperity at ease. Perhaps it was their obvious affection, perhaps their joy. Whatever it was, the nerves that had dogged her since stepping ashore now subsided.

"Your beau must be an officer then." Elizabeth pinned a straw hat atop her head.

"A lieutenant." Prosperity's heart quickened. Soon she would see David. Soon the two years of waiting would be over. "Lt. David Latham."

A cloud passed over Elizabeth's face. She looked up to her husband, who shook his head.

Fear knifed through Prosperity's heart. "Do you know him? Is something wrong? Has there been an accident at the fort?" How cruel to come this far and learn he'd perished.

"No, no. Nothing like that." Elizabeth smiled, but it looked forced. "I thought I'd heard that one of the officers married recently, but it must be someone else."

Prosperity breathed a sigh of relief. "I'm sure it was."

It had to be.

⁕

Aileen lay on a chaise longue situated on the front piazza, or veranda, of their quarters. David gritted his teeth. She hadn't even bothered to dress. Yet again. She'd thrown a silk wrapper over her nightgown, but her ankles and feet were bare. Completely inappropriate.

Her eyelids were closed, and one hand lazily waved an expensive silk fan that he'd never seen before. Perspiration drenched tendrils of her bright red hair and dotted her pink skin. She looked every bit the strumpet that he'd heard more than one officer's wife call her in whispered conversation.

He clenched his hands. Yes, Aileen was not educated or cultured, but she was still a child of God and deserved a chance to improve herself. He was giving her that chance, but thus far she'd shown little inclination to take advantage of that opportunity.

Her lids flickered open when he climbed the dozen steps to the main story. "Dahling," she purred. "What girl don't love a man who comes when he's called?"

"You should be dressed by now."

She waved the fan at him. "Too hot."

"The other ladies will talk."

"Let 'em. A rotten lot they are, all 'have to do this' and 'have to say that.' Not me, love." She curled her bare toes, stretched her arms, and yawned. "Me eyes is only for me man." Despite her heavy figure, she curved into a seductive pose and tapped the chaise. "Join me."

David could not muster a glimmer of attraction for the woman he called his wife. He prayed for her, he urged her to change, but his affections were reserved for the child she carried—his child, his future.

On that baby David could lavish the love he'd once saved for Prosperity. By now she must have received his letter. He could picture her sinking to a chair, a hand to her mouth to stifle the gasp of surprise. Her hand would tremble. Tears would fill her hazel eyes until they shimmered like stones in a stream. Her delicate throat would bob as she struggled to hold back the emotions, but in the end tears would course down her cheeks.

"Why ye standin' there like a fool?" Aileen snapped, pulling him from his thoughts. "Ye brung the milk, didn't ye?"

"Forgive me." He scurried forward and deposited the jug on the small table beside her. It was crowded with all the entertainments she required to get through the day. In addition to the silk fan, which would doubtless cost him yet another stiff bill from Greene's Mercantile, the tabletop housed molasses candies, a half-eaten vanilla cake, an empty teacup and teapot, a deck of playing cards, and the tarot cards he thought he'd thrown into the fire.

She ignored the milk and picked up instead a container of rouge, which she dabbed on her cheeks with her fingertips. Though he'd told her many times that her natural beauty did not require enhancement, she continued to brighten her cheeks as she had when working at the bawdiest grogshop in Key West.

"You don't need that," he attempted again.

She shrugged her shoulders. "Men like a pretty face." Her lips curved into a seductive smile, and her finger beckoned. "Come, love, stay with me a bit."

David choked down the bile. She had no idea how such talk repulsed him. Instead of tempting him, it reminded him of the depth of his sin. "I need to return to work."

Her lips drooped into a pout. "Ye just got here."

"I have men to direct and a fort to build."

She waved her hand. "That silly old fort can wait. They been working on it for years. What's a few hours here or there?" The seductive grin returned as she purred out the promise of relieving his tensions in terms that made him blush.

"The b-b-baby," he stammered. "Think of the baby."

She slumped back on the chaise with disgust. "I wish that d—" She cut off the profanity at his stern glance. Her lip curled with distaste. "I wish it was outta me."

He recoiled. "You can't mean that."

"I mean every word." She lifted a hand to her forehead and sighed. "Ye cain't imagine how much I suffer. The aches. The pains."

"I'm sorry." He felt helpless, as always. The women in his family and the wives of other officers never complained while with child. "What can I do?"

"Ye done plenty already. Yer the reason I'm in this way."

Again he apologized. "I want to help. Tell me what to do."

The pout vanished in a sly smile. "Sit down, love." She patted the chaise. "And pour some of that milk into me teacup."

He looked around. His superiors weren't near, so he poured the milk and sat down beside her.

"Ye best put the rest inside out o' the sun," she said, "and then come back ta me."

He headed into the house with the jug, but something about her demure smile unsettled him. Aileen was anything but demure. Based on her past performances, that smile hid her true feelings. He looked back through the window and saw her pour something from a small flask into the milk. His heart sank. He could demand to know what it was, but she would claim someone or other told her that rum or laudanum or whatever it was eased the aches of childbearing.

So he turned away and pretended he'd never seen it.

❦

Prosperity sent Elizabeth back to her husband when they reached the fort.

"Are you certain?" Elizabeth hesitated, glancing at the busy work site and guarded entrance. "I can stay with you until your beau arrives."

Prosperity shook her head. She did not want any spectators for this reunion.

"I can at least wait until you're certain he is here."

"Where else would he be at this hour?" The clanging of machinery and growl of engines filled the air. Laborers sang in time to the rhythmic pounding. Work was under way, and David, ever mindful of duty, would be supervising the men.

"Very well then." Elizabeth bade her farewell and walked back the way they'd come.

Prosperity waited until Elizabeth had disappeared from sight before gathering her nerve and approaching the guard.

He refused to let her enter. "No civilians."

"Lieutenant Latham will want to see me." The exertion of walking such a distance in blistering heat must be getting to her head, for she nearly blurted out that she was his fiancée. Goodness! The guard did not need to know her personal attachment to David.

"He did not give me your name."

Prosperity fought frustration. "He didn't know I was coming."

"I'm sorry, miss, but you can't enter the fortifications without permission."

"Perhaps you could send someone to fetch him."

That suggestion met the same flat resistance.

Without the trees to shade her from the sun, Prosperity wilted.

The black gown sizzled against her skin like a skillet over a hot fire. Perspiration ran from the equally scorching bonnet down her forehead and off her nose. "Please send a message to him. I can't bear this sun much longer."

At last a hint of compassion broke through the stern reserve. "I can't send for him, miss. Lieutenant Latham isn't here."

"He isn't?" The fear that he'd perished bubbled up again. "But where else would he be?"

"He went home to his wife."

3

Prosperity dropped her bag with a thud. She had never fainted in her life, but her head spun at the guard's words. Wife? David did not have a wife. He could not have a wife. He had pledged to marry her.

The guard must be mistaken. Perhaps he had misheard David's name. She did have a soft voice, and the machinery thundered nearby. She must speak more forcefully.

"I meant Lt. David Latham."

"Yes, miss. That's the one."

The quick response left no doubt. David had a wife. The O'Malleys had heard correctly. David was the officer who had married. How could it be? He would have broken the engagement by letter and waited an appropriate period of time for her response. He did not rush into anything.

The missing letters.

The landscape began to swirl as if she were caught in a vortex. What if David had written to her? What if he had broken off their engagement but the letter got lost?

She staggered backward.

"Are you all right, miss?" The guard reached out to steady her.

She pulled away. She couldn't talk to a stranger about this. She couldn't talk to anyone. The air pressed in on her, and the world was spinning out of control.

"You look pale, miss. Why don't you sit a bit? There's a bench in the guardhouse. I could set it here in the shade."

"You are too kind. I will be fine. It's just the heat." She mustered a smile to prove it, but her chin quivered.

He did not appear convinced. "Might I call a carriage for you?"

"No, thank you." She took a deep breath and picked up her bag. "See? I feel better already. Where might I call on them? Lieutenant and Mrs. Latham, that is?"

"Why, at the garrison."

"Naturally." Why hadn't she remembered that? David had written to her of the long walk between his quarters and the work site. "Thank you. I will call on him—them—there."

Her words faded behind the buzzing in her ears. Her vision blurred, and the ground heaved as if she were still aboard ship.

Don't collapse in public.

Whatever happened, she must not lose control of her faculties here, with only the soldiers near. She plodded away from the guardhouse, each step heavier than the last.

Only once before had she come near to fainting. She had been walking past the fish market when she overheard a fisherman say he saw her father's vessel go down in heavy seas. They found no survivors. She had clung to a hitching post and drew in the icy breeze until a friend rushed from the market to assist her.

Today no one would help her. She was alone in a strange land. The oppressive heat closed around her. Her knees wobbled. Cold and then hot sweats wrung the last bit of strength from her. Her bag felt like it contained lead, rather than a change of clothing and her Bible. It now took both hands to hold on. She must find shade. She must sit and collect herself. She must not lose consciousness.

The flowers and trees that had so delighted her on the walk here now blurred. The streets and paths spread out in too many directions. All looked the same. She could not think, could not find her way, could not stand much longer.

"Come with me." The directive came with comforting arms that gathered Prosperity and drew her toward the shade of a large tree.

Prosperity hadn't the strength to resist.

Elizabeth led her into the coolness where breeze and shadow met. "Let's rest here a bit." She spread a delicate handkerchief on the ground. "It's not much, but it will keep some of the dirt off your skirt." She guided Prosperity onto it.

The ringing soon eased, and Prosperity's head cleared enough to wonder why Elizabeth had come back. "How did you know to return? Did you overhear my conversation with the guard?" The idea that anyone had heard that terrible news made her stomach roll.

Elizabeth simply smiled. "After walking a short distance, my strength was sapped. I feared the heat must have affected you even more, since you are accustomed to a much cooler climate. I had to make certain you were well."

Prosperity had misjudged the woman. She blinked back tears. "I'm sorry."

"There is nothing to be sorry about." Elizabeth squeezed her hand.

"I-I can't believe it." She took a deep breath. Unlike Nantucket's cool breezes, this thick air did not calm. Images of David flashed through her mind. How serious he'd been when he'd asked for her hand in marriage. The relief when she'd agreed. The endearments in his letters. The way he'd smiled when she cut the lock of hair from his head and placed it inside the silver locket. *Until we have children.* They'd argued over names. He'd wanted to honor her parents. She'd wanted to honor his, but in the end gave in. He had grinned at that, and she'd told him what a fine father he would make.

He still would. But not with her.

"How is it possible?" Prosperity's agonized whisper thundered in the heavy air.

Elizabeth squeezed her hand again. What could she say? She had no idea what Prosperity was talking about, though she must suspect. After all, she had heard the news that an officer had married. David.

Prosperity gulped a breath to quell a sob. "We pledged to marry a-as soon as he finished his tour. He wrote of his love. He said he would send for me when he'd saved enough for the passage. That promise was made long ago, but he never retracted it. He never led me to believe anything was amiss. M-marry another? How can this be?"

Elizabeth hesitated before asking softly, "How long have you been apart?"

"A little more than two years." Prosperity undid the ties of the stifling bonnet and yanked it off her head. "But that shouldn't make any difference. David is as unchanging as the sea." Yet even as she said that, she knew its falseness. The sea changed constantly. Placid in the morning, it might rage by nightfall. The sea swallowed ships and men. It had taken her father and never spat him out. Tears welled again. To have lost father and mother and fiancé in so short a time was too much to bear.

"Then there must be an explanation," Elizabeth said.

Prosperity blotted an escaped tear with her plain cotton handkerchief. "He never said a word." She shook her head in disbelief. "David always insisted on honesty and integrity. His word was his honor. This is so unlike him."

"Then it might not be true."

Prosperity knew the hollowness of such hope. "How could it not? The guard confirmed that Lt. David Latham returned home to his wife. There cannot be two men of the same name and rank in the same regiment. No, as much as I do not want to believe it, it must be true."

Elizabeth didn't say anything at first. Birds chirped and croaked in unfamiliar songs. Leaves rustled, sounding like a torrent of rain. Prosperity wept silently.

Only after she had dried the last tear did Elizabeth speak. "Would you like to see him and discover the truth for yourself?"

"I-I can't. I can't bear to see him . . . with another woman." The tears welled again. "And yet I can't bear not knowing." She twisted the damp handkerchief. "What will I do?"

"I will go with you, if you wish."

Prosperity looked at Elizabeth O'Malley, really looked. Beyond the beauty of her features, she exuded understanding and compassion that far surpassed physical attractiveness. Elizabeth meant every word she said. She would brave this moment with her. A wave of gratitude soothed the pain. Prosperity had found a friend in this foreign land.

Yet no one else could bear this burden. Prosperity took a rattling breath and attempted a smile that came out rather poorly. "Thank you, but this is something I must do myself."

"Two are stronger than one, and a three-strand cord can't easily be broken."

"Ecclesiastes." Prosperity thought of her Bible tucked in the bottom of her bag. All her life she'd found answers there, but this time she wasn't sure God could speak to the mess she found herself in. She'd never considered what to do if David did not marry her at once. Mrs. Cunningham's admonition rang in her ears. She should have written ahead. Yet she could not have afforded to stay in Nantucket until a reply arrived.

Key West had beckoned, brimming with a bright future. David would gather her in his arms, reaffirm his undying affection, and give her enough money to let a room until the wedding. How fanciful those ideas now seemed. Without David's assistance, her few coins would not provide room and board for more than a night.

Where would she go? Where could she lay her head tonight? If she could find a room inexpensive enough to accept her paltry sum, where would she stay tomorrow? If David truly had married, then what?

Her head spun again. She squeezed her eyes shut and breathed out the dilemma facing her. "What will I do?"

Mr. and Mrs. Cunningham were the only other people she knew in Key West, yet they had not offered her any assistance. She might call on them and beg for a position in exchange for room and board.

Elizabeth wound her arm around Prosperity's shoulders. "First of all, you will have a decent meal. Then you will rest. This encounter can wait until tomorrow."

She thought Prosperity was worried about confronting David. She could not know her desperate circumstances. Prosperity took a shuddering breath. "I suppose you're right. I will find a room."

"You will stay with us. We have an extra room that will be perfectly comfortable until you get your bearings."

"I couldn't—".

"Rourke would never let me hear the end of it if you don't stay with us. He is always anxious to hear about far-off ports. Once you've rested a bit and regained your composure, perhaps you might tell him of Nantucket. He will have a hundred questions about its commerce and ships."

Somehow Elizabeth had managed to turn a charitable act into a welcome visit. If not for the ache in her heart, Prosperity would bubble over with gratitude. But all she could manage was a whispered thank-you.

"I shan't stay more than tonight."

"Stay as long as you wish." Elizabeth's mouth curved into an impish grin. "I would greatly appreciate a woman's help around the house, though I would understand if you prefer quieter quarters. You see, I have a rather boisterous infant son."

"A baby." Prosperity touched the locket at her throat. "How old?"

"Almost six months."

Six months. Elizabeth's son had been born during Ma's final decline. So often Prosperity had seen this cycle. An elder passes and a baby is born. "Hope for the future."

"And a challenge at times."

"I'm sorry I took you away from your baby."

"Not at all. He's visiting his aunt Anabelle and cousin Patrick for the afternoon." She stood and extended a hand. "Shall we?"

Tonight she would gather her strength. Tomorrow she would call on David.

❧

Disgusted by the smell of liquor on his wife's breath, David made an excuse about an urgent project and hurried back to the construction site. Work would take his mind off troubles at home.

When he arrived and learned that one of the cisterns had leaked during a test, all thoughts of Aileen vanished. The project was constantly beset with supply problems that brought progress to a halt, but thus far the engineering had held true. A leaking cistern invited the dual problems of salt water intrusion and undermining the foundation. It must be repaired. He pored over the plans with Captain Dutton, Lieutenant Ambleton, and the sergeants heading the work crews.

By the time a plan of attack had been agreed upon, darkness had fallen. Captain Dutton invited the lieutenants and sergeants to dine with him at an inn so they could discuss other potential issues. David felt a twinge of guilt for abandoning his wife, but in the army, work always took precedence over family.

"I'll send a message back to the garrison with Private Jameson," Dutton said.

With conscience eased, David enjoyed a hearty meal of stewed beef, a meat seldom seen on Key West. While dining, the men discussed progress in detail. Eventually talk drifted toward other problems.

"We've had another delay out of Mobile," Dutton announced. "Don't expect the next shipment of brick from those suppliers until mid-June."

The bad news raised a murmur among the men, but supplies seldom arrived on time or with any regularity.

"Engstrom reported a puzzling shortage of spikes," Lieutenant Ambleton added.

That caught David's attention. "I thought he'd made more than enough to last through June. Are the men using too many?"

The question was debated, but no one could agree on what

had caused the problem. Some cited the blacksmith's languid pace and thought he was covering up for laziness. Others believed the men had been overzealous in their use. A few drifted back to the problem of supply. Captain Dutton ended the discussion by charging David to look into the problem.

By the time the supper meeting ended, the Negro curfew had gone into effect, and the streets had quieted. While Dutton hired a hack to return to the garrison and the others lingered at the inn, David strolled through the residential area between the town center and the garrison, enjoying the stars above and the occasional domestic scenes in open parlor windows. As he passed one house, he thought he spotted a familiar figure from the corner of his eye.

Prosperity? His steps froze even as his heart raced. Impossible.

Though he watched the brightly lit parlor long enough to draw the attention of passersby, the only woman to enter the room had blonde hair. He must have been mistaken.

Disappointment settled in. Though he could never claim Prosperity for his wife, he selfishly wished for just one glimpse of her or one gentle word to console him that he'd made the correct choice.

Instead he plodded to his quarters where accusations doubtless awaited. Aileen had been upset that he'd left her that afternoon. The confrontation would not be pleasant. For an instant, he considered lingering in town or walking the docks. Alas, Aileen slept very little at night. She claimed it was due to her delicate condition, but he suspected she was accustomed to those hours from working at the grogshop. Though her indolence irritated him, he let the point rest. After all, he had caused this situation. He must shoulder the consequences.

After checking in with the guard, he slowed his pace. Experience taught him that one drink invariably led to another and another. Would she curse him, or had she passed out long ago? After her first drinking spell, he'd scolded her so thoroughly that she promised never to do it again. But instead of giving up liquor, she had taken to hiding it.

He dreaded what he might face. This sort of behavior could not be good for the baby. He must exact another promise from her and watch her more closely, no matter how painful. He would search her things each morning before leaving for work.

He crossed the parade ground. His quarters were dark. What a relief! She must have retired. There would be no vitriolic accusations tonight.

He climbed the steps onto the veranda and entered the dark interior. A lamp and matches should sit on the small table just inside the front door, but they weren't there.

"Aileen?"

No answer.

He waited for his eyes to adjust. Gradually, shapes came into focus, and he could navigate to the staircase leading to the upstairs bedroom. Again, guilt rippled through him. A true husband should join his wife, but he slept on the parlor sofa. Each night he dropped to his knees and prayed, but he could not love her as a husband ought to love his wife. He could not bear to touch her. Not yet. Perhaps after the baby was born.

Enough moonlight streamed through the open front door to delineate the staircase. He crept upstairs, his weight making each step creak. The door to her bedchamber was slightly ajar. No light shone from within.

"Aileen?" He rapped lightly.

No answer.

51

Inside this door should be another lamp and matches. He felt around in the dark. Thankfully she hadn't crowded the washstand the way she'd filled her veranda table. He grasped the lamp and fumbled with the matches but managed to take both from the room. After pulling the door mostly shut to guard against the sudden glare, he struck the match and lit the lamp. Light flared until he adjusted the wick. The oil was low, but the lamp cast enough light to illuminate the dusty hall crowded with piles of unwashed laundry.

He gently nudged the door open a little more. Her bed was untouched.

What? He pushed into the room, his heart pounding. Where was she? Had the birth pangs arrived? Had she gone to one of the officers' wives?

He stormed downstairs, through the house, across the veranda, and onto the grounds. None of the other parlors was lit. A lone bedroom lamp shone two doors down, but it blinked out before he reached their steps.

Where was she? He hurried back to his quarters. Perhaps she had fallen and was lying injured inside.

He plowed through the parlor, lamp swinging wildly from corner to corner until he could be certain she hadn't fallen—or fallen asleep. The downstairs and upstairs got a thorough search, but his wife was not in the house. Where had she gone?

His breath caught. What if she'd returned to the grogshop?

He collapsed onto her unmade bed. How could she throw away a good home and a respectable husband? He had given her everything, even his name. He'd pulled her from the dregs of society and turned her into an officer's wife. How could she return to such a despicable life, especially while carrying their child?

No one would do that. He'd jumped to conclusions. There must be another explanation. Perhaps she had sought the midwife over an unusual pang. Perhaps one of the wives had taken her in—but then a light would have shone from the woman's quarters. Unless Aileen had sought her old friends at the grogshop.

He raked a hand through his hair. Why would she return to the clutches of sin?

The next second he knew the answer. He had chastised her. He did not trust her. He had never been a husband to her.

The lamp sputtered out.

The missing lamp! She must have taken it with her. Then she truly had gone. As her husband, he must find her and bring her home—willing or unwilling.

His gut tightened. This would not be pleasant. If he did find her at the grogshop and she had been drinking, she would hurl threats and vulgarities at him. A drunkard or two might even come to her defense. He rubbed his jaw, anticipating the blows sure to come. Maybe his uniform would mean something. Then again, a man deep in his liquor did not respect a constable, least of all an army officer.

What if she was with a man? That idea made him nauseous. Surely not when she was so heavy with child. Father would say he had married a strumpet and must accept the consequences. Before this debacle, David had spouted on about saving sinners and granting second chances, but talk was hollow. Doing it was much more difficult.

Structures could be analyzed for weaknesses, but relationships defied analysis. So many flaws riddled this marriage that he could not begin to shore them up.

Nevertheless, he must rescue his wife from the throat of sin.

He inched through the doorway and toward the head of the stairs, feeling his way in the dark.

Footsteps sounded on the veranda below. The front door opened to laughter. Aileen's artificial laugh was echoed by one much deeper and definitely masculine. Only moonlight spilled through the doorway. The lamp had either gone out or been left behind.

"I told ye no one's here, love," Aileen purred.

The man's slurred and unintelligible murmur sent David's blood raging. He shot down the staircase. Two forms stood silhouetted in the front doorway. He clenched his hands.

"Welcome home, wife." Each word spat out like a musket ball.

Footsteps followed by a curse told him the drunkard was trying to make his escape.

David tore across the room, past Aileen, and across the veranda. The man had slipped into the shadows, surprisingly quick considering his inebriated state.

That left Aileen.

David spun to face her. The crescent moon revealed her standing with hands braced on her hips, her heavy state masked beneath a cloak.

"Never again," he said tersely.

"Who d'ye think ye be tellin' me what to do?" Aileen stood tall and unrepentant.

"I'm your husband."

"And I be your wife, fer what it's worth."

"A wife honors her husband."

She snorted derisively. "A husband loves his wife. Ye didn't come home."

"That's no excuse. Captain Dutton sent word."

"Aye, sent word, as if that's any excuse."

"It's no reason to resort to whoring."

Her sharp gasp sent guilt knifing through him. He shouldn't have said that.

She started to sob. "I'm no good. No good." Over and over she said it, punctuated by hiccups. "I try and try, but I'm rotten like me da always said."

Shame galloped in on the heels of anger. He'd asked too much of a woman berated her entire life and had given her too little. How could he expect her to change in a few short weeks?

He handed her a handkerchief and she blew her nose. "Why can't ye love me? Why can't anyone love me?"

He felt as helpless as a boy caught dragging his mother's clean wash through the mud.

"It's 'cause I was born bad," she choked out. "Me da said red hair's a sign of the devil, that there weren't a bit o' good to be found in a girl baby with red hair."

In four and a half weeks of marriage, David had never asked about her past, and she had volunteered little. They lived physically together but emotionally apart. He hadn't wanted to know her, hadn't wanted to fall in love with her. He might learn to love her after she repented, but what if she didn't? Every instinct screamed to wash his hands of her.

She hiccupped out another sob. "Jes' throw me out like he did, like the rubbish, that's what he called me."

"Your father was wrong."

She drew in a shaky breath and rushed into his arms, still sobbing. He instinctively held her.

Earlier tonight he thought he'd seen Prosperity, but she was only a dream—a lost dream. Aileen was his reality.

4

Never go to bed angry, Mother used to counsel Prosperity, yet she had done just that.

Removed from the distraction of conversation, her thoughts bounced repeatedly against the news of David's betrayal. Could it be true? How could it not? The night with its waxing crescent moon gave her no answers.

Her small room only reinforced what she'd lost, for it opened into a nursery filled with toy ships, wooden blocks, and a rocking horse—none of which the O'Malleys' little boy could use yet. She fingered the worn baby blanket lying folded on the back of a rocker. She and David had dreamed of children. When David gave her the locket, she had joked that it didn't have enough places for the many children they would have together.

His gaze had danced with delight. "As long as they're girls."

She had laughed then, but she could not laugh now. He had married another. Just a few months ago he had sworn undying devotion. What had happened? What could possibly have changed his mind so quickly?

Unable to bear the nursery a moment longer, she returned

to her simple bedchamber. She had set her Bible on the chair beside the bed, but she could not waste her generous host's oil simply to seek comfort in its pages. Instead she turned to prayer, but in the noiseless, interminable hours of darkness, nothing could stop the relentless waves of thought pounding against the same shoreline.

David was married. Life had come undone.

When first light grayed the horizon and cast the jagged leaves of the palms into silhouette, she rose, stiff from the many sleepless hours of kneeling and pleading with God to make everything right. Surely there was an explanation. David would not act in haste. He had never done so in his life. She would seek him. She would uncover the truth.

She dressed while the sky blossomed into crimson.

Red sky in morning: sailor take warning.

How often she had repeated that saying growing up. So often it had come true. There had been a red dawn the day Pa died.

With trembling fingers, she buttoned the bodice of her simple mourning gown, fit for a common woman in the lower classes. It did not require a maid to tighten stays or fasten the back. It marked her position in society as clearly as her simple bonnet. No one could mistake her for a woman of fortune. Here in Key West, where many of the tongues flowed with the languid ease of a Southerner, her speech marked her as an outsider. How she longed for something familiar.

How she longed to hear David.

She closed her eyes and envisioned him poring over his drawings, the spectacles perched on the bridge of his nose. That scholarly concentration and pensive look always stole her breath. He could get so deeply engrossed in his work that the rest of the world melted away. That was the David she cherished. That was the David she'd held in her heart the last two years.

She placed her Bible into her bag, hefted it from the bed, and slipped quietly from the room.

David would start for the fort early. She aimed to intercept him when he left the garrison, which Elizabeth told her was located within walking distance of the O'Malley house.

After leaving her last few coins on the hall table, she moved noiselessly toward the front door.

"Please keep your money. You are our guest."

Prosperity jumped. She whipped around to see Elizabeth in the nursery rocking her son. "I don't want to be a burden."

"You are a blessing."

The gentle words, coupled with Prosperity's fatigue, melted her resolve into building tears. She retraced her steps and gathered her coins. "Thank you."

"You are welcome to stay." Elizabeth did not add "if it doesn't go well."

Prosperity knew what she meant. If David was married, he could not help her. She would need food, lodging, and more than her tired mind could grasp at this moment. Still, she could not leave her bag here. That admitted defeat. She must trust that today's interview would end well. "Thank you, but I hope that won't be necessary."

"Would you like company?"

Prosperity shook her head. Perhaps she would find this had all been a dream. Perhaps God had taken care of everything in a way she could not imagine. Perhaps David was not actually wed. If so, she would forgive him as long as he regretted his actions. That's what love meant, suffering the bad with the good.

After a last look at the baby, Prosperity slipped out into the somewhat more tolerable morning air and hurried down the street. Soon houses were replaced by storefronts. The harbor appeared before her. She had ended up where she'd begun yesterday. Somehow she'd made a wrong turn and now had no idea how to get to the army post.

Nary a breeze ruffled the flag hanging in front of the customhouse. Even at this hour men hurried to work, sails were raised, and shutters flew open. The crunch of wagon wheels bit into the tangy salt air. Prosperity breathed deeply. It wasn't her Nantucket, but Key West smelled of the sea. She would find her way.

A distinguished gentleman with graying temples, top hat, and black frock coat walked past with a decisive stride. He nodded at her and continued on.

She hurried after him. "Pardon me, sir. Might you tell me how to get to the army post?"

The gentleman paused, and she realized he wasn't quite as old as she'd first thought. He looked careworn, to be certain, but his pale blue eyes twinkled, and his smile melted the fatigue away. "Staying there, are you?"

At her puzzled look, he nodded toward her bag.

"Oh. Meeting someone." She could not reveal more.

He accepted that. "You must walk in the opposite direction. Take Whitehead to Fleming and then head east. It will take you to the garrison."

Whitehead? Fleming? Prosperity was even more lost. "What street are we on now?"

He chuckled. "I've forgotten a very important step. You appear to be new to the island. If you would not be averse to joining me, I can take you to Fleming Street."

"Thank you," she breathed. "I would not. Be averse, that is."

The man's proper speech and manners flustered her.

Again he chuckled, putting her at ease. "Very well then. I am Dr. Goodenow, but you may call me Clayton."

"Clayton." Somehow that did not feel right on her tongue. "Thank you, Doctor. I am Prosperity Jones. Miss Jones. I hope I'm not keeping you from anything important."

His smile so reminded her of her father's that her heart nearly broke. "Miss Jones, you would only be postponing an exceedingly dull meeting with the surgeon at the marine hospital. Since I am heading toward Fleming anyway, your company would be a welcome addition to an otherwise dreary morning."

Reassured, she accepted his offer. "But once we reach Fleming, I must go on alone."

"Very well, Miss Jones. May I take your bag until then?"

"You are already carrying your doctor's bag."

He brushed off her concerns. "Never let it be said that Clayton Goodenow allowed a lady to carry her own bag." He doffed his hat and bowed as if she were someone important.

"I am not a lady of means. My father was a whaler."

"The sea is a noble profession." He took her bag and began walking. "Is it your father whom you mourn?"

"No. My mother. She passed in April."

"My condolences."

Even though he was a physician, she did not care to bring up Ma's illness. It was over now, but something he'd said earlier had piqued her curiosity. "Do you work at the marine hospital?"

"I am not on staff, but the physicians on the island do work in concert." He explained that marine hospitals were instituted to aid ailing seamen far from home. "But then with your father in whaling, you probably knew that."

"I have heard of them but never knew that they worked with other doctors in the community."

"I can't speak for everywhere, but on Key West, isolation necessitates cooperation."

"Cooperation." The word warmed her. "A noble idea. Working together, like in church."

He peered at her. "A peculiar observation, Miss Jones, but not one I'm willing to dispute at present." He halted on the street corner and returned her bag. "We have reached Fleming."

She looked both directions down the cross street, wondering which way to walk.

"To your left, Miss Jones."

"Thank you." She swallowed in a vain attempt to settle the tumbling in her abdomen.

"Good day, Miss Jones." With a nod, Dr. Goodenow departed in the opposite direction.

Prosperity drew a deep breath and headed toward the garrison. The street she'd walked with the doctor had looked somewhat familiar. Perhaps she had walked it on the way to the fort yesterday. If so, then she might meet David on his way to work despite the delay caused by going the wrong direction. If not, she would retrace her steps and head toward the fort.

One way or another, she would get her answer.

"Please don't leave." Aileen clung to David as he donned his coat and hat.

He carefully extracted his arm so he could slip it into the coat. "You know I must."

"But we need to be t'gether."

"Later." He had issued that response so many times that it rolled off his tongue automatically.

"That's all ye ever say." She crossed her arms.

David sighed. Though he could summon nothing nobler than pity for his wife, he had risen early to fetch breakfast for her. She had shoved the hotcakes away without tasting them.

"I can't eat," she'd complained. "Ain't nobody up this early."

Except those who must labor. David didn't point out that she was the cause of their late night. The shaky truce had taken hours to negotiate. David still wasn't clear on the terms, but she apparently thought it meant shirking duty.

Aileen stretched her arms and yawned. "Stay with me, love. One day won't make no difference."

In his exhausted state, David actually entertained the idea before shoving temptation away. "I must fulfill my duty to the United States Army."

Her lower lip poked out in the usual pout. "I hate the army."

"It pays for your gowns and gives us a place to live."

"This?" She waved her arms at their quarters. "Too small an' too far from town. It's like a prison the way they make ye say where ye're goin' and what yer business be."

"Best get used to it. I have six more years to serve here, and there's no certainty my next post will be any closer to a town." Before his wife could issue her counterpoint, he stepped onto the veranda and jogged down the steps.

Aileen trailed behind him but didn't take her usual position on the veranda's chaise longue. Instead she followed him across the grounds all the way to the guardhouse. "Ye'll come back early, then?"

He turned back long enough to issue a reply. "If my commanding officer allows it."

Ordinarily she would pout or complain, but today her expression lifted into a surprisingly pretty smile. "Until then, dear husband." She waved. "The baby and I anxiously await your return."

The response was so peculiar that David stared to see if something was wrong. She waved again, the very picture of the doting wife, though perhaps a bit less than properly dressed. Could last night's confrontation have changed her so much?

He shook his head, marveling at what had just happened. "Until later."

She waved yet again, her smile dimpling her plump cheeks.

He tentatively waved back, uncertain what had caused the change. Then he turned to head to the work site.

Standing not ten feet from the guardhouse was either a ghost or the very person who dominated his dreams and regrets. She carried a bag and wore mourning, which meant her mother had passed, but it was not her clothing that drew his attention. Her gentle hazel eyes had widened. Her countenance had blanched, and her free hand went to her abdomen in a reaction so familiar that it ached. She looked from David to Aileen and back again.

"Prosperity." He could barely get her name past his lips.

She shook her head.

He stepped toward her.

She backed away.

"Is it you?" It looked like her.

Her expression crumpled, her mouth worked, but nothing came out. Then she threw out her hand and ran.

He followed, calling her name, but she did not stop. A sob burst from her and struck him harder than a blow to the jaw.

"David, love," Aileen called out.

He let Prosperity go.

5

The unfamiliar streets turned into a maze, and Prosperity was soon lost. She stumbled this way and that, vision too blurred by tears to note a familiar landmark or read a street sign.

David was married.

The rumor was true. Moreover, he'd either been married longer than the O'Malleys indicated or he'd been living a sinful life with this woman, for she was heavy with child. David's child!

Prosperity clutched her free hand to her abdomen and struggled to draw breath.

She was supposed to give him children. *She* wanted to present him with a son. They would raise him together, instruct him in godly ways. Day after day, year after year, she had clung to his promise as to a lifeline. She had waited. She had kept her vow, but he had tossed his promise into the sea.

Oh, David. What have you done?

Though empty, her stomach still managed to churn.

"I waited," she muttered, drawing the attention of a gentleman passing by.

What did she care if strangers gawked? What was left of her? Mother, father, fiancé—all gone. All hope for the future gone. Tears burned against eyelids already swollen.

What had happened to the David she knew? This David looked older and more tired. The fine dashing figure of memory had been replaced by one burdened by heavy cares. Sin could crush a man. For but one instant had she seen the man she remembered. The moment he recognized her, the weight dropped away, but then it returned, even heavier.

She could not bear to look at him, could not stand the thought of his touch. He was married. Married! Husband and father. All the regret in the world would not erase the fact that this burden was of his own doing—and her undoing.

Hadn't Mrs. Franklin counseled her to write first? Hadn't Mrs. Cunningham and Elizabeth O'Malley warned she might not find the same man who'd left Nantucket twenty-six months ago? She had heeded none of it, clinging instead to what had proven to be a flimsy pledge. He had betrayed her.

The honor he had touted in Nantucket had proven weak in Key West. Like so many others, he had fallen prey to temptation. That woman—his wife—was pretty, in a cheap, tawdry way. How could he?

She curled in upon herself, head low as if walking into a gale. She had risked everything to join her love, and he had abandoned her for that . . . that woman. The sobs came faster and would not stop. She saw no one, heard nothing but the anger thundering in her ears.

She had lost everything.

A sob wrung out of her with terrible violence. Her arm ached from the weight of her bag. Her legs could not support her much longer. If she did not find someplace to rest, she would faint dead away in the street. She stumbled forward, vision blurred by tears. After swiping them away, she spotted a picket fence around a park-like lawn. Using the fence as support, she walked along it until she found an open gate and could enter. She collapsed onto the lawn, not caring who saw her.

David, oh David. Why?

The question repeated without an answer.

She allowed the tears to flow, hoping they would wash away the worst of the pain. Death she could face, but not betrayal. Not by the man she loved and trusted.

She pressed a sleeve against her eyes. What had she done? What could she do?

Carry on, Ma would have said. *Sometimes that's all you can do. Shoulder the burden and carry on.*

Until now, Prosperity had never realized how difficult it would be to follow that advice. Losing Pa had hurt, but they all knew the danger of the sea. It hung over every whaling trip like a black cloud. This was different. She had had no warning.

So she sat on the lawn staring numbly at the blades of grass, seeing nothing but that moment at the army post. He had been shocked at first and then had grown upset, calling after her with increasing urgency. Did he regret his actions? It no longer mattered, for what had been wrought could not be undone.

Eventually she spent the last hot tear, and her head cleared enough to remember Ma's counsel that the Lord didn't promise a life without suffering. Best thing to do was to turn hardship upside down by counting blessings. Digging a handkerchief from her bag, she blotted her eyes and tried to follow her mother's advice. She thanked God for good health and safe passage. Though her funds were low, God had blessed her with new friends who'd given her a place to stay. Over the years she had learned many skills that would help her find a paying position.

That's what she would do. She could cook, clean, or scale a fish. Someone here must need help.

She squared her shoulders. Tearful regrets would get her nowhere. God cared for the sparrow and the lily. He would help her find the job she needed.

"Miss Jones?"

Prosperity looked up to see Dr. Goodenow approaching. "Doctor?"

For the first time she looked at her surroundings. Before her stood a lovely two-story building with a long staircase leading to the entrance. Palm trees dotted the grounds, and brilliant red and pink flowers added to the cheerful appearance.

"Are you well?" the doctor asked.

Prosperity smoothed her skirts and offered a shaky smile. "Quite well, thank you. I got a bit lost, however. Is this the hospital?"

"Why, yes, it is."

His generous smile sparked an idea. God did indeed provide seed for the sparrow, but the sparrow still must gather it if he wished to eat.

"Might I inquire if there are any positions available?"

His eyebrows rose. "Dr. MacNees mentioned that one of the housekeepers left yesterday."

Prosperity gave silent thanksgiving. "May I apply for the position?"

The doctor's lips lifted ever so slightly. "Let me take you to the matron."

"Oh no, Doctor. I would not wish to take you from your patients. Just direct me, and I shall find her."

He chuckled. "Your concern for the patients is a mark in your favor." He then directed her to a Miss Stern, who proved as formidable as her name.

The stout, graying spinster grilled Prosperity on her background and abilities. She showed her the washhouse and which rooms in the hospital must be kept spotless. Then, while peering intently at Prosperity, she took a metal tray containing bloody bandages from an orderly.

"You would be responsible for laundering these as well as the bed linens."

"Yes, ma'am."

The woman grunted. "They must be boiled with the correct soaps. Gracie will show you the proper method. Some will be worse than this."

"I've changed many a bandage, ma'am, when my father got gaffed or cut open on his whaling vessel. And my mother—" Prosperity swallowed at the memory of her mother's distress over soiled bedsheets. "She was ill a long time."

Miss Stern gave no indication that impressed her. "Seamen are brought here with all manner of disease. Yellow fever, cholera, even smallpox." She paused, probably waiting for Prosperity to flinch.

She did not.

The matron grunted again. "As a newcomer, you are more susceptible, especially to yellow fever. If that concerns you, this is not the place for you."

"I'm not concerned. I nursed my mother for many years."

"Humph."

Though the woman seemed reluctant to hire her, she led Prosperity to her office. The tiny room was lined with supplies. The matron stood behind a small desk and jiggled the keys attached to her belt. "You would also attend to the dead, Miss Jones."

"Yes, ma'am."

Miss Stern peered at her more intently. "You're not afraid?"

"The dead can't hurt us, ma'am." *The living can.*

At last Miss Stern gave her a modicum of grudging respect. "I suppose you might do. But Dr. MacNees makes the final decision. Return tomorrow after the noon hour, and I will give you his decision."

"Thank you, ma'am." Prosperity gathered her bag and left Miss Stern's office.

Her heels clattered on the polished floors and down the many steps to the manicured grounds. Despite Miss Stern's unyielding countenance, Prosperity felt confident she would get the position.

David or no David, she would make a new life in Key West.

⌘

At the end of the busy workday, David sat alone in the cramped field office and tried to concentrate on the engineering drawings. One leaking cistern had turned into two. Their first attempts to shore it up had failed. Instead of making progress, the project was backtracking. He had to find a solution.

On top of that, the fuss over the lack of iron spikes refused to die. The smith insisted he'd made plenty. The men in charge of the stores insisted they had received only what they currently had. Someone was lying, but he had neither the time nor the inclination to determine who. The discrepancy was small, but the loss would set them behind until more iron stock arrived.

Through it all he couldn't get Prosperity from his mind. All day his thoughts wandered back to her, to her shock and distress, to the way she'd run from him.

She must not have received his letter. She couldn't have. If she was in Key West now, she must have left weeks ago. The ship bearing his letter would have passed hers as she sailed south. She hadn't undertaken such a dangerous voyage in response to his actions. She had stepped away from the security of home to join him.

That made his actions sting worse. Oh, the calamity one heedless night could bring! He could accept the burden, but the consequences should not fall on Prosperity. She had already suffered the loss of both parents. Mourning black signaled her mother's passing. She deserved the life he had promised her. Instead he had heaped pain on top of her sorrow.

He dug his fingers into his hair and tugged. Oh, that he could take the pain from her. If only he could turn back the clock, but that was not possible. Their lives, once intertwined, now sped in opposite directions. But he could not simply walk away. What could he do?

The lines of the drawings blurred. A clock ticked. The wind puffed against the insubstantial walls of his office. In the distance, the workers guffawed over some joke. Waves struck the shore, ushering in an intense longing for the simplicity of boyhood and home.

Home.

He leapt to his feet. That's what he could do for Prosperity. It wasn't much, but it might be enough.

While the thoughts tumbled around in his head, he rolled up his drawings. Prosperity's family had suffered a huge financial blow after her father died. John Jones had left no will or inheritance. The whaling gear that hadn't gone down with his ship was sold. Prosperity took in laundry, since that allowed her to stay home to nurse her ailing mother. Piece by piece their furnishings had disappeared. Though he'd offered to help, she'd refused to accept a single penny. Prosperity could not have much left after burying her mother. She had turned to him as her last hope.

If it took all he had, he would send her home.

❦

"No room," the woman at the boardinghouse stated. "Even if I did have a room, I wouldn't take in a lady like yourself."

"I'm a simple working woman." Prosperity had already assessed the lodging in the small town, and this boardinghouse appeared by far the best. "If you will not lease me a room, could you at least tell me which would be a good, Christian establishment?"

The woman shook her head, which was topped with a white cotton cap with gray curls peeking out. "A boardinghouse is no place for an unmarried woman."

Prosperity was at her wit's end. After learning that the inn was far too costly, she had walked around and around the town, rejecting every boardinghouse that had a seedy appearance. This one looked clean and well kept. "But I need someplace to stay, and yours is the finest in town."

The compliment drew a smile, but the woman stood firm. "I have a lot of sailors staying here. Wouldn't be right taking you in. You might try finding a room in a private residence. Last I heard, Captain O'Malley's looking for a boarder."

Prosperity lifted an eyebrow. Captain O'Malley, eh? Interesting that this woman not only knew the man but claimed to know he wanted a boarder—a fact that neither he nor his wife had mentioned yesterday. "Is he now? Their home seems rather small."

"I wouldn't know nothing about that, but he's offering a good rate, better'n you can get at the worst boardinghouse. A fair sight better'n I'd give you."

No doubt the O'Malleys had passed this notion to the boardinghouse proprietress out of kindness, but it still raised her dander. She did not need charity. "Your rooms aren't full, are they?"

"Like I told you, I got a fair many sailors staying here. You'd be safer with the O'Malleys. Take my advice, Miss Jones, and find yourself a room in a nice, Christian home. I wouldn't want you to come to any harm."

Prosperity gripped the handle of her bag, more than a little unnerved. Key West was not Nantucket. Not at all. "I won't keep you any longer, then." She backed away.

"The captain and his wife are good Christian folk," the proprietress called out. "You'll be right welcome there."

Prosperity faced the street, having lost her first choice. Before her, people and carts and horses passed in a jumble of noise and dust. She clung to the fence post to steady herself. The remaining options were unpalatable. She could let a room in a miserable and unsafe boardinghouse, beg the Cunninghams for a room, or humble herself before the woman who had already invited her.

Never be too proud to accept kindness, Ma had counseled. *In gracious receiving you bless the giver.*

Prosperity swallowed the sudden lump in her throat.

Yes, the O'Malleys would welcome her, but they would either refuse payment or charge a pittance. Accepting charity stung. How had she sunk so low? Tears burned in her eyes, and she bit her lip to quell them. A Jones bore hardship without complaint.

She would approach the O'Malleys but would only agree to stay if they would accept full and reasonable payment. Once she was offered the position at the hospital, or rather *if* she was, she could more easily afford a weekly rent, as well as save for . . .

What was she saving for?

The question hit with the force of a huge wave. Her entire future had been washed away. She had nowhere to go. No fiancé. No family. She dropped her bag with a thud and clung to the fence, breathing deeply until her head stopped spinning.

"Miss Jones?"

The familiar voice sent starch to her knees. "Dr. Goodenow." She affixed as much of a smile as she could manage. "It seems we are always running into each other."

"Indeed we are." He returned the smile with a great deal of warmth.

Prosperity couldn't help but notice that his frock coat was now rumpled, as if it had been casually tossed in a corner while he worked. Yet the top hat bore not a speck of dust. Formal and yet not. The contrast fit his manner quite well. Her feeble smile faltered.

Beneath the brim, his expression tightened. "Are you unwell? This climate can be difficult for those unaccustomed to it."

"The air is rather heavy."

"A common reaction." The inviting smile returned. "You need a cup of tea."

"No, I don't—"

"Ah." He held up a hand. "I will brook no dissent. Consider it an order, if you will." He stroked the graying sideburns that trailed down his jaw. "Ah yes, perfect." He bowed with an elegant sweep of his hand. "Miss Jones, would you care to join me at the home of one of my dear friends? She is always eager to learn what is happening at the hospital and will welcome the companionship of another lady." Without waiting for her reply, he picked up her bag and extended his arm.

Prosperity blinked, quite unaccustomed to having a man

take the lead. It had been more than two years since David left. Pa had been gone six. Prosperity had learned to seek her own guidance. How strange to once again accept that of a man, and not just a man but a comparative stranger who was carrying her bag and taking her to tea with someone she did not know.

"Your friend . . . is she married?"

"Indeed she is." He chuckled. "You need not fear propriety. She often has many at her tea table."

Prosperity accepted his arm, and they strolled away from the harbor. Who could this woman be? Her former shipmate came to mind. "Do you know Mrs. Cunningham?"

"Naturally. One cannot help but know her."

Prosperity puzzled over what that might mean. The lady did express her opinions freely and dressed like a bastion of society.

"Will she be there?"

"I cannot say." He slowed before an all-too-familiar house. "We are here. Mrs. O'Malley will be delighted to meet you."

6

I can't believe ye didn't say one word about her." Aileen sat on the chaise with her arms crossed, holding sentry over the front door of their quarters. "Did ye think I'd never find out?"

David hesitated on the top step, battling the desire to return to the work site rather than face this inquisition. Aileen, however, was his wife and deserved more of an explanation than he'd given her this morning.

"Your fiancée," Aileen spat. "When did ye plan to tell me?"

"She lives fourteen hundred miles away on Nantucket Island."

"Looks to me like she's livin' here."

David swallowed hard and began again. "I broke off the engagement. She must not have received the letter."

"Maybe she did. Maybe she thinks she'll take ye away from me."

"Prosperity isn't like that."

Aileen's expression hardened even more. "Why don't ye never say me name like that?"

"Like what?" But he knew. His feelings for Prosperity still raged.

"All soft and gentle-like."

"I'm sorry, Aileen. She caught me by surprise." He tried, really tried, to say her name with affection.

Aileen looked away. "Second-class. That's what ye think of me. Ye wouldn't have tied the knot with me if ye'd had a choice, would ye?"

Guilt rolled over him in waves. He dropped to his knees before her. "We're a family. We're making a life together."

He reached for her hands, but she tucked them under her elbows.

She stared into his eyes. "Do ye love me?"

He tried to hold her gaze but couldn't. "I promise to cherish and provide for you the rest of your life."

She snorted. "Just what I thought."

"We barely know each other."

"Whose fault is that? Did ye ask me anything about me family?"

"I'm asking now."

She pressed her lips into the petulant frown he'd come to know so well. "Ain't it a bit late?"

"No. No." Since he couldn't hold her hands, he clasped her wrists. "I care about you, Aileen. I care very much, but love will take time."

"Did it take time with her?"

David hesitated, trying to calculate her response. "We knew each other for many years, and yes, it took time for love to grow."

The corner of her mouth twitched, signaling he might have finally broken through her anger. "But it did."

"And it can for us." At least he hoped so.

She uncoiled into her usual sultry pose. "I can make ye love me. Let me show ye."

He battled to hide his disgust. "Perhaps later."

Her eyes shuttered again. "Ye're thinking of her, ain't ye? Is she coming back?"

"No. No." He rose to his feet and stomped away the tingling numbness. "I doubt she would ever return here."

Never see Prosperity again. The idea hurt more than it should.

"Then she's a fool."

"A fool?" David would never understand Aileen. One minute afraid of Prosperity's return and the next calling her a fool for staying away.

Aileen's lips curved into a smirk. "If she loved ye, she'd fight to get ye."

He almost countered that Prosperity had moral principles. Almost. But that would have guaranteed continued enmity. To move forward as a family, there must be no secrets between them. That meant explaining his plan and getting Aileen's approval.

He removed his hat. "I would like to help her, though."

Aileen stiffened.

David plunged forward. Once he explained, Aileen would see the sense in it. "She is very poor, and with her parents dead she cannot have enough money to return home. I would like to give her the fare for passage back to Nantucket."

As he'd expected, Aileen brightened at the prospect of losing her rival. Then a shadow crossed her face. "How much would it cost?"

"If you approve, I will inquire at once."

"Then she would be gone."

He nodded.

Her shoulders relaxed. "As long as it don't cost much, I give ye me blessing."

Blessing. The word sat poorly on the lips of a strumpet, but it also gave him hope. Perhaps the admonitions and prayers were beginning to have an effect.

"Very well. I will find out the amount and take it to her."

"Nay." Aileen shook her head vigorously. "Ye can't do it. Ye'd only bring her more misery. Let me."

"You?" David stared.

"Aye. I'll take it to 'er, to yer Prosperity."

David wavered. Getting the two women in the same room could not be good, but Aileen was right about one thing. Seeing him would only hurt Prosperity more.

"Should you do this . . . in your condition?" He choked back the fact that she had gone to the grogshop just last night.

She waved off his concern. "I be from hardy stock."

That wasn't his only concern, but he wasn't certain how to phrase it without sending Aileen into another bout of temper. He blew out a breath as he weighed the words. "She might not accept money from you."

Aileen snorted. "Is that what has ye in knots? Don't ye fret. I'll send one of me friends in with it."

David did not ask if that was the same friend who had escorted her home last night. The thought that she would return to a lover immediately after being discovered sent anger coursing through his veins.

"Don't get yerself outta sorts." She leaned close and ran a finger along the collar of his shirt. "One o' the girls will do it. For a price."

David supposed that was the best he could expect. But Prosperity might wonder at a gift of money from a tavern girl. He must make sure she knew it came from him. "I'll send it in a note." He must do at least that.

Aileen frowned.

"She won't accept it otherwise." He wasn't certain she would accept it even with the letter. "I must explain why I'm—we're—giving it to her."

Aileen did not look pleased. "I want ta read it first."

David didn't realize she could read. Perhaps he had misjudged her in other areas. As his wife, she was entitled to this much. He nodded. "Of course." He added an extra boon. "You may seal it."

Triumph curled her lip, and her neck arched a little higher. "Ye trust me?"

David closed his eyes, battling doubts. Marriage was built on trust. Even if he hadn't entered the state trusting her, he must begin to do so or life would descend into utter misery. This step wasn't easy. She hadn't proven at all trustworthy, and he was entrusting to her the future of the woman he loved.

"I thought so," she snapped.

He gathered his nerve. "I trust you." It was a miracle the words didn't stick in his throat.

***

Dr. Goodenow began to make introductions until Elizabeth told him she and Prosperity were already acquainted. Thankfully she did not ask how the meeting with David had gone. Prosperity could not bear to tell anyone of that disaster. Neither did Elizabeth remark on Prosperity's bag. She simply motioned for her housekeeper, Florie, to take it to the bedroom.

The tea would have been a painfully awkward affair had there been more than three other guests gathered in the parlor. Prosperity did not know the two older ladies. Mrs. Cunningham, however, rushed across the room with an extravagant greeting.

"Why, if it isn't little Prosperity. We traveled together from

Charleston. Such seas! I could not regain my balance all evening."

Her chatter leveled off into a litany of complaints, to which Prosperity nodded and murmured her regrets. At last she was introduced to the two other women, one of whom apologized for her husband's absence, but seconds later she could not remember their names. From the corner chair, she stared out the open window and sipped tea, wishing this would soon end.

David was married. Married. And soon to become a father. Apparently he had formed this unbreakable bond at the same time he claimed undying love for her.

Hot liquid drenched her lap, and she jerked the cup upright. Mrs. Cunningham glared but thankfully did not comment. The rest of the group was too entertained by whatever Elizabeth was saying to notice. Prosperity picked at the shortbread wafer on her plate, but it was too soggy to hold.

How could David lie to her? How could he betray their love? The David she knew had been honest to a fault. He couldn't even offer a less-than-truthful compliment to please a lady. What had happened to him? What had sent him down this sinful path? Had this place, filled with bawdy sailors and taverns, done this to him? Or did he truly love the woman? Then why pretend to still love her? Why the charade?

"Miss Jones will soon join the staff, if I'm not mistaken." Dr. Goodenow's mention of her name pulled her from the barrage of thoughts.

"At the hospital?" Mrs. Cunningham exclaimed. "Whatever for?" Her imperious gaze turned on Prosperity. "I thought you intended to marry."

Prosperity could not swallow the humiliation. "Not at present." She could manage no more, but both Elizabeth and Mrs.

Cunningham would be able to guess from the heat staining her cheeks.

"I'm certain Miss Jones will do well," Elizabeth said. "I can put in a good word, if it would help."

Gratitude welled inside Prosperity. Dear Elizabeth had stepped to her aid again.

The doctor followed along. "I spoke to Dr. MacNees on Miss Jones's behalf. Anyone who can wander all over town with that heavy bag is strong enough to handle any work at the hospital."

The two older ladies chimed in with a similar sentiment, but Mrs. Cunningham frowned.

"My dear Elizabeth, you must consider this carefully. If I understand correctly, Miss Jones is staying with you. All manner of disease festers in a hospital. You must consider your son."

Prosperity blanched. "I would never want to bring illness to you or your baby. I can find a room else—"

Elizabeth cut off her concerns. "My son's health is in God's hands, not in groundless fears."

Mrs. Cunningham appeared ready to counter, but Dr. Goodenow quieted her by pointing out that the laundresses had no contact with the patients. "In fact, it's forbidden."

Prosperity wondered how then she would clean the wards, but she supposed that would be revealed if she received the position.

"Then it's settled," Elizabeth stated. "We shall recommend Prosperity for the position."

"Thank you," Prosperity whispered past the lump that had formed in her throat. In the midst of unexpected betrayal, she had found friendship. "You are so very kind."

"As supporters of the hospital, we are self-serving," the doctor said. "Though the staff is small, the hospital struggles to keep housekeepers and washerwomen. Believe me, Miss Jones, you will be a most welcome addition."

The older women nodded, but Mrs. Cunningham pressed her lips into a look of disapproval reminiscent of Aunt Florence.

Prosperity clung to the doctor's statement instead. "Then you are certain I will be offered the job?" A sliver of light pierced through the darkness.

"The director must approve," Dr. Goodenow said, "and Miss Stern will give her opinion. She does favor colored women."

The ray of sunlight vanished. "Then nothing is settled."

The doctor set aside his teacup. "I cannot imagine any impediment, as long as you do not plan to wed." His gaze pierced her. "Do you have an attachment?"

Prosperity shook her head. The only attachment remaining was a painful one. Her fiancé had spurned her to marry another. She toyed with the handle of her teacup. Key West was not large. David's days as a soldier centered on the garrison and the fort, but he must walk through town to get between one and the other. He and his wife would go to market, to church, and to entertainments.

Perspiration beaded on her upper lip. Eventually their paths would cross. What if he grew ill?

"Do soldiers ever have need of the hospital?" she blurted out, clearly interrupting one of the older ladies.

"The army has its own hospital," Dr. Goodenow answered.

That removed one meeting place, but the island was too small to avoid David forever. Her stomach churned.

"Are you well, Miss Jones?" the doctor asked.

She looked up to see everyone staring at her.

"Forgive me." She touched a cold hand to her burning cheeks. An explanation for her odd behavior was expected. She forced a smile. "I would very much like this position."

"Of course you would." Elizabeth accepted the explanation without question. "Dr. Goodenow is right. The hospital would be blessed by your service."

Blessed was not a word Prosperity would have chosen, but it gave the position greater meaning. Perhaps her labors might bring comfort to the suffering. Perhaps God would ease her grief by giving her a new purpose. Perhaps in time the pain would ease.

"Miss Jones has earned my good word, Doctor," Elizabeth stated emphatically. "If Miss Stern has any questions about her character, she may speak with me."

Prosperity bowed her head. She did not deserve such confidence. If her character had been that impeccable, why had David abandoned her? Why hadn't she seen his true character? How had she failed so miserably? That fact would be ever before her, for she could not hope to avoid David and his wife forever. The knife that had stabbed her dreams would strike again and again. She had no choice but to accept it. After all, she could afford neither to leave nor to stay without this position.

She offered a tremulous smile. "Thank you all."

Elizabeth turned to the doctor. "Please tell Miss Stern that she may call on us here if she wishes an additional interview, since Miss Jones is staying as our guest."

Prosperity clutched the locket at her throat. Tonight she would remove it. Tomorrow she must begin anew.

Two days later David returned home to find Aileen missing. She must be delivering his gift to Prosperity. Before he'd left for the work site, Aileen had folded the painfully emotionless note around the money and sealed it with wax stamped with the Latham seal. Prosperity would recognize that even before she opened the note.

What would she do then? When she read his concise message, would she weep or give thanks? Would this small gesture relieve any part of her pain? He had agonized over it all night, wishing he could write something—anything—to comfort her. He could not. Aileen must read the note. So he wrote only his hope that she would purchase passage and signed it "Lt. and Mrs. David Latham."

That had hurt.

The ink shone like drops of black blood before he blotted it. Then he gave the letter and money into his wife's hands.

Did he trust her to deliver it?

Despite uttering the words the other night, trust did not come easily. Aileen had betrayed even the tiny fragment he'd carried into their marriage. From the first day, anything he offered was snatched away and tossed to the ground like a worm-eaten coconut.

His best hope was that she would want to send Prosperity north on the first ship.

Still, he paced the veranda until his wife returned. The hired hack splashed through the puddles left from the late-day rains as it crossed the parade ground to his quarters.

He descended the steps before the hack pulled to a stop. To all appearances, he was the doting husband eagerly welcoming his wife home from a day in town. He extended a hand to help her from the carriage, ignoring the unfamiliar and undoubtedly new bonnet she sported.

"Good o' ye to meet me, love," Aileen purred, her smile sly as a pharaoh's concubine. "Eager for me, are ye?"

David bit his tongue rather than reveal his concerns before the hired driver. He handed the man enough to cover the fare, and the hack drove off. He then escorted Aileen up the stairs to the veranda, where she tossed the new bonnet onto the table as if she couldn't wait to take it off.

"Well?" she questioned. "Ain't ye goin' to ask what yer dyin' to know?"

"I suppose it's too much to think you would tell me without asking."

Her laugh held no innocence. "Yer gettin' to know me, love." She ran her fingers along his jaw, but the scent of liquor stained her breath.

David shut his eyes and tried to ignore his wife's faults. He had wed her for better or worse. Much as he wanted her to change, she'd stayed exactly the same. Perhaps one day the better part would arrive. For now, if he wanted an answer, he must ask the question.

He drew in a breath. "Did you deliver the letter?"

Her lips curled into that familiar triumphant grin. "Aye, love. It's outta me hands now."

David swallowed his relief. "Good. Thank you."

"I know how ye can thank me." Her tone cajoled, but he could only think of Prosperity.

"How did she react?"

Aileen jerked her hand away. "How would I know? Ye told me to send someone else."

"I'm sorry. You're right, but I hoped she might have reported back to you."

All softness had vanished from his wife. "It be done, Lieutenant. I followed me orders. That's all ye need to know."

But it was not all he wanted to know.

7

Prosperity received the position at the hospital two days after the tea and without an additional interview. Apparently Dr. Goodenow's recommendation carried a great deal of weight.

The first days at work were a blur of finding her way, locating the supplies she needed, and laboring until every joint and limb ached. She had difficulty keeping her eyes open after supper, even when the baby cried. When she laid her head on the pillow each night, she dropped at once into a dreamless sleep.

That left little time to contemplate David, except on Sundays, when she scanned the congregation at church and looked for him on the walk there and back. Every army uniform caught her eye, but none were David. She ought to be relieved, but the desperate ache refused to dim as May gave way to June.

Laundry and scrubbing floors occupied her days. She'd thought her hands roughened back home, but the sheer quantity here left them raw. She heeded every snippet of instruction, even when it didn't make sense. There would be time to raise questions after she'd gained Miss Stern's confidence.

After she finished the workday, generally a little before sunset, she liked to walk the shoreline behind the hospital. Though the air carried a familiar ocean scent, it was not home. She missed the dunes and the crashing waves with their cool salt spray, but at least it was all the same ocean. Perhaps these waters had once touched Nantucket's shores.

"You'll turn brown as a coconut if you don't bring a parasol," Dr. Goodenow called out to her one day.

She stopped and held her hand to the brim of her bonnet to shield her eyes. He stood some thirty yards distant, dressed as always in the black frock coat and top hat.

"I don't own a parasol," she called back.

He strolled toward her. She waited until he drew near.

His eyes twinkled. "I didn't expect to find you here."

"I didn't expect you to seek me."

He chuckled. "Touché."

"Why are you here?"

"A meeting with Dr. MacNees."

"I hope nothing is wrong."

He shook his head. "Quite well, in fact. No cases of fever yet. We hope for a mild year."

She puzzled over his report. "I'd heard several patients were feverish."

"Not with yellow fever, or yellow jack as some call it. Recent cases have all proven the usual ague."

"Oh." She began walking the shore again.

"Find anything interesting?"

"Unusual shells." She unfolded her hand to reveal the fragment of a shell with a pearly pink interior. "It's beautiful."

"That's a tiny bit of the queen conch shell. You probably don't see those on Nantucket Island."

She shook her head. "It's all so unfamiliar. I don't even know the trees. What is that one, for instance?" She pointed to one near the hospital.

"A stopper. The berries are often used to calm the bowels."

That piqued her interest. "Do you know about herbal remedies?"

"They are often quite effective. For instance, the bark of that tree, the buttonwood, is astringent and can be used to cleanse wounds."

"Like the green bark of a white pine."

"Ah, you're a bit of an herbalist yourself."

"From necessity," she admitted. For several paces they walked in silence. She debated whether to explain that statement, and he perhaps waited for her to do so. Revealing that Ma had suffered consumption could jeopardize her hard-won position, for some feared the disease could pass to those who nursed the infected.

Dr. Goodenow did not press her. He simply walked beside her in silence, content to wait.

He had been a kind man, and his support had doubtless led to her receiving the position. Guilt pricked her. Withholding truth was also deception. Hadn't she suffered greatly from just such deceit?

She stopped and stared out at the ocean. "My mother suffered weakness and coughing for many years and finally succumbed this April. They say it was consumption."

She waited for the disapproval and the hurried excuse. They did not come.

"Ah yes, I do recall you mentioned that your mother had passed." He stood with hands clasped behind his back.

"I burned the linens, everything that was not hard surfaced—and those I scrubbed with vinegar. The rooms I aired with chloride of lime."

"Quite sensible."

Though he appeared unconcerned, she must be certain. "I show no symptoms of the disease, and it has been more than a month since we buried her."

"Rest assured, Miss Jones, that I have no fears that you are spreading contagion."

She breathed out in relief. "Then you will not inform Miss Stern?"

"Your mother's passing is a private matter, I believe."

"Thank you." Prosperity watched the gentle swells pull at the broken shells and white sand. "Thank you also for telling me about the trees. I want to learn as much as I can. Is there a book I can read on the plants of the island?"

Dr. Goodenow shook his head. "That knowledge is passed down by word of mouth."

Disappointed, she tried to concentrate on the shimmering horizon. "Then there is no way to learn."

He chuckled. "There are always ways to learn. You simply need to ask."

She looked at him then, noted the kindly gaze and the soft crinkles at the corners of his eyes. Like David. She shook away the thought. Dr. Goodenow was nothing like David. He was much older, for instance, but he did know which plants could be used for medicine. "Will you teach me?"

He simply smiled. "Allow me to walk you home. The sun will soon set."

Miss Jones's question had startled Clayton Goodenow. Their conversation had been pleasant, and he'd enjoyed probing the extent of her nursing experience and her knowledge of medicines. He hadn't anticipated the curiosity—or the attraction.

He walked her home that evening and then found an excuse to talk to the marine hospital surgeon every day that he was free. Patient visits were finished early enough to allow this little indulgence, though he took care not to raise the suspicions of Miss Stern, who tolerated no inkling of impropriety on her staff. More than one young housekeeper had been sent packing for becoming too friendly with a patient or orderly or physician. Miss Jones, shrouded as she was in mourning black, appeared to draw no interest from either staff or patients, but beneath that somber exterior was a lively mind. That was what attracted him.

At least that's what he told himself.

She ought not walk alone, whether on the shore or between the O'Malley house and the hospital. Since she clearly had no relations on the island and must have suffered a devastating end to an understanding with her beau, no one could protect her. He took it upon himself to ensure her safe passage, especially after dark. She did not know the island and could easily wander where she shouldn't, but in truth he craved her eager questions.

It had been too long.

"You are here again?" she asked when he met her at the workers' gate late in the afternoon many days later.

"Happened to be in the neighborhood." The overly buoyant reply surely rang as untrue to her ears as it did to his, but he could not seem to stay away. "May I walk you home?"

She closed the gate behind her. "The O'Malleys' house is very nice, but it is hardly home."

Her wistfulness caught his attention. "You miss Nantucket."

"It's not home any longer."

"Then you intend to stay?" Clayton held his breath.

"For now."

Again that wistfulness tugged at his heart. "You are most welcome here."

"Thank you." Her smile was weak. "And thank you for offering to walk me home, but I have an errand to run first. Elizabeth heard lemons arrived from Havana and asked me to get some."

"I could help. To carry them." The fumbled words and rush of heat startled him. That hadn't happened for many years.

Her puzzled expression only made him feel sillier.

"She only wanted a few, and the market is very close."

"Forgive me." He nodded stiffly to counter the momentary lapse. "If you agree, I will walk with you until I turn onto my street."

"Thank you, but it isn't necessary." She strode forward without him.

Though disappointed, he must acquiesce. If he pushed too hard, she would run away, and he would lose even the friendship they had developed over the last week. These feelings she drew to the surface were only an aging man's fancy, a way to relieve the unending ache of Sarah's loss.

Then she stopped and looked back at him, a grin teasing the corners of her mouth. "I didn't mean your presence would be unwelcome."

His spirits buoyed as if the sun had finally come out from behind years of dark clouds. He hurried to join her.

She gazed up at him with those luminous, innocent eyes. "Perhaps you can tell me more about the trees and plants that are suitable for medicine."

"Of course." There were worse things than medicine to draw two people together.

"If you are certain," she said.

"I am."

He had not been this certain in twelve years.

⌘

David worked late as usual. Though the laborers were released at sunset, he stayed an hour more to make notes on progress and set up the next day's work. The day had been fruitful, with new supplies of iron arriving that afternoon. He'd privately instructed the smith to mark the spikes, which would make them less palatable to thieves, if in fact the previous batch had been stolen.

By the time he left, supper had been served, and the work camp hummed with song, laughter, and raw jokes.

He walked across town toward the garrison, tarrying a moment outside the inn where his commanding officers preferred to dine. He would have liked to inform the captain of the new plan, but Captain Dutton was hosting several officials. Laughter filtered out the open door. David longed to once again laugh.

Before Aileen, he'd enjoyed returning to his quarters, had reveled in the fact that everything was in its place. Now he dreaded the residence. In addition to the disarray, Aileen would make demands until his head ached. For a moment he considered lingering at the inn, but that's how he'd gotten into trouble in the first place.

He sighed and moved on. If only he could remember that night almost nine months ago. If he had awoken in her arms, these questions would not linger, but he'd awoken in the bar-

92

racks without recalling a trace of what had happened the night before. How could he have done such a thing and remember none of it?

He strolled down the streets and purchased a loaf of bread from a baker who was closing his shop for the day. The walk between the garrison and fortification brought the only silence in his day. During this time he faced no demands. No worries. This time was his alone.

Near the turtle cannery, fishermen hauled their catch ashore. He watched for a while, wondering how it would feel to sail away from the world and its demands. One of the sailors whistled a tune, and David answered. The man cast him a grunt of appreciation before resuming his work scrubbing the deck.

David walked on, breathing deeply the flowery scent perfuming the night air. Jasmine, someone had told him. David didn't know one bloom from another. He only noted the cloying scent, so different from Prosperity's freshness.

Prosperity. She must have left by now on one of those ships. She would be standing on deck, watching the sun slip below the horizon. If he thought God would listen, he would pray that she found comfort back home.

A man escorted a finely dressed young woman toward the chapel. Wednesday evening. Ah yes, he remembered the prayer meetings well. Prosperity would sit attentively with the women. He had to sit with his brothers on the opposite side of the chapel. When Father wasn't looking, he would cast a look toward Prosperity. For a split second, their gazes would meet. Then she would duck her head, and pink would suffuse her cheeks in a way that only made her more beautiful.

Prosperity. Oh, the ache in his soul. To think of her gone

forever nearly killed him. Yet he must let go. That meant walking away from what could never be and accepting what was.

He turned from the young couple and left the docks. Too soon the garrison loomed ahead.

The guard stopped him at the guardhouse. "Lieutenant, I've been waiting for you."

"Is something wrong?"

"No, sir." The man grinned. "Mrs. Latham sent for the midwife."

"The midwife?" David instinctively turned toward his quarters. The lights blazed.

"Yes, sir. You're going to be a father."

David didn't wait for the guard to finish. He ran.

The house was in chaos. Shrieks and screams rent the stillness of night. Mrs. Ambleton, the other assistant engineer's wife, and the rest of the officers' wives filled the small parlor.

"There you are," she proclaimed when he stepped through the door. "I was about to send Will to find you."

David drove straight to the point. "What's happening?"

The youngest of the wives giggled. The oldest shook her head.

Mrs. Ambleton glared. "You're going to be a father."

"I know that." At her shocked expression, he added, "The guard told me. I meant to ask if the midwife is here."

Mrs. Ambleton shook her head. "We thought you were her."

"Who is with Aileen?"

"Mrs. Stormant's girl, Evie."

David wasn't certain the colored maid was up to birthing a baby. "We need to do something."

Another fit of screaming, followed by raw language, descended from the upstairs bedroom.

"I'm sorry." David felt his ears burn. Why couldn't his wife temper her tongue?

Mrs. Stormant, heavily jowled and resplendent in gold-colored silk, chuckled. "The best of us falter at such a time."

David glanced at the staircase. "Shouldn't someone, uh, else be with her?" He hoped they wouldn't tell him to go up the stairs.

"My Evie has birthed five babies," Mrs. Stormant said, taking the loaf of bread from him and handing it to another lady. "She will handle things until the midwife arrives."

"Should I go . . . ?"

"No!" the women said in unison.

"You must wait," Mrs. Ambleton confirmed, "until you are called in."

That was a relief, but it still left him with the uncomfortable dilemma that four—no, five—women inhabited his parlor. Somehow they'd managed to pull together a tea service. The table from the veranda was set up in the corner with the beginnings of a game of whist under way.

His wife shrieked again, the cries crawling up his spine and her language heating his face.

He tugged at his collar. "Shouldn't I do something? It sounds like she's dying."

Mrs. Stormant took pity on him. "Trust me, it's perfectly normal." She ushered him toward the door. "Generally the men congregate out of doors. Since this has just begun and might take hours, I suggest you go to our quarters. Cook will give you some stew. If I'm not mistaken, the colonel just returned. He will round up the rest of the officers to see you through the night."

David wasn't sure he wanted to spend an evening listening

to outrageous storytelling, but it was better than sitting in a parlor full of women.

"We'll send for you when the baby is born," the commander's wife said.

His baby. Perhaps a son.

For the first time, he found some joy in this painful marriage.

8

David clutched his head. The screams had died to whimpers and sobs hours ago, and still there was no baby. More than a full day had passed, nearly two according to Mrs. Ambleton. The entire time he had not dozed off more than a couple minutes before the slam of a door or a shout jerked him awake. Night blended into day and day into dusk. Work did not cross his mind, and no one suggested he go to the fort.

He had left the commander's quarters at dawn and took up his post at the base of the stairs. Occasionally a girl—Mrs. Stormant's maid, he believed—called down the latest. She and the midwife attended Aileen while the wives drifted in and out of his quarters. Someone left food on the table. He couldn't eat.

By the time dusk swathed the post again, he couldn't bear it. He couldn't imagine how Aileen did.

"Nothing yet?" Lt. Col. Reed Stormant poked his head in the front door.

David rose and saluted, though he was tired to the bone. "No, sir."

"Sit, sit." The commander did not enter the room. "Send word when you hear. Dora will want to know." He cleared his throat. "She's more than a bit concerned."

So was he. "Shouldn't the baby be here by now?"

"That's not my area of expertise, but Dora says the midwife claims it could take a long time."

David slumped. He'd hoped for better news. "What if . . ." He couldn't complete the thought.

"Don't let your thoughts drift that direction. Be the strong soldier."

David straightened, mindful of his duty. "Yes, sir. I will return to work in the morning."

"You will be with your wife come morning. That's an order. Good night, Lieutenant."

"Good night, sir."

The commander left.

The midwife called down. "Was that anyone with a carriage?"

David leapt to his feet. "Yes. The commander."

"I need you to be fetchin' the doctor." The woman stood at the head of the staircase, wiping bloody hands on a rag.

"A doctor?" David asked as his head spun.

"You heard me."

"Who? Where?" David had spent two uncommonly healthy years on the island, but the post did have a physician. "I'll check the hospital."

"That be as good as anyplace."

"All right." But what did he say once he got there?

The woman glared at him. "Hurry! We don't have time ta chat."

David flew out the door and across the parade ground. Each footstep felt heavy as lead, like those terrible dreams when he couldn't outrun the pursuing enemy. In the dreams, the enemy loomed tall and black, its shadow swallowing him. But this wasn't a dream. It was very real. He clattered up the steps and burst into the post hospital.

A weary attendant looked up from the book he was reading. "What is it?"

"Help. I need help. For my wife," David said between gasps.

The man wrinkled his nose. "Dr. Rangler's gone to Fort Jefferson in the Dry Tortugas. He said to send any serious cases to the marine hospital."

That must be why the midwife asked about a carriage. She must have known that the army surgeon was gone. David raced back across the parade ground to the commander's quarters. He burst through the door without knocking, startling their daughter from her piano lessons.

Colonel Stormant rose from his chair. "What is it, Lieutenant?"

"A carriage," David gasped, forgetting he was supposed to address his commander properly. "Fetch a doctor." His breath rasped against a dry throat. "Please."

The commander acted without hesitation. In seconds he had ordered the carriage readied. After donning his coat, he kissed his wife and promised to return as soon as he had finished fetching a physician. David blindly followed the man to the porch.

"Go home, Lieutenant."

"I'm going with you."

"Your wife needs you."

"But I must do something."

The commander gave a wry grin as the carriage arrived in a plume of dust illuminated by the lamps hanging by the driver's seat. "There's no room for you. Tell your wife that help is on its way." With a flick of his coattails, the commander climbed into the carriage, and it left.

David watched dully, his strength at such a low ebb that he could barely stumble down the steps to the parade ground. Only afterward did he realize that the carriage could easily carry more than two, but he was too exhausted to wonder why the commander had refused to take him. He must return home. In his quarters, the windows glowed, but not with the warmth of a new baby. No, they winked feebly, as if afraid of what was to come.

❦

Miss Stern had left early that day, if five thirty could be considered early. At the nurse's request, Prosperity helped carry food to the hospital's few patients, all fever victims. Through the open windows, the orange sun dropped toward the horizon as the nurse handed out the food from Prosperity's tray. One patient pushed the gruel away. She didn't blame him. It was tasteless stuff. The others at least attempted to eat.

Fever was a terrible thing. If only she had a balm plant. An infusion of the herb in drink had brought cooling relief whenever her mother suffered. Instead all she could offer was a comforting word.

"Don't let Miss Stern catch you talkin' to de patients," Gracie clucked when she returned to the kitchen, where the laundresses and cooks gathered at the end of a long day. "You be let go like de others."

That wasn't the first time Prosperity had heard of dismissed housekeepers, but she'd thought it would have been for something more severe than saying a prayer or giving encouragement. Surely Miss Stern couldn't be that harsh.

Her hand stilled as she handed the tray of barely eaten food to a scullery maid.

"Ain't ya gonna let go?" the colored woman scolded.

"I'm sorry."

The woman shook her head as she walked to the garbage bucket. "Ain't it a pity ta throw such vittles to the fishes."

"The fishes? Wouldn't the swine get the leftovers?"

"T'ain't no pigs here, missy." The woman clucked her tongue as she went about her work. "Dey be bringin' in a chile ta do a woman's work."

Prosperity wasn't exactly certain what the woman had said, but it sounded uncomplimentary. "Well, I'll be going back to work then."

"Shore, shore." The woman chuckled as she waved her hand. "Work."

Something about her tone sent shivers down Prosperity's spine.

"What did she mean?" she asked Gracie as they walked back to the laundry.

Gracie shrugged. "Don't take much ta get de rumors goin'."

"What rumors?"

It took some prodding, but she finally got the truth from the laundress. "Dat doctor you be seein'."

"Doctor?" She must mean Dr. Goodenow. "We're just friends."

"Maybe, but don't take much fo' rumors." Gracie leveled her gaze at Prosperity. "You be careful."

The caution wasn't lost on Prosperity. Any rumors pairing her with Dr. Goodenow were ridiculous. The only man who had ever captured her heart was David. Her David. She squeezed her eyes shut against the welling tears. The betrayal still stung.

The doctor, on the other hand, must be twenty years her

senior. He was more like a father than a suitor. He had the appearance of a professor. A teacher. That's all he was. He was teaching her the medicinal qualities of the plants on the island. How could that be wrong?

Prosperity slipped a sheet into the mangle. Darkness already shrouded the grounds. By the time she finished her work, it would be very late. Dr. Goodenow would doubtless insist on walking her home, as he had nearly every day. Though the strange sounds and smells terrified her, she could not accept his escort. She must not.

First she must complete her work. The stack of dried bed linens needed pressing.

Gracie eyed her nervously. "My babe be hungerin' by now."

Prosperity lifted the sheet from the mangle. Gracie had a houseful of small children, and the youngest was a newborn. "Go. I will finish this."

Gracie's worry split into a wide smile. "Thank ye, miss. Anytime I kin help, you jes' ask."

Prosperity waved her away, still pondering the rumors. If Miss Stern heard them, Prosperity's days at the hospital were numbered.

The work was so familiar that her hands completed it without a thought. Instead her mind drifted to the handwritten journal that Dr. Goodenow had loaned her this morning. It listed various plants and their uses. While eating the midday meal in the kitchen, she had pored over the notes. The cook had teased her, asking if she thought she would become a doctor, but Prosperity ignored her. It was all nonsense, for women did not become physicians. What patient would ever seek their advice?

Though innocent, that journal gave the impression of impropriety. It must be returned.

"Miss Jones?"

Prosperity jumped. "Oh! Dr. MacNees."

The surgeon headed the hospital. Prosperity had only seen him from a distance. Miss Stern had pointed him out with reverence. Prosperity was to obey any orders he might give her but to otherwise steer clear of the great man. Why would he be in the laundry? Unless he had heard the rumors also.

"Miss Jones." He peered at her from beneath great bushy eyebrows.

"Sir." She felt her face heat. "I will not leave until I finish all my duties."

"I am not here to critique your labors, Miss Jones. Dr. Goodenow requests your assistance. He is waiting for you at the main entrance."

Her ears buzzed. Was this a test? Was the head of the marine hospital saying this to determine if the gossip was true?

He clapped his hands. "Now, Miss Jones."

She jumped again. "I-I-I'm supposed to go with him?"

"That is what I said. You will be assisting at a birth. I assume you know something about birthing a baby."

Her head spun. A birth. If a doctor had been called, then either the mother or the child was in desperate straits. "Yes, sir. I mean, no, sir. I have never assisted at childbirth, at least a human birth. I did help with puppies."

Dr. MacNees looked unimpressed. "Why are you still standing here? Hurry along, Miss Jones."

So much for staying away from Dr. Goodenow. By tomorrow, the gossips would have them courting. Or worse.

⚜

Prosperity stood at the top of the hospital's entry, peering at the unfamiliar carriage. She didn't realize the doctor had a conveyance, least of all one capable of carrying four. Why own such a vehicle when he had no family?

"There you are." Dr. Goodenow opened the carriage door and climbed out. "Hurry."

She clattered down the steps. He extended his hand to assist her, but she hesitated. An enclosed carriage with only the doctor would raise speculation, especially since she'd left the hospital by the main entrance.

"Why did you ask for my assistance?"

The doctor's hat shadowed his expression. "I require a nurse."

"I am not a nurse."

"You will do admirably. Please get in, Miss Jones. Our patient is in a desperate condition."

Prosperity's heart pounded as she climbed into the carriage. She was surprised to discover another man inside. Dusk and the dark interior shielded his identity.

"Miss Jones," the man said. "Dr. Goodenow speaks highly of your nursing abilities. Thank you for coming at once."

Though he spoke like a gentleman, she pressed a trembling hand to her midsection.

Dr. Goodenow sat beside her rather than next to the gentleman. "It is our duty, as you well understand, Colonel."

Colonel. Prosperity's throat went dry. David's superior. What if the woman in labor was David's wife? Her head spun.

The man grunted a reply. "Blamed uncomfortable situation."

"Did the midwife convey the problem?" Dr. Goodenow asked.

"Only to fetch a doctor," the colonel said. "The company physician is at Fort Jefferson, or we would have sent him. Much quicker." He rapped on the roof of the carriage. "Hurry."

The driver must have obeyed, because the jolts and bumps bounced Prosperity side to side on the seat. She clung to the frame of the window so she didn't slam against the doctor. Yells and whistles came from up top, and the carriage careened around a corner. Buildings, their windows beginning to glow with lamplight, passed in a blur.

Then the carriage slowed. Prosperity flexed her stiff fingers.

"We have arrived," Dr. Goodenow said.

"Almost." The commander slid across his seat and leaned out the open window.

In the light of a lantern, a soldier saluted and then waved them on.

Prosperity fisted her hands. David's wife was heavy with child. How many wives lived at the post? How many were ready to deliver a baby? There could not be many, yet she prayed fervently that this was not David's wife. How could she be in the same room with the woman, least of all assist in bringing David's child into the world?

She squeezed her eyes shut and forced herself to take a breath. *Dear Lord, let it not be her.*

The carriage rolled to a stop. She looked out the window. They had halted in front of a building that looked more like a house than barracks. The receding light revealed a wide veranda at the top of a long set of stairs. These must be officers' quarters.

David.

The commander got out first. Dr. Goodenow followed. He extended his hand to help her from the carriage.

Prosperity trembled so badly that she could not stand. "I can't."

"Come now. There is nothing to fear," the doctor assured her. "I will do the difficult part. You only need to calm the patient and urge her to do as I direct. I have found a woman's presence most helpful."

"The midwife," she croaked.

"After this long, she will be exhausted. Our patient needs a fresh and calming presence like yours."

The doctor didn't understand, because he didn't know. If this was David's wife, Prosperity's presence would not bring calm. She could not forget the sharp look of triumph the woman had cast at her that first meeting.

"Come along, Miss Jones." The doctor's patient urging had sharpened. "If I'd thought you were the timid sort, I would never have asked for you."

Dr. Goodenow trusted her abilities. His confidence roused her from the numbing dread. He needed her. She must not fail him. Besides, she could not be certain this was David's wife. If she faltered, and it was another officer's wife, she would never forgive herself.

Lord, give me strength.

She slid across the seat and managed to get her feet under her. She grabbed the door frame and pulled herself upright. Outside, a lantern illuminated the single step she must navigate. She thrust out a foot and lost sight of the tiny step. Her resolve faltered.

"Be careful." The doctor braced her with both hands, giving her the benefit of his strength.

Somehow she descended from the carriage, though she did not feel her legs move or her foot on the step.

Dr. Goodenow patted her hand. "You will do famously, Miss Jones. I have complete confidence in you."

More than she had. Prosperity drew a deep breath. *Dear Lord, help me face whatever lies ahead.* It flashed through her mind that perhaps God did want her to face what she dreaded most, but she could not have entered the building if she knew David awaited her.

Ten short strides took them across the yard. A dozen more carried them up the steps and onto the veranda. The commander stormed into the house ahead of them. Dr. Goodenow released her hand and entered next. Prosperity trailed behind, taking deep breaths of the somewhat cooler evening air to steady her trembling limbs. Her hand brushed against the wood frame of the doorway and held on.

She did not look up. She could not bear to see who awaited them inside. The door had swung half shut, and she could hear the murmur of voices beyond it. She recognized the doctor's voice. The commander boomed his replies, but the third person . . . was it David? Fear mingled with hopeless anticipation, for she loved him still. How could she not? Their lives had been intertwined for years. She had never considered a future without him.

Once upon a time she would have recognized even his whisper, but two years had changed so much. The day she'd come face-to-face with him, she'd barely recognized him. His face was weathered and tanned like that of a farmhand or sailor. His hair, always closely cut and neat back home, was longer and wild as a tangle of dried grasses. It had turned much fairer than she remembered, and his brow was deeply carved by worry.

Where was the man she loved? How had this place stolen her beloved and left a stranger in his place?

She inched a foot over the threshold. One more and she would be inside. Such a simple action, done every day without thought, yet tonight laden with dread.

"Blood," a woman exclaimed. "More'n I ever seen, and I been birthin' babies for twenty years."

Prosperity quaked. She had seen her share of blood, but not in quantities. Ma had coughed up bloody sputum. Injuries on the wharves left men wounded. Once Pa's leg had been gashed by a harpoon, but the mate had stitched the wound together. Birthing naturally included blood, but this must be exceptional to draw a midwife's concern. A birth carried no small amount of fear. Women died far too often. Babies were born lifeless. The time of joy could end in terrible sorrow.

Would this night end in death?

"Oh blackest heart," she whispered. 'Twas akin to murder to wish evil upon another soul, yet her wicked thoughts had leapt at the hope that David's wife might perish. She clung to the door frame, trembling. "Lord, break my heart of stone. Spare her life." How those words stuck in her mouth.

"It's time, Miss Jones," Dr. Goodenow called.

Prosperity heard a gasp. She looked up.

David stood before her.

9

D avid's thoughts flew to the obvious.

Prosperity had not returned home to Nantucket.

Was she waiting for a ship headed north? Hadn't he given her enough to cover the fare? Regardless of the reason, here she stood, so beautiful and so vulnerable that every fiber ached to go to her. Her presence filled the room with radiance and his heart with regret. He could not hold her, could not console her. They would never rejoice in the birth of their son or daughter. He had thrown that away.

Still, his lips formed her name. He could not look away.

She wavered, and her eyes shut. He stepped forward, but the physician reached her first.

"Miss Jones?" The doctor eased her into a chair and urged her to breathe.

She smiled feebly. "I'm sorry. I feel better now."

"Do you need something to drink?" The physician, whose name had escaped David's mind, hovered over her.

"The patient!" the midwife demanded, her gray-streaked black hair wild about her shoulders.

Aileen screamed as if to emphasize the need, and David shuddered. She could not know that Prosperity sat in David's parlor. In *their* parlor.

"Go," Colonel Stormant barked. "I'll send Dora over with tea. That'll revive the girl."

David balked. Prosperity was not an ordinary girl, but there was no one to accept his protest. The doctor hurried up the stairs behind the midwife, who filled him in on every horrifying detail. The colonel barged out of the house, presumably to request tea.

That left David alone with Prosperity.

Her owl eyes stared at him.

What to say? What could he say? No apology could erase the pain he'd caused. Words and gifts fell terribly short. Faced with the opportunity he had longed for, David found himself speechless. He swallowed. He never expected to see her again. Why tonight of all nights? He reached out to her.

She jumped to her feet and stepped beyond reach. "I must attend the patient."

"Yes." Her voice mesmerized him. "Thank you." So inadequate.

"Dr. Goodenow expects me." Yet she did not move.

"You? Are going to help?"

"I will comfort . . . your wife."

The words slapped him. His wife. Prosperity would help Aileen. The irony was too bitter to bear. "You don't have to."

"The doctor expects me." Again she did not move.

"Do you work for him?" The words came out harsher than he'd intended.

"He helped me find a position at the marine hospital."

"As a nurse?" Though she had nursed her mother many years, no physician he'd met would allow a woman to nurse men.

"A laundress."

He finally noticed her chapped, red hands. "You shouldn't have to work."

"I always have."

"I wanted to give you more, a life of ease."

She turned away, a simple move yet laden with meaning. She rejected him.

"Prosperity." He reached for her, desperate to touch her once more.

She skirted around him, heading for the staircase.

"Don't leave," he begged. "One minute longer."

She hesitated at the bottom step, her expression unreadable. Upstairs, Aileen screamed.

"Your wife needs me." She turned her back to him and ascended the stairs.

✦

Where Prosperity got the strength to climb the steps, she could not say. God must have answered her prayer, for under her own power, she could not have walked away from David.

He had reached for her.

How often she had longed for his touch. For months and years, but especially since arriving in Key West. Part of her wanted to believe that every obstacle could be washed away if only he returned to her. Foolishness! He had married the woman who bore his child. Soon he would become a father. He would hold his son or daughter in his arms and kiss his wife. No one could tear them apart.

Except death.

Her wicked heart had leapt at the thought. It had urged her to accept one tiny moment of tenderness with the man she loved. No one would see a simple clasping of hands and think the worst of it. How tempting, but even if no person alive saw that embrace, God would. And not only the action but the tarnished heart from which it sprang.

So she stepped out of reach and climbed the staircase while David's wife cried out for him. Over and over the woman screamed his name. Each scream pummeled Prosperity. She wanted to run, yet onward she climbed.

The steps creaked beneath her weight. The polished railing slid under her fingers. As she drew closer, the voices of doctor and midwife grew clearer while David's receded. Their urgency drew her even as fear pulled her back.

Two rooms led off the dark and narrow hallway. The closest door was ajar, and light streamed through the opening. She hesitated.

What if her appearance did not comfort? The woman's triumphant air in announcing her bond with David suggested deep pride and possessiveness. Prosperity's hand trembled on the doorknob.

"Daaaaavid," the woman shrieked, followed by a string of obscenities that made Prosperity recoil.

Childbirth was hard and painful, and she had heard a woman could lose her mind.

The vulgarities ended with sobs and murmured voices.

"You be all right," the midwife consoled.

The patient—it was easier to use that term than to think of her as David's wife—answered with more vulgarities. Such a woman would definitely see Prosperity as a rival.

Prosperity could walk away now. Dr. Goodenow did not know her history here. He did not realize what effect her presence might have on a struggling patient. He had able assistance in the midwife. Moreover, he would expect her to remain downstairs until her head cleared. She could claim continued dizziness, but it would be a lie.

Moreover, David waited at the base of the stairs. He would pace the room, anxious for word. If she descended, he would plead for news, for hope. He would reach for her again. His desperate need for consolation must come from anguish. At each scream, he'd flinched.

He loved his wife.

If Prosperity had doubts before, they were answered in that moment.

"Fetch Miss Jones," Dr. Goodenow barked from inside the room. "I need her help."

The doctor needed her.

Prosperity pushed open the door. The dim light of a single lantern could not hide the horror of the scene. Bloody linens were heaped on the floor. The midwife looked up, her exhaustion evident. Dr. Goodenow appeared worried. The patient clung to the iron bedstead, pale as snow, with yet more bloodied linens affording a small amount of modesty. Her red hair was matted and snarled. Her swollen abdomen arched with agony as a birth pang ripped through her.

Then she noticed Prosperity. Her lips curved into hatred. "Get. Out."

Prosperity fled.

⁂

David jerked out of his muddled thoughts at the sound of footsteps hurrying down the stairs. He pivoted away from the windows in time to see his beloved rush out the front door.

"Prosperity!"

He ran after her, his boots clattering on the veranda, but she did not stop. Her black skirts billowed in the breeze, and her bonnet bounced against her back. Then darkness closed around her.

"Prosperity! Stop!"

She could not leave at this hour, alone and unguarded.

He hastened his steps, but she had always been fleet of foot. He could not catch her, not in the dark. No matter how many times he called her name, she did not stop.

Colonel Stormant stepped in front of him and caught his arm. "Let her go, Lieutenant."

"But she is alone. It's dark." His words came out in gasps. "Need to escort her."

"Your wife needs you."

Wife. David's thoughts careened back to the agony inside his quarters. Neither the doctor nor the midwife had followed Prosperity down the stairs. That meant Aileen's trials were not over. He did not have a child yet.

"But Prosperity—Miss Jones—cannot walk alone at this hour." David could not stand by and watch her walk into danger. "Ruffians will be out, and there's no moon to guide her steps. Anything could happen."

"I will find her. Return to your wife, Lieutenant."

His wife had doctor and midwife watching over her. Prosperity had no one, and David doubted the commander could catch up to her. "She has a head start."

"My carriage is at the ready. Do not fear. I will find her. Now return to your wife. That is an order."

"Yes, sir." David fought disappointment.

"My wife brought tea and some cakes." The commander clapped him on the shoulder. "Everything will turn out for the best."

David managed a weak smile. "Yes, sir."

He reluctantly returned, pausing in the doorway to confirm that Colonel Stormant had indeed fetched his carriage. Across the parade ground, Prosperity stood in the light of the guardhouse lantern for but a moment before vanishing into the darkness.

A piercing cry from upstairs drew his attention to the struggle inside.

David entered the parlor. Mrs. Stormant paused while pouring a cup of tea. Upstairs, the squalling continued with barely a gasp for air.

The commander's wife smiled. "At last, praise the Lord."

"At last?" Realization dawned. "The baby."

"Yes, you have a son or daughter."

He dropped to his knees.

Thank You, Lord.

His child had survived the ordeal. Exhausted, he buried his face in his hands, overcome by emotion. A child. Elation soon gave way to the huge sense of responsibility. A new life depended on him. He must feed and clothe and train this child. He must instill honor and integrity in him or her, even though the baby's mother displayed neither virtue.

Such a difficult road to travel. Nothing like what he had envisioned back on Nantucket Island. Now he must set the sternest example so the babe did not fall into the mother's ways.

"Lieutenant?"

The midwife's voice pulled David to his feet. She stood at the top of the stairs holding an impossibly small bundle that must be his child. The physician, dressed again in his black frock coat, descended the stairs, his expression grim. David's hopes sank.

"Will the baby . . . will Aileen . . . that is, are they all right?" David stammered out.

The doctor did not smile. "It's too soon to tell. Your wife is resting now, but she has lost a great deal of blood. The baby appears normal, but the labor struggle might have adversely affected him."

"Him?" Despite the grim news, David caught onto that promise.

"Yes, you have a son."

His somber expression sent a shiver up David's spine.

"Good night, Lieutenant. Send for me if problems arise."

"What problems? Where do I find you?" David must have been introduced to the man, but he didn't recall the physician's name, least of all where to find him.

"Forgive me. The night has been long. I am Dr. Clayton Goodenow. My office can be found on Fleming Street. Good night, Lieutenant."

The physician departed, and David closed the door behind him. A son. He had a son.

"Congratulations." Mrs. Stormant eased past him. "Send for Evie if you need anything. I will let myself out."

"Would you like to see him?" The midwife must have descended the staircase while he was bidding the doctor good night, for she stood by his side.

Mrs. Stormant glanced at the baby and hurried out the door. Odd reaction.

He looked down at the little bundle and staggered backward. "Is it . . . is it normal for a baby to be darker than his parents?" He hoped the coffee-colored skin and dark hair were a result of the traumatic birth.

The midwife hesitated.

David pleaded with his eyes. *Tell me this isn't a mistake.*

"Sometimes they lose the hair, and it grows in again in its proper color." She pulled the baby close.

"Then there's hope. And the skin color? Will it get lighter?"

She looked down at the child. "Sometimes they're a bit . . . darker at first."

"But?"

She didn't answer.

That's when David knew. He and Aileen were extremely fair-skinned. This baby was not. It couldn't be his. It had never been his.

He turned away, sick.

Aileen had deceived him.

10

Prosperity stumbled into the darkness, turning this way and that until she was utterly lost.

This night shook the foundations of the life she'd managed to build here. Hard work to help the sick and learning about local medicines had given her purpose. But a few minutes with David exposed just how shaky that new life was.

She could not forget him. Her wicked heart still longed for him, even to the point of wishing his wife dead. Cruel emotions! She must not let them master her.

She clung to a fence. The rough slats dug into her palms.

Get. Out.

His wife was right. Prosperity shouldn't have been there. She should have left the moment she realized who the patient was. A former fiancée should never appear at the birth of the couple's child.

Their baby.

Not hers. She choked back the pain.

Why hadn't she asked Dr. Goodenow for the patient's name? Why, when she realized it was David's wife, hadn't she told the doctor that she could not assist? Instead she let him believe she would help. When he needed her, she ran away. He wouldn't trust her any longer. He shouldn't. The faint glimmer of a future died.

Hot tears bunched in her eyes.

"Mama," she whispered. "Papa. Why did you have to leave me?"

They had been her source of counsel over the years. Even while ill, Ma had passed on her wisdom. Tonight, the rustle of palms, sounding so much like rain, was her only answer. That and the huff of a horse and the crunch of carriage wheels. Its lantern drew near, and she pressed into the shadows of this dark night.

Her heart quickened as the carriage slowed and the door swung open. A man stepped to the ground. What could he want but mischief? Fear pulsed life into her limbs. She picked up her skirts and ran.

"Stop, Miss Jones."

Dr. Goodenow. Why was he here and not at David's house? Had David's wife died? Had the desires of her wicked heart come true? She halted, her limbs trembling.

He drew near. "I didn't mean to frighten you. The commander and I have been looking for you."

"Why?"

"My dear, you cannot walk alone in the darkness. This is not Nantucket."

"That is not what I meant. The patient . . . ?"

"She delivered a son."

Prosperity drew a shuddering breath. "Then she lives."

"She survived the birth but is not out of danger."

Oh, how cursed the heart that wishes ill of another. Prosperity squeezed her eyes shut against that hope. "I will pray for her." Each word hurt.

"You know her."

How to answer? "I saw her once." She could imagine the doctor's raised eyebrow and the questions that danced in his mind. The woman had demanded she leave, after all. To all appearances, they were well acquainted.

"We ought to go." The kindly man did not press for an answer.

She would give it anyway, in the hope that saying it aloud would snap the thread that connected her to David.

"She married my fiancé." Her throat constricted. "My former fiancé."

He drew in a long breath, made more poignant by the pause. "I am sorry."

Nothing more could be said.

❦

"Don't you want to hold the baby?" the midwife asked.

David stared at her. This wasn't his baby. This wasn't his son. The memory of Aileen's lover raced through his mind. Was that man the father, or were there others? His wife knew no boundaries. Did she demand payment or did she give herself away to any man who showed the slightest interest?

His stomach seized violently, and he had to turn away to compose himself. He could not hold this child. Nor could he climb the stairs and face the woman who had stolen his life.

"Sir? Are you all right?"

He yanked open the door. "I must leave."

"In the middle of the night?"

"Yes." How could he explain? He didn't even understand himself. He only knew he couldn't stay.

"Where are you goin'? When will you be back?"

"I don't know." His tone came out too harsh, but he could

find no compassion within. Aileen had cost him the love of his life. Aileen had stolen his future to cover up her indiscretions. This baby spelled out that fact for all to see. No one could mistake what she had done, and he could not hide that he'd been deceived.

"But the baby and your wife. They need care."

David pulled every dollar from his wallet and thrust them at her. "Care for them. Hire a nurse if necessary."

The woman's eyes rounded. "Aye, sir." She snatched the money from his hand. "I'll take good care o' your wife and babe."

Not his baby. That much was certain. But he could not deny that Aileen was his wife. The marriage certificate proved it.

The midwife would not let it go. "But in the morn—"

"Hire someone."

He stepped across the threshold and into the breezy night. The door slammed shut, whether from his anger or the wind he did not know or care. He flew down the steps, eager to escape these quarters that had become a prison.

Overhead the stars twinkled. The tiny hint of a crescent moon, newly risen, cast little light. He stumbled across the parade ground, numb to all but the pain. Where would he go? What would he do? By morning everyone would know the truth.

"Where are you going, Lieutenant?" the guard asked.

David jerked out of his thoughts. "Where?" He had no idea.

"If you're going after the lady, the commander and the doctor said they were going to escort her home."

The lady. David laughed bitterly. What a contrast between the woman who ought to have been his wife and the woman who was. One brought gentleness and honesty. Every virtue detailed by the apostle Paul. The other? The blackest vices known to man. How grievously he'd wounded Prosperity. She would never forgive him. He wouldn't in her place. Small wonder she had fled. He was the last person she would want to see tonight.

"No, I'm not looking for the lady. I'm going to town."

He would let a room. Then he remembered that he'd given all his money to the midwife. The taverns and grogshops might give him credit, but that was where he'd run astray in the first place. That left his office. It would not be comfortable, but it was his last retreat.

"You'll be back later tonight?" the guard asked.

"No."

David wasn't sure he would ever return.

⁓✦⁓

The events of the night shook Prosperity so badly that she could not eat the supper Elizabeth had asked Floric to set aside for her. She excused herself due to a headache and slipped into bed. In the darkness she could hide, but it gave her no comfort. Though she was exhausted, sleep stayed away. Hour after hour she tossed this way and that, battling the echoes of this terrible night.

A couple times her eyelids drifted shut, but even those brief respites were pierced by the shouts of David's wife.

Get. Out.

The words reverberated until Prosperity pressed the pillow to her ears. Nothing could blot them from her mind. The hatred had spewed at her like a rushing wave, knocking her from solid ground. She flailed and searched for stability, but none could be found.

What had she ever done to this woman? She didn't even know her name. Prosperity ought to hate her, for this woman had stolen her future. This woman would join David wherever the

122

army sent him. This woman would welcome him home at night. This woman would watch their children play in the yard.

It should have been me.

Over and over. A thousand times the scenes repeated, but no peace would come. Tears dampened her pillow, leaving salt traces on her cheeks. She did not brush them away, too worn to even lift her hand.

She must never see David again.

As the sun sprinkled the trees with the promise of a new day, that resolution gave her strength. She must walk away from her beloved forever. If he sought her, she would turn away. If he spoke, she would ignore him. If he wrote, she would return the letters unopened.

It was the right thing to do. He had a family now. Their lives no longer intertwined.

That resolve gave her the strength to walk unescorted to her job at the hospital. It stiffened her spine when Miss Stern glared at her with lips pressed together. She repeated it with every stroke of the wash paddle in the boiling laundry tub.

"Miss Jones." At the midday dinner break, Miss Stern approached her. "I wish to speak to you in my office."

The woman's grim expression jostled her fragile confidence. Had she done something wrong? Every worker feared a call to the matron's office. Usually it ended in dismissal, but if that was the case Miss Stern would have asked her there when she'd first arrived. Unless some new accusation had formed during the morning hours.

The walk to the matron's cramped office was painfully short. After a sleepless night, Prosperity wasn't sure she could bear up under a verbal thrashing.

Miss Stern did not close the office door behind them, but she did proceed to her small desk surrounded by shelves of supplies and books. Prosperity glanced at the titles. *The Nurse's Guide. The Family Nurse.* Perhaps Miss Stern aspired to greater duties than presently possible. Perhaps they shared that small dream.

"Please sit." Miss Stern motioned to the wooden chair across the desk from her.

Prosperity sat. She carefully arranged her skirts and apron before folding her hands on her lap and straightening her spine so she could look the matron in the eyes.

"Let me get straight to the point," Miss Stern said. "Dr. Mac-Nees informed me this morning that Dr. Goodenow requested your assistance last night at a birthing."

Since the woman waited for a response, Prosperity nodded.

"This is not part of your duties. You are a laundress and housekeeper. Understand?"

"Yes, Miss Stern."

"Women do not assist physicians. Understand?"

"Yes, Miss Stern." Though Prosperity gave the expected response, her gaze drifted to the books. Dreams could be crushed, but Dr. MacNees had approved of Prosperity joining Dr. Goodenow. Surely he would not disapprove of Miss Stern's ambitions. "But a woman did assist Dr. Goodenow."

Miss Stern's expression tightened.

"The midwife," Prosperity added. "She was the one who sent for the doctor."

"That is not the point, Miss Jones."

Perhaps fatigue had emboldened her, but Prosperity could not let it go. "Women are fully capable of nursing a patient."

For the briefest of instants, hope flickered in Miss Stern's eyes, but it soon dimmed. "Our ability is not the issue, Miss Jones. Propriety is. Dr. MacNees assures me that your attendance was at his request and that of Dr. Goodenow. He seems to believe that excuses the breach in propriety. It does not."

Prosperity could not breathe. Her predecessor had been dismissed for impropriety. She closed her eyes and steeled herself for the words that were certain to come.

"I will not tolerate a repeat of such conduct. Understand?"

Prosperity's eyes shot open. Miss Stern was not dismissing her? "Then I still have my position?"

"As long as you abide by the rules, but let me warn you that any association with physicians or patients outside the strict guidelines of your position will be grounds for dismissal. Understand?"

"Yes, Miss Stern." Prosperity must not see Dr. Goodenow anywhere near the hospital. Their walks could not take place within Miss Stern's sight. Alas, his journal was still in her possession, and he would doubtless arrive this evening to escort her back to the O'Malleys' house. She must inform him of Miss Stern's directive and send him away. If anyone saw her hand him his journal, the gossip would send her back to the matron's office.

"Miss Jones?" The matron scowled at her. "You may leave now."

"Yes. Of course." Prosperity hurried away, deep in thought. How could she return the doctor's journal if they never saw each other again?

An orderly carried a tray with tea service toward the dining room. Tea! Of course. Dr. Goodenow often attended Elizabeth's teas, which she held every other Tuesday. That gave her three full days to wade through his scribbling and copy the parts that most intrigued her. Elizabeth had grown up on the island. She could point out the plants, and then Prosperity could connect them to the notes in the journal.

"There you are!"

She had been hurrying along at such a pace and so deep in thought that the man's exclamation made her jump. It took no time to spot the source of the comment.

"David."

He looked dreadful, even worse than last night. Dark circles underlined his eyes. His curls stuck out in every direction. His shirt hung loose, soiled by dust, its collar missing. So too did he lack a coat and hat. Any effort at military correctness was gone. He looked like a man who had spent the night in a tavern.

She instinctively backed up a step. "What do you want?"

His dry lips moved before any sound came forth. "To talk." His voice rasped like a planer against rough wood. "You are my friend. My only friend."

Oh, if a man's words could drive tears to her eyes, David's could. But she knew the futility of this path. "Your wife."

He turned away, overcome.

Her heart raced. Had her wicked desire come to pass? "She lives?"

He nodded, and she breathed out a sigh of relief. At least she was not guilty of murder with her thoughts.

"The baby?"

He looked back at her, eyes red and mouth twisted. "A boy."

A son. Her heart ached. It should have been hers. Theirs.

"Congratulations." Even to her ears it sounded hollow.

Yet, all was as it ought to be. Then why was he here? To stab her over and over with what she had lost?

She crossed the hall. "I must return to work." She tried to slip past, but he grabbed her arm.

"Prosperity."

126

She froze. His touch still sent shivers through her, but those feelings were wrong, so terribly wrong. "I can't talk."

"Tell me you understand. Tell me you forgive me."

She knew she should. She knew what the Bible taught.

Instead she pulled her arm from his grasp. "I'm not allowed to speak to anyone when on duty."

He wanted more, needed more. She saw it in his eyes. But she could not give it. Not now. Maybe never.

"Good-bye, David."

He stared back with pleading eyes, his shoulders slumped.

She ripped her gaze from him and hurried down the hallway. Would he follow? Half of her wanted him to come after her. Half did not. She could not bear to look back, could not bear to know. Instead she kept walking, body steeled as her shoes pounded on the wood floor. At the end of the long hallway, she headed down the steps. On the landing, she paused, heart pounding.

No sound of footsteps.

No pleas.

Nothing.

She crept up the steps and hazarded a peek.

He'd left.

11

David did not return home. He went back to his office at the work site and did not leave. Private Jameson brought water so he could wash. His coat and hat hung on the pegs where he'd put them before heading to the marine hospital.

Prosperity's rejection hurt worse than Aileen's betrayal. The pair of blows cracked the foundation of his life. Without a strong base, nothing could rise. The future loomed so bleak that he could not look at it.

He did not shave or comb his hair. He left his uniform hanging. Work alone could scour away the pain.

Saturday passed in a blur. If he ate, he did not recall it. Any sleep happened when he collapsed onto the desktop. Then the terrible dreams would begin. The screaming would wake him with a start. He would light the lamp again and try to work, but his vision blurred. He rubbed the spectacles on his shirt, but they were not the cause.

Still, he pressed on. There was nothing else he could do.

No church services this Sunday. God had forsaken him when

he'd cried out for help. Surely He could have revealed the truth before David married Aileen. Instead God had let him walk into the viper's den. Only work remained.

When a persistent knocking woke him on what must be Monday morning, judging from the angle of the sun and the workers busy on the site, it took long minutes to shake the grogginess.

"Yes?" He rubbed his whiskered jaw and stretched his neck this way and that to relieve the knot that had formed.

"Letter for you, sir. Came in on the packet last night."

David blew out his breath and rose. It was likely from his family. He had not heard from them since writing of his marriage. He cracked the door slightly. "I'll take it."

Private Jameson didn't hide his disdain for David's appearance, though he shoved the missive through the opening.

The terse handwriting revealed the letter was from David's father.

"That will be all, Private."

Jameson retreated, and David closed the door. He turned the letter over and over, hesitant to open it. His father's cramped yet perfectly formed letters stared back at him. He could guess what Reverend Latham would say.

A bitter laugh escaped at the thought of the stern abolitionist learning that he now had a colored grandson. That would stir the man's emotions.

He broke the seal and opened the letter. His father did not waste space with pleasant inquiries or statements about family welfare.

Your letter shocked your mother and me. You have broken your sacred pledge, apparently without informing your betrothed, for she has left Nantucket to meet you. I did not raise a son to shirk responsibility. First you disdained the ministry for the military. I could overlook that, considering you chose a profession held in generally high regard. However, I cannot overlook this latest insult. You broke your word. I find little to commend in your behavior and even less reason to call you my son.

He could read no further. The rest would expound on the wrong he'd done. If Father knew the entire truth, his rebuke would be even stronger, but David had not revealed Aileen's occupation in a grogshop and the shameful circumstances under which they'd wed. Once Father learned of the child's birth, even that shame could not be avoided.

He closed the letter and shoved it into his desk drawer. In the process, the army manual shifted to reveal his Bible. His hand shook. Inside that Bible rested the daguerreotype of Prosperity. One look. Just one look would not hurt. Her calm gaze might settle the unrest in his soul.

He removed the manual and ran his fingers across the Bible's cover. A finger hooked under the edge. He only needed to lift the cover and pages to where the plate created a break. Just one look.

His hand trembled, and he slammed the drawer shut.

Prosperity belonged in the past, and he could never return there.

Bleak as it was, this future with Aileen and her child was now his. He should return to his quarters. Three days away was enough. She had sent no message. No one had brought news. He must return to her.

How could he? His knuckles ached from gripping the desk. The anger exploded until he feared he would do something terrible. She had deceived him, had stolen his life in order to hide her sins. What man had fathered that baby? Did he know the man?

He slammed his fist against the desktop. The resulting pain felt good, real. It also revealed that he could not return yet. He must wait until the anger subsided.

Work would do that. He pulled the drawings of the first tier casemates from the shelf and spread them out on his desk. Verifying the calculations took all day. Food arrived. He ignored it. His sergeant reported. He responded by rote.

After dark, a brief knock ushered in Captain Dutton.

David plucked the spectacles from his nose and stood at attention. "Captain. I, uh, I'm sorry for my appearance." He scrambled to pull his coat from the peg and began to tug it on.

"Forget it." The engineer waved off David's efforts. "It's too hot for wool."

"Yes, sir." David dropped the coat onto the chair. "To what do I owe the honor of your visit? Is there a problem with the construction?"

"No. No. Other than an assistant engineer who is working too hard when he ought to be home with his wife and baby."

David noted that he hadn't referred to the boy as David's son. No one had used that term yet. It was obvious the child was not his.

He returned to his calculations. "There's a lot to be done."

"Nothing that can't wait. Come along, Lieutenant. I'm taking you home."

Home. David almost laughed. "I don't have a choice, do I?"

"No. Your wife needs you."

Aileen did not need a man who couldn't bear to look at her. She would know in an instant that he despised her. No, that wasn't correct. He despised himself for believing her. She was what she had always been. He had foolishly thought that he—and he alone—could turn a donkey into a racehorse.

"I suppose I must face the responsibilities at home." How that word stuck in his mouth. Home was never supposed to include an unrepentant wife and a child who was not his.

"Come along, Lieutenant." The captain clapped him on the shoulder, guiding him out the door at the same time. "We all must face unanticipated responsibilities. Life invariably deals each of us a bad set of cards sooner or later. It's what we do with them that counts."

David's cards couldn't get much worse.

The captain headed for a carriage that looked suspiciously like the post commander's. That meant Dutton had been sent to fetch him.

"Is there a problem?" He tugged on his coat.

The captain hesitated. "Fever."

David swallowed a surprising bolt of fear. "The baby?" Surely God would not punish an innocent for his parents' mistakes.

"Your wife."

❧

Dr. Goodenow did not arrive to escort Prosperity to or from the hospital Saturday evening or Monday. Had Miss Stern spoken to him? It did delay the inevitable. Their friendship could not continue.

Monday evening, Prosperity finished copying notes from the doctor's journal. Her fingers ached, but she was eager to find the plants he described. She brought the journal to the parlor, where Elizabeth was reading aloud to her son, though he was too young to understand.

Elizabeth closed the book and kissed her son's forehead. "He always falls asleep when I read to him."

The joy on her face sent a pang of regret to Prosperity's heart. She would never know a mother's love for her child.

Brushing aside the pain, she thrust out the journal. "Please return this to Dr. Goodenow at tomorrow's tea. He loaned it to me."

"You may give it to him yourself. I expect him at any moment. He wanted to see how Jamie is faring."

Prosperity frowned. Jamie, named after Rourke's late father, looked the picture of health with no sign of colic or croup. "I didn't realize Jamie needed a physician."

Elizabeth chuckled. "He doesn't. If you ask me, Dr. Goodenow likes to visit Jamie because he and his wife never had children."

"His wife?" Prosperity felt a sudden chill. She had assumed he wasn't married. If he was, she should never have spent time alone with him. "He never mentioned that he's married."

"Was, I'm afraid. His wife died in childbirth many years ago. He never remarried."

"How tragic."

Elizabeth nodded. "I think that's why he's so dedicated to his work."

The revelation swirled in Prosperity's mind. How difficult it must have been to watch David's wife struggle in childbirth. It must have reminded him of his loss, yet he had not said one word. He might have refused to go. He might have suggested the commander find another physician. He might even have asked Dr. MacNees to attend the birth, but he did not. Unlike her, he had faced the danger and helped the patient not only give birth but survive the travail.

"I didn't know," she murmured.

"He doesn't speak of it. Mrs. Cunningham cautioned me not to ask about his family and then proceeded to tell me why." Elizabeth shook her head. "I feared it was gossip, knowing how she enjoys the latter, but others confirmed that it is true."

"How very sad."

The doctor rose even more in Prosperity's estimation. She had not yet told Elizabeth where she'd been Friday night. All she'd said was that it had been a medical emergency. Elizabeth probably assumed she'd been at the hospital. With the doctor arriving, something might be said. She should tell her friend what had happened at David's house.

Prosperity took a shaky breath. How to begin?

A knock sounded on the front door.

"Ah, there's the doctor." Elizabeth lifted her son to her chest and kissed him again. His little arms reached for her, even in his sleep.

"Stay with your son," Prosperity said. "I will answer the door. It will give me a chance to return the journal."

She hurried from the room and the joy that drove daggers into her heart. Oh, she was happy for Elizabeth. She deserved this joy, but Prosperity could not help thinking of what she had lost and what would never be. A love as deep as the one she had for David occurred but once in a lifetime. The children she'd dreamed of raising with him now belonged to another woman.

The knock came again, louder and more urgent.

"Mrs. O'Malley?"

Prosperity recognized Dr. Goodenow's voice. She pulled open the door.

He drew back. "Miss Jones."

"Elizabeth is with her son in the parlor. She is expecting you."

"Please beg her forgiveness and tell her that I cannot stay." He appeared disheveled, even frantic.

"What is it, Doctor?" Elizabeth asked from behind Prosperity. "Is there a problem?"

He looked from Elizabeth to Prosperity and back again. "I fear there is."

"Then please don't waste time on a social call," Elizabeth pleaded.

The doctor licked his lips. "Actually, I hoped to convince Miss Jones to assist me."

Dread prickled up Prosperity's spine. "It's forbidden. Miss Stern would dismiss me if she learned I assisted you outside the hospital."

His countenance took on a grim expression that chilled her even further. "I realize I am asking for a great sacrifice, but you are already exposed."

Elizabeth frowned. "Exposed to what, Doctor?"

"Fever. I can't be certain of its origin, whether contagious or not, but in the event it is, I must take precautions."

Prosperity drew in a sharp breath. Fever could decimate families.

Elizabeth did not flinch. "I will pray for the afflicted. If Prosperity cannot attend you, I shall."

Elizabeth's response shamed Prosperity. Instead of fear, Elizabeth had turned to the One who could heal any disease and then offered to humbly serve.

"I will go," Prosperity said. "Allow me to fetch my bonnet."

"Of course."

It took but a moment to return to her room and don the bonnet. She then followed the doctor to a hired hack. He assisted her into the carriage before sitting beside her. The driver slapped the reins, and the hack jerked forward.

Only then could she ask the one question he had not answered. "Who has fallen ill? Someone at the hospital?" It was the only place where she might have come into contact with fever.

His jaw tensed. "Mrs. Latham."

David's wife.

12

David stared at the woman he had once loved deeply and loved still.

"Prosperity." Her name rang out like a bell on a church steeple.

From the moment she entered his quarters in the wake of the doctor, she had averted her gaze.

"Miss Jones," she now murmured.

Her words cut deeper than the sharpest sword.

"Miss Jones," he echoed, the name sitting ill on lips accustomed to tender familiarity.

The doctor barely spared him a glance. "When did the fever begin?"

"I'm not certain." How could he admit his neglect for three days? "I was at the construction site when word arrived."

"You noticed nothing this morning?"

David swallowed. "I rose early." That much was true, though his guilt must show. "The midwife is here. She is taking care of . . . things." That much he'd managed to ascertain before sending for a doctor. He had not expected Captain Dutton to fetch this particular doctor, nor to see Prosperity with the man. Did she work for him in addition to the marine hospital?

"Upstairs, Miss Jones." The doctor climbed the staircase.

She moved to follow, gaze still averted.

David caught her arm. "Please look at me."

"I am needed upstairs."

His hand trembled. "I'm sorry." It was a pitiful expression of his guilt.

She pulled away.

"I never wanted to hurt you," he cried, desperate to stop her for a moment longer. "I never intended this to happen." How he wanted to tell her all, how Aileen had deceived him into marriage, how he had no memory of a liaison with her, but to reveal his wife's duplicity meant shaming the woman he had bound himself to until death. "I'm sorry for everything."

The ragged apology hung between them.

For a moment she hesitated. Then she turned toward the stairs.

"I can't expect your mercy," he pleaded, "but I hope for it anyway."

She paused but did not look back. If she considered responding, she decided against it, for her foot landed on the first step and was soon followed by the next.

The baby began to squall, and the frazzled midwife yelled over the crying that Mrs. Latham had been feverish when she'd arrived. His love hurried up the staircase to save his wife.

❧

This time David's wife did not recognize her. Though the room was dimly lit by a lamp, in her feverish state she would not recognize anyone. The fever had closed her eyes and muddled her mind. Unintelligible sounds slipped past her lips. Her body shook. Perspiration drenched her bedclothes, but it was the smell that made the bile rise in Prosperity's throat.

The smell of death.

The midwife stood beside the bed jiggling the bawling baby, whose cries not only didn't abate but got worse by the minute.

Dr. Goodenow placed a hand on the patient's forehead and barked out an order. "Fetch the coldest water you can find."

Prosperity turned to obey, but the midwife thrust the baby into her arms. "I'll get the water. You take him."

Him. David's son.

Prosperity trembled.

The small bundle was so well swaddled that only his anger-darkened face showed. He did not feel damp and did not smell, but the squalling did not stop. She could think of only one other reason. "Has he been fed?"

The midwife paused in the doorway. "Do it look like he's been fed? Who's gonna feed him? She can't." After gesturing toward David's wife, she hurried away.

Prosperity had not tended many babies, but she knew all infants needed milk. Unfortunately, this one's mother could not supply it. "What do I do, Doctor?"

He looked up and blinked as if just realizing she was there. "About what?"

"Feeding the baby."

As if in response, the baby wailed with such piercing intensity that Dr. Goodenow winced.

"Find some milk." He resumed his examination. "If we don't get this fever down, the patient might not survive the night."

That stopped Prosperity's heart. Suppose David's wife died. What then? She did not wish for it. Truly she did not. This woman's death would not solve anything. Prosperity had realized that downstairs when David pleaded for forgiveness.

She lifted a prayer for the poor woman's life.

The woman tossed and moaned. A garbled word came out, backed by desperation, but Prosperity could not understand it.

"Hush, hush," Dr. Goodenow soothed. "Save your strength. Fight for the sake of your baby and husband."

Prosperity edged out of the room. The baby's cries had settled into a heart-wrenching series of sobs and gasps for breath. She must find milk.

"It's stifling in here," Dr. Goodenow called out. "Have Lieutenant Latham open every window in this house. We need to cool these rooms. And see what's taking that midwife so long."

Prosperity hurried down the short hallway, relieved that she was not needed with the patient. Though her mouth had prayed for healing, her heart would not follow. Easier to focus on the baby.

David's son. Prosperity paused at the top of the stairway.

He waited below. He would try to talk to her again, would beg her forgiveness once more, but she could not give it. Not yet. Not while her heart wrenched this way and that.

The baby gasped for air between piercing cries. She jiggled him and pulled the blanket over his eyes in case the brighter light downstairs would bother him.

Poor child, born into such turmoil. It was not his fault that his father had betrayed her. This innocent babe must never know what had once been.

She descended the stairs, taking care not to stumble.

Lamplight spilled from the parlor, where David paced before the darkened windows, hands clasped behind his back in a posture so familiar that her breath caught in her chest. David.

Dearest David. How many nights she had lain awake recalling his every inflection and movement. When puzzled, he would clasp his hands behind his back while his brow scrunched low until he found the answer.

At her appearance, he halted, brow still furrowed. "What happened?"

"Open every window."

He did not move.

"The doctor said we must cool the house."

He strode to the parlor and threw open the windows.

"Also, your son needs milk."

David visibly flinched but did not answer.

"Do you have cow's milk?" she persisted, appalled by his lack of interest in his son.

He waved toward the back of the small house and a dark doorway. "If there's any, it would be in the pantry."

"May I have a lamp?"

Rather than lighting another, he took the one from the small table beside the sofa and led her back to a closet lined with shelves. A few dishes and even fewer foodstuffs sat upon those closest to the door. He opened a stoppered jug and sniffed.

"Smells fresh." He handed it to her.

Prosperity hesitated.

"Marnie must have brought it," he said. "It's not my jug."

"Marnie?"

"The midwife."

She felt a little better. Maybe the midwife had sent for milk when she realized the child's mother could not nurse.

"It must be warmed." She remembered that much from the one time she'd assisted a friend whose milk had slowed. The mother had mixed something with the milk, but Prosperity could not recall what. She scanned the pantry shelves. Biscuit. A tea chest. A moldy lemon. Sugar. That was it. A little sugar to sweeten the milk. "Where is the cookstove?"

He stared. "Why did you stay?"

The sudden shift of direction threw her off-kilter. "What?"

"Why didn't you return home?"

She could not admit destitution, that he had been her last hope. His abandonment had left her without any resources. She might have despaired if not for the kindness and generosity of the O'Malleys and Dr. Goodenow.

Fortunately, the baby wailed again.

"I need to warm the milk," she repeated.

David looked confused. "The cookhouse." He waved vaguely out toward the back door. "We eat what the men eat."

That explained why the pantry was so bare. It also left her without a ready heat source. The jug felt as warm as the room. The baby's screams grew more desperate. It would have to do. "A little sugar."

They reached for it at the same time. The brush of his hand sent a shiver of pleasure down her spine. She backed away, horrified by her reaction. This could not be. It could never be.

He appeared not to notice. "How much?"

She swallowed. "A little of the loaf." Giving direction helped dispel the unwelcome sensation. "Pour some of the milk into a cup and stir the sugar into it."

He did as directed. She tasted the milk. Not sour.

The midwife burst through the back door carrying a pot of cold water and a kettle of boiling hot water. "Make way."

Prosperity dared not miss her chance to ensure the source of the jug. "Did you bring the milk?"

"Aye, when I seen she weren't nursing. New milk." Marnie glared at David. "I'm expecting to be paid for it."

"Of course."

The midwife set down the hot water and then barged on toward the staircase with the cold water the doctor had ordered.

"I think it's ready," David said.

"Pour some of the hot water into that bowl." When he did not obey, she added, "The milk needs to be warmed."

She set the cup into the bowl. It wouldn't take long. While waiting, she considered how to administer it. Her friend had trickled the milk from a spoon, but her baby had been much older. A newborn wanted to suckle. She looked around for a feeding tube or bottle and saw none. The midwife must not have brought a means to feed the wee one.

She tested the temperature of the milk and lifted the cup from the hot water. "It's ready."

David swallowed. "What do we do?"

"Hand me the spoon you used to stir in the sugar."

Once again their fingers brushed. Once again that startling sensation made her pulse pound. Or was it fear that she would harm this child?

She brought a spoonful of milk to the baby's mouth and attempted to trickle the fluid in, but he was crying so hard that it dribbled out onto the blanket. "Oh dear, let me try this in better light."

They moved to the parlor, and she settled onto a stiff-backed chair. She pushed aside the blanket that covered the boy's face and gasped. The baby's skin was unnaturally dark.

"Is something wrong?" David hovered over her.

"No. Nothing." He must see what she saw. Ma had once said a baby might look redder at birth, but this was not red.

This baby's skin was definitely dark. That meant . . . She could not contemplate it now. This poor babe needed nourishment. She again filled the spoon and lifted it to the baby's mouth. He refused it, spitting out the little she'd managed to get in. The babe must suckle.

"What now?" David sounded nearly as desperate as the child.

What a pair they were, helpless before a squalling infant. Prosperity racked her memory. Once with kittens, she had dipped a sponge into milk and let them suck that.

"Do you have a clean sponge?"

"I think so."

"Scald it with the hot water."

He disappeared into the back of the quarters with the lamp, plunging her into darkness. Long minutes later, he returned with a small piece of damp sponge and the lamp.

Prosperity pulled aside the blanket that swaddled the baby's head. Black hair and olive skin. David had blond hair. His parents and brothers were all fair. His wife had the red hair and fair skin of the Irish.

"Is something wrong with him?" David asked.

A chill raced through her. David had flinched when she referred to the baby as his son. He referred to the wee one impersonally, without a name. She tugged more of the blanket away, freeing tightly fisted hands. The light was not good, but it was strong enough to see what everyone else must see.

This was not David's son.

⁓

David cringed when the baby's fisted hands punched at the air during another agonizing squeal. A baby. He knew nothing about babies. That's why God put mothers in charge of nurturing children. They handled everything in the sanctity of the nursery. Husbands stayed away.

He had seen Prosperity's expression change when the lamplight revealed the baby's dark skin and hair. Everyone could see that this child was not his. Word had doubtless spread through the post the past three days. It explained the bubble of calm that had surrounded him at the fort. They had avoided him like a leper.

Prosperity, on the other hand, recovered her composure without saying a word. She didn't need to. He could read her shock as clearly as an engineer's drawing. Kind soul that she was, she did not point out the obvious. That only intensified the pain. This was the woman he ought to have married.

She dipped the sponge into the milk and put it in the baby's mouth. He quieted for the instant he could suck in milk. Over and over she dipped the sponge. Judging by the rate and intensity of sucking, the baby was famished.

"You must hire a wet nurse," Prosperity said. "He needs regular nourishment."

A wet nurse? He knew nothing about such things. "I can get fresh milk every day."

"It will do in a pinch," she said in that Nantucket lilt that made him long for home, "but he needs mother's milk."

"How does one go about finding a wet nurse?"

Though she spoke to him, her gaze never left the hungry little boy. "I know someone who might be willing. She works with me at the marine hospital."

"And with the doctor?" Irrational jealousy surged to the surface. Did Prosperity love the man? Was he courting her? Is that why she hadn't left Key West?

"Dr. Goodenow does not work at the marine hospital."

"Yet he helped you get work there."

She looked at him sharply. "Yes, he has been a good friend."

And he hadn't. "I suppose I deserve that."

"Deserve what?"

He should stop, but the line between love and hate was thin, and his hold on the former was slipping away. "I love you."

Her eyes widened. "Do not say such things."

He must. He might never get another chance. "I never stopped loving you."

She rose, her distress obvious. "You're married."

"Lies. All lies." The fever caught hold of him, blistering all sense from his head. He grasped her shoulders.

She stiffened. "Release me, Lieutenant, and do not touch me again. You have lost that privilege."

He let go. Condemnation scorched worse than the hottest furnace. He had lost his head and driven a wedge between them. All because of Aileen's treachery. "You don't understand."

With a glare so intense it wilted the last of his desperation, she snapped back, "No, I don't. Nor is it any of my concern. Your wife and son need you." She deposited the baby in his arms. "I suggest you begin by feeding him. Tomorrow I will inquire about a wet nurse and send her here. You will need her until your wife recovers and is able to nurse again."

Gentle Prosperity had changed. She now took command.

The baby resumed wailing.

"Dip the sponge in the milk and let him suck it," she directed.

"I can't. I don't know how much." Surely his father had never done such a thing. He held out the baby.

She stepped back. "He will let you know when he is done."

David stared in disbelief. She was leaving him with a baby.

She cocked her head, a faint smile teasing the corners of her lips. "He won't stop bawling until you feed him." Then she walked toward the door.

"I don't know anything about babies."

She paused long enough to look back. "You will learn."

That was no consolation. "I need someone to help me. Can't you . . . ?"

"No. Ask the other officers' wives. They will know. As I said, I will try to find a wet nurse."

He would rather have the woman he loved, but he had utterly ruined that. "I'm sorry."

"Lieutenant?" The doctor strode past Prosperity and into the parlor. His clothes and hair were rumpled, and fatigue lined his face. "Give Miss Jones the baby. You need to see your wife."

The severity of the man's words rippled over David with the force of a hurricane. "Is she . . . that is, will she live?"

As much as he hated Aileen's actions, he did not want her to die. She had done what she needed to do for the sake of her unborn child. She'd wanted the boy to have a father and a good name.

David was barely conscious of the baby leaving his arms as he repeated his question. "Will she live?"

The doctor mopped his forehead. "That is out of my hands now. There's nothing more I can do for her."

13

Prosperity clutched the baby to her chest, though she could only give him milk with the soaked sponge. In time, he was satisfied and slept. She settled him in a stuffed armchair with another butting up to it, seat against seat so the baby would not roll out.

She stared out the dark window. Nothing could be seen even if she was looking, but her thoughts had turned inward. Why had David claimed his marriage was a lie? Had he not truly wed the woman upstairs? That thought made her even more nauseous. Surely the army would not allow a woman to dwell with an officer unless a relation or his wife. He could not prove the former, so he must have married her. His claim made no sense.

Even worse, he'd declared his love for Prosperity. That thought ignited a storm of emotion. How could he say such a thing with his wife languishing upstairs? What if she died? What would he do then? The faint hope she'd tried so hard to dash wriggled back to the surface.

It was wrong, horribly wrong. This baby needed his mother

and father, even if David was not the birth father. This baby's needs must come first. To forget her confusion, she focused on him.

The empty hours of the night trickled past. David and Dr. Goodenow had climbed the stairs ages ago. It was now the wee hours of morning, when darkness took its deepest hold and hope seemed out of reach. Not one sound had come from upstairs, not even the creaking of someone walking across the floor. No wails or cries. Nothing.

She gave up pacing so she wouldn't wake the baby and settled in the straight-backed chair. Pray without ceasing, Paul had told the Thessalonians, but words could no longer overcome fatigue. Her mind constantly rambled, and her eyelids kept drifting shut. Each time they did, she jerked awake and then checked to make sure she hadn't woken the baby.

How peacefully he slumbered in the midst of strife. She stroked his tender forehead. This little one did not know the turmoil surrounding his parents. He must never know it.

The stairs creaked, and she stood expectantly.

The midwife appeared, carrying the kettle of water. At Prosperity's questioning look, she muttered, "Won't be long now."

Prosperity followed her out of the parlor. "Then there's no hope?"

The midwife shook her head. "Her head's clear at the moment, but she's lost too much blood."

"Isn't a clear head a good sign?"

"Seen it happen before, jest before the end."

Prosperity drew in a sharp breath. "Then there's little time."

"Aye." The midwife pushed out the back door. "He be payin' his last respects."

Prosperity could not even swallow. She ought to apologize

for her wayward thoughts. She ought to console David's wife that her baby would have a good father, but her feet would not move toward the staircase. How easy it sounded to offer a simple word of hope. A stronger woman might march up those stairs. Prosperity remained rooted to the spot.

This moment must remain between husband and wife. Her presence would not bring the peace this woman needed. So she watched the midwife disappear into blackest night and offered a prayer for the soul of David's wife.

More creaking sounded from above.

Prosperity moved back to the parlor and discovered the baby rubbing his fists against closed eyes. She picked him up and cradled him close, humming the lullaby her mother had sung to her. He drifted back to sleep.

Footsteps rang on the staircase.

She looked up to see Dr. Goodenow, dressed in black coat and hat. He carried his medical bag. Either David's wife had died or the fever had broken.

"Is she . . . ?" She must hope for the best.

He shook his head.

Gone. David's wife was gone. Once again everything she'd counted as certain shifted. God had granted her heart's blackest desires.

◦✠◦

David knelt by the bed and stared at Aileen's still body. Peace at last, but at such cost. He shuddered over the violence of her delirium. Over and over she had begged for her child. He had promised . . . he didn't know what he'd said. With her last gasp, numbness had settled in. Unrepentant until the end, she had used her moment of clarity to curse him. The words—uncharacteristically free of vulgar language—still rang in his head.

I hope you suffer the way you made me suffer.

He had recoiled and instinctively looked to the doctor. The man was gone. No one else heard Aileen. Only him. No one else witnessed her bitterness. He could be thankful for that. She had no right to curse him. He had given her a home and his name. She was the one who had lied and cheated. Not him.

Instead of unleashing the anger, he forced himself to turn back to her. At the threshold of death, blame ought not be affixed. This shaky marriage had been built by two willing participants. She'd needed a father for her baby. He'd believed her tale, believed himself capable of such sin, and offered her the answer she sought. Yet he'd never been a husband to her.

David took her lifeless hand. A stranger to death, he knew not its character, but even he recognized the chill in her flesh. Still, he held on, staring at her for untold minutes, waiting for some sign that this too was one grand deception.

It was not.

The doctor returned to confirm what David already knew. Aileen was dead.

Their two-month marriage had been excruciating and exhausting. The child he'd hoped to gain from their union proved his mother a deceiver. He had nothing to celebrate from their time together and no direction for the future.

"What now?" he managed to ask.

"You will need to make funeral preparations."

He didn't know where to begin. Other than grandparents, his family had not known death's cruel sword. He had no experience with its responsibilities. Perhaps Prosperity would help. She had buried two parents.

He began to rise. Then sank again.

Foolish thought. After the pain he'd caused her, she would not look at him, least of all help him. No, he must do this himself. There was no one to notify beyond Aileen's few friends at the grogshop. She'd never attended a church and had no kin on the island.

He groaned and buried his head in his hands.

The doctor placed a hand on his shoulder. "You'll get through this. I lost my wife many years ago. It's difficult, but you will survive."

The man did not know that he harbored no love for Aileen. David would not mourn her as much as he would mourn his failures with her. That would be impossible to forget.

"I don't know what to do," he whispered.

"You must live for your son."

"My son." David brushed away the doctor's consoling hand and strode to the window overlooking the other officers' quarters. "You know as well as I that he's not my son."

The doctor paused so long that David would have thought he'd left if not for the man's reflection in the window.

"He is your son by law."

"Did you ever raise a child that wasn't yours?" David spat.

Again the long pause. "My wife died in childbirth. The baby was stillborn. I would have given everything to have my wife back. I would have even given up my insistence on a child of our own, but it was too late. I had refused her wish to take in an orphan. If I had listened to her . . ."

David could not absorb another man's pain. Not now. "At least your wife loved you."

"Perhaps too much." The doctor shook his head. "I didn't

deserve such devotion. We are selfish creatures by nature, and I am no exception. But that baby downstairs needs a father."

David couldn't bear to look at the boy. What sort of father could he be? "How can I?"

"You give him a home and a future," the doctor said.

David turned away, even though he knew the doctor was right. Caring for Aileen's child was the greatest thing he could do to atone for his sins, the one thing he could still promise her. It would also be the most difficult.

❦

David's wife had died, and Prosperity had wished it. For that she could never forgive herself.

"We will go now, Doctor?"

He shook his head. "You must watch that child in your arms until another can be summoned."

Her heart sank. One more moment with David might break her resolve. Yet what woman threw herself at a widower on the night of his wife's death?

"I know this is difficult." Dr. Goodenow stood at her side now, hand upon her shoulder. "Think of the child, not his father."

How easy to say and hard to do. Her thoughts ran wayward, unbridled in their conflicting passions. "Another officer's wife?"

His somber expression softened. "The hour is late, but if a light burns in another window, I will inquire if someone might come to assist you. But I must caution you that dawn is not far away. Doubtless everyone is sleeping."

"The midwife, then."

"I sent her home, as there was nothing more she could do." He drifted toward the door.

A creaking on the stairs sent her heart racing and her gaze

flitting upward. David appeared, step by painful step. His shoulders now bowed. His countenance had aged. His gaze passed over the doctor and landed on her. Oh, those blue eyes! Bright as a summer sky and deep as an ocean. They said more than words ever could. Regret and pain and sorrow.

She caught her breath at the immensity of his anguish.

His gaze drifted down to the babe in her arms, asleep still, unaware that his mother had left this world and its sorrows behind.

"Thank you," he croaked in words barely audible.

She swallowed the protests that rose instinctively to her lips—that it was nothing, that any woman would do the same, that she had only done what must be done.

"Please stay," David said, looking not at her but at the baby. "I cannot."

Surely he knew that, but his gaze rose again to her face, and she nearly cried out at the torment in his eyes.

"I don't know what to do." He licked his lips. "The baby. Everything. Please help. As a friend."

No words could be crueler. Every part of her longed to agree, but that would be terribly wrong. "Your wife has passed."

He flinched as if she had just fired a musket, but her statement wiped away the anguished husband and rejuvenated the soldier. "I will need to make arrangements. For the burial. And for the child."

A shiver ran down her spine. She preferred the despairing husband to the emotionless soldier. "I will ask Gracie—she's a laundress at the hospital—if she will nurse the boy."

He stared at her.

"Your son will require a wet nurse." She was certain she'd said this before, but he seemed to have forgotten. "Gracie is nursing her own and might be able to take on another baby. If not, she may know someone who can."

He nodded, but she doubted he would remember come morning. She looked for the doctor, who would confirm the need for a wet nurse, but he was gone. He must have slipped out to find another officer's wife.

"Mother's milk is best."

David avoided looking at her. "Then do make inquiries, Miss Jones."

The stiff formality slapped her across the cheek. She could barely draw a breath. This was as it should be, but not as she wished. "I will."

It was the only proper thing she could do.

14

Prosperity was true to her word. Later that day, before the last of the officers' wives left David's quarters and returned home, a wet nurse arrived to take the squalling baby.

The buxom Negro girl looked barely twenty, if that. Gracie by name. A slave, most likely, hired out to the hospital. Her wages would go to her master. For this service, David wanted the fee to stay with her. After all, she was giving of herself, perhaps diminishing what she could give to her own baby in order to sustain Aileen's child.

The girl expertly quieted the babe with a few soft words and jiggles, much as Prosperity had. For the briefest instant, a fierce longing swept through him. Prosperity. Dear Prosperity. His betrothed and beloved. Now no longer his.

"You be needin' someone ta nurse dis boy every day," the girl said, drawing David from his regrets. "Every three ta four hours."

He dragged a hand through his tangled curls, painfully aware of the depth of his exhaustion. "I will pay handsomely."

He named a price, and her eyes rounded. He must have offered too much. Too bad he hadn't thought to ask the other officers what was a reasonable rate.

"I got my own babes," she protested. "An' I does laundry at de hospital."

"I realize that."

"I kin only nurse him early in de mornin' an' before supper. I cain't be leavin' my babes ta live here."

"That's not what I intended." But he had no idea what he intended or what needed to be done. A widower could not raise a baby, even if he wasn't a soldier. David's work meant long hours away from home. What was he supposed to do with this child all day? No matter what the doctor tried to impress upon him, this product of Aileen's wild ways was not his responsibility.

"Ya need someone ta take care of dis boy, ta feed him when I cain't be here."

"I know." His head split from the piercing squalls, well-meaning condolences, and ricocheting emotions. He drew a deep breath and began again. "I realize that must be done, but I don't know how to do it." He wished to wake from this nightmare that heaped on difficulties like bricks. "I need someone to take care of him until I figure it out. Could you take him for just a few days?"

The girl glared. "Don't you be shovin' your chile off on me. Miss Prosperity done tole me what ya done ta her, how you be runnin' off with a no-good woman. She too proper ta say anything, but I ain't got no problem speakin' my mind. This babe needs ta be fed. You pays me for dat, but I ain't gonna raise yore chile for you."

"I'm not asking for that." Wasn't he? Didn't he want every trace of Aileen wiped from the house? He had not shed a tear when the doctor laid a sheet over her. He'd quickly agreed to the commander's offer of a plain pine casket. He looked forward to the body's removal to chapel. He'd already contemplated burning everything she'd purchased, but the child would still remain.

"He need a mama," the girl asserted with the conviction of a matron of forty.

Prosperity. No other name came to mind. No other woman could bring peace and proper balance to his wildly careening life, but she would not even look at him.

"How?" he croaked.

The girl shrugged. "Do what ya must."

David had seen this often enough. A widower was soon surrounded by women eager to become his next wife. He need only select among the prospects. That would likely prove true here also—if he didn't have the responsibility of a mixed-blood baby. That narrowed the field considerably, even to nothing.

"I nurse him as long as I kin," the girl added, "but I cain't promise ta do it fer long."

"Do you know someone else?"

She shrugged.

His desperation grew. "There must be someone who would take him."

The girl's expression twisted. "Ain't no one gonna accept dis babe. Ain't white. Ain't colored."

The truth of her words pushed past the pain and exhaustion. This baby had no future. None. That's what the doctor had been trying to tell him. If he didn't give this boy his name, the little one had no chance.

The revelation cleared the fog from his head. "I must be his father."

She nodded with what appeared to be approval. "He still need a mama."

David had been given his marching orders. Find a wife. Not only a wife, but one who would accept a mixed-blood child *and* meet the approval of his commanding officers. He might as well have been asked to build a tower to the moon.

⚜

Gracie reported that she'd agreed to nurse David's son before and after her workday. That ought to have brought Prosperity comfort, but the girl added that she'd prodded David to remarry.

"Remarry!" The idea vexed her. "He is newly widowed."

Gracie shrugged. "Gotta git that po' chile a mama."

Of course. Marriage was a practical necessity. Some woman would be dazzled by the adventurous life of an army engineer's wife. That woman could not be her, though it stung to think of David married to yet another woman.

Each day she asked Gracie if anyone visited David. Each day the answer was no.

Her heart buoyed, though she managed to hide that reaction from Gracie.

Eventually she must make peace with David, but the pain was still raw. Anger, fear, despair. The emotions swirled like the rushing tide through an inlet. Each night she prayed for guidance. Prayer brought conviction but no easy path. She must face David before she could move on.

To that end, she determined to pay a visit with Gracie after work on Friday. "Might I go with you tonight to Lieutenant Latham's quarters?"

The woman clucked her tongue. "Gracie cain't tell Miss Jones what ta do."

Her hands paused from folding bed linens. "Are you saying that it's not proper? I'm simply paying my condolences."

"Mm-hmm."

"No one would have cause to gossip."

"Do it matter what people say?"

It did. It mattered a great deal. Her tenure at the hospital was already on shaky ground. "Perhaps I'll wait."

"He not wait fo' you, no sir."

That did not sound like David. At least not the David she knew. "Love is patient."

Gracie harrumphed. "Fo' a fool."

"Do you think me a fool?"

Gracie picked up her empty basket. "Love done make every one o' us a fool at one time or t'other." She gave Prosperity a stern look. "Alls I'm sayin' is don't be doin' nothin' rash in the heat o' things jes' ta ease the ache in yo' heart. Else you find yourself with a whole pile mo' heartache."

The truth of her words sank into Prosperity over the following days. In the calm of dawn after morning prayers, her thinking was much clearer. In those hours she could lay out David's character and actions without the confusion that dogged her later in the day. David had betrayed their vows. Not only had he wed another, but that marriage had been necessary because he had been with this woman in a sinful way. Even though the child was not his, he must have believed it was. Betrayal in thought was as wrong as betrayal in deed.

Still, on her daily walks to the hospital or to market, her gaze wandered to every uniformed soldier she passed, alternately hoping and fearing that it would be David. Her breath would catch until she was quite certain it was not him. Then her fragile hope would collapse.

"Come now, Miss Jones," Dr. Goodenow said as he walked her to the hospital one Monday morning. "Enough of the gloom."

She paused on the corner of Fleming and Thomas, where they now parted ways. "Is that an order, Doctor?"

He laughed. "It is. Come, let's continue to the hospital."

"I thought you understood . . ."

"You may walk ahead of me if you wish, but I must go to the hospital this morning."

Her curiosity piqued. "You have a meeting with Dr. Mac-Nees?"

"Have you heard of the sorry business aboard the *Philadelphia*?"

"Cholera, right? I heard Dr. MacNees was not pleased the city refused to allow the ill to be brought ashore." Dread shivered down her spine. "You're going to help? Are you going out to the ship? Or are the sick being brought to the hospital?"

"Neither. The ship carries a surgeon. Dr. MacNees is joining the mayor to examine those passengers put off on Sand Key."

"Those not infected." She had wondered at that drastic measure, which was doubtless done to remove the healthy from infection. But the conditions could not be pleasant since Sand Key had no shelter beyond the lighthouse, which could not possibly house all those set ashore there. "Is he looking to see if the contagion has spread?"

"Very perceptive, Miss Jones. In his absence, he has asked me to oversee the hospital."

"He has?"

"Don't seem so surprised." But a smile threatened to break his artificially stern expression. "Without an assistant, he has little choice but to turn to a local physician. It will be a brief tenure, however. I expect him to return by nightfall."

161

"Very brief indeed." But still fraught with danger. "I do think it best if I go on ahead."

He swept his hand forward. "As you wish."

If their connection that day had ended with the morning conversation, nothing might have come from the chance occurrence, but by ten o'clock, Miss Stern appeared at the laundry. Cook was taking a break to chat with Gracie. At Miss Stern's appearance, the cook pretended she was fetching clean table linens.

Miss Stern ignored the cook and focused on Prosperity. "The doctor requests your presence, Miss Jones." By her expression it was perfectly clear that she did not approve.

Prosperity lifted the mangle and pulled the sheet from it. "Do you know why?"

"It is not our place to question a physician's orders. You had best remember that. Now put on a clean apron and follow me upstairs."

Upstairs. That meant the wards or the dining room or even the surgeon's office. Prosperity's hands trembled as she untied the knot behind her back and slipped into a starched white apron.

"Hurry, hurry," Miss Stern urged.

Prosperity rushed after her while tying the apron strings. Even so she could not miss the sneer that twisted the cook's expression. Tales would be spread, but Prosperity could not dwell on what she could not change.

"Do you know what he wants?" she dared to ask.

Miss Stern harrumphed. "To assist him, he says."

Prosperity gasped.

Miss Stern halted. "Let me warn you, Miss Jones, that one misstep will cost you dearly. Listen carefully and obey orders to the letter, but do not make one step beyond what is necessary. Do you understand?"

By now her pulse was racing. She nodded, though she had no idea how she could counter the friendly banter Dr. Goodenow was certain to employ.

They arrived at a supply closet, and Miss Stern unlocked the door. She then handed Prosperity a metal tray filled with bandages, instruments, and small bottles of medicine. "Take this to the first ward. The doctor is already there."

Prosperity's hands shook, and the metal instruments rattled against the tray.

"Don't stand there gawking," Miss Stern said tartly. "Go."

Prosperity did not want to enter the wards. She didn't fear illness or even the seamen suffering there. She feared the repercussions. Hadn't she made it clear to Dr. Goodenow that they must have no contact in or near the hospital? Yet he'd breached every rule by asking her to assist him. Her stomach knotted as she walked down the corridor.

The ward was far from full. Two men occupied the beds closest to the door.

Dr. Goodenow looked up from tending to one of the patients. "Ah, there you are. I was beginning to wonder if the matron would refuse to let you leave the laundry."

Prosperity edged into the room. "I'm sorry, Doctor."

"Come here. I need one of the medicines on your tray."

"Yes, sir." She tried to hold the tray steady, but the instruments and vials rattled with every step.

He smiled when she stopped beside him. "You may breathe now."

She let out her breath. "Yes, sir." She wanted to ask why he had sent for her, why take such a huge risk, but Miss Stern had made it clear she was only to obey directives and answer direct questions.

Dr. Goodenow picked up one of the bottles and measured out a small quantity. "Tincture of rhubarb will help ease dyspepsia and restore the bowels."

Prosperity knew she ought to pay attention, but she could not concentrate more than a few seconds. Entering the ward had recalled the painful memory of David's wife lying amid bloodied sheets.

". . . often used in dysentery and the latter stages of cholera. Miss Jones?"

Prosperity pulled her thoughts back to the present. "Forgive me. What do you need?"

"I was explaining the properties of the medicine. Didn't you ask to learn this?"

Her cheeks heated. Was that why he'd called for her? Oh, careless tongue. She regretted ever speaking her mind. "I'm sorry, Doctor."

Dr. Goodenow eyed her a long moment. "I am the one who is sorry. I've asked too much." He guided her out of the ward. "I will speak with Miss Stern."

Her hands shook so badly that he took the tray from her and handed it to a passing orderly, who gave Prosperity a knowing grin before going into the ward as directed. Oh dear, the gossip would spread terribly.

"Please understand that I meant no harm," Dr. Goodenow whispered.

His nearness made things even worse. She avoided his gaze. "I should return to the laundry, sir."

"You deserve better."

In other circumstances, that statement would have delighted

her, but she could not shake the fear. If she lost her position, she would have no money to let a room. Elizabeth would insist she stay, but Prosperity could not accept charity. Her lip quivered.

"Don't be afraid." Thankfully he did not reach for her. "Dr. MacNees did approve of this and will tell Miss Stern when he returns. That should smooth things over."

The knot in her stomach began to unravel.

Dr. Goodenow lingered a moment longer. "Forgive me, Miss Jones, but if the officials allow the passengers from the *Philadelphia* to enter Key West tomorrow, as I suspect they will, I may not have another opportunity to ask you to join me at tea this coming Saturday afternoon."

Though the corridor was hot, it could not account for her discomfort. "I'm not certain . . ."

"It is a social, Miss Jones. A benefit for the temperance league."

If only she didn't have this Saturday off. Instead she must find a kind way to refuse. "I don't know if it would be wise."

"Your friend Mrs. O'Malley will be attending. It is to be held at the Cunninghams' house."

With Elizabeth in attendance, the event would be above reproach, and she *was* curious to see where the Cunninghams lived. Mrs. Cunningham had talked extensively of her porcelain vase collection from the Far East.

Down the corridor, Miss Stern tapped her toe, watching every moment of their interaction. Already the woman disapproved of her friendship with the doctor. If this conversation continued—and Dr. Goodenow would not rest until she agreed—Miss Stern might seek dismissal.

"Very well then. I accept."

Dr. Goodenow smiled. "I shall look forward to it. Expect me to call on you at three o'clock."

"I will walk with Mrs. O'Malley." That was safest.

"We shall walk together then."

If she had the tiniest feelings for him, her heart should have tumbled at his insistence, but she felt nothing. Perhaps in time her affection for him would grow, but not yet, not until she broke free from the past.

❧

David dreaded the social, but Colonel Stormant had required every officer's attendance. Mourning carried little weight with the colonel. A black armband marked David's status, but Ambleton had already warned him to expect a goodly share of feminine attention. He left the baby with Mrs. Walters, whom he'd hired to replace Gracie, and arrived with the other officers in his stifling wool dress coat.

Perspiration dotted his brow, and not just from the heat. He had not attended many socials before joining the army. His father considered such functions the breeding ground of gossip. This afternoon many ladies graced the parlor, veranda, and expansive garden. Light fabrics turned billowing skirts into frothy confections. Though most necklines were modest, the heat prompted many ladies to wear shorter sleeves than would be considered proper back home.

The other officers had been swept away by some acquaintance or other, highlighting the seclusion David had put himself in since arriving on the island. Work consumed his days. Solving each unforeseen issue with the construction gave life meaning. His only foray into society had resulted in destruction. He was not eager to dip a toe into that pool again.

He glanced around the room, looking for a familiar face. Shy girls and hopeful ladies caught his gaze for a moment before darting away. Their mothers didn't bother to hide their disapproval, leaning close to their charges to impart some words of wisdom. David could imagine what they were saying. It was not kind, for eyes widened and then those same young ladies whispered to their friends behind their fans. After another quick glance, they settled their attention on one of his compatriots.

No mistake about it. This tea might be billed as charitable, but its real aim was to match young ladies with eligible young men. At best, he'd been deemed ineligible. At worst, the matrons viewed him as scandalous. Finding another wife—at least one of quality—would be nearly impossible.

"Come this way, Lieutenant." Captain Dutton appeared at his left elbow and drew him toward the garden where another segment of Key West society mingled.

This was a decidedly older grouping without the hysteria of the marriage mart. Matrons sipped tea while relaxing in lavish chairs that probably belonged in the parlor. Gentlemen in ivory-colored suits congregated to the side, telling tales and negotiating deals.

Captain Dutton tapped him on the shoulder. "The mayor is asking about progress at the fort. You can provide the detail he wants."

The captain must have already endured a barrage of questions if he'd resorted to sending in an assistant. The afternoon just got more arduous.

Dutton mustered a grave smile. "You know how best to handle, er . . . indelicate questions."

David wasn't at all certain what his commanding officer meant, but now was no time to ask. The mayor stepped forward, waving his hand and calling out Captain Dutton's name. David walked slightly behind the captain, who would make introductions. Though he tried to focus on the mayor, his eye was drawn to a small group seated beyond the man.

He drew in his breath.

Dr. Goodenow was seated between a lovely woman with golden hair and another who far outshone her in spite of the plain gray dress and unadorned bonnet. Prosperity.

Every ounce of strength seeped away.

She was listening intently to the doctor, her lips slightly parted as if the man's words amazed her. Compassion shone from her brighter than the lighthouse's lantern. Her every move revealed grace greater than a queen.

David tried to speak her name, but his voice stuck in his chest. He tried to move to her, but his feet did not budge.

Then God had pity on him. Perhaps it was the twitter of a bird or the flutter of a butterfly, but whatever captured her attention, he silently blessed it, for her head tilted upward, and she looked straight at him.

15

D avid." His name escaped Prosperity's lips in a whisper. She smoothed the skirts of her dove-gray gown, which she had donned simply because she could not bear the black mourning gown in the day's heat. Her hands trembled, but she could not look away from him. She had both longed for and feared seeing him from the moment the first army officer arrived this afternoon. With Elizabeth and Dr. Goodenow surrounding her, she'd felt safe, but that sense of security vanished the moment she saw him.

David. Every hope had been tied to him, and every tie had been ripped from her grasp. He stood beside his superior officer, silent, the black armband marking his grief. The captain motioned to David from time to time during his discussion with Mayor Carmody and Captain O'Malley, yet David's gaze kept drifting toward her.

Such longing and regret and suffering shone from behind his too-stiff countenance. He had lost a wife and discovered her infidelity mere days apart. Though he stood a few feet from Prosperity, he had retreated within himself.

Her feet stirred, instinctively urging her to go to him.

Dr. Goodenow lightly touched her sleeve. "You need not acknowledge him."

Her nerves jangled, caught between the kindness of one man and her longing for the other. "I must." David needed her.

The doctor turned to Elizabeth. "Please tell her to act sensibly, Mrs. O'Malley."

Elizabeth glanced at her and then the doctor as a gentle smile graced her lips. "I have never known Prosperity to act anything but sensibly."

The comment was meant as an affirmation that she would choose the proper path, but Prosperity felt a deeper truth, one that Elizabeth could not have known. A lifetime of sensible choices had ended with her voyage to Key West.

She rose, letting the doctor's caution fall behind her. Two short strides brought her near. "Lieutenant."

Something flickered in his eyes before he bowed stiffly. "Miss Jones."

Her fickle heart buoyed with that flicker, willing it to be hope for their future, all the while knowing that nothing could wipe away the mistakes of the past.

He nodded, and his gaze darted toward the garden paths. "Would you care for a stroll?"

The way he could not hold her gaze disconcerted her. She hesitated.

He offered his arm, still without any outward sign of affection.

She had hoped too much and too soon. The doctor was right. She need not speak to David. The dictates of propriety gave her an excuse. She could simply offer her condolences and return to the comparative safety of her friends, but that would not quench the irrational longing that consumed her days. Perhaps one last conversation would put an end to it.

"Miss Jones." The doctor must have risen behind her. "If you would like to see the grounds, I would willingly escort you. There are many plants here with medicinal qualities."

She looked back at him, surprised at the pang of curiosity that rose in her. The doctor treated her with greater respect than any other man, yet this one time she must decline.

"I will return shortly," she said. "Then perhaps you might explain more about the plants."

She placed her hand on David's arm, and awareness shot through her like lightning. He trembled. Did he feel it too? If so, he said nothing.

As they walked, that once-familiar scent of soap and sea revived the David of her youth, brimming with strength, honor, and unwavering seriousness. The old desire to tease him into a smile returned.

"Are you emulating your fort with that straight back?"

His glance betrayed confusion. "An officer must display proper composure."

She stifled the urge to smile. "Especially an army engineer."

"All officers, regardless of rank or position."

She couldn't hold back any longer. "Oh David, don't you recognize my teasing anymore?"

Like before, many emotions crossed his face, but today she could not ignore the underlying sorrow that hollowed his cheeks.

"I'm sorry," she whispered. "Jesting is not appropriate, not now."

His throat bobbed behind the rigid collar. "I don't mind. It reminds me of how things used to be."

Used to. The past. How foolish she'd been to think she could recapture it.

They turned back toward the main gathering, and she spotted several women quickly look away. Their promenade had not gone unnoticed. Whispers and rumors would form. Gossip would flow. Mrs. Cunningham's pointed frown made it perfectly clear what she thought. Prosperity should not have indulged her whim. David was not yet three weeks into mourning. To walk with any woman so soon after his wife's death naturally invited speculation, especially since he had a son.

His son. Yet not his.

Gracie had nursed the baby a little over a week before he dismissed her. Why?

Prosperity glanced at David, who stared straight ahead, his jaw working as if he struggled to find something to say.

"Your son," she began.

"He is not mine."

The coldness with which he spoke drove a spike through her. That poor baby needed love, but David would not give it. "He is your son in the eyes of the law."

"Don't lecture me like your doctor friend."

The sting of his words shattered her illusion that they could resume where they'd left off two years ago. She'd been holding on to a cord that led nowhere. It was time to let go.

She released his arm. "I wish to return to those friends."

"Prosperity—"

"Miss Jones, please. The time for familiarity is over."

His countenance paled. "I'm sorry. That didn't come out right. I didn't mean—"

She could not listen to excuses. "Goodbye, Lieutenant. I wish you well."

He sucked in his breath.

She left, dropping the cord that had once connected them. Let the winds carry it away.

⌒⌒

That had gone as badly as David could have imagined. He had let anger at Aileen and jealousy of the doctor drive a wedge between Prosperity and him. She had approached him and walked with him against the doctor's advice. She didn't seem to see it, but the man was clearly enamored with her. David had not counted on competition. He also had not counted on the depth of her compassion for Aileen's child.

That miscalculation led to the inexcusable blunder. She had every right to walk away. He'd been consumed with his own agonies and never once thought of the bold grace she'd extended before women who would flay her reputation. What a cursed idiot he was!

The hostess, a dark-haired, arrogant woman, stopped Prosperity for a word. The woman's glance in his direction and satisfied expression suggested she'd congratulated Prosperity for walking away from him. Deserved humiliation heated his neck.

He straightened his spine and walked back toward Captain Dutton, who looked annoyed that he'd been left alone with the mayor. Yet another miscalculation. The captain had counted on him to calm the mayor, but how could David calm anyone when he couldn't manage a simple conversation with the woman he loved?

He passed a group of ladies huddled together in deep conversation.

". . . a colored baby," one lady whispered none too softly.

"Scandalous, but what can one expect when marrying that type of woman?"

The insult struck with the force of a musket ball. Anger flared like lit gunpowder. David clenched his fists, but responding would only bring worse condemnation. Turn the other cheek, Jesus had instructed, but David's every instinct urged him to defend his honor. Yes, he had made a bad choice, but he had done so with honorable intentions. He did not know of her duplicity. Though he longed to explain, honor forbade sullying the reputation of the dead.

So he focused straight ahead and passed the group with haste. Still, he could feel their pitying gazes upon his back. He stood a bit taller. Like any good soldier, he had learned to build walls between his personal life and work. Emotion had no place in the life of a soldier. Reckless emotion ensured death. David must not fall to the enemy today. He focused on joining his commanding officer.

Captain Dutton broke off his conversation with the mayor long enough to cast an urgent look at David. It was not a plea for rescue but instead hinted that something serious had happened. David's thoughts immediately leapt to the fort.

Upon his arrival, the mayor was asking what additional problems to expect. David wasn't aware of any problems that impacted the civil authorities.

"As I stated earlier," the captain addressed the mayor, "Lieutenant Latham is in charge of the day-to-day details of the construction. He will answer your question. Lieutenant, meet me in front of the house as soon as you finish. We have business to address." He then bowed out of the conversation.

David fought back his curiosity and did his best to concentrate on the question, but Prosperity stood directly in his line of sight. She did not lift her gaze to him. Instead she placed her hand on the doctor's arm. A twinge of regret hit his already battered heart. His idiotic responses had driven her to the man. The doctor led her onto the same paths David had just walked.

"Pretty girl," the mayor mused, his gaze following Prosperity, "if plainly dressed."

David hadn't noticed her gown. Even if she wore sackcloth she would shine brighter than any other woman. Prosperity's beauty did not lie on the surface but shone from deep inside. He had never seen another woman who could compare. Yet the mayor did draw his attention to the fact that she was wearing gray instead of mourning black. Had she already transitioned from full mourning? He tried to calculate the weeks and failed. "She lost her mother in April."

"You know each other?"

David would never reveal the depth of the attachment to a stranger. "We are both from Nantucket."

"Ah. An islander, then. It must resemble our fair isle in some respects."

"Yes, sir." To direct the conversation away from Prosperity, David asked the mayor what concerned him about the progress at the fort.

"I understand you ran into some construction problems," the mayor said. "Will you need additional labor?"

That was all? At first glance, Captain Dutton's discomfort made no sense. Then David considered the ramifications of bringing in more men from outside the island. Many in Key West hired out their slaves to the public project. In return, they received their men's wages. An influx of hired labor from the mainland might displace those Negroes, especially during times when supplies dwindled and work slacked.

"I haven't received any word that additional men are required," David said delicately. "The current labor force is keeping up quite well."

"What do you say about the rumors that men will be sent here from Fort Jefferson now that funding has dried up for that project?"

David was woefully unprepared to debate appropriations or the movement of men. He'd been so preoccupied the past few weeks that he hadn't heard about the stoppage at Fort Jefferson. He glanced toward the house, where Captain Dutton paced on the rear veranda.

"I shouldn't keep the captain waiting." It was the only excuse he could muster.

The mayor looked displeased. "You can't tell me what will happen, then?"

"If Captain Dutton does not know, then I certainly do not. I'm sure that he will keep you apprised of any changes in the quantity of laborers needed for the project."

The man's mouth ticked. "Well then, I suppose we must leave it at that."

"Yes, sir." David bowed and departed before the man could think of another unanswerable question.

By that time, the captain had made his way through the house to the street. Judging by his pacing and furrowed brow, whatever had happened was of grave importance.

At David's approach, he halted. "We return to the garrison." He took off at a brisk walk.

David followed, doing his best to match the captain's strides. Though he longed to ask what had happened, he must wait. The captain would speak when he was ready.

When they reached a quiet street, the captain slowed his pace. "Command suggests you find other lodging for your infant."

The statement slapped David with the force of an anvil. What had happened? Had the colonel or captain overheard the whispered slurs and decided to act? That wasn't like his commanding officer. No, this decision sounded like Colonel Stormant's doing. His wife had acted much more aloof since the birth. "Are you suggesting I live outside the garrison?" He had no idea how he could afford to let a house or rooms that would allow for an infant.

"You might consider settling the child with its nurse for the time being."

David's insides knotted. "May I ask why, sir?"

This time the captain looked him in the eye. "Fever. I received a report this afternoon that Ambleton's wife has taken ill. Fever. Possibly yellow jack. The surgeon wants to take all precautions."

David felt sick. Georgina Ambleton had been among the wives who visited his quarters the night Aileen died. "Shouldn't the baby be under the surgeon's care?"

"Dr. Rangler has no experience with infants. You would do better with a local physician, should the need arise. Moreover, there is the problem of nursing the child. The army hospital is not equipped to deal with that, especially if this incident turns contagious."

"Others in the garrison are ill?"

Captain Dutton's expression was grim. "We are attempting to prevent this from spreading to the men, but you know how easily the fever touches newcomers."

David caught his breath. Prosperity. She too had spent time at his quarters the night Aileen died. If the contagion had gotten into the air there, she might fall ill. Since this was her first time in the tropics, she was particularly susceptible.

Someone needed to warn her. David's gut clenched. Would she listen to him?

∽⚹∾

Clayton basked in the satisfaction that Prosperity had not only left her unfaithful fiancé but that she had accepted his own offer to show her the flora on the same garden path. At first her attention drifted, but once the lieutenant left the garden, she listened to his description of each plant and tree with great interest.

"What is poisonwood?" she asked when he commented on the use of gumbo-limbo bark to counter its rash.

"A tree that is very similar to your poison sumac. Every part is poisonous to the touch, but rest assured that there are none in town." He noted with pleasure the lightness of her touch on his elbow. "They may be found in the wild parts of the island and on the other Keys."

"Then I shall not go there."

He smiled at her practical if overly cautious solution. "I could show you how to discern them should you ever find yourself exploring the wilderness."

She laughed then, her light hazel eyes sparkling in the sun. "You need have no fear of that. I prefer the town."

"Not a quiet shore?"

The idea must have tantalized her, for she hesitated. "Would you show me that quiet shore?"

His pulse beat faster than it had in many years. "Of course. We shall plan a picnic and make a day of it."

She nibbled her lower lip, a sure sign something had vexed her. "But would it . . . that is, I wouldn't want to feed the gossips."

"We shall invite a group of friends. Perhaps the O'Malleys and the Cunninghams."

Naming her friends and acquaintances wiped away the concern. "Then do plan this picnic."

"Perhaps Captain O'Malley might take us to a neighboring Key," he mused, "such as the Marquesas. The Dry Tortugas would be too far."

"Tortugas?"

"Named for the turtles that nest there. Dry because there is no source of water other than rain. If not for the building of Fort Jefferson and the lighthouse, no one would live there."

She puzzled over that a moment. "If there is no water, then how can anyone survive?"

"Cisterns, my dear, the same as they have here. Have you not noticed how rainwater is collected and funneled off roofs into deep cisterns?"

"Broken cisterns," she mused.

"I would hope not."

She smiled softly. "That is from the book of Jeremiah."

"Ah." He looked away, uncomfortable with her mention of the Bible. He had not opened one since his wife's passing. He could not believe in a God that let the good and the innocent die. Science gave solid answers. Science would succeed where religion failed. "I am not familiar with that passage."

She gasped. For a moment he thought his response had distressed her, but then he noticed that her attention had flitted to the street.

"I wonder where he is going in such a hurry."

Clayton spotted the lieutenant. Annoyance floated to the surface. Would she never give up this fruitless pursuit of a man who did not deserve her? "Doubtless duty calls."

179

His dismissal did not appear to ease her concern. First a frown settled. Then she slipped her hand from his arm. "I should inquire if something has happened. Perhaps there is trouble with his son."

She stepped away, but he caught her arm to save her from a grave mistake.

"Please take care, Miss Jones." He released her arm, since many eyes had turned toward them. "Rushing after a young man will fuel gossip."

He pointedly glanced to their left, where Mrs. Cunningham watched their every move. She followed his gaze and, as he'd predicted, flushed that lovely shade of rose, delicate as the petals of the roses his late wife had planted back home many years ago. Even now, twelve years later, the thought of her brought a wave of sorrow, though not as crippling as it had once been.

Prosperity brought him back from that lonely place. Her innocence and faith reminded him of Sarah and better days.

She bowed her head. "I'm sorry. I did not think."

"It's all right. No harm done." He longed to console her, to take her in his arms and hold her close as he had once held Sarah, but sense won out over longing. "Might I offer a word to the wise, gleaned over many years of life?"

She nodded.

Oh, how sweet the trusting of youth. She had not yet suffered the indignities that a lifetime would hand her.

He offered a soothing smile to brace against the harsh words. "The lieutenant is capable of caring for his own family."

The pointed remark had the desired effect, though he regretted causing the slump of her shoulders.

"I suppose you are right," she murmured.

He held out his arm, and she returned her hand to it. How

gentle her touch. He quaked at the thought of all he'd lost. Could fate bring it back? For a moment he could almost believe in such an unscientific idea, but providence had shown itself a devouring beast. It took and took until the giver had nothing left. Survival required a strong will and the cunning to seize opportunity when it arrived.

"Come with me, Prosperity," he whispered with the gentle smile she seemed to enjoy, "and I will show you the world."

"The world?"

She did not understand. Perhaps he had spoken in haste, caught up in the moment. He glanced toward the guests. No one watched them now, and the realization made him rush where perhaps he ought to take his time. Was it too early to declare his feelings? Perhaps not, given she had walked away from her former beloved. Yet he must tread carefully.

"I would give you the world if I could."

Her smile set his heart pounding. She understood! She knew what he wished and had seconded it with that single gesture.

He took her hand in his. "Dearest Prosperity—and you are dear to me—I will not promise more than I can conceivably deliver. As you know, I am a simple physician. What you see is who I am." He ought to look in her eyes, but he could not risk losing his composure, not now when so much was at stake. "I would strive to make you happy, my dear Prosperity."

He felt the tremble of her hand but dismissed it as his own. He had gone this far. He could not stop now.

Romantic notions called for gentlemen to drop to one knee. He could not and would not do such a thing in front of those who would disparage the moment with gossip. No, this was best stated purely and simply.

He cleared his throat, gathering his nerve. Amputating an

injured leg was easy compared to this. His life hinged on the answer to this question, but her clear, hazel eyes looked up at him with such trust.

"What is it?"

Those eyes spurred him to spill the question in a single rush. "Would you do me the honor of becoming my wife?"

Her gasp told him he'd made a mistake.

16

"What?" Prosperity choked out.

How had a pleasant afternoon stroll turned into a declaration so stifling that she could not draw a breath? She stared at Dr. Goodenow, not believing what she had just heard. Surely her ears had deceived her. He could not have proposed marriage. She had given him no cause to do so. He was a kind man who insisted on escorting her to the hospital and back whenever possible, but marriage?

They were not even courting. He had never suggested they should. Not in so many words. True, he had suggested familiarity by using her given name, but she had never called him anything but *Doctor*. He was a deserving gentleman and would make a fine husband, but she could not think of him in that manner.

She did not long to see him. Her thoughts did not linger on him after they parted. His presence was generally pleasant except when he prodded her to step outside the bounds of her position at the hospital. That had made her worry over his intentions, but never with any thought toward personal attachment. He did not plague her dreams like David did. She could not draw a breath without thinking of David. Even though she must move on, she could not step away from him one moment and fall into the arms of another man the next.

"I've startled you," he said.

"No. No." She slipped her hand from his and tried to settle her thoughts. "You are a good man, a fine man . . ." She could not look at him.

"But not a suitor. Is it the difference in our ages?"

"No! Not at all." How could she explain without crushing his feelings and ending the fellowship between them? She swallowed. "Your respect and friendship mean a great deal to me."

"But that is not enough."

She backed away. "I—I'm sorry."

His crestfallen expression raised such regret within her. She did not wish to hurt him.

He swiped his mouth with the back of his hand, as if to erase the disappointment. "The fault is mine, Miss Jones. I thought . . . well, I assumed incorrectly that you shared my affection."

"I had no idea."

His smile was wry. "Again, the fault is mine for misinterpreting your words and actions."

"My words?" What had she ever said to encourage such a thought? "I could not consider marriage, not now." Not so soon after leaving her hope of a life with David.

He nodded ever so slowly. "You are in mourning still. I ought to have waited, but I thought the change of gown meant you were coming out of deep mourning."

"No, that is—" She couldn't explain what had never occurred to her. She simply couldn't abide the black dress in the heat.

"There is no need for you to explain. I was mistaken. We shall not speak of it again."

The stoic manner in which he bore his defeat touched her. "I'm sorry, Doctor. You are a good man. I'm simply not ready for marriage."

"I should have realized that, considering the betrayal you recently endured."

That stung, and she instinctively stiffened.

"Pardon me for mentioning a sore subject," the doctor hastened to add. "After watching you with the young lieutenant earlier this afternoon, I assumed you had resolved matters between you."

Prosperity stared at her clasped hands. The doctor spoke of heartache as if it could be treated in the same way one treated a cold. "Does a broken heart ever heal?"

He must have heard her whisper. "Never entirely. After twelve years, I still miss my late wife, but I have learned that one must carry on."

"March on," she murmured, thinking of David on his way back to the garrison. Is that what he was doing, trying to continue on after losing so much?

"That is one way to think of it. Look at me, Prosperity."

She could not.

He continued anyway. "Though you are not yet ready, my offer still stands. If at any time in the future you change your mind, you only need tell me."

She ought to say something gracious, but she could only think of David. If he had proposed, would she have answered differently? Yes. A thousand times yes. If he had asked before dismissing that tiny babe. She could not love a man who would not cherish an innocent child. Since her own fickle heart still cried out for him, she could not trust it. Not with David. Not with anyone.

"The heart is deceitful above all things," she murmured.

"What did you say?"

That was another reason she could not consider Dr. Goodenow's proposal. Her husband must live by God's Word.

She smiled softly. "Another passage from Jeremiah. Please take me to Elizabeth. I wish to return home."

❦

Mrs. Walters eyed David warily. "You want me to take him with me? I don't need another babe squallin' and keepin' me awake at night."

She had never mentioned a Mr. Walters, and David didn't ask. Her wild locks sprayed out from under a washerwoman's scarf, and her apron bore testimony to the large brood she had at home.

"I can't take another child." Her hands braced her hips with finality.

"Please? Just until I can find someone else."

He wished Prosperity could help him. She would know what to do. She would take care of everything. But she was not here, and if this afternoon's meeting was any indication, she wanted nothing to do with him.

"No, sir. No, sir," she repeated, shaking her head to emphasize the point.

"I will pay double," he offered. It was more than he could afford, but he was desperate. He didn't know where else to turn, and command had made it clear that he was to remove the baby from the officers' quarters at once.

"Double?" Mrs. Walters hesitated, apparently tempted yet still skeptical. "Why're you willin' to spend that much?"

He thought through his answer. Admitting the presence of fever would only send her running. He began slowly. "My commanding officer asked me to find a place for him in town."

"Why? 'Cause the child's colored?"

"Because he needs a mother."

"I ain't this boy's mama. If you ask me, it's 'cause he's colored. Ain't no white commander want a colored baby in his camp."

"The commander has never shown any prejudice—"

Mrs. Walters snorted. "It's there, plain as the nose on your face. All right. I'll take the poor thing with me, but only for two weeks. After that, you gotta find someone else."

Though relief surged through him, it was brief. Two weeks would pass quickly. Maybe the threat of fever would end by then. If not, he'd have to find another wet nurse willing to take the boy into her house. Tending to this boy might be the honorable thing, but it was proving extremely difficult.

"Thank you, ma'am."

"Thank you," the woman mumbled as she gathered the boy's things. "If you wanted to do right by this boy, you'd give him a name."

David recoiled. If he gave the baby a name, the boy would be his. As long as the boy remained nameless, he was just another of Aileen's mistakes.

Mrs. Walters lifted the baby to her shoulder. "A boy needs his papa."

Her glare echoed Prosperity's and told him he'd failed in this too. Mrs. Walters might not realize the child wasn't his, and he couldn't bring himself to tell her.

"What papa doesn't name his boy?" the woman said pointedly. "A child cain't go through life without a name." She bounced the boy lightly. "We call you David after your papa."

"No. Oliver." The name blurted out. He had once dreamed of naming his child after Prosperity's mother, but that was while they were courting. They had spent happy hours contemplating the possibilities. Prosperity wanted to honor his family, but he'd been adamant. Olivia for a girl, and Oliver for a boy.

"There now." Mrs. Walters nodded. "Oliver. That be a good name." Her wide grin revealed crooked teeth. "Yes, sir, Oliver's a fine name." Cooing softly to the baby, she made her way to the door. "Two weeks, Lieutenant Latham. Then I return little Oliver to you."

Two weeks to win back Prosperity.

c⁓ɔ

Sunday afternoon, Prosperity and Elizabeth kept each other company since Captain O'Malley had left on a wrecking voyage with his former chief mate and brother-in-law. Later, Elizabeth's sister and her son would join Elizabeth for supper. Though this was the first time the two captains had left their families since Prosperity arrived, in rough weather they made these forays more often. According to Elizabeth, the women always banded together at the O'Malley household, for Anabelle and John's house could not accommodate everyone.

Prosperity looked forward to Anabelle's arrival, for she had not yet met the sister that Elizabeth spoke of with such fondness. Until then, they occupied the time playing with little Jamie, who loved to bang his wooden blocks together. He was just beginning to crawl, which kept Elizabeth busy.

"You garnered a great deal of masculine attention at yesterday's social," Elizabeth commented while directing her son away from the nursery door.

"Not so much."

Prosperity cherished these precious moments of family life, despite the regret that she no longer had a family of her own. This was the life she had dreamed of having with David. They would chase a toddler around the house. He would put his son on his shoulders to show him the world from a different vantage point. Her locket ought to contain the images of their children. Oliver and Olivia, he had insisted. Instead it would remain empty unless she accepted the doctor's proposal.

Yet how could she marry without love?

"No other lady attracted the notice of two gentlemen," Elizabeth said as she carried her son back to his pile of wooden blocks. "And both of them are highly desirable. Did you notice the looks of envy the other women cast your way?"

Prosperity would not call what she'd seen envy. She'd witnessed the hurried whispers and unconcealed smirks. Mrs. Cunningham had made it quite clear that Prosperity's stroll with David had inspired scandalous gossip. She had not passed on the same result after Prosperity's walk with the doctor. In fact, Mrs. Cunningham could barely contain her jubilation. If Prosperity hadn't quieted her, she would have bubbled to her friends that they were courting. Oh dear. Did Elizabeth suspect the doctor's proposal? They were dear friends, and he might have mentioned his plans to her.

"There is no need for anyone to envy me," Prosperity whispered.

Elizabeth kissed Jamie on the forehead when he placed a block atop another. "Because you are still in mourning?"

Prosperity breathed out with relief. If Elizabeth had known of Dr. Goodenow's proposal, she would have mentioned it then. "I am not ready."

"I understand." Elizabeth stroked her son's golden curls. "I

189

mourned my mother for some time, but I also used the mourning period as an excuse to fend off an unwelcome suitor. I must warn you that society here does not hold strictly to convention. Gentlemen will approach you and ladies will speculate."

"There is nothing to speculate about." Prosperity picked up her sewing. She was embroidering a nautical motif on a baby tunic as a gift to her hosts, who still refused to accept full payment from her. "I am not looking to marry."

A twinge of guilt pricked her. Perhaps that wasn't entirely truthful. If David had proposed . . . no, she could not answer that with any certainty. She no longer knew her own mind.

"I don't know how it is on Nantucket, but in Key West it does not matter if you seek marriage or not. You are new to town and of marriageable age. People will pair you." Elizabeth's eyes twinkled. "Perhaps they will match you with the lieutenant or the doctor, since they both singled you out at the social."

"Too much so."

Elizabeth laughed. "You can never have too much attention from deserving gentlemen."

Deserving. That was the question, wasn't it? Prosperity nibbled on her lower lip. Could Elizabeth help her sort through her confused feelings?

"Do you think they're both deserving?"

Elizabeth dangled a bright red ball in front of little Jamie, who tried to grab it. "I know the doctor a bit better, but I have heard enough about Lieutenant Latham to believe he is a man of strong character."

"You have?" Prosperity was surprised, for she had heard naught but derogatory statements of late. "You heard something good?"

"Sometimes it's less about what is said and more about what isn't."

Prosperity frowned. "I don't understand."

"I have learned not to judge people by public opinion. Two years ago, when I returned to Key West, my own father stirred up vicious lies about Rourke." A deep sadness settled over her usually calm expression. "He attempted to separate us forever."

"But they are not at odds now."

"Arriving at that point was not easy, and it did come at a cost. I thought I'd lost both men." Elizabeth stirred, as if troubled by the memory. "It hurt a great deal at the time, but in the end the price was worth paying."

Prosperity let out her breath. How much of a price was she willing to pay? The doctor offered a life of comfort and affection. Sense told her that was a good match, but her heart could not substitute companionship for true marriage. Not now. Not yet. She closed her eyes and tried to think. Mere weeks ago, she had risked everything for David. Now? "I don't know what to do."

"What does your heart tell you?"

"I wish I knew." Prosperity set aside the embroidery and paced across the small room to the window. It opened onto the side yard shaded by coco plum and lined with a picket fence. Security was enticing, but then why did she long for the brilliant orange blooms on the other side of the fence?

"The doctor is good and kind," Prosperity said slowly. "He respects my abilities more than anyone ever has."

"But?"

"But I don't feel anything for him beyond affection."

Elizabeth did not reply at once. "Is that because the lieutenant still claims your heart?"

She must admit that much. "I wish it wasn't so, but I cannot stop thinking of him. Even when he disappoints me, I cannot get him from my mind. I spent too long last night trying to make sense of what he said when I should dismiss it and move on."

"What did he say?"

Prosperity could not repeat David's words to a woman playing with her child. Elizabeth would not understand. Prosperity herself barely understood. He hurt from his wife's betrayal, evidenced by that poor child. "What he said matters not. His pain is what hurts. Even while his wife lived, I could not stop thinking of him. Now . . ." She could not complete the thought.

"Now that he is widowed," Elizabeth said, "your hopes have returned."

She bowed her head, ashamed.

Elizabeth rocked Jamie, who had grown sleepy. "Did he love her?"

Prosperity recalled the tension between them the day she first arrived at the garrison. David's wife had boasted loudly, trying to draw his attention. Instead he had followed Prosperity. On the other hand, he had worried the floor with his pacing during the birth and stayed at his wife's bedside in her final moments.

"I'm not certain. I did not know them well." Prosperity swallowed the bitterness. The screaming curses still resounded in her ears.

"It's impossible to know another's heart. He did appear distracted at the social, though you were the only lady he singled out."

Prosperity did not want to recall the painful conversation with either man. "It's too soon."

"Because he's grieving."

"It's too soon for me."

Elizabeth's expression softened. "You must miss your mother dearly. Were you close?"

Prosperity blinked back a tear. "We talked over everything. She was my dearest friend and confidante."

"You are fortunate to have had such closeness. I loved my mother, but we spent too much time apart to grow close. I last saw her when I was sixteen. I wish we could have had the kind of bond you had with your mother. What would she tell you to do if she were here today?"

"She would never have agreed to let me sail to Key West. Ma was a Nantucketer through and through. No other place on earth could compare."

"She sounds very loyal and sure of her beliefs."

"Very much so. She was such an example of kindness and Christian hospitality. Even when we had nothing, she would offer a cup of tea." Prosperity swiped at a tear.

"Did she approve of your engagement?"

"Oh yes, she was so proud of David and his position in the army corps. She told all her friends that he was an engineer building a great fort that would defend the nation."

"It sounds to me like she would have wanted you to be together."

Prosperity bowed her head. "Everyone assumed we would marry. We'd been close for years and years. Since I was thirteen and he fifteen years of age. I planned my entire life around him, including a houseful of children. How foolish that seems now."

"We often think we can see our future when we are young. I know I did, but God is the only one who knows the path we will follow."

Prosperity looked up, startled by the truth that she had ignored for so long. "I wish He would tell me."

"Perhaps He will. Trust Him."

Prosperity couldn't believe that Almighty God would tell her whether to accept the doctor's proposal or wait for David. If she even could. She rose and paced to the window. "I still love David, but how can I trust him after he broke our pledge?"

"Trust is a fragile thing. It takes tremendous faith to recover."

"I used to think I had that kind of faith."

"None of us knows until we are tested." Elizabeth rose and laid her son in the cradle that was shaped like a rowboat.

A knock sounded on the front door. Since Elizabeth always gave Florie Sundays off, no one hurried to answer.

Elizabeth's brow wrinkled. "Anabelle wouldn't be here yet. Will you watch Jamie while I answer the door?"

"I can get it."

"No, no." Elizabeth waved her off.

Prosperity knelt beside the cradle and gently rocked the little boy. His eyelids fluttered open a moment but then fatigue pressed them closed again. Seconds later he relaxed and drifted into peaceful slumber. His little mouth dropped slightly open. She brushed a curl from his forehead. Her son might have looked like this. With David's coloring, he could easily have fathered a boy with curly blond hair and blue eyes. A pang squeezed her chest until she could not breathe.

Oh David. Why?

"Stewart wanted to bring it to the garrison, but I insisted it belonged in her hands." That strident voice could only belong to one woman.

Prosperity left the nursery to greet Mrs. Cunningham, whose straw bonnet sported yards of ribbon. "Thank you for inviting me to the social yesterday."

"You must get out in proper society more often."

Prosperity bit back a retort. The memory of the woman's scathing assessment of David was still fresh in her mind.

Mrs. Cunningham opened her bag and withdrew a letter. "This arrived on the mail ship. Stewart was gathering the post to take to the garrison when I happened to notice that this one belonged to you." She held out a small letter that was battered and torn.

Prosperity caught her breath. "Who would write to me?" Perhaps Mrs. Franklin or another of the women from Nantucket. Certainly not Aunt Florence or her cousins. They had not written when she lived within a day's sail.

Elizabeth slipped past her to check on Jamie.

Mrs. Cunningham smiled smugly. "Read it and see."

Prosperity examined the address, and her heart stopped. That was David's hand, each letter looped with precision so none was larger or smaller than its mates. The return address directed it to the garrison, but her address . . .

"It was sent to Nantucket," she breathed out.

"And returned here when it could not be delivered."

Prosperity tried to wrap her mind around what had happened. "It must have taken weeks and weeks to go back and forth."

"I imagine so." Elizabeth returned to her side. "The mail packet from Charleston takes two weeks under good conditions."

Prosperity calculated the time in her head. At least two months had passed since David had written it. She turned over the letter. "The seal is broken."

Mrs. Cunningham's chin jerked upward just a little. "Understandable after so much travel and rough handling. You'll notice the creasing and dirt, as if someone trampled on it."

"True." Prosperity still suspected Mrs. Cunningham could not have resisted opening it.

"It's from that lieutenant, isn't it?" Mrs. Cunningham sniffed. "Too late, I say. There are far more respectable prospects to be had, as you well know."

The nudge toward the doctor didn't make this any easier. Prosperity stared at the letter. David had left her for a—a strumpet. There was no genteel way to put it. She unfolded the sheet. Perhaps his words might excuse his actions.

"Would you care for a cup of tea, Mrs. Cunningham?" Elizabeth offered. "We might take it in the parlor while Prosperity looks after Jamie. I would dearly like your opinion on which china to set out for the benefit later this month."

Faced with the choice between new gossip and the opportunity to voice her opinion, Mrs. Cunningham hesitated. When Prosperity folded the letter again and slipped it in her apron pocket, the woman went with Elizabeth to the parlor.

With their departure, Prosperity slipped into the quiet of the nursery and settled in the rocker. She fingered the broken seal. She could not abide the thought of Mrs. Cunningham or anyone else reading words intended only for her. Though the army might at any time open David's letters, no other letter had been touched.

Her hand shook as she unfolded the paper. The date stood out since it was written in a heavier hand than the rest. April 20. The day of her mother's burial.

After years of suffering, Ma finally had peace. Prosperity did not. The journey to Key West was supposed to have solved everything, but instead it had brought sorrow and turmoil.

"Ma, what do I do?" she whispered into the quiet before looking back at the letter.

Her eyes scanned the words, but they jumbled together into nonsense until she reached the very last sentence.

I will marry tomorrow.

A cry burst from her lips before she could stifle it. David had written. He had tried to tell her. He had acted honorably.

The room was suddenly too small. All thought of meeting Elizabeth's sister vanished. She must see David. She must talk to him. Nothing else mattered. She ran out of the room, past the startled ladies, and out of the house.

17

As was his habit, David spent Sunday afternoon at the work site reviewing the week's progress and noting what changes and corrections needed to be made on the morrow. His father would be appalled. The Sabbath was a day of rest. He ought to have stayed away from the fort, but he could not abide the usual occupations of the officers on a Sunday afternoon. The families banded together for a large Sunday dinner, complete with children playing ball and other games on the parade ground and married couples sitting in the shade of a canopy.

So instead he focused on work, which was much easier to set in order than the maelstrom of emotions that threatened to undo his stiff reserve.

"Come now, Lieutenant," Captain Dutton had urged rather halfheartedly, "you don't see any of us at work on a Sunday."

"No, sir." Yet he had still made his apologies, and the captain had let him go.

The idle work site could not revive his spirits, for Prosperity's pained expression tormented him day and night. After a promising start, he had driven her away. She had teased him like in the old days. Her eyes had sparkled. Then he had to open his mouth. She'd first paled at his refusal to talk about Aileen's baby. Then he'd compounded the problem by accusing her of lecturing him. What if she had? He deserved it.

He scrubbed his face, sticky from the thick air and ever-present dust.

"Prosperity." Even speaking her name constricted his throat.

She had meant so much to him, everything, and he had ruined any chance of regaining her trust. She had proven that by running straight into the arms of the good doctor.

He tossed down the pen. He couldn't concentrate. His mind drifted here and there, untethered to anything solid. Frustrated, he leaned back in his chair and looked out the window at the construction. The most difficult portion, the foundation, was done, and the first level was rising. At this rate it would take years more to complete. Then came the second and third levels. Cannons must be put in place. Permanent quarters built for soldiers and officers. Armories, furnaces for shot, and countless other smaller buildings. Then Captain Dutton had proposed five towers elsewhere on the island. This project would last his entire eight years and more.

Within that time, Prosperity would surely marry. She would gather with friends on a Sunday afternoon to watch the children play. He would still be here, alone. Dampness touched his little finger. Ink. He'd pressed the nib so forcefully that it spilled its ink onto the desktop.

He reached into the drawer for a blotter, and something sharp bit into his hand.

David hauled everything from the drawer to find the culprit. It was in his Bible. He heaved it onto the desk and opened it.

The binding cracked, twisting the pages into two disjointed halves. Wasn't that the case with everything in his life? Broken. Impossible to mend.

Prosperity's calm gaze looked back at him. The engagement daguerreotype. How nervous she had been, afraid she would ruin the picture and waste his good money. He'd had to console her, telling her it cost pennies when in truth it cost a great deal, but the price had been worth it, for he had carried her with him from Nantucket to Key West.

She had been his rock until he cast her aside. What now?

He reached to turn the plate upside down and then realized the Bible was open to the final chapter of Proverbs.

She openeth her mouth with wisdom; and in her tongue is the law of kindness.

Prosperity. He stared at the verse. By chance he had placed her image atop the verses extolling the virtues of the noble wife. If only he had read that chapter before throwing it all away on a night of drunkenness.

He slammed the Bible shut and shoved it back in the drawer. In his youth he'd believed God blessed him and guided his every step. No longer. He had fallen so far that nothing could bring him back.

How fruitless to try to work today. He put away his pens and drawings and left his office.

The soldier on guard bid him a good evening.

"Evening?" Surely it wasn't that late. David peered west. The sun hung low, but at least an hour of daylight remained. Plenty of time to walk back to the garrison before dark.

Within a few blocks he could hear the lively jigs and chanteys drawing men to the grogshops. Squeals and laughter permeated the late-day air that hung heavy as a cloak over the island. The streets began to take on a different appearance at this hour, transforming from daytime business to nighttime revelry.

David walked past the very grogshop that had wreaked such havoc in his life.

"Eh there, Cap'n." The sultry voice came from a saucy wench who doubtless intended to lure him into her employer's establishment.

"No thank you, ma'am."

"Ma'am!" She hooted. "I ain't married." She grinned, revealing a missing tooth. "I might have something you want, Cap'n."

David ought to walk away, but something made him pause. Poor Aileen had been in the same condition. He'd tried to rescue her without success. Perhaps this one would leave her occupation if another means of making a living might be found. "I'm sorry, miss, but I am only a lieutenant, not a captain."

She cocked her head, and the light struck her face. That's when he realized she was far younger than she'd first appeared. And her tooth wasn't missing. Rather, her teeth were gapped, making her less than comely to men not deep in their cups. Sorrow swept over him. If only something could be done so women didn't fall into this terrible trap.

"Lieutenant, eh? Aileen's lieutenant?"

A chill shook him. "Yes."

The girl's gaze narrowed, and she crooked a finger toward him. "Come out back, soldier, an' I'll give ye what ye want."

She pointed toward the alley behind the grogshop. No doubt this is where the ladies made the bargains that their trade demanded. Squalid shacks lined the far side of the alley. He did not care to know what happened inside those rooms.

"C'mon. Ain't what ye're thinkin'." She touched a finger to her lips.

She wanted to talk. The realization made David's mouth go dry. Even if she was simply after money, he would attempt to dissuade her from the sordid trade. Decades earlier, Commodore Porter had driven the pirates from Key West. If only the military could scrub away the other vices.

He followed her.

She led him into the quiet alley and pressed a finger to her lips. Obeying her warning, he did not speak, only waited.

"Don Louis," she whispered after looking around to ensure they were alone. "From Havana. Told 'er he'd marry 'er, but when she went to the docks, the ship was gone. He left without 'er."

David drew in a sharp breath. "Aileen?"

She looked at him like he was a fool. Perhaps he was.

"I didn't know," he said.

"'Course ye didn't."

Aileen had told him nothing of her life. He worked the question in his mouth before spitting it out. "She knew she was with child at the time?"

"Aye." The girl's eyes darted left and right. Apparently deciding no one was near, she leaned close. "When she seen ye, she knew ye'd raise the babe as yer own."

Though meant as a kindness, the words still stung. Aileen had used him for her purposes, and those of her child.

"Then she . . ." He could not bear to ask if she'd ever loved the man who'd gotten her in that state.

The girl understood what he needed to know. "She lost 'er head over 'im. We all told 'er he weren't the kind ta trust, but she thought he'd come back for 'er. She kept comin' back here lookin' fer him."

Those disappearances and late-night excursions. He'd thought she was plying her old trade in spite of her condition, but apparently she'd come here looking for the man she loved. Don Louis. The name didn't sound right. Spanish mixed with French. The girl might be pronouncing it wrong, but it didn't matter. At the moment, he only cared about Aileen's past. "He never returned?"

The girl shook her head. "But another one loved 'er."

He recalled the drunken man who'd stumbled into their quarters with her. "She loved him too?"

"Naw, but he helped 'er."

In exchange for . . . His blood boiled. He squeezed his eyes shut against the knifing pain. Aileen had known no bounds. Marriage vows meant nothing to her. She used anyone within reach to accomplish her ends. This man was clearly a drunkard, yet she'd coerced him into coming to their quarters. Why? What did she need from him?

"How did he help her?" He opened his eyes.

The girl was gone.

⚜

On a Sunday, David would be at the garrison. Prosperity must see him, must tell him how mistaken she'd been. He had honorably broken off the engagement. She should never have doubted him.

She raced through the streets, letter clutched to her midsection. Passersby stared, as well they might, for she had not donned cap or bonnet. Her hair spilled from its pins. Her chest heaved from the exertion, and her face burned.

These streets did not look familiar. Lively music spilled from open doorways and windows, mingling with laughter and shouts, many in language unfit for a lady's ears. She had turned onto the wrong street. Four soldiers stumbled toward her, their hats askew and coats unbuttoned. The sort of confidence instilled by spirits raised their voices in slurred boasts.

"Thank 'e fer sharin' the fruits of yer labor," the largest of them said to one whose countenance could capture the attention of many a lady.

The four laughed, repeating *labor* in such a way that made it clear there had been no labor involved at all.

As a whaler's daughter, Prosperity had seen her share of such behavior, for the taverns crowded as near as possible to the wharves. When her father found one of his men stumbling out of a drinking establishment, he'd grab the rascal by the jacket and haul him back to the ship to sleep it off.

Pa could not protect her today.

She crossed the relatively empty street.

They crossed also.

She turned back.

They cut her off and surrounded her.

"This one's purty," the burly one slurred.

"Excuse me, gentlemen." She attempted to slip between them, but the burly man caught her arm and squeezed until it hurt. She drew in a shaky breath. "Please let me go."

"Dun't ya wanna talk?" His breath reeked of spirits and tobacco.

She stood tall, knowing from experience that cowering only fed a rascal's appetite for mischief. "I want to go to church."

That ought to have silenced the men into reverence, but instead it brought guffaws. Three of them crowded closer.

"Ta church," the short one squealed.

"I'll take ya ta church," the balding one snorted.

The brawny man jerked her closer. "She's mine. I seen her first."

Perhaps Dr. Goodenow had been right to insist on escorting her. She tried to tug her arm from the man's grasp. "Please, let me go."

"Not today." His rancid breath gagged her. "A girl in these parts is lookin' fer a man, and this man is lookin' fer a woman."

A chill ran down her spine. "I am not that type of woman." That only drew laughter.

"As you can see, I'm in mourning," she stated as calmly as possible.

"I know how ta raise yer spirits," the brawny man chortled.

It was more than she could bear. No act of will could stop the trembling that seized her limbs. She looked to each man, hoping one had enough integrity to stop this. The three leered at her, and the handsome one made no move to help. With no gentleman near, she must save herself. Lacking her father's brawn, she could only rely on wits. Pa had often appealed to the men's better nature or even their relations.

She squared her shoulders and stuck an accusing finger in the burly man's face. "Would your mother approve of this behavior?"

The man's grasp loosened ever so slightly. "Me mum is gone."

"I'm sorry for your loss. May she rest in the Lord's arms."

Her words had a somewhat sobering effect on the men. The short one stared at his boots. The balding man cleared his throat. The burly man released her arm.

The fourth man, whose darkly handsome visage appeared behind the short man, surveyed her from head to toe. "Too self-righteous, boys."

"Jameson!" barked a familiar masculine voice. "Urich, Smeech, and Drenth."

The men shot to attention and stepped away from her.

"Back to the garrison at once." The lieutenant's voice carried unquestioned authority.

Prosperity knew she should withdraw, but she could not rip

her gaze from David, strong and commanding, not broken as he'd been the last time she saw him. Excitement rippled through her. Then she recalled the letter in her hand and the accusations she'd held in her heart. The thrill of pleasure turned to trembling.

"Aw, Lieutenant," the brawny man whined. "We didn't mean nothin' by it."

"If you linger one minute longer," David snapped, "I will report you to Colonel Stormant."

The four soldiers scurried away.

That left her face-to-face with the man she'd wanted to see when she bolted from the house. That desire had not taken into account her rude dismissal of him yesterday afternoon.

He did not smile. His eyes were cold as ice.

She would not find forgiveness.

⌒⊶⊷⌒

When David spotted his men harassing a woman, he expected to find them arguing over one of the girls who plied their trade inside and outside the grogshops. He'd never expected to see Prosperity.

Her hair had tumbled from its pins. Her skirts were dusty, and she clutched a letter to her midsection. Her cheeks were flushed and her eyes wide.

His hands fisted. If one of his men had hurt her, he would pound him senseless. Jameson should know better than to associate with those three. That no-good Smeech had been closest to Prosperity. He would kill the man.

"David." It came out of her in a gasp, as if she was more terrified of him than the louts who'd been pestering her moments before. She stepped back.

The blaze inside him died. She feared him. Not the men who had hounded her. Him.

He swallowed. "Did they hurt you?"

"No." She touched a hand to her hair. "I-I left the house in rather a hurry."

"You're alone?" He looked around but did not spot the doctor. She averted her gaze.

"You shouldn't walk alone . . . in this part of town." He amended what he'd wanted to say, that she shouldn't walk alone anywhere, for Prosperity had an independent streak. She walked Nantucket without fear, but there her father's reputation had kept ruffians at bay. Here she had no such protection, other than the doctor whose seemingly constant presence thwarted most of David's attempts to talk to her. "This is no place for ladies."

"I got turned about."

"Why are you out at this hour? Dusk will fall soon."

She bit her lower lip, that painfully familiar gesture that signified uncertainty.

He would give her time. "Allow me to escort you to your destination."

She lifted her face, eyes brimming, and it took all in his power not to run to her. After the debacle at the social, he must use restraint.

"At the very least, we must leave this area."

She nodded but did not move to take his arm.

"Where to?" he prompted. "Church? Or a friend's house?"

She straightened her neck, though she did not look at him. "Point me in the direction of Greene Street, please."

"In that direction a few blocks." He extended his hand, hoping she would accept his arm. Instead she seemed to suddenly realize that she still held a letter in her hand and folded it.

"News from home?" he asked.

She paled, and her hand trembled. Surely not more bad news. He searched his memory but could think of no other relative of hers on the island.

"What is it?" he asked. "Has a friend fallen ill?"

She shook her head. "Your last letter. It arrived today."

His throat constricted and his hand dropped. "You never received it." He had speculated as much when he first saw her here, but to know she'd traveled to Key West assuming they would wed shoved aside the pain of the last few weeks and replaced it with the ache of what he had done to her.

"Until today," she repeated.

"I am sorry." Nothing could erase the pain that the letter must have renewed.

Her lips quivered. "I misjudged you."

Hope shot through him with an arrow's accuracy. Then he recalled his blunders. "You had every right. I gave you nothing but heartache."

She looked away. "Why?"

Such a simple question, yet impossible to answer. He would not speak ill of the dead. For all her faults, Aileen deserved that much. Yet he must answer. Prosperity deserved that much.

Boisterous laughter billowed from the grogshops and re-inforced the root of his sin. "I failed." He swallowed against his dusty, dry throat, but it did not help. "I failed you."

"We all fail those we love," she whispered.

"But I tried to make amends once I realized you had come to Key West. Why didn't you purchase passage home?"

"With what?"

"I sent you enough for the fare."

The widening of her eyes told him the truth. Aileen had

promised to get it to her. Aileen! Why had he thought to trust her in this vital mission when she had proven untrustworthy in every other way? He recalled the new dressing gown and trinkets for which he'd never received a bill. She had spent the money he'd intended for Prosperity.

"You never received it," he said dully.

Her back stiffened and her eyes flashed. "'Tis cruel to claim assistance that was neither requested nor given."

"B-but," he stammered. What could he say? Nothing. Not one word would prove his innocence when prior actions stated his guilt.

She cut off further conversation with unusual vehemence. "You might lie to your family or your men, Lieutenant Latham, but do not lie to me. I thank the Lord that I learned your true nature before we wed."

His jaw dropped. He had no answer.

She did not wait for one. Shoulders squared and head held high, she strode off.

He deserved her silence. He deserved shunning, yet he still followed close enough to ensure her return to a safe part of town.

She did not look back once.

18

What had provoked David to claim he'd sent her money? Or to believe she would have taken it? For passage back to Nantucket, he'd said. He wanted to send her away, to blot out their past completely. Amends! Money could not erase heartache. Pretending he'd sent it only deepened the pit he'd dug. Either David had changed completely, or she had never truly known him.

Prosperity shoved the stack of clean linens onto the shelf. Three days had passed, yet she could not shake the anger that boiled inside her like wash water. Hadn't he hurt her enough without adding dishonesty to the roster of grievances? Perhaps once a man got mired in sin, he sank deeper and deeper. The Bible taught that she must forgive, but forgiveness could not come in the midst of anger.

"Straighten those sheets, Miss Jones," Miss Stern barked, "or you will press them again."

"Yes, ma'am." Ordinarily Prosperity took great pride in her work, but stewing over David had made her careless. The torrid

July heat drained her strength. She could not waste the little she had left this late afternoon redoing work that had already been completed.

She smoothed the sheets under the matron's watchful gaze.

Perhaps Mrs. Cunningham was right and she should accept the attentions of the worthy doctor. Though Dr. Goodenow did not touch her heart, he would not lie to her.

This time she set the sheets on the shelf with care that no corner or edge folded.

"Better." Miss Stern scowled above the high collar of her simple gray dress. "With yellow fever season approaching, we won't have time for this sort of carelessness. The beds will be filled and the days long. Do you understand, Miss Jones?"

Prosperity nodded, but a chill shivered through her at the mention of yellow fever. In her short time on the island, she had heard fearful tales of this disease that mostly struck newcomers. Sailors making their first foray into the tropics would often contract the fever and be put off at the hospital's long pier. Though the men would never set foot in town, the disease seemed to filter into streets and homes.

Yet not every victim was new to the island. Elizabeth's mother had perished from it, and she had lived here over two decades. According to Elizabeth, at the first hint of fever some of the men would send their wives and children north on the first packet. Elizabeth would never leave.

"To what purpose? We are ultimately in the Lord's hands."

Prosperity might have thought differently had she a son to consider.

When Dr. Goodenow met her on their appointed street corner at the end of her shift for the walk home, she asked him about the disease.

"It does more often strike those who are new to the tropics." He extended his arm.

She slipped her hand around it but again felt not the slightest attraction. Why couldn't she fall in love with him when he was clearly the better man?

"Are you afraid?" he asked.

"No." That wasn't quite true. "Perhaps a little. Did you ever contract it?"

"If I did, the symptoms were so inconsequential that I could not tell the difference between it and an ordinary ague. Often it is like that, particularly in younger people." He waved at a swarm of the annoying mosquitoes that gathered in earnest at dusk and dawn. "Clean everything thoroughly. Disease spreads through filth and foul air."

Again that chill skittered down her spine. She handled the soiled bed linens. "Are there any cases of yellow fever now?"

"None that I know about."

Prosperity swallowed. Fear was getting the best of her. "C-can I get it from doing the wash?"

He frowned. "Unlikely."

She breathed a little easier. "How is it treated?"

"We treat each symptom as it emerges."

That did little to remove the weight that had settled on her chest. "Can it be cured?"

"Some do recover."

"Yet others do not." Prosperity had watched her dear ma suffer through chills, fatigue, and wracking coughs until the last bit of strength left her. "Like consumption."

"Not at all. Why would you think that?"

"Because of my mother's struggles."

Tenderness softened his gaze. "Ah yes, you mentioned she

suffered from that disease. I am sorry for your loss. Caring for her must have been difficult."

Though she appreciated the sympathy, it did not inspire any feelings for him beyond friendship. Yet Ma would surely have approved him as a suitor. Prosperity wished her mother was still alive. Ma would have known what to do.

"I could not save her." She choked down the lump in her throat. "No one could."

"Unfortunately, we physicians do not yet know how to heal all our patients, but one day scientists will discover the cure for every illness and disease."

"All of them?" The claim rang hollow. "How is that possible when every manner of evil runs wild upon this earth? Do you not believe we live in a fallen world?"

"A fallen world?" He laughed. "That is superstition, my dear."

"It is written in Scripture."

He seemed not to hear her. "One day soon superstition will give way to science. Then such nonsense can be forgotten."

His reply unsettled her. She stopped walking and pressed a hand to her abdomen.

"Are you unwell?"

She shook her head, wishing they had arrived at the O'Malleys' house and this walk could be over. "Just tired."

"You must rest more and eat properly. More meat for strength. I will speak to Dr. MacNees about lightening your duties."

"No! No, please." She would never make enough to afford a room of her own if her duties were cut.

"Don't worry about Miss Stern. Dr. MacNees will handle her."

"It's not Miss Stern. I don't want to leave the hospital without sufficient help in what I hear is a busy season."

"Remarkably generous," he murmured, "but you give too

much of yourself, dear Prosperity. I love that about you, but it also worries me. If you were my wife, you would not need to work."

Wife. The word shot through her with deadly accuracy.

"We agreed not to discuss this." Emotions aside, she could not consider union with a man who did not believe in God. He'd called her faith superstition, but that was all she'd had to cling to during the darkest hours of her mother's illness. Faith gave her the peace and assurance to step forth into the unknown. Knowing she would one day see her mother and father again comforted her during the long, lonely nights.

"I will never stop loving you, Prosperity."

She could not promise the same.

✦

"I can't keep him here." Mrs. Walters thrust the baby at David. "I got my own babes to consider."

David swallowed his frustration and took the fussing boy. Had she heard about Mrs. Ambleton's fever and assumed yellow jack, or did prejudice change her mind? David had searched long and hard to find a woman willing to nurse the baby. Most had turned him away. Now Mrs. Walters had too.

"But he needs to live with a wet nurse. Where can I find one?"

Mrs. Walters appeared sympathetic even while handing him the small sack containing the few items he had purchased for the baby. "Hire one of the darkies."

David cringed at the term. "I've already tried." Even before his son had been evicted from the garrison, he'd been unable to find a Negro willing to nurse him. More than once he'd wondered if Gracie had said something to the African community that turned them against him. "I don't know who else to ask."

Mrs. Walters shrugged. "One of the owners."

That bitter taste intensified. Approaching a slave owner meant stealing milk from a Negro woman's baby in order to line the owner's pockets. Moreover, if the owner had heard rumors of yellow fever, he would never let one of his slaves near David's son.

"I don't know which women would be available to nurse." He couldn't bring himself to call them slaves.

Mrs. Walters clucked her tongue as if scolding him. "Men don't know nothing about nothing. Talk to the midwife." She told him where to find the midwife who'd assisted Aileen. "She'll know who lost her babe."

Then she closed the door in David's face. As if appalled to be left in the arms of a soldier, little Oliver let out an ear-piercing shriek followed by gulps of air. His face contorted and reddened with every howl.

David jiggled the boy. "Hush. Quiet." More jiggles. "Shh." Passersby stared.

He shot them an apologetic look. What was he supposed to do with a crying baby? Prosperity had worked wonders with the baby the night Aileen died. What had she done? He tried to picture her and recalled the sponge she'd dipped in milk. She'd fed him.

That was the one thing he could not do. Not now and maybe not ever. Until Dr. Rangler was certain Mrs. Ambleton hadn't contracted yellow fever, the commander would not allow the baby back onto the post.

"Be quiet," he commanded.

His plea did not have the slightest effect. His men took orders. This baby did not.

He had never been alone with an infant. Panic crushed him like a two-ton block of granite.

A few passersby looked his way with sympathy, but none of them offered to assist. Meanwhile, the baby hollered louder and louder. With each escalation, his breath grew more ragged until David feared the boy would suffocate himself.

Then he felt the wetness and smelled what could only be described as the vilest of latrines. The baby had soiled himself, and David had no idea what to do.

Where was that midwife? Fleming Street, Mrs. Walters had said, only a couple blocks away. He rushed down the street, ignoring the curious glances and growing stench. Only a couple blocks. Then he could at least get relief from the immediate problem. But when he reached the area Mrs. Walters had indicated, two buildings matched her description.

He had no choice but to knock.

Since the first was in much better condition than the second, he chose it. When he lifted his fist to rap on the door, he noticed the sign: *Dr. Clayton Goodenow.*

The man vying for Prosperity's affection.

He lowered his hand.

No matter the need, he could not turn to the competition. He could not let the doctor see how incompetent he was, for the man would surely tell Prosperity. David would never win her back if she thought him unable to manage a tiny baby.

He backed away from the door.

"May I help you?"

David barely heard the man's voice above little Oliver's bawling. He spun around to see the doctor, and the immediate problem slipped behind the fog of jealousy. "I don't need your help."

If the doctor was offended, he did not remark on it. "Is your son ill?"

David recalled the lecture that the doctor had given him after the baby's birth. The man had insisted the boy was David's son, whether by blood or not.

"Let me check for a fever," the doctor said.

David jerked the baby away from the doctor's outstretched hand. "He's not sick."

The corner of the doctor's mouth inched up a fraction. "Perhaps a change of diaper would remedy the situation."

"Naturally," David said, though he could not admit that he had no idea how to accomplish that much-needed task. His neck heated, betraying his incompetence. No doubt the good doctor would tell Prosperity that little detail. "But first I need to find the midwife."

The doctor pointed to the house on David's right. "She lives next door, but if the door is closed she is with an expectant mother."

"I didn't notice the door."

"Let me check." The doctor returned to the street, and David took the opportunity to leave the man's veranda.

"Hmm. That's peculiar," the doctor murmured. "Even the shutters are closed."

"Closed?" David repeated, still trying to calm little Oliver so he'd stop howling.

"Marnie would never close up the entire house in such heat." He knocked on the door, cocked his head, and then pushed the door open. "It's not locked. Follow me."

It felt wrong to enter a home without invitation. "I'll wait here."

"If something's wrong, I might need your help."

David stepped into the stuffy interior. The rooms were dark with the shutters closed and smelled faintly of vinegar and something else vaguely familiar that he could not place. At least the change of scenery had piqued Oliver's interest enough that he stopped crying.

The doctor slipped through the rooms as if he knew them well. "Marnie? Are you here, Marnie?" He pushed open a door and stiffened. "What happened?"

The doctor moved into the room, but David stopped at the doorway. The midwife lay in bed, pale and shaking beneath a thin coverlet.

The doctor immediately placed a hand on her forehead. "Fever."

"Cholera," she whispered. "From that ship. I helped one of the women."

The doctor whirled toward David. "Get the baby out of here at once."

Instead David stood gaping, the soldier in him wanting to respond.

"Go," the doctor barked.

This time David obeyed. Only when he reached the veranda did he realize he'd been holding his breath since the midwife first mentioned cholera. One of the dreaded tropical diseases. He'd seen men felled by cholera and prayed he didn't join them. In over two years, he'd been fortunate, blessed with natural resistance and fortitude, Captain Dutton had claimed.

"Some are," the man had said. "Others fall at the first hint of illness. Watch the men closely. An epidemic will set back progress even further."

He had followed the captain's advice, instituting measures of cleanliness that made the men grumble. He didn't listen to a single complaint. As far as he was concerned, if God required his chosen people to wash before a meal, so could the men under David's command.

Oliver let out another wail.

David pushed the blanket from his damp cheeks. The baby must be dreadfully hot. Or . . . His stomach leapt into his throat. What if the boy had a fever? He touched the baby's forehead but couldn't feel anything other than a squirming bundle of displeasure.

The doctor stepped onto the narrow veranda. "Go home, Lieutenant."

That he could not do, not with a baby. "Is there another midwife?"

The doctor shook his head. "Not since Linnie O'Neill passed. Now with Marnie sick, there's not a midwife to be found on the island except some of the colored women."

David was desperate. He could not return to the post with the baby, and he could not find anyone able to take on the poor child. Fear or prejudice had closed every woman's door. "Tell me where to find one of them."

The doctor's gaze narrowed. "Why do you seek the services of a midwife? Is one of the officers' wives in need?"

"No." David knew what he must do, but admitting weakness stung. No Latham ever bowed to need, but a baby's life depended on him. "I need to find a wet nurse t-t-to take care of him." He felt heat clear to the roots of his hair. "To change him."

There. He'd said it. Now the doctor could take the upper hand with Prosperity. David would lose her, all for the sake of a baby that wasn't his.

The doctor's eyebrow arched. "I thought Miss Jones had recommended someone."

"That was two nurses ago." Desperation tinged each statement. "No one will keep him, and the commander won't allow him in the garrison." He stopped short of mentioning the prejudice he'd encountered. "Oliver needs milk. He needs someone to care for him."

"Oliver?" The doctor's expression softened. "You have accepted him, then."

Had he?

"He is my responsibility." It was the most he could admit.

The doctor nodded. "Very well, Lieutenant, I shall see what I can do."

"Thank you," David managed to say, though the words stuck in his throat.

"Return in two hours. I will have an answer for you then."

If the doctor succeeded, David would be indebted to him. The price would doubtless be relinquishing all claim to Prosperity's heart.

David stood in the street watching the doctor walk toward the heart of town, his top hat dark against the setting sun. He absently rocked his squalling son, fully aware that he still had a diaper to change and no idea how to do it. Engineering a fort in the middle of the ocean would be easier.

❧

Something was wrong with her. Prosperity dreaded the touch of a decent man who wanted to heal the ill and longed for a kind word from the man who had betrayed her trust.

On Nantucket, she had known what she wanted—a husband and family to love and nurture. Since coming to Key West, her entire world had been thrown upside down. She'd thought helping the ill would replace the dream she'd lost, but she felt uneasy in the wards and had run from the one woman who needed comfort. Nothing fit together as it ought.

Rather than enter through the front door, she skirted the

O'Malleys' house and entered from the rear. Her room was just inside. Here the shade granted a measure of coolness. She tugged at the ribbon beneath her chin, still upset by the doctor's insistence on the supremacy of science. The ties knotted. Frustrated, she pulled the bonnet off and sent her hair tumbling around her shoulders. She tossed the wretched bonnet on her bed. The knots could be dealt with later. Now she needed to find calm.

She sank to her knees beside the bed.

Even when Ma was terribly ill, she insisted that one's knees were the pathway to God. One morning Prosperity had found her shaking from the cold while kneeling beside her bed. How Ma had managed the strength to crawl out of bed mystified her. She'd intended to chide her for such a foolish action, but Ma's fervent prayer had brought tears to her eyes. Instead of asking for healing, Ma had prayed for her daughter to grow in faith and confidence.

Think first of others. Ma had urged that more times than Prosperity could remember.

"Who, Ma?"

The whispered plea met no response.

Prosperity lifted the Bible from the chair beside her bed and opened it to several different places. Some days the words spoke clearly. Today they muddied and swirled like dirty wash water.

Which man did God intend for her?

She tried to think through biblical examples, but many of the marriages were arranged. Abraham had sent a servant to a far-off land to get a wife for his son Isaac. The servant prayed for a sign, and God gave it at once. If only He would answer her so clearly.

She closed the Bible, no closer to an answer than when she'd left the doctor.

Perhaps Elizabeth could help. She knew Prosperity's dilemma and did not promote one man over the other. Others, like Mrs. Cunningham, voiced their opinions freely, but their advice had failed to dim her love for David.

She sighed. Her mind was hopelessly tangled unless Elizabeth could make some sense from it.

Her friend had a visitor. Prosperity had heard the murmurings of conversation when she first entered the house. They were probably in the parlor. Since the nursery was empty, little Jamie must be with them too. Surely the guest would leave soon, since the supper hour approached.

Despite Elizabeth's assurances that Prosperity was always welcome to meet her friends, she usually kept to her room. She hadn't the lively temperament of her friend and knew little of the goings-on about town. She had always been a homebody, content among family and close friends, preferring solitude to the confusion of large gatherings.

Still, just this once, she would approach the parlor and accept the introduction to one of Elizabeth's acquaintances.

The floorboards creaked as she edged forward. She hesitated outside the room.

"Is that you, Prosperity?" Elizabeth called out. "Do come in."

Having received the invitation, Prosperity stepped into the room and immediately halted.

A tall, strikingly beautiful Negress stood in the center of the room with Elizabeth at her side. They appeared to be looking at one of Jamie's tunics. At their feet, little Jamie played with a slightly older boy who must be the Negress's son. Both women looked up at her.

"I'm sorry." Prosperity backed away. "I didn't realize you were busy."

Was Elizabeth hiring new help? But then why would the woman bring her little boy? And what had happened to Florie? Prosperity wasn't accustomed to the ways of those who could afford servants, never having had any herself, but she doubted few employers wanted the servants' children running about their home.

"Not at all. We were just admiring your handiwork on Jamie's tunic." Elizabeth glided toward her with outstretched hands and the welcoming smile that always made her feel like a dear friend. "It's simply too beautiful to use."

"But I meant it to be used. I can make another."

Elizabeth brushed aside her worries. "Come in and meet Anabelle. I have been talking on and on about you, but we seem to never cross paths, what with your work at the hospital. Prosperity, this is Anabelle, my dear sister."

Sister? Elizabeth's sister was colored? Prosperity's jaw dropped.

Anabelle extended her hand. "Pleased to meet you, Miss Jones."

The woman spoke with the gentility of a wealthy heiress, not at all like Florie. Prosperity scrambled to gather her wits before she made a fool of herself. She shook Anabelle's hand. "I've heard much about you."

Anabelle returned a tight smile. "But not my color, apparently."

"Goodness!" Elizabeth cried. "Forgive me. I never thought to explain that Anabelle is my half sister, as well as my dearest friend. We shared everything as children." Her eyes glistened. "Still do."

Their close bond was obvious even to an outsider. "I never had a sister."

Elizabeth chuckled. "I didn't think I did either. Not until two years ago."

So much seemed to have happened at that time, but Elizabeth

did not explain. Prosperity tried to wrap her mind around the fact that the two openly admitted kinship. That sort of thing was generally stuffed under the carpet, even in the North. She never dreamed to see such an open display in the South.

"You're free?" The thought slipped out of Prosperity's mouth before she could stop it. "Forgive me. I shouldn't have asked such a thing."

Neither woman appeared disconcerted.

"I am free," Anabelle stated in a rich voice very different from Elizabeth's.

Prosperity looked from one to the other. The sisterly resemblance could be seen in their height and noses, but it wasn't obvious enough that a casual observer would notice. An awkward silence stretched for seeming minutes but was probably only a few seconds before a sharp rap on the front door drew their attention.

"I'm not expecting anyone." Elizabeth looked to Prosperity. "Are you?"

Prosperity shook her head. Every bit of her irrational feelings longed for it to be David, but how could it be after the way she'd treated him? Momentary anger had cost her any chance of reconciliation.

Florie hurried down the hall to answer the door. Prosperity crossed to the window, hoping to spot the caller. She pressed against the glass, but the lush vines blocked her view.

"Anxious to see someone?" Anabelle asked.

Prosperity stepped away from the window. It would not be David, could not be. Based on the steady flow of Elizabeth's friends and acquaintances, it wouldn't even be someone she knew.

A man's voice rang through the hall. "I must speak at once to Mrs. O'Malley."

Prosperity knew that voice.

19

Clayton noted Elizabeth O'Malley's surprise when she burst into the hallway and dismissed the maid. After all, he had just joined her for tea yesterday.

"I'm sorry to bother you at this hour." He closed the door behind him.

"No bother. It must be urgent business. Did you wish to see Prosperity?"

"Not this time." He removed his hat. "I seek your assistance."

Elizabeth's half sister drifted into the hall, her son on her hip. "I should be heading home."

Clayton knew the former slave's story, though he had never met her. "If you can spare a minute, you might know someone who could help."

He had both women's attention now.

"I need to find a wet nurse willing to take a newborn into her home." He considered how best to broach the sticking point with Elizabeth's sister present. "The infant is of mixed blood." There was no kinder way to state it.

Neither of the women blanched, as he had suspected would

be the case. The sister was mulatto. The two were close. Their husbands had worked together for many years.

Elizabeth puzzled a moment. "Wouldn't Marnie know who has lost her baby?"

"She is ill, I fear, and isn't in her right mind."

The sister looked at him sharply. "Fever?"

"She claims cholera, but all the symptoms are not yet present."

"We shall pray for her," Elizabeth stated in a tone that accepted no fear. "Any illness is difficult to bear in such heat. May our Lord heal her fully."

The sister nodded.

Clayton did not believe that prayer cured anyone, but it comforted some, especially women, so he said nothing to contradict them. "The boy's father will pay. He is in rather desperate need, since he is not allowed to take the boy into the garrison."

Something flickered in Elizabeth's eyes. "He is a soldier then."

"Is—is it David?" The tremulous question came from Prosperity, who stood framed by the parlor doorway, Elizabeth's son in her arms.

Clayton hesitated to bring Prosperity into close proximity with the lieutenant. On the way here, he had debated the repercussions over and over, but in the end decided the welfare of the child must take precedence. Perhaps under the microscope of daily contact, her childish infatuation with the lieutenant would fade.

"It is David, isn't it?" Prosperity breathed, stepping closer.

He nodded.

Elizabeth sprang into action. "I have enough milk for two, and we can supplement it with sweet milk."

Prosperity's eyes widened. "Here?"

Elizabeth nodded. "Together we will be able to watch him. Perhaps Anabelle might sit with him from time to time."

"B-but should we?" The agitation was spelled out clearly on her fine features. "Won't it mean . . . ?" She didn't need to finish. Everyone knew this meant increased contact with the lieutenant.

Clayton saw his plan falling into place.

"Perhaps it's for the best," Elizabeth said firmly. She focused on Prosperity. "One can't make informed decisions on any matter without hearing all sides."

Prosperity blanched, and her reply came out in a whisper. "I suppose you're right."

Clayton saw an opportunity to both ease her fears and strike a blow against the lieutenant. "I doubt the father will stop by often. The last wet nurse indicated he visited just once in the two weeks she had the boy. In fact, she had to send word for him to fetch Oliver."

"Oliver," the ladies said in unison.

"That's the name he gave the boy," Clayton confirmed.

Prosperity wavered, her lip quivering. "The name we chose."

"You and David chose the baby's name?" Elizabeth asked.

Clayton winced at the use of the lieutenant's given name.

"We talked. Long ago. He wanted to name our firstborn after my mother. Olivia if a girl, and Oliver for a boy." Her hand rose to her throat. "We hoped to have many children."

This intimacy was almost more than Clayton could bear. He had to turn the tide. "There is something I must point out before you make a decision."

He gained the attention of all three women.

"The lieutenant was asked to take the boy from the garrison due to a possible case of yellow fever."

Prosperity gasped, but Elizabeth stood firm. "He is an infant. The fever is mild in children, and Rourke and I have already had it."

"We must consider Miss Jones," Clayton pointed out.

Prosperity squared her shoulders. "I am not afraid. The Lord will see us through."

"Then all is settled," Elizabeth said. "Bring us little Oliver."

As Clayton closed the door behind him and stepped off the veranda, he wondered again if he had made the right decision.

⌒⊹⌒

David had managed to talk Mrs. Walters into showing him how to diaper the baby. The messy process nearly made him retch, but at least little Oliver stopped bawling once he was swaddled in a clean cloth.

"Men," Mrs. Walters had harrumphed as she demonstrated how to line up and secure the cloth so it would stay in place.

David struggled to concentrate. His mind wandered to the dilemma he found himself in. It seemed no one on this island would accept a mixed-blood baby, yet he could not bring the boy back to the garrison.

He moaned. "What am I supposed to do?"

Mrs. Walters looked up sharply. "Pay attention."

He shook his head. This wasn't just about diapers. "I can't care for an infant."

"Any fool can see that. You need a wife."

"That is not simple to do."

Mrs. Walters harrumphed again. "Seems to me you had no trouble the first time."

That was true, but Aileen had come to him. Prosperity ran from him. "It can't be just anyone. She must adore children. She must be loving and kind. Calm, gracious, and thoughtful." He'd just described Prosperity. "Even so, we would still need a wet nurse."

Mrs. Walters clucked her tongue. "Trouble, trouble. You could ask one of them men with darkies if they won't take him on for a bit."

"Never." The line between freeman and slave could easily blur. David would not lose Aileen's child. He could promise her that much.

"Then you got yourself a problem." She handed the boy to him.

He sighed. "Thank you for taking care of Oliver."

"I cain't feed him."

"I understand."

"My milk's drying up."

"I understand." It might be the only thing he understood.

⌘

It was too soon.

Prosperity paced the hallway. She wouldn't have agreed to do this if she hadn't learned David named his son Oliver.

She closed her eyes and imagined again the picture she had painted of their life together. She and David would share a small whitewashed house with shutters and a trim little porch. She would chase the children from the kitchen while pulling the roasted turkey from the oven. David would insist on carrying it to the table, where the glowing faces of their six children eagerly awaited the feast.

A shaky breath could not calm her nerves. That fantasy would never exist. She no longer lived on Nantucket Island, nor was she likely to ever return. David had married another and now had a son to raise. And he had named him Oliver.

In the face of that and Elizabeth's courage, she had agreed to take care of the little one. It wasn't Oliver's fault that his father had broken her heart. He was innocent.

Think first of others.

"That's what I'm doing."

"Pacing the floors?" Elizabeth asked from the nursery where she was feeding Jamie.

"No, I was thinking of my mother's advice to consider others first."

"Sound advice."

And yet it carried hidden danger. David. Illness. Loss.

Prosperity bit her lip. "You're not afraid of fever? For Jamie, I mean?"

Elizabeth set Jamie in his cradle and joined her in the hall, softly closing the nursery door. "I meant what I said. We are all in God's hands. Of course I'm concerned, but no parent can protect her baby from everything. We can only do our best and trust the rest to our Lord."

Prosperity blew out her breath. "You're right, and I'm worrying about nothing."

"You're thinking of David."

Prosperity looked away, but Elizabeth would not let her go. "You must face him sooner or later. Until you talk through everything, you will never have the answer you seek."

Prosperity knew her friend was right, but . . . "It's difficult."

Elizabeth squeezed her arm. "The most important things in life are often difficult. Think of those long, hard days caring for your mother. Difficult."

"And yet precious. I would not wish away a single moment."

"You are strong, Prosperity. Whatever happens, remember that you have friends here who love you and will stand by you."

A lump formed in her throat, but she hadn't time to swallow it before the dreaded knock sounded on the door. Elizabeth hurried to open it.

David had arrived.

The golden-haired woman from the social opened the door wide. "Welcome, Lieutenant. Dr. Goodenow has told us everything. I am Mrs. Elizabeth O'Malley, and we are delighted to help."

"Thank you, ma'am." He could not have asked for better. Every movement and inflection exuded Southern grace and civility. She might not live in the largest house in Key West, but this generosity placed her higher in his estimation than any society belle. "I will pay, of course."

She chuckled as she ushered them in. "No recompense is required. We are blessed with more than enough and wish to share with those in need."

Then her response was urged by Christian duty. Mere weeks ago, that would have embarrassed him, but desperation drives a man to accept any help extended. He only wondered if she knew Oliver's parentage. One look and she might retract the offer.

He pushed the blanket from Oliver's face. The boy had settled down enough to gaze with interest at the strangers around him. David watched Mrs. O'Malley's reaction.

She smiled and stroked the boy's cheek. "What a lovely child."

He breathed out in relief. Not one trace of prejudice crossed her lips. "I intend to raise him once he's weaned."

She took David's statement in stride. "Of course you do."

He had to be blunt. "I don't want Oliver treated differently because he has darker skin."

Sadness crept over her face, and he thought he heard a strangled gasp from the shadowed doorway behind her.

Mrs. O'Malley addressed his concerns. "You may be assured

that he will receive the same care as my son. You see, my sister is mulatto. I am all too aware of the cruelties society inflicts on those who do not fit their narrow qualifications for acceptance."

He must trust her.

She took Oliver and pressed a hand to his forehead. She then nodded at the doctor. "No fever."

Why did everyone think Oliver was feverish? "He is not ill."

She smiled softly. "Of course he isn't."

The doctor shook his head. "It is too soon to tell. Symptoms might take a week to show."

Panic clutched David's abdomen. The doctor had found someone to care for Oliver, yet now he was trying to drive her away. Would he lose this kind woman's help? "Oliver is not ill. He has never been ill, and he's had no contact with any of the men at the post. There's no need to be alarmed."

Mrs. O'Malley shifted her gaze to him. "We are not afraid, Lieutenant. Have no fear, we will care for your son."

"We?" Some of the wealthier families kept a nurse, whether hired or slave, for their children.

"Miss Jones will help look after your son." She moved aside and handed Oliver to Prosperity, who stepped from the doorway behind her.

David could not breathe. He could not move. He could not stop watching her. She gazed into Oliver's eyes with such compassion that he could have collapsed from relief. Prosperity. Dear Prosperity would care for little Oliver. No one better existed. When she kissed the boy, joy flooded over him. This was more than he could have hoped for and all that he had wanted. "Thank you, Prosperity."

She did not look up. "I am doing this for Oliver's sake." All her compassion flooded onto his son. "He is an innocent and should not suffer for what others have done."

A hammer strike couldn't have hurt worse. Her meaning was clear. David was to blame, not just for hurting her but for harming Oliver. How could she think that of him? "I would never hurt my son."

"I'm sure that's not what Prosperity meant," Mrs. O'Malley soothed.

It was exactly what she'd meant. She had taken his hope and skewered it with veiled accusations. Though she had agreed to nurture his son, the deal did not come with a relationship attached. This act of service was not offered because she still loved him or because she hoped for a future together. No, she thought he would do to his son what he'd done to her. Didn't she understand? Hadn't he told her how he'd tried to help? She knew he'd written and sent money. He'd apologized. Yet she turned every attempt at reconciliation into another dagger.

"I will always regret the pain I brought you." He meant every word. Could she not see?

Prosperity did not look at him. "I will care for your son."

"Together we will," Mrs. O'Malley said.

David couldn't rip his gaze from Prosperity, who was cooing and tickling the baby's chin. Little Oliver responded with a sound David had not yet heard from his son—a happy sound that made his heart ache for what might have been if only he had not strayed.

"I'm sorry," he said.

She still did not look up. Her eyes were for Oliver alone. David might as well not exist.

"Thank you," he attempted.

Prosperity looked to Mrs. O'Malley. "He looks hungry. I

233

will prepare the sweet milk." Then she disappeared down the hall with the baby.

David leaned against the plastered wall, spent. He had grasped for the wind, and it slipped through his fingers.

Mrs. O'Malley sighed sympathetically, but the doctor seemed to take great pleasure in Prosperity's reaction. Naturally. The man probably figured he now had the upper hand.

Goodenow tamped down his hat. "If all is settled here, I must check on Marnie."

"Please tell her we are praying for her," Mrs. O'Malley said. "With Miss O'Neill gone, women only have her to rely upon."

"I will ask her if I might look in on those who are in confinement. If you hear of anyone in need of her services, please ask them to see me until she recovers completely."

"Thank you, Doctor, and thank you both for entrusting little Oliver to our care."

The doctor nodded and slipped out the door.

Much as David hated to admit it, Goodenow was not an evil man. He was worthy of Prosperity's affection. He did not discriminate against Oliver. He'd found perhaps the only nursing mother in Key West who would treat his son with dignity. He cared about those who were suffering. In so many ways, the doctor surpassed him. In comparison, David's tally came up very short.

No wonder Prosperity turned away.

"Good evening, Mrs. O'Malley." David placed his hat upon his head and turned to leave.

She held him in place with a touch. "Don't give up hope."

"Hope?" Fear raced through his veins. "Oliver will be all right, won't he?"

"That is not what I meant." Her gaze offered encouragement.

"All the work on Fort Taylor was washed away in the hurricane of '46. Rebuilding that foundation took time."

He had no idea what she was talking about.

"Great monuments can be lost in a day, Lieutenant, but it takes time to rebuild. So too with relationships."

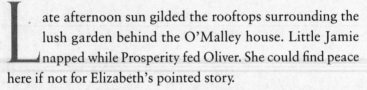

20

Late afternoon sun gilded the rooftops surrounding the lush garden behind the O'Malley house. Little Jamie napped while Prosperity fed Oliver. She could find peace here if not for Elizabeth's pointed story.

"I struggled to forgive my father, but in the end it was essential." Elizabeth finished with a summation that would make her attorney father proud.

For over two weeks Elizabeth had attempted to change Prosperity's opinion of David. Prosperity understood the point her friend was trying to make, yet their situations were not the same. In some ways, Elizabeth had suffered greater betrayal, but her father had repented and begged forgiveness. David's apology had been delivered in his usual unbending manner, as if spoken from duty, not regret. Never once had he explained why he'd abandoned her for a woman of ill repute.

She continued to drip milk into the baby's mouth with the peculiar glass bottle that Captain O'Malley had procured from an apothecary. The oddly shaped vial with the metal tube delivered just enough milk for the baby to swallow, though it did nothing for little Oliver's need to suckle. He kept reaching for the glass.

"He prefers mother's milk," Prosperity noted.

"That he does, but if anything my milk is lessening."

Prosperity shot her friend a concerned glance. Elizabeth already couldn't keep up with Jamie's voracious appetite, and she had been supplementing with sweet milk before Oliver arrived. Seeing her sacrifice for an unrelated baby had spurred Prosperity to take in the little boy, but a baby needed mother's milk. "What will we do?"

"Though it's best to begin weaning in the cooler months, I will start now."

Prosperity shook her head. "Don't put your son at risk. We can hire another wet nurse."

"That poor boy has already had too many nurses."

"Then we will continue as we have for as long as we can. Oliver takes sweet milk without problem. I will feed him more often." She could not give up this little one who had wormed his way into her heart. She kissed Oliver's forehead, soft and sweet smelling.

Florie took the empty feeding bottle back to the cookhouse for boiling.

"You did a fine job of changing the subject," Elizabeth noted. "You must understand why I told you about my differences with my father."

A fool could tell. Though Prosperity had many faults, she hoped foolishness was not one of them. "You want me to forgive David."

"I'm simply pointing out that I couldn't move forward with my life until I forgave my father."

"I know." Truly she did. The Bible said that one must forgive to be forgiven. "But that doesn't make it any easier, especially when he isn't sorry for his actions."

"Why do you say that? He said he regretted hurting you."

"Words are not enough. It must come from the heart."

"I see." Elizabeth plucked a coco plum from the nearby tree and dropped it into a basket. "I had to forgive my father before he repented. It wasn't easy. I had to say the words over and over to convince myself."

"That doesn't sound like forgiveness to me."

"Forgiveness is an act of will. Speak the words, and ask God to help erase the hurt."

Jamie awoke with a cry. Elizabeth hurried to his cradle, which they had set in the shade.

Prosperity had always thought forgiveness must come from the heart, that she must first feel compassion for the one who had wounded her. Elizabeth seemed to be saying the opposite. Yet how could she extend forgiveness when the pain still kept her awake at night? Perhaps that pain was her answer. David was no longer the man with whom she had pledged to share her life. Dr. Goodenow would never cause her anguish, for she felt nothing but pleasing friendship with him. Without passion, she could not suffer pain.

Little Oliver clasped her finger. Poor child. Not David's son by blood, certainly, and subject to a lifetime of cruelty. The ignorant and vicious would slander his mother and thus him. Some would even say he should never have been born. What would David's father say? Reverend Latham favored returning the Africans to their native lands. How would he react to this baby, who was likely not Negro but certainly had mixed blood? She could not envision Oliver on Nantucket or in the fearsome minister's home. Then where would this poor child go? Everywhere, lines were drawn on the basis of skin color.

"Jamie is asleep again." Elizabeth settled in her chair.

The hushed comment pulled Prosperity from her thoughts. "Where does your sister live?"

Elizabeth drew in her breath, clearly surprised.

"I'm sorry," Prosperity said. "You don't need to answer."

"It's not a secret. She lives in the colored section, beyond the hospital."

"Separate."

"We asked them to live near us, but they said they were more comfortable there."

Prosperity kissed the baby's forehead. "What is going to happen to him?"

"A lot will depend on the love he receives from his parents."

"His mother is dead. David must not know the father, or he would have contacted him." Prosperity doubted anyone knew.

"Parents do not need to be blood relations. They just need to love. The lieutenant seems to have accepted Oliver as his own. That's a good sign."

"Is it?" Prosperity nibbled on her lip. "Won't it be difficult for Oliver to grow up with a white father?"

"Perhaps. He will need strength and character to shrug off the slurs. His parents can teach him that."

"I heard some of the women at the social."

"There will always be ignorance and cruelty, but love can prevail."

Prosperity wasn't so certain. Poverty had cast her in a different light than her aunt and neighbors. Many looked down on her family. Aunt Florence's criticisms always stung, yet how mild those were in comparison to what this little baby would face. "He will need to be strong."

"And that strength must be tempered with love and forgiveness."

There was that word again. Prosperity involuntarily shuddered.

"Try," Elizabeth counseled. "Simply try. For little Oliver's sake if not for your own."

Jamie howled again, and Elizabeth slipped away.

Alone again, Prosperity gazed at the babe, whose eyelids had drifted shut. In a short time, this little one had captured her heart. She could not bear to see him hurt even a little. Animosity between her and his father would harm this precious child.

For Oliver's sake. Prosperity could not forgive David for his sake or hers, but she would try for the sake of this little baby.

Closing her eyes, she whispered, "I forgive you."

Each word hurt.

Elizabeth said she had repeated it over and over.

"I forgive you."

But she wasn't thinking of David. To mean it, she must picture him when she said the words.

"I—" She choked.

Take a breath. Blow it out. Smell the sweetness of the baby sleeping. Do it for his sake. Her nerves calmed.

"I forgive you, David."

Oh, how it sliced through her, with pain so fresh it took her breath away. She had remained utterly faithful, but he had not. She had counted on him, had placed all her hope in him, and he failed her. When she needed him most, he was not there.

Yet the moment his wife died, he'd expected her to return as if nothing had happened. She'd seen that hope in his eyes, as if she could forget what he had done. Impossible. The last wet nurse said David did not visit his son. She had to send word asking him to fetch the boy.

Those were not the actions of a loving man.

She pulled little Oliver close. She could never leave this innocent boy with such a man. Never.

cᴏᴛᴏ

David mopped the perspiration from his brow and puzzled over his calculations. It was easier than thinking about Prosperity. He had visited his son at the close of each day since leaving him with her three weeks ago. She never joined him, nor would Mrs. O'Malley give an explanation for her absence. He suspected Prosperity hid in her room rather than see him. If she was working late, Mrs. O'Malley would have told him.

He must be grateful for the help he'd received and forget the hope he'd once held.

This afternoon another ugly mess arose. Missing tools. He had acquired plenty of chisels for the masons, but they insisted they'd run short. Tools dulled and broke, but the craftsmen had shown him their failed tools and a tally that showed the new chisels had arrived. Yet the storeroom was empty. He had gone over supply lists and counted all the chisels he could locate on site. He had recalculated three times. The figures were correct.

The thief had struck again.

This time he stole a different item, which meant either he knew David had planted a trap with the spikes or he was exceedingly careful. Either way, the problem remained. His stonemasons had no tools to fashion the granite blocks.

David ground his teeth. Captain Dutton had given him the responsibility to stop the thieving, but David had allowed personal matters to cloud his judgment. No longer. He would find the man responsible and see him punished.

That meant confronting the men.

He strode across his office and opened the door. His sergeant stood on the other side of the expansive parade ground, directing his work crew. David looked around and spotted a familiar figure lounging in the shadows of the completed casemates.

"Private Jameson!"

The handsome idler stepped into the open. "Lieutenant!" The crisp salute was regulation, but the grin was not.

David scowled. The man had gotten away with idling for too long. That was about to change. "Assemble the men."

"Even the darkies?"

David cringed. "Just the soldiers." A Negro would have great trouble selling army supplies.

Jameson's eyebrows shot upward. "In the middle of the afternoon? The sun is blistering."

"Your place is not to question orders, Private. Continue to do so and you will be charged with insubordination."

Jameson stiffened and snapped another salute. "Assembling the men, sir!"

The man irritated David. He did just enough to glide by, yet he seldom resisted an opportunity to question direction. David had been too lenient, allowing the men leeway when it came to army protocol. He disliked senseless regulations. After all, he had joined the army for the engineering corps. But he was beginning to see why his superiors demanded strict adherence to regulation. Leniency had led to idling. And worse.

He hated to think any of his men capable of criminal activity, but the army paid poorly, the pay hadn't arrived for nearly two weeks, and the opportunity to earn a little extra might prove too enticing.

Especially to a man with debts.

He stepped back into his office to retrieve his hat and coat.

David considered which men frequented the grogshops. Jameson, Urich, Smeech, and Drenth must have been in one while he spoke with Aileen's friend. Any one of them might have found himself in sufficient trouble to consider theft. One indiscretion often led to worse, as he had learned the painful way. Drunkards might become gamblers unable to pay a debt.

Jameson knocked on the door frame. "The men are ready, sir."

David glanced out the window at the assembled workers. Most slumped. Some mopped foreheads. Very few stood at attention.

He walked out of his office and into the yard.

More of the men snapped to attention, but a goodly number made a weak showing of it. A quick tip of one finger to the forehead, a smirk or comment to a neighbor, and the ever-present slump marked those who didn't respect leadership.

David took a deep breath, intensifying his scowl, and stalked down the line. "Shoulders back. Chin up!"

More men obeyed, but a few found the commands humorous.

"A week in the stockade will take the edge off your joke, Smeech," he barked.

The man stiffened, though his expression still betrayed doubts. "Yes, sir."

David glared at the men. Only when he had every last man's attention did he speak. Then he did so in a soft tone. He'd learned early on that this change of tone caught the men's attention.

"Certain supplies have turned up missing." He paced down the line, keeping an eye on their reaction.

No one betrayed his complicity. Yet.

"Iron spikes. Chisels."

Urich glanced at . . . David followed the man's gaze. Jameson. That David could believe, but he had to have more evidence than a foot soldier's glance.

"If anyone sees or hears one word about where they went, report to me. If the guilty party is in this platoon, his punishment will be less severe if he confesses." He paused.

The men remained closemouthed.

"Very well. You know where my office is. Dismissed!"

The men disbanded at once, much quieter than before. Some huddled together in whispered conversation. Others shook their heads and wandered back to their particular patch of shade. Jameson did not head toward his cronies but to the barrel of drinking water. No one angled for David's office. None had betrayed guilt. He must have patience and allow the guilty to feel the sting of conviction. If the man had a conscience, he would either betray his guilt or confess it.

David returned to his office and closed the door. In the late afternoon light, no one could see into the room unless they stood directly outside. David watched the men. Their movements were all natural. Urich, Smeech, and Drenth congregated, as was to be expected, but none of them approached Jameson, and he stayed a goodly distance from them. When the sergeant called the men back to work, they all plodded off as usual.

David had learned nothing. Frustrated, he returned to his supply lists. They had run low on brick again. The preferred brick makers constantly fell behind with their shipments, and the army had not given them leave to secure a different source.

He puffed out his breath. If he could suggest a more reliable source, the captain might be able to plead their case. He needed the name of a reliable brickyard. Just six months ago he could name dozens, but the sticky heat muddled his memory.

"Remember," he urged himself, swatting at yet another mosquito that had taken up residence in his office. The insects were a terrible nuisance, and his skin reacted with fierce red bumps that itched so badly he wanted to tear his skin off. If only the wind would blow strong enough to take the pests away. He scratched at a new bite.

A sharp rap on the door caught his attention. Was one of the men ready to confess?

He crossed the tiny room in three strides and flung open the door.

Every ounce of irritation evaporated at the sight of the man in front of him. He opened his mouth, but nothing came out. Hundreds of questions flew through his mind, but none nestled on his tongue. Instead he stood like a fool, gaping.

The tall, black-clad figure did not offer so much as a smile. "Good afternoon, son. Are you going to ask me in?"

⌒⟶⌒

Clayton strolled toward the marine hospital at six o'clock that evening, content with the way things were going. Over the previous three weeks, Prosperity had given him more and more of her attention. Though she still slipped away the moment they arrived at their destination, she left him with a smile instead of the frightened expression she'd worn following his ill-advised proposal.

Elizabeth said the lieutenant visited his son every evening, but Prosperity avoided him by leaving the house or closing herself into her room. Though Elizabeth was concerned over Prosperity's inability to forgive the lieutenant, Clayton saw that as an advantage. Soon enough the last of Prosperity's reserves would fall, and she would be his.

He brought welcome news tonight. Marnie had not contracted cholera and was back on her feet. Mrs. Ambleton had merely gotten the ague. Malaria touched nearly every newcomer, but with treatment, most survived. Prosperity would be relieved.

Under her care, the boy had gained weight. Giggles replaced bawling. If Clayton had any fear, it was that Prosperity would grow too attached to the child.

Another bit of news promised to turn her attention elsewhere. He could not wait to extend the invitation. This time he expected she would accept. That made his step lighter as he approached the hospital. Since his chat with Dr. MacNees, Prosperity allowed him to meet her outside the hospital grounds. The picket fence separated them, and with the surgeon's approval of the situation, even Miss Stern could not object.

Prosperity was not waiting. That meant either she hadn't finished her duties or the matron had kept her late due to an influx of patients. Clayton hadn't heard of any disease-bearing ship, but then he had been busy with one particularly cantankerous invalid most of the afternoon. A ship might have sent men directly to the hospital without word reaching town yet.

In any case, he must wait, and that urged even a seasoned man's nerves a little higher. He pressed his handkerchief to his palms, but they simply grew damp again. He walked to the small gate used by hospital staff. From here he could see a corner of the building housing the laundry. Smoke trickled from the chimney. Surely the bulk of laundering was done for the day.

Then he saw her, diminutive in her gray gown and spotless white apron, which she was in the process of removing. How Prosperity managed to stay so impeccably clean was a mystery. The moment she spotted him, a faint smile curved her lips and her step hastened.

Yes, she was beginning to enjoy his company. This invitation would only help.

"Doctor." Her voice was eager as she stepped through the gate.

He closed it behind her. "You look well after a hard day's work."

Indeed she did. Her cheeks were pleasantly flushed, and her eyes shimmered in the late-day sun.

"Work was not so difficult today."

"You ought not work at all." He held out his arm, and she accepted it.

"I would enjoy spending the entire day with Oliver."

That was not the direction he wanted to travel. "One day the boy must return to his father, and you will need to direct your attention to other worthy projects."

Her shoulders drooped, as if she'd just realized this time with the baby would end. "What could be more worthy than caring for a helpless babe?"

He could never counter the maternal need to nurture, but he hoped to distract her from it. "You might discover a new treatment to ease someone's suffering."

"Me?"

Her incredulous response made him smile. "It is possible, with the right guidance and assistance."

Her brow puckered. "Whose?"

"Perhaps someone involved with the botanical society."

That caught her attention. "A botanical society? Here?"

"What better place? We have much to learn about tropical plants. Some could have unexpected medicinal uses. They might even publish a treatise on what is currently known of native plant uses."

As he'd expected, her eyes widened. "That would be worthwhile indeed, but how might someone like me publish anything? Surely someone much more learned should study the plants and write the article."

"I might be persuaded to help." Clayton didn't mention that he was the one who'd proposed the society a few years ago and served as its president.

"Help?" Her hand drifted to her throat as it always did when an idea startled her. "I could not lead such an important project. You should do it. You would be marvelous."

He shook his head. "I am busy with my practice and can't devote the time necessary to accomplish this."

A cloud darkened her eyes. "My duty is to little Oliver."

Clayton groaned. It would be months before the baby could be weaned.

"And the hospital," she added. "I cannot leave them short of help during fever season."

"It is the opportunity of a lifetime." He could not let this go so easily. A dream must first be planted. "If you discover a new species, you would have the honor of naming it. You might name it in memory of a loved one, such as your mother." That got her attention. "Think about it for a few days. There is no hurry. In addition, you might wish to meet the members of the society. They gather once a month, and this month is their soiree."

Her head bowed, and he could no longer gauge her reaction.

"I could present you to the members," he offered.

Her head snapped up. "What do I have to offer? I know so little about native plants."

"You know more than you realize, and you would learn. Speak with the members and listen to the lecture."

She gnawed on her lower lip, a sign he had begun to sway her. "I would enjoy that."

"Then say you will join me." He would bring up the dinner and music later, after he spoke with the seamstress about the gown he'd commissioned for the occasion.

"I would like that, Doctor." She even smiled.

He only wished she would call him by his given name, but his attempts to guide her in that direction had failed.

Patience. That was his advantage. The lieutenant rushed and blundered, chasing his quarry away. Prosperity was a skittish doe. It would take patience to gain her trust.

21

David stared at his father as if he were an apparition. Had Father not cut him off with his last letter? Not one note had followed that caustic missive denouncing his marriage, not even after David sent word of Aileen's death. Had Father received that news? He quickly calculated in his head. Perhaps. Perhaps not.

Why was Father here? He never traveled, even to the mainland. That he stood at the door of David's office was inconceivable. Yet here he was, older and grayer but still formidable.

"Are you going to invite me inside?" Father's blunt question harbored no compassion.

The Reverend Myles Latham never smiled. Like his fiery sermons denouncing vice, he confronted opposition with force. This afternoon his expression betrayed no kindness, forgiveness, or joy at seeing his eldest son. David was expected to obey. By choosing his own path, David had run astray. This would be no prodigal son reunion.

David stepped back. "Of course. Enter."

His father ducked through the doorway just as David always

did. Temporary military structures were made for shorter men than the Lathams. The minister's black shoes clattered on the wooden floorboards. His assessing gaze traveled the room, settling on its chief attributes: the desk and the plans for the fort, which were nailed to the wall and strewn across the surface of the desk.

"Efficient." Father's steel-blue eyes settled on him.

David swallowed. He ought to invite his father to sit, but that could usher in a lengthy discussion. Moreover, the room had only one chair. The afternoon sun had heated the structure to boiling, and little breeze blew in the open window. A pleasant conversation was not likely.

"Mother came?" David could not imagine her leaving his brothers, though all were old enough to care for themselves, the youngest now fifteen. Like Father, she had not set foot on a ship since their arrival on Nantucket Island before David was born.

"Of course not. Why should I drag her away from home and children merely to witness her eldest child's debauchery?"

David bristled. "Marriage is hardly debauchery."

"Breaking one's word is sin—both against your honor and against the woman you pledged to marry."

Since Father made no mention of Aileen's death, he must not have received David's latest note. Then what had driven him to leave his congregation and sail fourteen hundred miles south? Certainly he had not endured the discomfort and expense simply to berate his son in person. Yet that was precisely what he was doing, despite having denounced David's engagement two and a half years ago.

"You never liked Prosperity."

His father brushed that away with a wave of his hand. "I

thought you could have done better, just as I believed you made a mistake joining the army. Building forts? The efforts of men always fall short. True protection comes from the Lord."

David gritted his teeth, though he could not disagree with the sentiment. "God didn't call me into ministry." Yet he'd felt the need to rescue Aileen from her sinful ways. "Can we not serve God elsewhere?"

Father ignored his question while taking a more thorough assessment of the office. "I never thought you would throw away everything and everyone dear to you. I should have guessed, considering you rebelled against my authority in the first place."

"I am a grown man. My decisions are mine alone. They do not affect you."

"Everything you do affects your family."

"Is that why you came? To criticize?"

His father's gaze narrowed. "You are to honor your father and mother."

"Why are you here?" The stark question filled his limbs with strength, like the rush of a brisk wind on a hot day. When his father did not answer at once, the momentary courage seeped away. "It is a long journey."

"I came to meet your wife. A peace offering."

Father didn't know.

"You will introduce us." Father did not ask—he stated.

David swallowed. "There is something you should—"

Father cut him off with a lifted hand. From David's earliest remembrance, that had been the signal that no further discussion would be tolerated. One time he had continued to plead his case. Just once. For the next two days he'd felt the sting of the strap every time he sat down.

"Your mother convinced me that I might have written in

haste." Father squared his shoulders. "A closer examination will tell." He glanced at the window. "The light is low. The guard said the workday ends at sunset."

David crossed to the window, buying time while he figured out how to tell his father what had happened. Aileen's death was easy enough, but after that would follow questions. Soon Father would unearth her less than respectable past, not to mention her illegitimate baby. David had failed Aileen in life. He could grant her a measure of dignity in death.

"Shall we leave?" Father demanded.

David focused on the workers. Lieutenant Ambleton had called his men to the west side of the site, where the walls afforded a bit of shade. He was probably giving final instructions. David ought to do the same with his men, but he had no instructions to give beyond the admonition not to steal. A moment later, the men scattered to their quarters, whether at the fort, in town, or at the garrison.

"The men have been dismissed." He turned from the window only to meet the piercing gaze of his father.

"We shall go then."

There was nowhere to go. He must tell his father what had happened. This was as good a place as anywhere.

He pulled out the room's single chair. "Please sit."

Father eyed it with suspicion. "Your wife will wonder where you are."

That was one thing Aileen had never done. She'd pouted and begged, but she never cared where he'd been or what he'd done. When he talked about work, she didn't listen. At first opportunity she interrupted to demand he get her something or do her bidding. He drew in a shaky breath. He should have realized that their conversations were always about her.

"No, she won't wonder where I am." Truth was bitter. "I must speak with you before returning to the garrison."

Father removed his black hat and eyed the stiff wooden chair. "I will stand. You sit."

David sat. With his father towering over him, he felt like a child about to get a scolding. He stood. "I need to tell you about Aileen." He paused, uncertain how much to reveal.

"What about her?"

David had forgotten how direct his father could be. He never tossed out pleasantries or compliments. David's mother must pass inspection before appearing in public, but even when every article of clothing was in order and every lock of hair covered, he did not praise her. David wished more than anything that he had told his mother she was beautiful and kind and loving before he left. She more than made up for Father's sternness with her deep well of affection.

David swallowed. "Mother is well?"

"When I left her nearly a month ago. Speak, boy. What do you have to tell me about this woman you wed?"

David could hardly reveal the whole truth. The olive branch would be withdrawn the moment Reverend Myles Latham learned his eldest son had married a fallen woman. He stared out the window at the orange sky. There was only one way to say it.

"She is dead."

"What? How?"

David drew his attention back to his father's dark form. The man never wore anything but black. With his height, he created an imposing, fearful presence. In this heat, he must also be sweltering. "From fever."

Father blew out his breath. "God's will."

David could not see divine will in the death of someone so young, nor did a simple statement dismiss the agonies and pain of that moment.

"One of those tropical fevers?" Father asked.

"I do not know." David held back revealing the baby. His father would calculate the timing in an instant, and any chance for reconciliation would be lost.

"When?"

David hesitated. Would his father visit the graveyard? If so, he would see the stone David had placed on Aileen's grave calling her a wife and mother. Then he would know of the child that David had not mentioned in the note. At the time, the morning after Aileen's death, he had wanted nothing to do with the baby. Fatigue led him to think the child would somehow go away, perhaps taken by someone. His thoughts had been so confused.

Yet he must answer, for his father waited. "A month and a half ago."

"And you said nothing?"

"I wrote. You must have left before the note arrived." Just like Prosperity had. David's mouth grew dry. The similarity was eerie.

Father rapped his hat against his thigh. "Then all is over."

David nodded. In many ways, it was.

"You have resumed your courtship of Miss Jones?" The formality of the question and the look of distaste betrayed his father's low opinion of Prosperity.

David licked his dusty lips. Prosperity had given him no opportunity. He had tried to see her when he visited Oliver, but she was always gone. Avoiding him. But he would not give up hope. He had written an apology a dozen times, but the words were never quite right. When he managed to get them perfect, he would go to her with the note and the most expensive necklace he could afford. Until then, he could neither confirm nor deny his father's question.

"I saw her," he said carefully.

"Then you will marry as originally planned." Again the piercing gaze.

David looked out the window. The blaze had dulled to a pale peach color. "I hope to."

His father grunted. "Do not let this gift slip away, son. You have been given another chance. Use it wisely."

"You approve of courting Prosperity?" He'd never dreamed to gain his father's approval.

"I was not speaking of courtship. God has given you a chance to redeem your life. Get on your knees and pray for direction."

God would not speak with him. Though David had not fathered Oliver, he had still fallen.

"I should return to quarters." Hopefully his father did not expect to stay with him, for then David could not visit Oliver—and possibly Prosperity—this evening.

"Won't they let you dine with your father?"

David breathed out shakily. Father must have let a room. Though supping with him would be painful, he could not compound his sins by lying. "I know a decent eating establishment at the Admiralty Inn."

"Precisely where I have taken a room. We shall dine and have a long conversation. I have much news from home."

David tried to hide his disappointment. This would be no short meal. His father could talk for hours.

Prosperity would wonder why he did not visit his son this night. She might think he did not love the boy, when in fact each day knit them closer together. The doctor would gain the advantage of another day.

Fear wound its icy fingers around his heart. Time was running short. If he did not change Prosperity's opinion of him soon, he would lose her.

❧

"I don't understand." Prosperity stared at the woman standing on the O'Malleys' doorstep. She was simply yet beautifully dressed in an exquisitely constructed gown. Despite the mugginess at this very early hour, she conveyed an airy ease. "You must be mistaken. I did not request a gown." She certainly could not afford one.

The woman's lips pinched into a tight smile. "The doctor said that would be your response."

"Doctor?" Realization dawned. "Dr. Goodenow?"

The woman nodded.

"He should never have presumed." She wracked her brain for a polite way to dismiss the seamstress who must have gone out of her way to call on her before they'd broken their fast. "I am in mourning. I do not need another gown."

"The fabric I selected is quite proper for half-mourning. At least let me show you."

Before Prosperity could react, Elizabeth swept in from the dining room and pulled the door the rest of the way open, revealing the sun's first glow on the palms.

"Mrs. Evanston," Elizabeth cried with genuine delight. "I thought I recognized your voice. It is always a delight to see you, but whatever would bring you here at such an early hour?"

"A fitting, naturally."

Elizabeth looked just as surprised as Prosperity had been.

"I don't recall ordering a gown. Has my husband been up to something without my knowledge?"

Mrs. Evanston chuckled. "Not this time. Dr. Goodenow has commissioned an evening dress for Miss Jones."

"Commissioned?" Prosperity choked. Did that mean he was paying for it? "Evening dress?" She gave Elizabeth a pleading look. Even though she was forcing herself to spend more time with the doctor, this went too far. "It is not appropriate. I cannot accept such a gift."

"I assure you that I have taken your mourning period into consideration," Mrs. Evanston hurried to assure her. "Do look at the sketches. We can adjust anything that does not meet your expectations."

"I have no expectations, because I do not need an evening dress. Where would I wear it?" Prosperity bit her tongue. That botanical society meeting the doctor had mentioned must take place in the evening. Had he said something about a soiree? She felt the color drain from her face.

"It can't hurt to look at the sketches and fabric." Elizabeth breezed into the dining room with the seamstress. "We can lay everything out on the table."

Prosperity trailed behind them. "But . . ."

Mrs. Evanston spread out her sketches and a swatch of the loveliest silk Prosperity had ever seen.

"I have never seen quite that shade before. Somewhere between black and deepest violet. Beautiful," Elizabeth exclaimed, handing the cloth to Prosperity. "It almost shimmers like the night sky."

Faced with Elizabeth's approval, Prosperity could not admit her initial reaction—that the color was too bright for mourning. "It's beautiful, but it would cost too much."

Mrs. Evanston peered at her. "I thought I made it clear that the doctor is paying."

That was the problem. "I cannot agree to this." Prosperity pressed a hand to her roiling stomach. "It—it's not proper."

"I believe you will see that an evening gown can be quite proper." Mrs. Evanston placed a sketch before her. "Note the appropriate neckline. Any ornamentation can be left off, though no one here would consider a little lace extravagant, even in full mourning. In fact, gray lace would denote your status."

"That's not what I meant. The cost—" How could she explain it? "I do not wish to be beholden to anyone. I'm afraid I cannot accept this."

Mrs. Evanston blanched. "But the fabric is already purchased."

"It is?"

"Last week."

Prosperity trembled. Dr. Goodenow had asked her to attend the botanical society meeting just yesterday. If the fabric had been purchased a week ago, then he must have commissioned the gown before he knew she would accept. Why would he lay out such a sum on an uncertainty?

Elizabeth squeezed her arm. "Don't fret. If you do not want the gown, I will take it."

That certainly brightened Mrs. Evanston, but it didn't relieve Prosperity's misgivings.

"The doctor must have paid for it already."

"I will reimburse him," Elizabeth assured her.

"That's not it. Well, that's not the entire problem." Prosperity could not explain with Mrs. Evanston watching. "It's, well . . . it's presumptuous."

Elizabeth appeared unrattled. "Talk to the doctor, then, before making your decision."

"I've made my decision. I can't accept this." Prosperity drew a deep breath. The whole business was turning her empty stomach.

"That would disappoint him," Elizabeth said softly.

Prosperity knew that, but she also realized that accepting such a gift drew her one step closer to marriage. Wasn't that precisely what she had worked out in her mind as the best choice? Still, her heart balked.

"A giver wants his gift to be received," Mrs. Evanston seconded.

But a gift could carry with it certain expectations. Aunt Florence and Uncle Harold expected her never to approach them for money in the future. Invitations to dine must be reciprocated. Something as personal as a gown required a personal response, one that struck dread in the pit of her stomach.

Elizabeth touched her arm. "My offer stands. If it does not suit you, I will purchase the gown."

That eased her mind a little, for indeed she had wondered what to wear to the botanical society meeting. Moreover, the fabric looked much more comfortable than her mourning gowns. Perhaps she might wear it just that once and then give it to Elizabeth. She lifted her gaze to tell her friend this new plan and spotted a very large problem. "You are much taller than me. How could it fit both of us?"

Elizabeth turned to Mrs. Evanston. "Do you have enough fabric for the extra inches?"

"Indeed I do. Your figures are similar. With flouncing in such favor, I can construct an extra tier that can be buttoned into place." She quickly sketched out her idea.

"Why, that is brilliant, isn't it, Prosperity?"

She had to admit the solution would work.

Mrs. Evanston smiled. "Very well. Then all I need this morning are some measurements, Miss Jones."

Prosperity hesitated. Now that the dress was closer to reality, her nerves fluttered even more alarmingly. Accepting this gown would surely lead to expectations she could not fulfill. What if the doctor sought a kiss? Or asked to court her? The very idea made her stomach churn.

Yet she had never owned such a gown. Her dresses were serviceable . . . and old. She had dyed her blue dress and bonnet black for mourning after her father's death. She had worn the gray one for years. The seams were fraying and the elbows were shiny. Neither would do for a soiree. She ran her fingers over the silk. What would it be like to feel such fabric against her skin? Would her entrance into a room draw notice?

She shook her head to clear away those untoward thoughts. Prosperity Jones was no society belle eager for the next ball. She was a simple woman who had dedicated her life to serving others as Christ had served in His time on earth.

"There is little time to ponder, given the deadline," Mrs. Evanston said.

Then the gown *was* for the soiree. Prosperity clutched her midsection.

Elizabeth must have noticed her distress, for she asked the seamstress for privacy. Mrs. Evanston slipped into the hall.

Elizabeth drew Prosperity to the far end of the room. "You are reluctant to accept the gift because you believe Dr. Goodenow will expect something in return."

Prosperity felt her cheeks heat.

"Listen to me." Elizabeth caught her hands. "I know the doctor well enough to allay your concerns. This is truly a gift, meant in kindness and friendship. He will not expect what you fear. He would never press you to accept his offer of marriage."

"I didn't realize my feelings were so obvious."

Elizabeth pulled Prosperity close and whispered, "Ask yourself how you would feel if the lieutenant had given the gift."

Prosperity squeezed her eyes shut. That was the problem.

⌘

David hurried toward town at an outrageously early hour. He had to believe two infants would rouse the O'Malley household before sunrise. If not, he would wait.

A whiff of fish brought a sudden pang for home. He'd often walked the wharves at sunrise to see what the night catch had brought in. When young, he'd dreamed of whaling like so many of his classmates. His father had other plans. David was to use his education to advantage in the church, but that vocation did not promise the thrill of the sea.

Perhaps that's why he'd found Prosperity so engaging. He could listen to her father's tales of daring for hours. Though she confided that many of those stories had been embellished, they still rang of adventure he would never see in clerical robes. Pursuing engineering through the army had been a compromise that ultimately fit better than either the ministry or the sea.

Still, the wild smell of the ocean stirred his blood. This morning he diverted his path to walk the docks lining the seaport. Fresh planks had been laid in front of the newest pier. The scent of hewn timber tickled his nose.

He glanced down.

The new spikes already boasted a coating of rust, the curse of the salt air. Some had been pounded so hard with a sledge that the rust was worn off.

He slowed.

That last spike bore a mark.

He knelt and brushed away the sawdust and dirt. The sledge had flattened the head of the spike, but the mark could still be read easily.

The back of his neck prickled. This was the marking the blacksmith had agreed to use. But that had taken place after the spikes went missing, and the man hadn't reported another theft.

He checked the remainder of the new planking and found only one other with the mark. A few missing spikes might escape notice. He looked around. Fishermen unloaded their catch, laughing and jesting over the amount each man had hauled ashore. Stevedores made their way to a schooner headed to the next wharf. Wagons had already lined up for the cargo. The cannery hummed to life. He could not spot any other dock construction, nor could he tell who owned this wharf.

Sunlight began to dust the tops of the trees. If he didn't hurry, he would miss another chance to see Prosperity. He hurried down the streets to the O'Malley house. Lamps burned inside, meaning the family was awake. He clattered up the steps to the veranda and crossed the expanse in two strides. Two raps on the door brought answering footsteps.

The housekeeper opened the door.

David pulled off his hat. "I hope to see my son." It still felt odd to call Oliver his son, though it was getting easier. "Is Miss Jones awake?"

The housekeeper nodded. "You wait here."

She disappeared into the house, leaving the door wide open. David could hear her calling for Prosperity, and his heart leapt. Maybe this time she would look at him. Maybe this time she would talk. His mouth felt dry, but swallowing did not ease it.

Prosperity appeared in the hall, her face flushed and her hair so hastily pulled back that wisps framed her face. Even in the glow of oil lamps, her hair shone with streaks of gold and red. Her hazel eyes shimmered gold, as they always did in such light.

"Prosperity." It came out in a breath.

Instead of ducking away, this time she met his gaze.

He wanted to tell her she was beautiful. He wanted to tell her how much he missed her. He longed to reveal his heart. Instead he asked if Oliver was awake yet.

A trace of what looked like disappointment crossed her face before she turned away. "Of course. I'll take you to the nursery."

He entered the house and closed the door before following her down the hall.

When he passed the dining room, he noted an unfamiliar woman making notes on a piece of paper. Drawings and fabric covered the table. Apparently Mrs. O'Malley was having some article of clothing made. Aileen had loved new gowns, which he could not afford. Yet somehow she'd always managed to acquire new things. Often he'd receive the bill later, but not always.

His step slowed. Perhaps he should reveal this much. "I know where the money went."

Her brow furrowed. "I thought Elizabeth—Mrs. O'Malley—refused payment."

He blinked. "Mrs. O'Malley? What does she have to do with—oh." Prosperity thought he was talking about his payment for Oliver's care. "She did until I suggested she set it aside for a young mother in need."

The stiffness left Prosperity's posture. "You did?" Her eyes shone with admiration.

He should have known that generosity would touch her heart more quickly than apologies.

"That is so generous." She swallowed. "Thank you."

Though he reveled in her response, he could not take credit. "She would not accept payment any other way."

"She is a generous soul."

He agreed.

Her brow furrowed. "But if you weren't talking about payment, then what money were you talking about?"

"The money I sent to you when you first arrived."

Her back stiffened. "Please stop bringing this up."

"But—" He cut himself off. Tempting though it was, he should not tarnish Aileen's memory. It would do nothing to win over Prosperity. "I'm sorry, you're right."

Her shoulders eased. "Thank you. I am sometimes correct."

"Often."

He thought he saw a trace of a smile, and his heart buoyed.

"You didn't visit Oliver last night," she whispered. "Did something happen?"

The trouble over the missing spikes and lost money faded under the reality of his father's arrival in Key West. If Father paid Prosperity a visit, David would lose ground again. His head spun, and he had to brace himself against the wall.

"Are you well?" Her eyebrows drew together with concern. "You look pale."

Indeed he felt like he had run from the garrison to the O'Malley home. "A little lightheadedness. It will pass."

"Did you eat this morning?"

"I wanted to see Oliver."

Was that approval he spotted in her gaze? "I'll have Florie bring you something."

"No. It's not necessary."

"Elizabeth would insist."

She'd moved close enough that her hair, which always smelled of the fresh ocean breezes, tickled his chin. He leaned against the wall and closed his eyes, overwhelmed by desire for the woman he loved and the future together that had once been assured.

A soft hand pressed against his forehead.

"You are a little warm," she said.

He leaned into her touch, relishing this tiniest of compassionate gestures. "It's the wool uniform."

She removed her hand.

He opened his eyes to see her gazing into them. "The wool is hot, even at this time of day."

"A poor choice." But the words barely left her lips.

How sweet those had once been, like springtime rain, soft and gentle, promising renewed life to come. He leaned closer, longing for just one kiss. One. Yet he knew that one would never suffice. He wanted more. He wanted to claim her, to sweep her into his arms and promise undying love. Yet if he gave in to that surging desire, he would lose her. His head knew it, but emotion clouded reason.

He brushed a stray lock from her forehead and let his fingertip glide down her cheek.

She trembled but did not pull away. Her lips parted, and the emotional battle played out in her eyes.

He must say something to persuade her. He must find the one thing that would turn her back to him. If only he could pull his scattered thoughts together enough to speak with eloquence. If only he could convey that her name rested on his lips a hundred times a day and a thousand times each night. A poet could find the words that would wipe away the pain and bring her back to him. An engineer had only precision.

"I still love you." His statement echoed in the hall, ricocheting off her with enough force to make her step back.

"Don't say such things."

"I must, or I will die." He reached for her.

She backed beyond reach. "Don't you see how impossible it is?"

No, he didn't. He couldn't give up or he would not be able to go on. "I only see how much I hurt you and how badly I want to take that pain away so we can build a future together."

Her chin quivered, and for a second he thought she would come to him.

Instead she squared her shoulders and jutted out her chin. "Your son is waiting."

Then she left. Only after the door closed, leaving him alone in the hallway, did he realize he had neglected to tell her that his father was in town.

22

It took all in Prosperity's power to walk away from David. Her cheek still tingled where his finger had brushed it. She wanted to believe him, wanted to forget what had happened and return to the past, but life could not be found in dreams and wishful thinking. He was not the same man, and she was no longer the woman who had entrusted her heart to him.

The baby lying in the nursery was proof of that. She could not look at Oliver without seeing David's betrayal. Though the boy was clearly not his, he must have believed the woman was carrying his child to marry her. That meant . . . well, that meant David had broken his pledge and dissolved the bond between them before he sent the letter.

They couldn't go back. She must move forward. Though she did not love the doctor, they shared much in common, and he treated her with great kindness. He would make a fine husband if only he believed in God.

While Dr. Goodenow escorted her to work, she tried to force David from her mind by recalling the other unexpected event in this new day. "Mrs. Evanston's arrival this morning was quite a surprise."

He appeared pleased she'd brought up the subject. "I hope you will forgive this old man for indulging my whims by commissioning the gown. Our dear friend Elizabeth tried to talk me out of it, but I insisted on thanking you in a tangible way."

"Thanking me for what?"

"For assisting with Mrs. Latham, of course."

The mention of David's late wife only brought back painful memories. "I did very little."

"You did as requested and likely saved that child's life with your quick thinking."

"Oliver." At last David was calling his son by name, but now Dr. Goodenow was not.

"What about him?"

"The baby's name is Oliver."

"Yes, of course. As I said, your assistance was vital."

The compliment did not sit well. "The midwife or one of the officers' wives would have done the same."

"But they did not." He patted her hand. "You were there through the most trying circumstances."

She couldn't accept that the small amount of assistance she'd offered was worthy of anything but a word of thanks. "Nevertheless, your gift is too dear."

"That's what Elizabeth told me you would say." He sighed. "Please indulge me. I have not had the pleasure of bringing joy to a woman since my wife's passing. Twelve years. It's been a long time."

Though he'd meant to ease her misgivings, he'd only increased them. She didn't care to be the object of a man's attention. Nor could she reciprocate his joy. She felt nothing but the comfort of friendship. He was a good man. She could not let him think her feelings matched his.

"I'm sorry, Doctor." The beginning was simple enough, but the next words stuck in her throat.

"No apologies, please. You are dear to me, Prosperity, dearer than anyone I have met in many years."

He was making this even more difficult.

She struggled against rising panic. "I cannot love you." She looked away. They had arrived at the hospital gate. It would be so easy to slip through the fence and escape, but that would not be fair. "I'm sorry."

To her surprise, he chuckled.

She stared, perplexed. "You aren't upset?"

"I know you are not ready to love, but I cannot hide my affection. You have suffered much loss in the past months. I simply want you to know that you may lean upon me. You can trust me." He tipped up her chin so she looked into his eyes. "I will not hurt you. I promise."

She wanted to believe him. "But I cannot return your love."

"Not now, but I am a patient man. I will wait in the hope that our friendship will one day grow into something stronger."

She still could not get rid of the feeling that she was somehow betraying David, which was utter nonsense considering he had abandoned her. "The gown. The soiree."

He touched a finger to her lips to still the protest. "For your enlightenment and comfort, my dear. Nothing more."

His gaze was sincere. She should believe him. After all, his words echoed what she'd hoped deep inside.

"Thank you." Her gratitude was whispered, but she echoed it with a quick embrace, that of two friends parting. "I must hurry to work or I shall be late."

He smiled, and the lines of his face highlighted his joy. "Until this evening then." He clasped her hands in a final farewell.

"Until then." She pulled away.

"Miss Jones!" a man scolded.

The severe tone sent a shiver down her spine. Worse by far than Dr. MacNees. She knew and feared that voice from Nantucket, but he could not be here. It was impossible. David's father never traveled farther than Boston. Yet it was his voice, and he knew her name. Slowly she turned around.

"Miss Jones." Reverend Myles Latham, dressed as always in black, scowled at her. "What are you doing with this man?"

❧

Since David could not do anything to change Prosperity's mind until evening, he turned his attention to the problem of the missing supplies. Spotting the mark on the spikes this morning had given him an opportunity to discover who was behind the thefts.

He spoke to the dock workers, who sent him to the foreman, who pointed him toward the warehouse owner, who insisted the spikes had been purchased from a legitimate source. A ship that left port yesterday, the *Joseph M*, had salvaged the spikes from a schooner that sank a year back. Though David insisted that was impossible, the owner stood by his story. David could learn nothing more until the *Joseph M* returned to port. Since she was a wrecking vessel, that could take some time.

Lacking evidence, he must formulate another plan, one that would trap the thief in the act. He'd thought his previous plan foolproof, but this man was more clever than he'd estimated. The thief had avoided suspicion by stealing such a small number that no one noticed. The spikes could have been strapped to a leg or hidden beneath a coat. He eyed the work crews, both hired and military, laboring on the fort. Who had done this? Whoever it was, the man was arrogant enough to think he could pilfer right under David's nose. That arrogance would be the thief's undoing.

By the time Captain Dutton stopped for the daily progress report, David had a plan in place. The next shipment of iron was due to arrive within a week, weather permitting. It was a large amount, for they were ready to cast the shutters for the embrasures. A little carelessness coupled with a hidden lookout should bring the thief right into their hands.

"Good work, Lieutenant," the captain said when David had finished outlining the details. "With any luck we'll nab them in the act and send them to the stockade. If we were in wartime . . ."

Captain Dutton didn't finish the thought, but David understood. The man took the theft personally, for he had poured all his energies and countless hours into the building of this fort.

"We will get the man or men," David assured him.

"Who do you suggest for the watch?"

David wasn't completely certain who to trust. Ever since the problem began, he'd been watching his men and those of Lieutenant Ambleton. Every one of them had wandered off on his own at some time, all except the Negroes on David's team. But suggesting a colored man for the watch would not sit well with some. It must be a soldier.

"I will be there, of course," he volunteered, "along with men-at-arms, preferably those not working on the fort."

"Ah." Dutton drew out the syllable. "That makes sense. Except for you. If you eliminate everyone who works here, then you cannot participate either. I will speak with the colonel. I'm sure he can recommend a reliable watch."

David understood the captain's reasoning, but control was slipping away. If he didn't join the watch, how would he know if the men were trustworthy or not? "Who will command them, sir?"

"Perhaps I will."

David did not point out the obvious, that the captain was also present at the construction site. He opted for another route. "In that case, may I join you? Your presence would assure everyone that I am not involved."

The captain nodded. "So be it. I trust you recall how to fire a musket?"

"Yes, sir." At least someone trusted him. "And thank you."

But after the captain left, a chill settled in his bones. He hadn't considered the possibility of gunfire. This could go very wrong and leave his son an orphan. He must make provisions beforehand in case of the worst.

He pulled open his desk drawer and removed the daguerreotype of Prosperity from his Bible. He could think of no one better to raise Oliver. She had spurned his attempts at reconciliation, but she had agreed to care for his son. This morning she had not immediately pulled away. Compassion shone in her eyes and her touch. Perhaps she could set aside her misgivings for the sake of an innocent baby.

Tonight he would ask.

The door to his office burst open. David looked up, expecting to see the oft insubordinate Private Jameson. Instead his father filled the door frame. His tall, black form blotted out all light.

"You lied," Reverend Myles Latham boomed with righteous indignation, his finger pointed at David's chest.

David stumbled to his feet. "About what?"

"Even now you deny your sin. Repent and be saved."

David bristled at the rebuke. "I haven't lied to you or anyone else."

"More lies." Father's steely gaze hardened even further. "The wicked are blinded by their unbelief."

"I have answered your every question, even those that pry into private matters. I place honor and integrity above everything. I told you no lies."

"Omission is also deceit."

David shivered despite the heat of the room and the perspiration on his brow. He had not told Father everything. "You did not ask."

"I asked about your wife. You only told me she had perished. You did not tell me she was a whore."

David recoiled at the bald word. Despite what Aileen had been, in spite of her treachery, he must defend her honor. "Did not Hosea marry a fallen woman?"

"At God's direction. Do not compound your sin by insisting God told you to wed a strumpet. An alehouse wench." Father's lip curled with distaste. "My son would never do such a thing."

Ice flowed through David's veins. Nothing would calm his father. Nothing could make him understand why David had married her. Nothing would ever wipe away the stain that Father believed had tarnished him and his reputation.

"It is done," he whispered, "and cannot be undone."

His father stared at him. "I should never have listened to your mother. Your defiance will break her heart."

David tried to respond. He opened his mouth, but what could he say?

Father spun around to leave and then looked back one final time. "The fruit of your iniquity must never know. I will ensure it." He stormed from the building, coattails flying.

David stumbled after him, but his legs gave way. Father knew about Oliver. Somehow he knew.

Prosperity. Father must have found and questioned her. David had failed to warn her this morning. Even if he had, she would have answered Father's every question, for she could never withhold the truth.

What did Father mean that he would ensure Oliver never knew about his parents? Would he try to take the boy away? For all his exhortations against slavery, Father would never raise a mixed-blood child. Neither would he send the baby into slavery, but he might give Oliver to someone. He might send the boy so far away that David could never find him.

Could he? Was it even possible? David was not the boy's birth father. Anything was possible.

With a groan he crushed his head between his hands. The fragile life he'd constructed here had just shattered.

⌒⊰⊱⌒

"Miss Stern be askin' for you," Gracie said while Prosperity donned her apron. "My oh my. She look madder'n a hornet done lost its nest."

Prosperity panicked. Though she'd left Reverend Latham as soon as she could, she was late for her shift. That must be why the matron was upset. She did not tolerate tardiness. Given earlier warnings, Prosperity was already on shaky ground. This interview would not end well unless she begged forgiveness. After the unsettling meeting with David's father, she did not relish facing an angry Miss Stern.

"Where is she?"

"Her office," Gracie said, "but I wouldn't be hurryin' her way iffen I was you. Let her settle. Send up Lillian with a pot o' her favorite tea." Lillian worked in the kitchen. "See if they got one of them butter biscuits she likes so much."

All good advice. Yet Prosperity stood frozen to the spot, twisting her apron ties. "Did she say what upset her?"

"Lawd, you think she done tell someone like me what she got on her mind?" Gracie's laugh did nothing to ease Prosperity's trepidation.

"Best get it over."

"You jes' wait here. I'll go send Lillian on up with the tea. Wait a bit and then you go."

Prosperity could not allow anyone else to face Miss Stern's wrath. "Thank you, Gracie. I appreciate that you want to protect me, truly I do, but I must do this myself."

Gracie shook her head and clucked her tongue. "There ain't no fool like . . ." Her sentence trailed off as she headed into the laundry.

Prosperity closed her eyes and prayed that the Lord would give her the proper words to calm the matron. She felt a little better, but the momentary peace disappeared with every step toward Miss Stern's office. Her pulse raced as she crossed the yard already hot with the fires and boiling laundry. Her heart pounded against her rib cage with each step into the main hospital.

Miss Stern's office was located at the near end. The waxed wooden floors echoed with each step. Closed doors lined the hall, leading to storerooms and offices, the pharmacy, and the surgical room. Miss Stern's door stood open.

Prosperity stopped to gather her courage. She closed her eyes and tried to sense the Lord's presence. What would He have her do? Extend grace and compassion. Speak the truth. She had done so when David's father questioned her. Between the doctor's reassurances and Reverend Latham's questions, she'd arrived late. She would explain the circumstances and ask forgiveness. Hopefully Miss Stern would understand.

Did not the Lord's Prayer urge all mankind to forgive as they had been forgiven? Her mind slipped to another verse: *Thy will be done in earth, as it is in heaven.* That was more difficult, for it meant accepting the course God directed, regardless of the outcome. She cowered at the thought of more pain and suffering, yet the little she'd endured was nothing compared with what Jesus had endured for her sake.

"Thy will be done," she whispered.

At last, elusive peace enveloped her.

She rapped on the door frame.

Miss Stern looked up from her reading. Spectacles rested on the bridge of her nose, but they could not hide the matron's displeasure.

"Miss Jones." The matron's rigid posture conveyed no sympathy or compassion. "At last."

"I am sorry for arriving late. An acquaintance from Nantucket stopped me outside the hospital." She saw no reason to identify David's father. "I could not turn him away."

"I did not call you here to discuss your tardiness or an acquaintance from Nantucket."

"You didn't?" Hope leapt inside Prosperity.

Miss Stern's frown intensified. "Did I not warn you to restrict any contact with physicians?"

Prosperity felt her face heat. "He is not employed by the hospital."

"Do not think you can rewrite policy by changing a few words. Dr. Goodenow has attended patients here and will likely attend patients in the future." Miss Stern spread her hands on the desktop and pushed to her feet. "You have ignored my rules and will pay the price."

Prosperity fought back. "We were not on hospital grounds."

"You stood outside the gate, in full view of anyone who might look your way. Moreover, your behavior was shameful. Such intimacies are not allowed. Period. I made that clear more than once, and you assured me it would not happen again."

Prosperity had no response. She had been careless, had believed Dr. Goodenow's assurances.

"Hand me your apron, Miss Jones."

The air grew heavier than her leaden feet. "My apron?"

"You are dismissed. Return your apron."

As a child, Prosperity had tried to sneak aboard her father's whaling vessel, intending to join her papa in spite of his refusal to take her with him. The gangway was wet and her foot had slipped. She'd fallen over the side and into the murky waters between the dock and the ship. Her dress dragged her down. Though she struggled, she could not find the surface. Her lungs ached, and her thoughts muddled until blackness took over. One of the men had heard the splash and dove overboard to haul her to the surface. When she woke, her dear papa held her in his arms, alternately sobbing and scolding her.

Today Miss Stern was pulling her underwater. Dismissed. Prosperity had lost her position, and with it the chance to live on her own terms.

"The apron, Miss Jones." Miss Stern held out her hand.

Prosperity drew a breath, and life flooded into her limbs. Though still numb, she managed to unknot the ties and hand the apron to the matron.

The woman sneered, "You may marry now without concern for the hospital and its regulations, since that is clearly your aim."

Prosperity opened her mouth to defend her actions, but then she remembered the friendly embrace she'd given Dr.

Goodenow. From a distance, it might appear they had kissed. Her face burned from both embarrassment and indignation.

"You may leave now, Miss Jones. See the paymaster for the wages due you." Miss Stern shooed her out of the office and closed the door behind her.

That was it. Once again Prosperity had been set adrift.

23

David did not care about the dictates of duty. Let the army court-martial him. He must protect Oliver. That was his only thought when he left command of the men to his sergeant. He ignored Ambleton's scowl and Jameson's ticked eyebrow. David's superiors would hear of this. So be it.

All that mattered was his son. *His* son. The child had come to mean more to him than he'd imagined possible that first desperate night when betrayal crashed in on him. It wasn't simply his guilt-wracked promise as he knelt beside Aileen's lifeless body. He couldn't bear the thought of someone—even Father—taking Oliver away.

He ran through the streets, too frantic to think of anything but protecting his son. He skirted pedestrians, dodged dogs and noisy roosters, and avoided the occasional cart. Perspiration drenched his uniform, but he could not shake the chill that had settled in his bones. He could not lose Oliver. That fact pounded into him with each thudding footstep.

"Watch where you're going," a woman called out when he narrowly missed her.

He spun away and careened into a robust sailor.

The man steadied him. "Careful, soldier."

David muttered an apology and raced onward. He must get to his son before Father.

He approached the O'Malley house. His breath came in gasps now. His feet slowed. He blinked to clear his blurred vision.

The house looked quiet. He halted and leaned his hands on his knees, trying to draw in enough air to settle his voice. If he appeared at the door looking like a madman, Mrs. O'Malley would turn him away. Prosperity would be at the hospital. He'd glimpsed her walking away with the doctor this morning. David thought he'd made progress, but she'd returned to his rival.

Oliver deserved a mother like Prosperity, even if she married another. That thought pierced the fog of emotion like a saber. It would hurt beyond belief to step away, but the welfare of others must take precedence over his wishes.

Steeled for what he must do, he climbed the steps and crossed the veranda. He knocked but heard no sound of footsteps. What if Father had already arrived? He could be persuasive, especially in clerical garb. He might have said anything to wrest Oliver from Mrs. O'Malley's grasp.

Visions of the boy being taken aboard ship mingled with fears of Father handing Oliver to strangers. Father had said the boy would never know the truth about his parentage. The only way to ensure that was to remove Oliver from Key West—and from David.

He banged on the door with both fists.

The door swung open, and David had to catch himself on the doorjamb.

"Yes?" the Negro housekeeper asked.

David searched his scrambled memory for her name. Florence? No, that was Prosperity's aunt. The housekeeper's name was similar but not the same.

He gave up and forged ahead. "I wish to see my son."

"Again? Missus Lizbeth with him."

David released his breath, quite unaware he'd been holding it in. "Then he is still here."

"'Course he here. Where else he be?"

"I don't know." He had to admit the remark did sound peculiar under ordinary circumstances. "May I see him? And Mrs. O'Malley?"

"Come in."

She ushered him inside and down the hall to the nursery. As they drew closer, David realized things were not as quiet as he'd thought. A child giggled. Oliver cooed. Mrs. O'Malley sang. Though her voice was lovely, David found himself wishing for Prosperity's rich tones.

The housekeeper stopped in front of the doorway. "L'tenant Latham ta see ya, ma'am."

The singing stopped. "Please show him in."

The housekeeper stepped aside, and he entered the room. Mrs. O'Malley stood, Oliver resting in her arms. The rocking chair still swayed slightly.

"Lieutenant. What may I do for you?"

He removed his hat. "Thank you for seeing me, ma'am. I have a matter of grave importance to bring to your attention."

"Well then. Pull a chair near, and we will talk."

David did as directed. She settled again in the rocker.

He set his hat on his knee, but his thoughts scrambled. How to say this without frightening her or making her think him mad?

"What is it?" she asked.

He licked his lips. "My father has arrived on the island."

"So I understand."

"You've heard already?"

"News travels quickly on the wharves, especially when one's husband owns a pier and warehouse."

"Of course." He had forgotten that. "Has my father been here?"

She shook her head. "You have not seen him?"

He breathed out in relief even while calculating what that meant. If Father hadn't seen Oliver yet, he might not know that the boy was not Latham blood. That gave David a ray of hope.

"Father and I met." He would not reveal the trying details of their encounter, simply his father's aim. He glanced at Oliver. The baby would not understand what he was saying. Not yet. "My father believes my son needs to be removed."

"From this house?"

"He doesn't know Oliver is here, at least I don't think he does. He wants to take my son away from me and from any chance of learning who his mother was."

Mrs. O'Malley sighed. "He worries about people's opinions."

That sounded particularly condemning for a minister, but it was true. Though David had never quite thought of it that way, his father had always cared about the opinion of others. "I'm afraid so." He studied his hat, stained and dusty. "I don't know what to do."

Mrs. O'Malley was no fool. She understood that life did not deliver the future in tidy packages. Oliver grasped her finger with his tiny little ones. Dark against light, both beautiful.

She sighed again. "Some find it difficult to accept the failures of those they love, so they try to hide the result. It never works.

Even if the truth doesn't surface, the secret eats away at the very people they'd intended to protect. God knows, and deep down we all realize that."

"It sounds like you're speaking from experience."

She rocked slowly as Oliver nodded off to sleep. "Shame can bind a man or woman as securely as iron."

He waited for her to explain.

"They think it impossible to ever escape and in their agony draw others in, hoping to spread out the pain."

"Wallowing in misery."

She nodded. "Sometimes. Other times they enact a veneer of righteousness."

That sounded like Father, but David had never known his father to err or stray. "Maybe he is righteous. Maybe that's why this is so difficult."

Her smile was tinged with sadness. "Saint Paul said we must measure everything against Scripture. How would our Lord have handled this matter? What would He have done?" She set the sleeping Oliver in one of two cradles shaped like boats.

Fishermen's boats. The thought struck from nowhere. Simple, yet carrying precious cargo. Jesus had ridden often in a boat and had calmed stormy seas, always bringing the boat's precious cargo safely to shore. Could He bring this precious boy to safety?

"I'm not certain." He had seen too much evil to trust that good would always prevail.

Mrs. O'Malley handed a block to her son. "'Behold the fowls of the air: for they sow not, neither do they reap, nor gather into barns; yet your heavenly Father feedeth them.' He watches over this little one."

Scripture couldn't reassure David when his father was waiting to strike. He gripped the arms of the chair until his hands ached. "Please don't let my father see Oliver. Don't let him take my son away."

She eyed his hands and then looked deep into his eyes. Surely she sensed his desperation. "He is your son. You decide who will see him."

That was what he'd needed to hear.

"Thank you." He rose. "You will tell Prosperity?"

"Tell me what?" Prosperity's tremulous voice came from behind him.

He whirled to see her red-eyed and distraught. She had pulled off her bonnet, and her hair had sprung loose from its pins. If that doctor had done anything to her, David would hunt him down and—

"Did he hurt you?"

Prosperity stared at him blankly.

Mrs. O'Malley went to her, arms outstretched. "What happened?"

Prosperity burst into tears, and Mrs. O'Malley held her. David had never felt so helpless.

❦

The implications of losing her position had tormented Prosperity on the long, hot walk home. Home! That too would disappear. Though Elizabeth would insist she stay as a guest, Prosperity could not accept charity, even from a friend. She must leave. But where could she go? Her final wages would not support her more than a week.

She'd sobbed in the seclusion of a thick garden until she'd thought she could weep no more. She'd tested and discarded every possible solution except one. She must marry Dr. Goodenow. That was the only choice left to her.

Though the idea weighed on her, she must face the future without complaint. Many a woman settled for far less. The doctor adored her. He treated her well. He would never strike her or berate her. She had seen no indication of vices. If only he loved the Lord, she might give her heart without reservation. On the other hand, she could be the light that guided him from the imprecision of science to the perfection of God.

This evening she would walk to their usual meeting spot and give him her answer. Until then she could hold little Oliver and find solace in his desperate need for her.

Then she walked into the nursery and saw David. His presence reminded her of all she'd lost. Instead of that once-cherished future, she must accept a lesser vision with a man she did not love.

The sobs returned with humiliating force.

Then Elizabeth enveloped her in a caring embrace. Prosperity buried her face in her friend's shoulder and prayed David would leave so she would not have to reveal her humiliation to him. Dismissed! For embracing Dr. Goodenow as a friend for the briefest of moments.

Standing before Miss Stern had been difficult enough, but she could not bear to tell David. Would he crow with delight that Dr. Goodenow had caused her dismissal? Would he reiterate the claim that he'd sent her money? Their last tender moment could not remove the sting that he'd tried to buy her removal.

She wanted to sink into a corner and hide.

Instead David touched her shoulder. She felt it as surely as one senses the difference between feather bed and horsehair. His caress worked deep into her, awakening that part of her she was trying to keep dormant.

"Tell us what happened." His voice had softened from normal, reminding her of that moment years ago when he'd pledged his undying love. "I will do all in my power to right any wrong."

Didn't he know how impossible that was? No one could change Miss Stern's mind, not even Elizabeth. Or Dr. Goodenow. Certainly not David.

"I must catch Jamie before he scoots out the door," Elizabeth said softly. "Will you be all right?"

Though Prosperity would rather hide in her friend's embrace, she nodded and accepted a handkerchief, which she pressed to her face.

Once again David touched her, this time with a firm grasp of the shoulder. "Was it my father?"

That startled her enough to drop the handkerchief from her face. In her distress, she had forgotten about David's father. The reason for her tardiness. "You know that your father spoke to me?"

"I suspected he would. I should have warned you." He looked ashen, as if he would collapse. His gaze was wild. He grasped both of her shoulders. "What did you tell him about Oliver?"

"Oliver? He didn't ask about Oliver. He asked about your wife."

He let go of her, visibly relieved. "Only about Aileen."

"Your wife."

David raked a hand through his hair, squeezed his eyes shut, and blew out in exasperation, precisely what he used to do whenever his father had said or done something hurtful.

She'd long been aware of the tension between them. Since David was the eldest son, she supposed that was natural. Reverend Latham seemed difficult to please, but David would never speak ill of his father. When the reverend informed the newspaper that David had graduated from the military academy at

West Point, she'd thought David had finally won his father's respect. Yet David had trembled before telling his father about their engagement. When she'd asked how he'd taken the news, David had assured her that his father was pleased. After the reverend's scathing interrogation this morning, she wondered if that had been the case.

David opened his eyes. "Thank you for not telling him about my son."

My son. The simple words shook her, for he said them with a desperation that could only come from love.

"You don't want him to know about Oliver?"

His desperation seemed to increase. "It's too late. He already knows."

"He did not hear it from me."

"I know. I believe you, but I wouldn't have blamed you if you had told him. He can be . . . persuasive."

That wasn't the word she would have used. He terrified her.

Again David raked his fingers through his hair. "You need to know—that's what I asked Mrs. O'Malley to tell you—that Father threatened to take Oliver away."

Prosperity could not breathe. Even though she must marry Dr. Goodenow and leave little Oliver in Elizabeth's capable hands, she'd expected to be able to visit. If Reverend Latham took the baby to Nantucket, she would never see him again.

Elizabeth rejoined them. "Do not fear, Lieutenant. We will not hand your son to anyone without your consent."

"Thank you." Yet he still looked worried.

Elizabeth changed the subject by turning back to Prosperity. "Perhaps now you can tell us what happened at the hospital."

How selfish she was to lament the loss of employment when she had a roof over her head and a man willing to marry her.

She forced a weak smile. "It's nothing of import."

"Clearly it is if you have returned midmorning," Elizabeth noted.

David watched her.

Prosperity could not look at him. "I'm sorry for going on so."

"We want to help." Elizabeth circled an arm around her shoulders and led her to the rocking chair.

Prosperity sank into it, her limbs shaky. "There is nothing to be done." She swallowed against the rising tide of embarrassment. Failure must be borne in the open in order to be conquered. Did not the Lord say that He would work good even from the bad? There was no use hiding what could not be kept secret. She took a deep breath. "I was dismissed."

"What?" David and Elizabeth said in unison.

His brow lowered. "They are fools. No one could make a better nurse."

"You are too kind," Prosperity whispered, "but I was only a laundress."

"Then you deserve better." He knelt before her. Now she could not avoid the blue eyes that reminded her of Nantucket skies. "They should have recognized your abilities. I have never known a better nurse. Your mother would have perished years ago if not for your care."

Ma. Thinking of her made Prosperity's throat constrict. She blinked back a tear.

"I'm sorry. That was thoughtless. I meant to share my admiration, not bring sorrow. In your care, Oliver has grown. He now laughs and—" David's voice broke, and he looked away, clearly overcome with emotion. "And I have you to thank for it."

Her heart went out to him. Without thinking, she wrapped her arms around his shoulders. That response came by instinct, but the reaction inside her carried far deeper meaning than simple consolation. The tie between them vibrated like a cord on a violin—stretched to the breaking point, yet in the hands of a master, eliciting such sweetness that the hearer longs for the tune to go on forever.

She cupped a hand under his chin, so familiar yet different. She once knew every curl on his head. When had the hairline receded that little bit at the peaks? His shoulders, broad and straight, now bowed. Where had that determined confidence gone? If only they could turn back the clock to when she'd teased him. If only they could run atop the dunes once more. But that time was gone. They must step forward, each on a different path.

She must marry Dr. Goodenow, and David must carry on, raising his son and building the fort.

"I'm sorry." She withdrew her hand and stood. "I should help Mrs. O'Malley with the children."

Elizabeth had taken Jamie from the room, leaving her alone with David and the sleeping Oliver.

David would not let her walk away. "I miss you."

Miss. Not missed. The simple words struck harder than Miss Stern's dismissal. Yet how could she give her heart to him again? Only a fool plunged into the same shallow waters. His love for Oliver had nearly swayed her, but it was not enough to wipe away the sins of the past.

"I can't."

That shook him. She not only saw the tremor but felt it as her own heart tore in half. Better to lose all feeling than to ever hurt again. That's what life as the doctor's wife promised.

She walked to the cradle. His son slept, lids closed and mouth slightly open, trusting completely. She prayed David would not betray that trust.

He had not moved, as if waiting for her to change her mind. She could not. "You should leave now."

He drew in his breath but said nothing. Then she heard him walk away.

⁕

Prosperity must be confused. David had to believe that was why she'd first clung to him and then sent him away. Goodenow must be to blame. The man had succeeded where David had failed. Even Oliver could not sway Prosperity's heart.

For the first time, he had to admit that he might never win back her trust. That prospect sent chills through him despite the hot sun. He wrapped his coat tighter and hurried down the street toward the fort.

What could he do? Elizabeth O'Malley said that the answers he sought could be found in the Bible. Mother felt the same way. Sometimes she would console him with Scripture that contradicted the way his father had instructed him. She must have seen the hypocrisy yet said nothing against her husband, choosing the path of obedience. Or least resistance.

Elizabeth O'Malley was quite different. Perhaps that came from growing up in Key West, where colors and nationalities mixed. Spanish, Portuguese, and French might be heard on the streets, along with tongues he could not recognize. The exotic frontier town invited bold speech and actions—even from women. Mrs. O'Malley might be strong enough to keep Oliver away from Father. Her faith was certainly solid.

He could not say the same. When he'd witnessed the hypocrisy of those who claimed godliness yet lied and cheated, he'd closed his Bible in disgust. Only after pledging to wed Prosperity had he picked it up again. Her faith so far outstripped his that he was ashamed to enter marriage so much unequal. When he'd had to abandon that future, he'd closed the Bible again, blaming God for his bitter circumstances. But it wasn't God's fault. It never had been. The fault fell squarely on his shoulders.

As David checked in with the guard, he decided to pull that Bible out of the bottom drawer and see what it actually said. That was the only way he could know how Jesus would have handled this problem with Father.

The workers swarmed the casemates. Wagons carted brick onto the site. Another shipment must have arrived. Lieutenant Ambleton eyed him with irritation. Since the man approached at a rapid rate, he must have news of great import. David changed course to meet him.

"Your man has gone missing again," Ambleton stated.

"My man?" David tensed, fearing another confrontation over the Negroes. He mopped his forehead, now so hot he wanted to strip off his coat at once. "I have several men under my command."

Ambleton's mouth curled in disgust. "Jameson. I've never met a lazier soldier."

David recalled Jameson's participation in the group harassing Prosperity and set his jaw. "He will be disciplined the moment he is found. Forty lashes."

Ambleton jerked and gave him a strange look. "You don't think that too severe?"

"The man's insubordination has gone on long enough." All his frustration and anger over the confrontations with Father and Prosperity boiled over. "We must set an example."

"He's your man." Ambleton headed back to direct where to unload the next wagonload of brick.

David slogged across the dusty parade ground to his office,

his legs like lead. The office's window was open, letting in dust and insects. It should be closed. He always closed it when he left. He must have been in too much of a rush.

He pushed open the door and stepped inside. It took a moment for his eyes to adjust to the dimness but much less time to realize the room was a shambles. The drawers had been pulled out of his desk, and their contents were strewn across the desktop and floor. Standing behind the desk stood a single defiant man.

"What are you doing?" David demanded.

Jameson smirked. In one hand he held the daguerreotype of Prosperity and in the other a knife.

24

"Give me that." David lunged for the daguerreotype. The idea of even an image of Prosperity in that worthless man's hands infuriated him.

Jameson stepped out of the way. David flew past him and crashed into the makeshift bookshelf. The books tumbled to the floor, but he managed to stay on his feet.

He swiveled to meet the private. "That belongs to me."

Jameson laughed and scratched the plate with the knife.

"My fiancée." He could not believe his eyes, for Jameson dug the knife into the plate over and over again. He grabbed for the knife and missed. "Why?"

"I loved her."

"Prosperity?" David didn't think they even knew each other. "Then why would you ruin her image?"

"Seems to me that you're the one who ruined it," Jameson sneered.

The blood pounded in David's head. He had not ruined Prosperity's reputation. Never. He flexed his hands. He had the advantage of height and reach. A punch to the jaw might knock Jameson senseless, but David had never boxed. And Jameson had a knife. "Leave Prosperity alone."

"The way you left my love alone?" Jameson taunted.

"Your love? What are you talking about?"

"You think she married you from love? She wouldn't have even considered you if it hadn't been for me."

"You?" In spite of his sluggish mind, David figured out who Jameson must mean. "You and Aileen?"

"Of course Aileen. Who else did you wed?"

Something Jameson had said stuck in David's mind. "What do you mean she wouldn't have considered me? She said I'd fathered her child." Which was clearly false.

"What would you expect her to say?"

David's head spun. "Was I ever even with her?"

Jameson sneered. "A little too much liquor, a pretty woman, it's easy enough to believe."

"Because she was a—" He stopped before he spoke the word.

Jameson wasn't so kind. "A whore? Is that what you thought of her? No wonder she hated you. Yes, hated." He threw the daguerreotype to the floor and ground it against the accumulated sand with his heel. "If I was an officer like you, she would have married me."

David tried to piece it all together, but his mind slogged forward at a painfully slow pace. He shook his head and ended up dizzy. Only the desk kept him from falling.

"What's wrong, Lieutenant? Too much liquor in the middle of the day?"

David swung for Jameson and missed. Perspiration drenched his shirt and ran down his forehead. This room was too hot, even with the window open. "That is insubordination, soldier." But his words sounded far away, as if spoken underwater. He swiped his forehead with his coat sleeve.

"What are you going to do? Charge at me again? Try it and you'll bleed your last drop on the floor of this office."

David's vision blurred. He shook his head again. "You wouldn't dare touch an officer."

"Wouldn't I? I'd be off this island before anyone found you."

David sensed the truth of the statement. A daguerreotype was nothing compared to the real woman. Jameson wanted to harm Prosperity. Somehow David must stop him. How, when he had no weapon and Jameson held a knife? He tried to think, but he couldn't concentrate.

Love your enemies, bless them that curse you. The fragment of Scripture floated into his mind, but what did it mean? How could he love a man threatening to destroy those he loved? Love him? Bless him? He didn't know if he had it in him, but he could do nothing else.

David raised his hands. "I don't want to hurt you."

That only made Jameson snort in derision. "How weak and blind you are."

David blinked and squinted. Why wouldn't his eyes focus?

"You never knew," Jameson continued. "Never saw what was right under your nose."

In a brief moment of lucidity, David realized the man wasn't talking about Aileen or even Prosperity any longer. The scattered papers. The supply lists on the desktop. Jameson was looking for something or to remove something. "You're the thief."

"A man using his wits to advantage."

"Thief." His mouth felt like cotton and his ears rang. He

clung to the desk to hide the fact that his knees were giving way. "You will face court-martial."

"I don't think so." Jameson sheathed his knife. "Once the colonel finds the missing spikes and chisels in your quarters, you will be the one in the stockade. Forty lashes, was it?"

David stared, speechless. Jameson had not only heard every word he'd said, but he had rigged everything to cast suspicion on him. While David's attention was focused on Oliver and Prosperity, Jameson was destroying David's career.

"Why?" he croaked.

"For Aileen. She deserved better."

"You?" Somehow David made the connection. "You're the one she brought to our quarters that night."

Jameson didn't answer, but the truth was clear. Aileen had turned to him for comfort.

"What else did you two share? The money meant for Prosperity?"

"You threw money at another woman while denying your wife. I made sure Aileen got what she deserved."

David's head spun. No wonder Prosperity had thought he was lying. Every incident of the past months made sense now. When Aileen rejected Jameson in favor of David's rank and wages, the man had wrought revenge first by making her his mistress and now by destroying David's reputation. Jameson didn't need to physically harm Prosperity. David's dishonor would sever any possible reconciliation.

His knees gave way, and he fell to the floor, knocking his head against the corner of the desk. Blood trickled down his temple as terrors licked at his tinder-dry mind.

Jameson cast a pitying look at David and strode across the

room to open the door. "Farewell, Lieutenant, and a speedy trial." He stepped out and closed the door.

David tried to follow, but he could not even crawl. He fell face-first on the floor, the destroyed daguerreotype beneath him.

"Prosperity." Her name came out a bare whisper.

All was lost. Crushed like sandstone beneath a sledgehammer. Prosperity, Oliver, family, and career. Jameson would reach Colonel Stormant first. David hadn't the strength to pursue him. He couldn't even get to the office door. All vigor had unaccountably drained from his limbs.

Once Father learned of this disgrace, he would seize Oliver. No judge would deny him. David had already lost Prosperity. Now he would lose his son *and* his honor.

He dug his fingernails into the wooden floor. If only he could drag himself far enough to send someone to warn Prosperity. Sand bit beneath his nails, pressed against his cheek, stuck to his damp skin, but he hadn't the strength to move a single inch. He do could nothing.

Help me, for I am lost. The words gathered on his lips, but he lacked the strength to utter them. All was lost. No one would help him.

You have Me.

The words rang clearly in his muddled mind.

"Who?" he gasped out.

But he knew. Deep down he knew. Years of neglect and rebellion had separated him from those he'd once honored: his father, his mother, Prosperity, and soon his son. Now it would even separate him from the army and his last shred of honor.

He had nothing.

Yet One remained.

I will never leave you nor forsake you.

Had he heard that, or was his mind playing tricks on him?

His Bible lay within reach, where Jameson had tossed it. With his last ounce of strength, he pulled it close. Too exhausted to open the cover, he clung to it, the last solid rock in a sea of quicksand.

⋯⟡⋯

She had no choice, Prosperity told herself the following Monday. David had not visited Oliver all weekend. She'd thought he loved his son, but this sudden stoppage meant she was wrong. He had only visited in the hope of seeing her. Once she squashed the possibility of reconciliation, he stopped coming to the house. She could not respect a man who did not love the innocent child entrusted to his care.

She stood on a low stool in the center of the nursery, the partially finished silk gown swirling around her. Circumstances had forced her hand. It was the best choice for all involved. Still, her nerves tumbled and rolled. A weekend of prayer had not made her feel any better about her decision. She must simply jump, and the sooner she did so, the better.

"Are you certain?" Elizabeth asked while she assisted Mrs. Evanston with the fitting of Prosperity's new gown.

Fortunately, Mrs. Evanston spoke before she had to answer. "Arms out to your side so we can adjust the bodice."

Prosperity lifted her arms, hoping the dressmaker wouldn't poke her with one of the many pins bristling from her pincushion. The woman must have worked all weekend to get so much done so quickly. With the soiree just five days away, it would take every minute of those days to finish the dress. Her future could be cemented in much less time.

"I am." She would tell Dr. Goodenow tonight.

Elizabeth did not look pleased. "I'm not sure you thought through this decision."

"I did nothing but think and pray," Prosperity said with what she hoped sounded like conviction. At least agreeing to marry the doctor—Clayton, she must begin to call him—would assuage her guilt for accepting the new dress.

"You will need a crinoline and more petticoats," Mrs. Evanston noted.

Prosperity did not own a crinoline.

Elizabeth must have noticed Prosperity's alarm, for she said, "You may borrow mine. I have extra petticoats and a spare crinoline."

"But they would never fit. You are so much taller."

"We will pin them up." Elizabeth shrugged off any difficulty with her usual assurance. "If that troubles you, I will ask my friend Caroline if you could borrow hers. She is about your height."

Leave it to Elizabeth to find a solution. At least discussing the dress had put an end to the uncomfortable conversation about Prosperity's decision. It was the right thing to do.

"You may put your arms down now," Mrs. Evanston said. "I'm finished except for the length of the skirt. Are you accepting the gown, Miss Jones?"

Prosperity nodded. Instead of a flush of excitement, dread made her stomach heave and her head spin.

The dressmaker's eyes widened. "Please step down. You look faint."

Indeed she felt unsteady on her feet. "Perhaps I should sit a moment."

"We will have you out of the dress in no time." Good to her word, Mrs. Evanston removed a few pins and slipped the gown, such as it was, over Prosperity's head.

Prosperity sank into the rocking chair.

Oliver kicked his feet and arms in the cradle, gurgling to be picked up, but she didn't dare trust herself. Jamie tugged at his mother's skirts while she helped Mrs. Evanston.

"Don't you need to measure the length?" Elizabeth asked.

"We can take that from the gown Miss Jones is wearing." Mrs. Evanston began to measure the length of Prosperity's skirt.

"Can it be completed that quickly?" Elizabeth asked.

"Do not fear, the dress will be ready in time for the soiree." Prosperity drew in a shallow breath. Perhaps her lightheadedness was due to the unfamiliar tight corset. Fashion dictated a small waistline, and Mrs. Evanston would not budge on that point. Prosperity longed to loosen it, but it laced in back, and she could not undo it herself.

"Good afternoon, ladies," Mrs. Evanston said when she finished packing everything into her bag. "Stop by my shop the morning before the event for the final fitting. There will still be time for small adjustments."

Judging by the distance between Mrs. Evanston's upheld finger and thumb, any adjustments had better be miniscule.

Elizabeth and Jamie escorted the dressmaker from the house, while Prosperity bent over the cradle to stroke little Oliver. The baby brought such joy, from his little hands and feet to the wisps of dark hair curling on his forehead.

"You are so handsome, little one," she cooed, unable to resist his smile.

He grabbed for her hair and gurgled, as if knowing his tugs reminded her of the future she hoped to have. Dr. Goodenow was nearly double her age but not too old to have children, provided he desired them. She nibbled her lower lip. Perhaps she ought to ask. He had lost his first wife in childbirth. He might fear losing another. She hoped he wanted children. Perhaps witnessing the miracle of a child would draw him closer to God.

She cherished that thought until Elizabeth returned holding Jamie.

"That went well," Elizabeth said. "I've asked Florie to set out dinner. We are all famished. Shall I help you change into your dress?"

Prosperity untangled her hair from Oliver's grasp. She was grateful for front-buttoning gowns. They might not be fashionable, but for a woman of her class, they were practical. "I would like to remove the corset. It hurts to breathe."

Elizabeth chuckled as she unlaced it. "It takes practice."

"After this soiree, I will never wear one again." She took a deep breath now that the uncomfortable stays were gone.

"A physician's wife will be expected to present a proper appearance."

Prosperity had never considered that. "I suppose a lieutenant's wife must also."

"I suppose you're right." Elizabeth squeezed her hand. "I hope you will be very happy with Clayton."

Happy. That had never once crossed Prosperity's mind. "I will be content."

"Most women hope for more."

"After all the turmoil of this year, contentment would be a blessing." Indeed she longed for stability. Dr. Goodenow offered that, while David never could. He was attached to the army and would move here and there. In wartime he would take up firearms. He could die. Prosperity could not bear to lose another person she loved.

She slipped into her gray gown and buttoned it. Oliver cried out, and as she reached for him, sorrow wormed its way into her heart. This poor boy stood little chance of a contented life. Even in the best of families he would face scorn and ridicule. She pressed her eyelids closed against a sudden rush of emotion.

Elizabeth touched her shoulder. "Are you all right?"

"It's all too much," she whispered.

"There is no rush."

Prosperity knew her friend meant well, but she did need to hurry. The gown obligated her. She could not make her own way without a good-paying position. This would resolve matters with David once and for all. No, there was very much a need to rush.

"Ma'am?" Florie appeared in the nursery doorway. "Der's a man ta see you. A minister."

A minister? Prosperity's eyelids flew open. Elizabeth's pastor or David's father? Her already roiling stomach clenched even harder.

"Did he say who it was?" Elizabeth asked.

Florie shook her head. "But he a fearsome man, all in black."

"Reverend Latham." Prosperity clutched at her throat.

"Oh dear," Elizabeth said. "I'd better see to him. Prosperity, stay with Oliver. Florie, make sure Jamie stays in the nursery until I send the man away."

"What if he asks to see Oliver?" Prosperity could barely breathe.

"I will send him away as your David instructed. Under no circumstances are you to bring Oliver out of the nursery." Elizabeth paused in the doorway. "In fact, lock the door behind me and don't open it until he is gone."

That frightened Prosperity. Reverend Latham could easily push past Elizabeth. All three of them could not stop a man his size. Even if a locked door stopped him, the windows would not. She picked up Oliver, held him close, and began to pray.

25

The nursery window had no view of the front veranda, but Prosperity could hear Elizabeth through the locked door. She rejoiced at her friend's confident refusal and cringed at Reverend Latham's strident response.

"He's my grandson. You have no right to keep him from me."

He did not know the truth about Oliver. He must not, for his volume rose with each syllable. Under such forcefulness, Prosperity would have withered, but Elizabeth held firm.

"I am simply following his father's wishes. You may visit little Oliver with your son."

Under other circumstances, that might be a reasonable request, but the reverend had told Prosperity that he and David had a falling out. Reverend Latham said he'd tried to reconcile, but David had refused to listen. That was why he'd sought her. The reverend's gaze had skewered her like bait on a hook. She had been glad when Dr. Goodenow interrupted. Unfortunately, the doctor's continued attentions probably contributed to her dismissal.

Oliver began to fuss.

"Hush, hush." Prosperity moved away from the nursery door. If Reverend Latham heard Oliver cry, he might push past Elizabeth. She rubbed the little boy's back and settled in the rocker. He might be hungry, but she didn't have a feeding bottle ready. "Soon, little one." She prayed Elizabeth would send the minister away before Oliver progressed from fussing to bawling.

The poor babe needed a mother who would be with him day after day for the rest of his life, like Ma had been for her. Tears burned in her eyes, this time less for what she'd lost than for what this poor babe would never have.

She stroked his soft cheek. "You deserve a real mama."

Oliver responded by scrunching up his face and wailing.

She pressed him to her chest, though she hadn't a drop of milk to feed him.

Florie looked up and shook her head. Both knew the baby's cry would tempt David's father to barge into the room. Would a lock hold him back? She tensed. Florie eyed the door, the whites of her eyes stark against her beautiful mahogany skin.

A knock sounded on the door.

Florie jumped. Prosperity curled over Oliver and held him tightly. No one would take him from her.

"It's me," Elizabeth said. "He's gone."

Florie released the privacy latch. Prosperity held her breath, fearing the reverend had forced Elizabeth to say that. Thankfully, when the door opened, only Elizabeth entered.

"He was not pleased," Elizabeth said after Florie left and she had settled into feeding Oliver. "He threatened to seek legal recourse."

"Would he succeed?" Prosperity breathed out.

"I don't know, but my father might."

Prosperity puzzled out the situation. "Does Reverend Latham know that Oliver is not related by blood?"

"Do you believe it would matter?"

Prosperity wasn't certain. "He is not an easy man to know." She had trembled the first time she was invited to the Latham table. His steel-blue eyes searched her for faults. She counted it a blessing that he remarked only on the threadbare state of her dress. "He is accustomed to getting his way."

"Then the moment Rourke gets home, I will send him to ask Father's opinion."

The remainder of the afternoon Prosperity paced the parlor and tried to pray. Every noise out of doors made her jump. Elizabeth glanced at her but made no remark. When Captain O'Malley arrived home from work, Elizabeth sent him off to ask her father if Reverend Latham could force them to grant him access to Oliver.

"It will ease our minds." Elizabeth gave her husband a kiss before he left.

Their intimate affection always left a hollow place in Prosperity's heart—one that she hoped would soon be filled by Dr. Goodenow. Clayton. She had intended to give him her acceptance this afternoon at their usual meeting place near the hospital, but she could not leave Elizabeth alone in case David's father returned. Accepting the doctor's proposal would have to wait another day.

A knock sounded on the front door.

Prosperity jumped. Had David's father waited for Captain O'Malley to leave before approaching the house? She hugged little Oliver close. "I should take the baby to the nursery."

"I think I recognize that knock." Elizabeth rose, but Florie whisked down the hall to answer the door.

Moments later, the housekeeper returned. "De doctor, ma'am."

Dr. Goodenow entered the parlor on her heels. Unlike his usual impeccable self, he looked frazzled. His jacket was wrinkled and his tie askew. Even his hat sat unevenly, as if he had plopped it on his head in haste.

"What is it, Doctor?" Elizabeth asked. "You look as if calamity has struck."

Prosperity noted the doctor's pallor and the tiny jerk he'd given at Elizabeth's words.

His gaze drifted to her. "No one is ill?"

"No." Prosperity hugged little Oliver even closer. "Why do you ask?"

"It's Lieutenant Latham."

Her mouth went dry. "David."

"He visited last Friday morning," Elizabeth said, "and seemed well then."

Prosperity recalled the wildness of his expression and the perspiration on his brow. "What is it?"

The doctor's expression grew grimmer. "Yellow fever."

❦

Prosperity was supposed to be getting ready for the botanical society soiree. Elizabeth had laid out several sets of gloves for her to try on. The dress would arrive tomorrow. Instead she stood at the army post's guardhouse explaining her request yet again with the same result.

The guard shook his head. "Only family can enter the hospital."

"But he has no family here," she explained for the third day in a row, "except his father, and they are estranged. He needs to know that someone cares."

"I have my orders, miss."

She heaved a sigh, searching for some reason that might sway the guard. "We were engaged to marry." She had already tried that, but maybe this time it would make a difference.

"If you aren't his wife, you can't enter."

Frustration drove her to the brink of tears. "I don't understand. I was allowed to enter the garrison when his late wife was in childbirth and again when she was feverish and dying. Why can't I visit him now?"

"Orders, miss."

"What orders?"

The guard hesitated, giving her the first hint of an opening. She seized it. "There's something else, isn't there?"

The guard looked around. No one was near. "He's under guard, miss."

She didn't understand. "Do they think he will wander off and spread contagion?"

He shook his head. "Court-martial."

Her head spun. David? Under military arrest? It made no sense. Even Reverend Latham could not provoke that much trouble. Something must have happened under David's command. "What is the charge?"

"Theft."

"Impossible."

The guard's expression told her it was not only possible but fact.

"It must be a mistake. David—Lieutenant Latham—is the most honest man I know. He would never take so much as an extra biscuit."

The guard shrugged. "That's not for me to decide."

No, his superiors would make that decision. She didn't know

how a military court-martial worked, only that its consequences could be severe. "He would never harm anyone."

That wasn't entirely true, of course. He'd broken his vow to her, but he'd had reason. The night she received the news of David's illness, she had reread his letter to her. *I fear that I must break our engagement*. Must. Not wished. He'd written the day of Ma's burial, which meant Aileen had been far along before David decided he must marry her. David always acted swiftly to right any wrongs. He could not have known of this unborn child until shortly before he wrote. That meant he did not love Aileen. Regardless of the circumstances of their marriage, he could not have loved her. Heartbreak dripped off his pen onto the page. He'd thought the baby was his son. That was why he'd married her. That was why he'd recoiled when he first saw Oliver.

That night Prosperity had retrieved the locket from the washstand drawer and clasped it around her neck. Perhaps one day it could contain an image of his son.

"His son," she gasped now, realizing she did indeed have a reason that might sway the guard to allow her to enter the hospital. "Lieutenant Latham entrusted me with the care of his son."

As she'd expected, the guard wavered. "Is there a problem?"

She wanted to say there was, though neither Oliver nor anyone else in the household had shown any sign of fever. Now that a week had passed since they'd last seen David, Dr. Goodenow assured them they had not contracted the disease. The biggest threat to Oliver's well-being came from David's father.

That was her answer.

She stood tall. "The baby is in danger. I must speak to his father."

"Why didn't you say that?" The guard had her sign her name on a register and then called for a soldier to escort her to the hospital.

Her fingertips tingled. Soon she would see David. What would she say? And how could she save him from court-martial?

⁓⁂⁓

David's condition shocked Prosperity, though the orderly would not allow her beyond the guarded entrance to the isolation room. He was bathed in perspiration, shaking and delirious. He did not recognize her or even that she stood at the door.

"I wish to talk to him," she begged yet again.

The orderly shook his head. "He wouldn't hear you anyway."

"He would know."

The orderly glanced at the guard. "It's not allowed."

"Then who do I see to get permission?"

"You could try the surgeon, Dr. Rangler, or the commander, but I doubt either will allow you in the room. I'm surprised you got this far."

The commander had intimidated her the last time they'd met. The surgeon in charge might prove more sympathetic. "Where may I find Dr. Rangler?"

"He is sleeping."

"Then I will see him in the morning."

Since nothing further could be done that night, she returned to the O'Malley home. Her mind tossed over all she had learned but could come to no conclusion. When she entered, she found the family gathered in the parlor with Elizabeth's father, Charles Benjamin, esquire.

Prosperity trembled. "What happened?"

Instead of answering, Elizabeth asked how David was faring.

"Too ill to see visitors."

"Very unfortunate," the attorney said, his brow furrowed. "As I told Elizabeth, Reverend Latham approached me this morning. I refused to assist him, but there are many attorneys who would help. Have you told him of his son's illness? Great distress can change relationships." His gaze softened as he gazed at Elizabeth. "It did ours."

She squeezed his hand but spoke to Prosperity. "My father is right. We should find Reverend Latham and tell him how ill David is. It might change his heart and lead to reconciliation."

"David is not in his right mind."

Prosperity's statement sobered those in the room.

She explained further, "They allowed me to look in upon him from the entrance of his room. He could recognize no one."

Elizabeth remained ever hopeful. "When I drifted in unconsciousness, I could still hear my father plead for forgiveness."

Prosperity wished for reconciliation, but she had never seen Reverend Latham admit he'd erred, least of all plead for forgiveness. But once he knew of David's illness, he would see his son. Her hands shook at the thought of the bile David's father would spew on him.

Elizabeth touched her sleeve. "Are you all right, Prosperity? You look pale. Perhaps you should lie down."

"I am well." Prosperity shook off the fears of the moment. She must help David. That meant taking Elizabeth and her family into confidence. "David is under guard. Apparently he has been charged with theft and faces court-martial."

Mr. Benjamin frowned. "That is a serious charge."

"They're wrong. David would never take anything that wasn't his, even if he was starving."

"Circumstances might change a man," Mr. Benjamin said.

"I won't believe it. I can't."

The attorney seemed to accept her plea on David's behalf. "That will be for the military court to decide. Our immediate problem is that Reverend Latham could very well use this accusation to his advantage. The slightest inference of criminal activity, even if unfounded, could sway a judge to grant custody to someone of impeccable credentials."

Prosperity could hardly breathe. "But surely he would not seek custody if he knew Oliver was not of Latham blood."

"I hope you're right," Mr. Benjamin said, "but the fact that his son has taken responsibility for Oliver might in fact spur him even more to remove the boy."

"But why?" Prosperity gasped.

"To remove foreign blood from the family line," Rourke O'Malley stated bluntly.

Prosperity felt ill, for Rourke had struck upon a terrible truth. Despite his abolitionist preaching, Reverend Latham would not want even the appearance of colored blood in his own family tree.

26

Prosperity met Dr. Goodenow in the morning, not as she had planned but as she must. At her suggestion they walked the shore like they once did. He brightened, no doubt expecting a positive response to his earlier proposal. Instead she presented her plea.

"Will you help me get into David's sickroom?"

The doctor's hopefulness disintegrated, but she could not pretend any longer.

"I'm sorry," she whispered. "I did not wish to hurt you."

He sighed, looking off to sea as if expecting an answer to appear on the horizon. "It puts you at risk, but I suppose you realize that."

"I do."

"Very well, then. I will speak to Dr. Rangler."

The doctor kept his word and by later that morning had somehow secured permission for Prosperity to visit David's bedside.

"I told him of your nursing skills." A sad smile caressed his lips as he assisted her up the army hospital's steps. "But I must caution you against visiting the lieutenant."

"It's a risk I'm willing to take. I must give him hope."

The doctor's lips twitched, but he gave up trying to dissuade her. Instead he guided her to the isolation room and then told her he needed to speak again with the army surgeon. Prosperity gave him a grateful smile. He left, and then she stood alone in the tiny room.

Sunlight filtered through closed shutters, outlining the sparse furnishings of the sickroom. Inside the shutters, the windows were open, and a steady breeze stirred the air. Prosperity settled into the straight-backed chair at David's bedside. The iron bedstead and scent of illness reminded her of those last days with Ma. She laid her hand on his.

"Please don't leave me," Prosperity whispered.

Ma had not heard her. Could David? Elizabeth said she'd heard her father even in the depths of unnatural slumber.

David felt hot, and his curls stuck together from perspiration. He did not respond to her touch, other than the faint and soundless movement of his lips. A basin of cool water and a compress sat on the small table beside the bed. She plunged the soft cotton cloth into the water, squeezed out the excess, and placed it on his forehead.

When would the fever pass?

Dr. Goodenow had told her and Elizabeth what symptoms would indicate they had been infected. Sudden chills would begin the downward spiral. Then terrible pains and vomiting would accompany the fever.

Elizabeth and Rourke had suffered a mild bout of fever years ago. So too Florie. Those who had endured yellow fever and survived need not fear it again. Only Prosperity and the babies had been at risk. She'd turned Oliver's care over to Elizabeth and rejoiced when he did not fall ill. Now that she had been admitted to David's bedside, she would not set foot inside the house but would sleep on the back porch and take any meals in the yard.

Reverend Latham had not visited again, but Elizabeth promised to keep Oliver from him, regardless of any legal judgment he might win. She did intend to tell the man of his son's illness, still believing it would lead to reconciliation.

First David must get well.

He did not hear her through the delirium of fever and the haze of laudanum used to check the vomit, which thankfully had not yet turned black. According to Dr. Goodenow, black vomit and yellowing of the skin signaled the final, irreversible stage. Before that would come a lull in the symptoms. At that point, the patient would either recover or take a turn for the worse.

David cried out, and his feverish eyelids popped open.

"Hold on," she begged, grasping hands that could not feel her.

He shook from the tremors and stared into space with great, empty eyes.

"You must hold on for your son's sake." Over and over she repeated it, believing that would give him the will to fight. "He needs you."

Though she had not held Oliver since learning of David's illness, she heard the baby's cries. This morning she had automatically risen to fetch Oliver before recalling that she should not go near him. She missed the feel of him in her arms and the way he reached for any stray lock as if afraid she would leave. Now David's father threatened to rip the boy from her hands. The thought of never seeing him again tore a hole in her heart.

"He will be all right," she whispered. "He must be."

David had closed his eyes again, sunk into a world she could not share. Was it too late? If she had forgiven him, they might have become a family by now. Precious weeks had been wasted. Her selfish need to cling to the hurt might have cost them their last chance at a life together.

"Forgive me." She leaned over David and turned the compress. "I should have forgiven you. I should have told you that I still love you, that I never stopped loving you, that I've dreamed every day of a life together. If you can hear me now, my answer is yes. Yes, I would marry you. A thousand times yes." Tears flooded down her cheeks.

He did not make even the slightest movement. Her confession had come too late.

All her knowledge of healing plants could not conquer this foe. The doctor said the disease must run its course. A man's survival depended on his strength. And God. That's the part the doctor ignored.

She slipped to her knees and held on to David's shaking hand. "Almighty Father, please heal him."

David thrashed, tossing his head from side to side. The compress flew off. She retrieved it from the sun-dappled blanket, dipped it into the cool water, and placed it again on his hot forehead.

She felt helpless. Utterly and completely helpless. As she had been the day she learned her father's ship had gone down with all hands. Unwilling to believe God would take her pa, she had run to the harbor and then the dunes looking for him. For months, even after the funeral, she had scanned the horizon for the familiar silhouette of his whaling ship. It never returned. Then her mother had slipped from the bonds of this world into the next, her skin translucent, each blue vein visible. The last sigh had been so peaceful that Prosperity couldn't believe her mama had left her.

Even then, there had still been David. Until she learned of his marriage, hope had held fast in the stormy sea. She had clung to God's Word, praying that He would make good from all this. Then David's wife had died, and Oliver had arrived in Prosperity's arms. David had begged for forgiveness, just as she'd hoped and prayed, but she had been too caught up in bitterness to grant it. Now she might lose both Oliver and David.

"Heal him, Lord." It was the most she could manage.

Many survived yellow fever. Elizabeth and family, for example. Yet others perished. Elizabeth's mother. Many newcomers whose graves bore testament to their suffering.

Would she yet again plead for a life that would end up being taken? Would God leave no one untouched?

She turned the compress. David's forehead burned, and his eyes stared at nothing. He hovered on the edge of a vast abyss. At any moment he might fall, and she could do nothing to prevent it. He was in God's hands. To Him alone could she plead.

She knelt again. The wood floor made her knees ache, but what was that compared to the suffering David endured? Nothing.

"Spare him, Father. Please?" She drew in a shaky breath, painfully aware of her ineffective pleas.

Greater love hath no man than this, that a man lay down his life for his friends.

Must David die for her to know true love?

She buried her face in her hands. "Forgive me for clinging to bitterness, for not extending forgiveness." She had wallowed in her own pain, unable to see David's. How great it must have been! Yet he had never once spoken ill of Aileen. He had never once accused her. He had taken on her child as his own. "I'm so sorry, so, so sorry. You gave so much, and I didn't see it."

He could not hear her now, could neither brush away the tears nor condemn her. She would gladly have taken either rather than this silence that could stretch unto death.

"Grief will not heal him."

She looked up to see Dr. Goodenow standing at the foot of the bed. She did not wish to speak to him. Not now. "I was praying."

"Dr. Rangler insists you leave."

As usual, he ignored her faith. Why had she not given that greater account in her decisions? Faith stood as a chasm between them.

She removed the compress and swept a curl from David's temple. "My place is here."

"I can't convince you." It wasn't a question.

She shook her head.

"I thought as much." He paused. "You still love him."

She sucked in her breath, shocked that he had seen what she had tried so hard to hide.

"You always have, but I was too much a fool to see." He gave a wry chuckle. "Forgive an old man his dreams."

She rose then, tears building behind her eyes. "I wanted to make it work."

"I know. But it never would have." His gaze shifted to David. "I hope he survives. That little boy needs a father and a mother."

The first tear crested her lid and dribbled down her cheek. "I'm sorry."

"Don't be, my dear. It was a glorious fantasy. For two short months I felt like a young man. You gave me that gift, Prosperity. Never regret it."

Then he put on his hat and walked away.

❦

The army surgeon would not hear her arguments. Once Dr. Goodenow left, he insisted Prosperity follow. He would have the guard remove her if necessary.

The parade ground was quiet at the midday hour. She supposed the men were either dining or at the fort. David's project. A pang rippled through her. He took such pride in his work and agonized over every failure. He'd often written of his quest to find brick of better quality. He would have accounted for every item. The charges against him made no sense. David would never steal from the project he loved.

Fearing she would not be readmitted to the garrison if she left, she strolled the grounds. She hadn't gotten a good look at the officers' quarters last time. They looked welcoming with their verandas and many windows. A ball at the bottom of one set of steps marked the presence of children. She blinked back tears and walked on.

Her steps slowed as she rounded the larger buildings that must be the soldiers' barracks. Ahead, in the shadow between buildings, four men played cards. Judging from their whooping and hollering, gambling was involved. One man, dark-haired and handsome, rose from the makeshift table and chairs created from crates and shoved something into his pocket.

Prosperity recognized that man. He had been one of those who'd accosted her when she wandered into the wrong part of town. David had rescued her, but the incident still sent a shiver down her spine. She backed out of sight, painfully aware of how vulnerable she was. David could not save her today.

She hurried back toward the officers' quarters. The families there brought a measure of safety. A fragment of memory drifted past. She wracked her mind. What had it been?

Soldiers streamed out of what must be the dining hall, ready to return to their labors.

Labor! That was it. The men on that terrible day had congratulated the dark-haired man on sharing the fruits of his labor. The way they'd said it made it perfectly clear that he had not labored at all. Were they talking about gaming, or were these men the real culprits behind the thefts? If the latter, the dark-haired man was the leader. What was his name? David had shouted it with anger, and the man had responded with contempt. At the time she'd thought the dark-haired man behaved like a child, like Jamie when he didn't get his way. Jamie. That was it. The man's name was similar. Jameson.

Her pulse pounded. Perhaps she could clear David's name.

⚜

Since neither the commander nor the surgeon would allow Prosperity to return to David's bedside, she had no place to go but the O'Malleys' garden, where she could stay away from the family.

Clouds had filled the skies during the time she waited for and then spoke with Colonel Stormant. The colonel had listened politely and promised he would question the men. She prayed he did.

The leaden skies turned afternoon to dusk. Rain was on its way, just like the day Ma passed. Ma used to call rain "tears from heaven." On that day, heaven had wept with Prosperity. *Not again. Please, Lord, not again.*

320

She would have tarried in town, but spitting raindrops sent her to the O'Malleys' house to seek shelter in the cookhouse.

By the time she arrived, the darkened skies shrouded the home in shadow. A carriage waited at their gate. Few carriages traversed Key West. The impending rain must have convinced the visitor to employ his or her conveyance.

She slipped through the gate, intending to skirt around the house to the back garden. Lamps burned in the parlor, revealing Elizabeth, an infant in her arms, in what appeared to be a heated discussion with someone who stood out of view. With the doors and windows open, she could hear the visitor's strident demand.

"I will not take no for an answer this time."

Reverend Latham had returned. Her stomach churned. She must protect Oliver, but where was he? Did Elizabeth hold him, or was he in the nursery?

She slipped off her shoes and tiptoed onto the veranda. Through the open door she saw Florie step out of the nursery holding Jamie, her eyes wide. That meant Elizabeth held Oliver.

Prosperity crept along the veranda to the open floor-length windows.

Inside the parlor, the reverend faced Elizabeth with the determined stance Prosperity well recognized. Elizabeth's jaw was set, and she clutched Oliver to her chest. Rourke was not there.

Prosperity's pulse raced.

David's father had come for Oliver. If Elizabeth gave the baby to him, they would never get Oliver back. Only women stood between Reverend Latham and David's son. He clearly expected them to give in. Prosperity could not.

"Stop!"

All eyes turned to her, but she focused on Reverend Latham alone. "You cannot take Oliver."

Displeasure drew his countenance into an ugly expression. "I can and I will. I have the legal authority right here." He waved some papers.

She looked to Elizabeth for help, but she could give no answer. Prosperity turned back to David's father. "This baby does not need to be uprooted again. He needs stability. He needs love."

"He will get a proper home," the minister stated.

"He has a proper home."

Reverend Latham approached Prosperity at the open window, allowing Elizabeth to slip behind him toward the parlor entrance.

The man's gaze was so fixed on Prosperity that he didn't notice. "A child needs a good Christian home—"

"Which this is," Prosperity said.

"With his kind."

A sudden chill made her tremble, but Prosperity was not ill. She was angry. Rourke had mentioned this possible motivation, but she had not truly believed it. To hear David's father speak it aloud infuriated her.

"I am his kind." She punctuated each word with a shake of her index finger. "We are both human beings set on this earth by our heavenly Father. Oliver is the child I always wanted."

The reverend did not relent. "I am sorry for what you endured at my son's hands, but this is not your concern."

"But it is. I love Oliver, and I love David."

"Irrelevant." He whirled around to face Elizabeth. "Hand the boy over."

Elizabeth turned that unflappable smile on the reverend. "As I said, you must wait for my attorney to arrive."

That must be where Rourke went.

Reverend Latham shook the papers in his hand. "This is a judge's orders. You don't need an attorney to read that I have been granted custody of Oliver Latham."

"But what about your son?" Prosperity gasped. "Don't you care about him?"

The minister's blue eyes bored through her. "Why should I care about a criminal?"

"He is innocent!"

Elizabeth seconded that. "In this country a man is innocent until proven guilty."

"No," Prosperity said. "You don't understand. He *is* innocent. I overheard soldiers boasting about another soldier's illicit gains. He could be the culprit. The commander is questioning him and having his quarters searched. He assured me that one way or another, the truth will come out."

The reverend's righteous indignation deflated a little more with each statement.

"But I do not need proof to know David is innocent," Prosperity continued. "He is not capable of dishonor even in the worst of circumstances. You see, he protected someone who harmed him." She swallowed against the tears. "He would not see her honor destroyed even though it cost him his." The last barely squeaked past the lump in her throat. "Is that not the very definition of honor?"

The fight had gone from Reverend Latham, but he refused to surrender. "Even if David is proved innocent, he could not raise a child. My son is a soldier. The army is his calling. Without a wife, he could not possibly keep an infant."

"If David lives and will still have me, he will have a wife."

Elizabeth gave a gasp, immediately followed by a brilliant smile. She kissed Oliver's forehead. "As it should be."

Reverend Latham, however, stared in disbelief. "What do you mean, if he lives?"

"As I tried to tell you, Reverend," Elizabeth said, "your son suffers from yellow fever."

That shook the minister. "Is he very ill?"

Prosperity nodded. "But I place my hope in the Lord that David will recover. I love your son, Reverend Latham, and always will. Now, what will you do with those papers? Will you support your son and grandson, or will you heap more grief upon his shoulders?"

His hand trembled.

"Either way, I will not stop loving them." The words seemed to flow from someone else, a woman confident and certain, and the sensation was exhilarating. She looked David's father in the eye, no longer afraid of his imperious gaze. "If you take Oliver away, I will search for him the rest of my days."

He looked down, his shoulders bowed. "I wish to see my son."

27

David heard her. Somehow through the memories and images swirling in disorder, he heard Prosperity's cry. She loved him.

She wanted to marry him.

All he'd ever wanted would come to pass. If only he could get out of this deepening pit. But something pulled him down into the darkness. Taunting, insisting what he'd heard was not real.

He gulped for air and drew in nothing.

The darkness suffocated like a blanket pressed over his head. He tried to push it away. Tried with all his might, but he was too weak. It would smother him, and he could do nothing to stop it.

He tried to cry out for help. The words formed in his mind but refused to pass his lips. They were so dry. So terribly dry. His eyes would not open. More people spoke, but he could not make out a single word. He strained to hear, and the voices faded away.

The temptation to give in nibbled at his fingers. But if temptation existed, so too must a way out. Did not the Holy Word say so?

Help me!

The cry echoed in his mouth and nowhere else.

Yet he began to sense someone at his side, someone holding him steady, pulling him up inch by inch.

"Look up," that person seemed to say, though he heard nothing.

Above streamed a brilliant light like the rays of the midday sun. Suddenly from darkness to light. He blinked, blinded, and squeezed his eyes shut.

"The fever has broken," a man said.

A hand cupped his forehead.

"Praise the Lord."

That from the sweetest voice he'd ever heard.

⟳✦⟲

Elation surged through Prosperity, cut off the next moment by a thought. Dr. Goodenow had mentioned a lull. Had that already passed, or was this the critical moment? "Will he survive?"

Dr. Rangler hesitated. "It is not yet certain. If the symptoms do not return within a day or so, he will recover."

Then this was the lull. Prosperity smoothed the damp curls from David's forehead. "I will remain with him."

The surgeon started to dissuade her but ended up shaking his head. "All right, but only until nightfall."

"I have no intention of leaving his side until he is recovered."

"This is not a private home, Miss Jones," the surgeon snapped. "This is an army hospital, subject to regulation. You will leave."

"Colonel Stormant will grant my request."

The surgeon growled. "Then get that permission. In writing." He stormed from the room.

David's father, standing on the other side of the bed, shook his head. "He ought to realize by now that you will stop at nothing to get your way."

"To gain what is right," she corrected him.

He nodded soberly. "Will you grant me a moment alone with my son?"

Though she hated to leave David's side, a father was entitled to time with his son.

She stood. "Please call me if his condition changes. I will be right outside the room."

"Do not fear, Miss Jones. You have shown nothing but love for my son and grandson." His throat bobbed as if struggling to say more, but he did not.

His grandson. Not some nameless, unconnected child. His.

Tears rose as she stumbled out of the room and into the ward with its handful of patients. Between last night's confrontation and this morning, Elizabeth revealed all that had happened when Reverend Latham appeared at the house. He had been shocked at first by Oliver's appearance, but that surprise did not alter his course of action. In fact, it seemed to reinforce it. Rourke had indeed gone to fetch Mr. Benjamin, leaving Elizabeth alone to fend off David's father. The tide had turned the moment Prosperity arrived and the reverend realized how much she loved little Oliver.

Still, Reverend Latham had not relinquished his claim to Oliver. This very moment he might be forcing the issue with a weakened David.

She leaned against the wall of the ward, eyes closed, praying for reconciliation between father and son.

The isolation room was no longer guarded, the commander having found proof of Private Jameson's dealings with the merchants and shippers in town, as well as a few items in his trunk.

David was free, his rank and honor reinstated, but none of that mattered if Reverend Latham still intended to take away Oliver. Though fear clutched at her exhausted mind, she must trust in God's plan. She must have faith.

Prosperity grasped the locket. It still contained a lock of David's hair. It needed a lock of Oliver's hair.

Would David still want to marry her?

She had been overwrought when she revealed her heart to David and presumptuous when she told his father that they would marry. What if he could not forgive her constant refusal? What if she had hurt him too much, pushed too far?

The door to the room opened. Reverend Latham stepped out. He looked different. His shoulders weren't quite so straight, his back not quite so stiff. Red-rimmed eyes met her gaze.

"You may return. I have said my piece. Good day, Miss Jones." He nodded and left.

The formal address did not bode well. Had David given up his son? Had the fever returned? She drew in a breath and stepped into the room on trembling limbs.

Though pale, David tilted his head toward her.

"Prosperity." Her name barely rasped from his dry throat.

She rushed to his side and picked up the glass of water to give him a drink. That's when she saw it. The document that granted custody of Oliver to Reverend and Mrs. Myles Latham had been torn to pieces.

⸎

David did not speak to her that day. By the time Prosperity turned to him with the glass of water, he had slipped into slumber. Peaceful this time, his skin cool and the color returning. She sank into the chair and watched his regular breathing.

Each day cemented his recovery. None of the symptoms reappeared. Little by little he grew stronger.

Yet he did not address what she most longed to discuss.

Patience. She must wait until he was ready. She certainly deserved the delay, for she had kept him at arm's length for months. If David had been the teasing sort, he would hold out until she could no longer bear it.

But bear it she must. She visited each day. Once the lull passed without return of the fever, he was moved to the general ward. When he could walk, he was sent to his quarters, though not yet required to resume duties. There they would pass the time seated on the shady veranda, discussing the books he had read since leaving Nantucket as well as the progress at the fort. She once brought Oliver, who never came down with a fever.

"He is of sound stock, like me." She laughed. "I never seem to grow ill."

David smiled, but his attention was all on his son, who kicked his feet and waved his little arms. "I missed him."

"He fares well."

"I can see that."

"He takes mainly sweet milk now," Prosperity admitted. "He does so well on it that we don't think you'll need to hire a new wet nurse when Elizabeth can no longer nurse."

They spoke of such mundane things, yet she treasured each word shared. Sometimes she read to him while he closed his eyes. Other times he chattered on about his work at the fort. Never did they discuss the future.

They had time, she reasoned.

Yet as August slipped into September, and the daily downpours occasionally led to storms that lashed the island, she began to fear he could not forgive her. Never did he ask of her plans. Never did he look ahead. Instead he seemed content to dwell in the present.

But the present never lasts. In time, demands come and life moves forward. Prosperity took a housekeeping job that reduced her visits to three days per week.

One morning when she arrived, she found David bustling around his quarters.

"I can't find the brush to knock the dirt from my coat." He raked the hair off his forehead in a painfully familiar way.

"You are leaving?"

"I have been recalled to duty."

Her heart sank. Though she'd known that day would come, she had hoped they still had some time. "Are you well enough?"

"I cannot shirk duty."

She managed a tremulous smile. That was her David. "Naturally, but I shall miss our time together."

He looked up as if startled by what she'd said. "Are *you* leaving?"

"I meant the days spent in conversation. They are already too few."

"I am a soldier."

"I know." Again she smiled. "I am proud of that."

His frantic search paused. "Aileen hated my work."

Aileen. In their discussions following his illness, he never mentioned his late wife.

She looked him in the eye. "It's who you are. An engineer and a soldier."

"Then you do not regret my commission?"

"I cannot regret anything, for it has brought us to where we are now." She hesitated. "It is what you wanted most of all."

"Not most." His gaze shifted downward as if he were suddenly abashed. But then he looked up again. "While I was sick, I dreamed . . ." His voice trailed off before he regained strength. "I dreamed you said you would marry me."

Now that the words were before her, she could not find the right answer.

He reached for the doorknob, the brush forgotten. "I should be on my way."

"It was no dream."

"It wasn't?" He looked back.

She shook her head.

"But the doctor—"

"I never loved him. Not in that way. He is a good man, like a father."

"A father." He ran a hand over his jaw. "A father!" He laughed. "What a fool I was!"

"No. I was the fool. And—and I stretched the truth. I told Dr. Rangler and your father that we were engaged to marry." How that confession heated her cheeks. "I'm sorry."

He stared at her a long time, and she feared he would chide her for leaping to unwarranted conclusions.

Instead he shook his head. "That explains a great deal." A smile teased his lips. "You were a bit presumptuous, though."

"I did what had to be done." The next would be more difficult. "I will not hold you to it, however, as you were not in your right mind at the time."

His laugh barked out, and his lips curved into that glorious smile she so treasured. "Don't think you can wiggle out of this that easily." He grew serious and took both her hands. "I have never stopped loving you. I had to marry Aileen." He looked away, stricken.

"I know."

Her whisper drew him back. "I owe you an explanation."

"No, you don't. I know you, David Latham, and I know you would only act with honor. That is good enough for me."

His Adam's apple bobbed. "I don't deserve you."

"Nor I you." She smiled, hoping to ease his tension. "We are a pair, aren't we?"

His lips pressed together for a moment. "Any future must include my life in the army and my son. I will not give up Oliver."

"Nor will I."

He seemed pleased though still reserved. "I heard how you fought for him. But you must realize that it will be difficult. You will face hardship and ridicule."

"I know both."

"Many won't understand . . . about him . . . why he's different."

Tears gathered in her eyes. "Those who matter most will."

His throat bobbed again, and she thought his eyes misted. "I will love you unto death, Prosperity Anne Jones, and would be honored to make you my wife."

"I love you, David Latham, and I wish to make my life with you, for better or worse."

All the trials of the last few months slipped away. Once again he was the young man afraid to ask her to sit with him at the church social or the awkward gallant offering his coat to her in the midst of a cloudburst. Joy bubbled up until she felt giddy.

He caught up her hands. "Will you marry me?"

Though her hands trembled, she had never been more certain of anything in her life. "I would be honored to call you my husband."

He drew her close, duty and dusty coat forgotten. His lips brushed hers, sweet as a summer shower and full of promise.

Then he kissed her, firm and filled with a passion born from trial, a passion she had thought lost but that was now found. When the kiss ended, he continued to hold her, silent. Nothing needed to be said. She rested in the embrace, secure in his arms as the breeze rustled the leaves of the mahogany tree.

Though she wanted to stay like this forever, they could not. He had a duty to fulfill, and she had a hundred questions.

"When?"

His eyes twinkled. "Would tonight be too soon?"

"Tonight! We must speak with a minister and make necessary arrangements. I don't need anything grand, but we must secure a time at church. And Elizabeth and Rourke will be terribly upset if we don't include them." Her thoughts raced ahead of her tongue, ending with a jumble.

"Not tonight then?" His grin told her he had been teasing.

She shook her head and gently swatted his arm. "Since when did you become a tease?"

He sobered. "I don't want to wait a minute, Prosperity, but I will wait for as long as you need. Until the end of mourning or even longer."

"That is not necessary. Ma would want us together, especially with Oliver." She squeezed his hands. "I suppose then that we first must find a minister."

"My father is still on the island."

The thought of Reverend Latham officiating made her more than a little nervous. "Would he approve?"

"Don't be afraid." David smoothed her hair. "He adores you. He asks every day when I'm going to seize the gift that God set before me. That's you, Prosperity—you are my treasure."

Once again her eyes filled with tears. "Then he will be perfect."

He smiled and bent for another kiss, but a bugle call on the parade ground pulled him away. "Duty calls. Now, where is that brush?"

Prosperity plucked it from under the pile of gloves and hats on the nearby table. "I believe, Lieutenant, you are in need of a wife."

"I believe, Miss Jones, that I have found the perfect match."

"At last."

"At last," he echoed.

Her reflection danced in his eyes, precisely where it belonged.

Keep Reading for a Sneak Peek of
Book 3 in the

KEYS

— OF —

PROMISE

Series

Prologue

Early June 1856
Staffordshire, England

Catherine Haynes set her jaw and returned her cousin's glare. By very subtly lifting her gaze above his piercing gray eyes and fixing it on the portrait of her mother hanging behind Papa's desk, she could maintain the illusion of control.

"Well?" Ugly red suffused cousin Roger's neck. "I am waiting for an answer."

In the months since he and his family first arrived at Deerford, she had learned one important trait about her cousin. He expected compliance. This time she would not bow. Nor could she find words of refusal.

The mantel clock ticked off the seconds.

Roger braced his hands on the desktop, leaning forward like a snarling lion eager to capture its prey. "Your reply."

Not a question.

Catherine drew an imperceptible breath and imitated Maman's calm. "I cannot."

"You cannot?" The sentence exploded with unspoken threat.

He would force her into this marriage.

Again the ticking of the clock filled the silence.

What would Maman do? Faced with similar prospects upon her return from the grand tour all those years ago, Catherine's mother had abandoned her chaperones in the dead of night and eloped. Catherine had no such escape available.

Roger's smile menaced. "If you continue in this stubborn refusal, you will lose what is left of your family."

Meaning him. She had no one else. Not here. Maman's family was in faraway Louisiana, and the decision to elope had cost her all contact with them. No letters. No word of any kind. How the separation must have hurt, for Maman often regaled her with stories of plantation life, of balls and soirees and golden days running between the tall rows of sugarcane. Catherine had begged her mother to take her there, but Maman said it was not possible. Then she'd died.

Only the portrait remained. Maman's rose-colored gown flowed from her waist like that of an empress. At her throat rested the ruby brooch Catherine had often run her finger across when she was very young. *H* for Haynes, Maman had explained, a gift from Papa on their wedding day. Catherine had not found it with Maman's jewels. Papa must have buried it with her.

Dear Papa. Catherine tugged at her heavy black sleeves to hide the welling of tears.

"I suggest a different answer," Roger prodded.

Catherine brushed away the past. It could not solve this dilemma. She chose her words with care. "Mr. Kirby does not suit me."

"Does not suit? You act as if you would bring an heiress's fortune to your marriage. May I remind you that the terms of your father's estate leave you but five hundred pounds?"

"And fifty pounds per year." Eight months had not changed that fact. The passing of time had only increased her cousin's urgency to be rid of her.

"Until you wed."

That was the crux of it. Once she married, the annual payments would cease.

Roger settled into Papa's chair.

She clenched her jaw against a wave of revulsion. Roger might have gained the estate through settlement, but he did not belong in her father's place.

"I do not intend to wed. Allow me to manage the estate—"

He snorted derisively. "Is that what you call your playing around in the accounts?" He filled a pipe from Papa's tobacco jar.

Angry words rose to the tip of her tongue and stopped there. Very few men considered a woman intelligent enough to manage accounts, least of all an estate. Roger was not one of them.

"If you examine my entries—"

"I have." He slammed shut the open ledger before him. "Some might consider them adequate, considering your gender, but I found them entirely insufficient."

"Insufficient! Compare my skills to any man—"

He cut her off. "Use those skills to benefit your husband."

She choked. "I am in mourning and cannot consider marriage."

"You have worn black long enough. It's time to move on. I suggest you change into something more cheerful." His cold gray gaze, fixed above fashionably long sideburns, bored into her. "That would be welcomed by our guests."

Mrs. Durning, whose husband had just left to provision his ship for the crossing to the West Indies, and Mr. Kirby were expected. Neither cared about her attire, but at least it gave her an excuse to leave this unbearable interview.

"If you will excuse me, then." She reached for the doorknob.

"Not quite yet." He drew a breath on the pipe and exhaled a cloud of rich smoke.

If she closed her eyes, she could imagine Papa sitting there, his spectacles resting on the tip of his nose, where they would slide after hours of agonizing over the accounts. Papa had been a kind and generous man, often excusing debts and allowing rents to remain in arrears far too long. Of course, she hadn't known that until he fell ill and she had to take on the accounts.

Roger cleared his throat. "At three and twenty you will soon slip from a marriageable age."

"Apparently not, if Mr. Kirby is still calling."

Roger's jaw tightened. "His long association with the family places him in a rather fortunate position."

"Fortunate? That is a matter of perspective, is it not? As you just stated, I bring a pittance into any marriage."

"Precisely. Few would consider a wife who brings only five hundred to the marriage."

She could not resist poking at his unstated desire. "You might continue the fifty pounds per year. We are cousins, after all."

"Let me spell out what you could never have gleaned from your pitiable scribbling in the ledgers. Your father's estate is in ruins."

She opened her mouth to protest, but he lifted a finger to silence her.

"Even if I manage to collect the arrears, which I fully intend to do, it will not offset the losses."

Catherine would not be set down so easily. "Then how do you intend to pay the dowry?"

His lips twitched, signaling triumph. "I intend to sell the estate."

"Sell Deerford?" The words barely escaped her constricted throat. "You can't!"

"As you well know, I can. In fact, a buyer is at hand."

"A buyer?" She clawed at hope. "Mr. Kirby?" Perhaps she would agree to marry him if it meant saving Deerford.

He laughed. "Certainly not."

"Then who? Will he continue the tenants' leases? Will he keep planting the land as always?"

"This clay soil was never suited to farming, dear Catherine. It will fare much better in the hands of the pottery manufacturer that is buying it."

"A factory?" Her head spun. "But, the house."

"It would have been too costly to maintain."

"What will happen to the tenants? You must take care of them. They have worked Deerford land for generations."

He leaned back and blew out a plume of smoke. "They can apply for employment at the factory."

"But they're farmers." Each face flashed through her mind, from old widow Evans to the two-year-old Herring twins. "They don't know anything else."

"Then they can move elsewhere."

His cold statement sent shivers down her spine. She must help them, but how? The few guineas in her possession wouldn't feed them long. They needed lands to tend.

"You must find them new homes," she pleaded.

"Sometimes progress demands change. For them and for you." He paused. "Deerford is extinct. You have nowhere to go, dear Catherine. Perhaps a husband—especially one as charitably minded as Mr. Kirby—would find a place for your tenants on his father's or future patrons' lands."

Her throat closed. How carefully he had crafted the snare. If she hoped to help the displaced tenants, she must marry Eustace Kirby.

Roger seized his advantage. "I suggest you give full consideration to Mr. Kirby's suit."

She sank into the closest chair. "But he's a clergyman."

Roger's brow quirked. "Do you harbor resentment against that noble profession?"

Cousin Roger would not think so highly of the ministry if he had been forced into it as Mr. Kirby had been.

"I wouldn't make a good minister's wife."

"Let us hope Mr. Kirby doesn't see that fault before the blessed event. I shall give him my blessing."

"But I did not agree to marry him."

"You would destroy your father's hopes for you and leave your beloved tenants without a future rather than commit to a life of serving the Lord?"

Put that way, it sounded rather selfish, but she could not marry Eustace Kirby. The mere thought of kissing him made her stomach turn. Having children? Settling into a country parish? Impossible.

"There must be another answer." Yet she could not see it.

Roger leaned back with a contented smirk and puffed the pipe. "Make no mistake, dear cousin, fifty pounds will not go far. Once you have no home . . ." He let her imagine the result.

She clawed at the pit that was swallowing her. Above Roger, Maman's portrait smiled placidly at the terrible scene unfolding below. She would never have agreed to this manipulation. *You have my wits,* Maman had often told her, *and your papa's compassion.* What to do?

She tried to breathe, but the strictures of both garments and circumstance made it difficult to draw in enough air. Papa's halting words on his deathbed echoed in her mind. *Forgive me for losing what was yours.* Now she knew what he meant.

"So you can see," Roger was saying, "Mr. Kirby has presented a most opportune offer. I suggest you accept."

He had left her no escape. Her head spun, and spots danced before her eyes.

"Are you unwell?" Roger rose.

She shook her head rather than admit weakness. Several short breaths restored her vision, though her stomach still quaked.

He moved toward her, a glint in his eye, and brought to mind a shadowy memory from childhood. A stranger, dark as tea, had cast her the same look when he passed her in the hallway en route to Papa's study. Papa had closed the door behind them, but she'd crouched outside to listen. Murmuring voices grew heated, and then the door burst open. The dark stranger's victorious smile, like that of a king, claimed her imagination. He swept past, carrying a strongbox, and rode off on a black steed like an avenging knight.

She peppered her father with questions, but he would tell her nothing, only that it did not concern her.

But perhaps it did. What if this dark stranger had come from Maman's glorious plantation? What if contact had not been cut off forever? His glance toward her had not borne malice. No, it seemed to say that she belonged with him.

The study door opened.

"Excuse me, Miss Catherine, Mr. Haynes." The housekeeper dipped into a slight curtsey. "Mrs. Durning has arrived, and she says that Mr. Kirby will be here shortly."

"Good," Roger said. "Tell Mr. Kirby to join me in the study. We have business to discuss while Catherine entertains Mrs. Durning."

The housekeeper bustled off.

Roger drew again on the pipe. The set of his jaw meant the decision had been made. With or without her permission, Roger would give his consent to Eustace Kirby's suit. He believed he had trapped her.

Well, Roger could give all the blessings he wished. He was not her only family, and Mrs. Durning could very well give her the escape she desperately needed.

She stood, reinvigorated. "I request the annual sum due me."

He set down the pipe with a thud. "What?"

"The fifty pounds specified in Papa's will."

"You will waste it on the tenants?" he sneered.

She could no longer help them. Unless . . . . "And an additional ten pounds per tenant family."

He guffawed. Then paused, surprised that she didn't waver before him. "You are jesting."

"I am not."

"It's not in the terms of the will."

"I propose new terms. In exchange for the ten pounds per tenant, I will waive all future annual payments."

"You will anyway, once you marry." The smirk was back.

She drew in a deep breath, never more certain. "I do not intend to marry. I am rejoining my mother's family in America."

He stared, struck silent for the moment, but soon she saw the gleam of self-interest as he calculated the benefits of her plan. This would spare him not only the continued fifty pounds per year but also the five hundred upon her marriage, for she would have difficulty claiming it from America.

She assumed all the risk, leaving dull security for the unknown. Surely her mother's family would welcome her. Surely Maman's sin did not extend to the next generation.

Note to the Reader

I hope you enjoyed reading about this unique place and time in history as much as I enjoyed researching and writing about it. Though all the events and characters in this story are fictional, Fort Zachary Taylor and the marine hospital did exist. The hospital was built in 1844 and operated until its closure in 1943. Today the remodeled building is the site of private condominiums, but the exterior of the structure looks very much like it did when still a hospital.

The fort also stretches back to 1844 when the site was chosen. Construction began in 1845, but progress was wiped out in the hurricane of 1846. As was the case with the town, the Army Corps simply got back to work under the direction of Capt. George Dutton. Since he was such a key figure in the building of the fort, I wanted to keep his name in my story. His vision and energy pushed the project forward despite setbacks from weather, supply and labor shortages, funding issues, and disease. After he finished his eight-year tour of duty, a succession of commanders followed. Work on the fort and towers continued through the Civil War. By 1866, advances in armament had made brick-and-mortar forts obsolete, and work was ordered to cease. Before the war with Spain in 1898, the top two tiers were removed, so the structure you can visit today looks very different from what was so diligently built 150 years ago. One of the most obvious changes is that it is no longer out in the water. Filling and natural changes in the shoreline have landlocked the structure, which is the centerpiece of Fort Zachary Taylor Historic State Park.

Both are worth seeing if you visit Key West. You can also find many digital images online in the Monroe County Public Library's Keys History photo collections.

Acknowledgments

My deepest gratitude goes to the Lord, the Creator of all things, who grants me the privilege of writing down these stories. I am honored and humbled.

How privileged I am to work with the amazing team at Revell. Andrea Doering and Jessica English make the story clearer and so much better. Your discerning eye is so very much appreciated. I am hugely indebted to Michele Misiak and the entire marketing team. Cheryl Van Andel and the visual communications department create the most wonderful covers. Of course, everyone in sales and publicity is priceless. I am so blessed to work with you.

Once again I have to give a shout-out to Tom Hambright, the historian at the Monroe County Public Library's Florida History Department in Key West. Your knowledge is truly amazing! Stop by the library website (www.keyslibraries.org) for a fascinating glimpse into Keys history.

Kathy and Jenna, you're the best writing friends a gal could have.

To my husband, who puts up with the long hours and less-than-gourmet meals—thank you!

Christine Johnson is the author of several books for Steeple Hill and Love Inspired, in addition to her books with Revell. When not writing, she enjoys quilting and loves to hike, kayak, and explore God's majestic creation. These days, she and her husband, a Great Lakes ship pilot, split their time between northern Michigan and the Florida Keys.

Christine Johnson

WHERE ADVENTURE LEADS HOME

ChristineElizabethJohnson.com

 Christine Johnson Author

ChristineJWrite

More adventure and romance
await in book 1 of the
Keys of Promise series!

Can a girl enamored with the adventurous seas
ever be content with the tame life of a Southern belle?